GALLANT SCOUNDREL

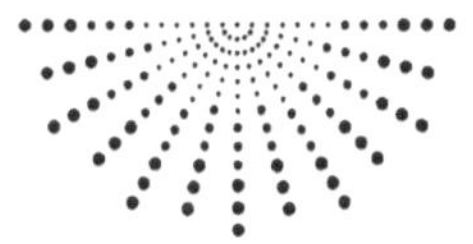

BRENDA HIATT

dolphin star
PRESS

GALLANT SCOUNDREL
The Saint of Seven Dials
book 5

Copyright 2016 by Brenda Hiatt
Cover art by Dar Albert

This is a work of fiction. Though some actual historical places, persons and events are depicted in this work, the primary characters and their stories are fictional. Any resemblance between those characters and actual persons, living or dead, are purely coincidental.

Dolphin Star Press

ISBN: 978-1-940618-32-6

ALSO BY BRENDA HIATT

The Hiatt Regency Classics

Gabriella

The Cygnet

Lord Dearborn's Destiny

Daring Deception

Christmas Promises (a novella)

Christmas Bride

Azalea

Americana Dreaming

Azalea

Ship of Dreams

Bridge Over Time

The Saint of Seven Dials

Scandalous Virtue

Rogue's Honor

Noble Deceptions

Innocent Passions

Saintly Sins

Gallant Scoundrel

CHAPTER ONE

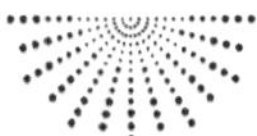

LONDON—NOVEMBER, 1816

"WELL, LADS, BELIEVE I'LL HEAD OUT BEFORE M'LUCK TURNS." HARRY Thatcher swept his winnings into a kerchief in his lap, then stuffed them into his pocket. "Give you all good night."

Sir Barney Phillips leapt to his feet with a scowl. "Never say you're going already, Thatcher? Bad form to leave at the top of your game, don't you know. Only sporting to give us a chance to win a bit back first."

Harry cocked an eyebrow at the irritating young dandy. "Bad form? When you've done the same more evenings than I can count? I'll be back soon enough. You can have your chance then."

He stood, long practice preventing him from swaying even the slightest bit despite the prodigious quantities of claret and port he'd consumed over the past six hours. Fortunately his credit was still good at the Guards' Club, or they'd have cut him off after the first bottle. Tonight's winnings would assure that credit remained sound for another month, at least. Till his next army cheque, if he were careful.

Not that he often was.

"I tell you, you must remain for at least one more," Sir Barney insisted pugnaciously. "I'll not have you waving my voucher about, saying God knows what about my ability to pay."

As Phillips had done precisely that to Harry barely a month ago, he might well worry. The obnoxious popinjay had gone out of his way to discredit him since their earliest days serving together in the war, when Harry had mercilessly tweaked Phillips over his complete humiliation at the hands of a woman.

Smiling at that memory, Harry shrugged rather than give him the assurance he clearly craved. "Shouldn't bet more than you have on you, then, eh?" He made no attempt to moderate his voice.

"Wouldn't have, had I known you were using more than luck to win. S'pose it stands to reason, though. Why should I expect half a man to have a full sense of honor?" Phillips nodded significantly at Harry's empty left sleeve.

An indignant murmur broke out around them. Well known for his heroism as a major in the recent wars, Harry was held in far more respect by the members of the Guards' Club than Sir Barney, who'd sold out after his first real battle.

"Still haven't learned your lesson about insulting those who are more than your match, have you, Phillips?" Harry drawled. "This 'half man' may have cuckolded a dozen or so husbands but he's never before been accused of cheating at cards, if that's what you're implying. But perhaps I misunderstood you?"

The younger man sneered. "Surely you're not threatening me, Thatcher? Lord Peter Northrup isn't here tonight to fight your battles for you, in case you hadn't noticed."

"I only let him knock you down because he needed it, Phillips." That incident had occurred last month, when Peter was suffering over a woman he'd married less than a week later—poor blighter. "If you fancy I can't do the same, I invite you to give me reason right now. Unless you'd rather name your seconds?"

As Harry's aim with a pistol was legendary, Sir Barney fell back on bluster. "A fine fool I'd look dueling a one-armed man."

"And a fine coward you look refusing," Harry taunted, using the same epithet Phillips had applied to Peter last month—though it had been a barb aimed at Harry himself that had finally broken through his friend's vaunted calm.

Sir Barney possessed no such claim to levelheadedness. "Not even a cripple calls me coward here," he exclaimed, lunging forward in an attempt to strike Harry in the face.

Harry easily sidestepped him while simultaneously planting his right fist squarely on Phillips's nose. With a surprised grunt, the baronet fell with a crash to the general sound of cheering from the avid onlookers. For a long moment Harry stood over the man, half-hoping he'd get up so he could knock him down again. Apparently one blow was enough to jar a modicum of sense into the insufferable pup, however, for he merely sat there, scowling.

"Right, then, I'm off." Draining his last half-glass of port, Harry headed for the door.

"You ain't heard the last from me, Thatcher!" Phillips shouted after him.

"I should hope not, as you owe me forty-five pounds," Harry said over his shoulder as he continued out to St. James's Street. Though it would be worth forgoing twice that to have Phillips finally barred from the Guards' altogether.

Not until he was halfway back to his lodgings did Harry finally pull out the evening's winnings to count it properly. Despite being as drunk as he could remember since his stint at the Congress of Vienna, he found that his quick mental tally at the table had been correct to within a farthing. Three hundred twenty-two pounds, all in cash except for Phillips's voucher. A tidy sum. Even so, he'd need to pace himself a bit better to make it last.

He could almost hear his best friend's voice echoing that thought. Over the past few years Peter had begun habitually voicing such cautions—which Harry just as habitually ignored. Not that Lord Peter had time lately to act as Harry's conscience, what with the new demands of married life.

While Harry appreciated the respite from Peter's continual nagging, he couldn't deny that without his friend's steadying influence, his drinking and gambling had begun to get just a bit out of hand. No one's welfare but his own was at stake, however, so what did it matter?

Up ahead, he caught a glimpse of a dark-haired woman just entering a house. A fleeting resemblance again put him in mind of the time Phillips had been bested by a woman back in Portugal, though now he recalled the incident with more poignancy than amusement. For he had been quite a different man then. Before meeting—and later losing—Xena Maxwell.

With a shake of his head to banish such regrets and a half-rueful chuckle, he continued on to Swallow Street, where he turned into the mews that offered easiest access to his third story flat above a haberdasher's shop.

"Oi! You there, cripple!" came a rough voice from behind.

Harry wheeled around with a curse. He normally ignored passing slurs about his missing arm, but this one sounded confrontational.

"You'll move on if you know what's good for you," he informed the looming figure blocking the exit to the mews.

"Or what?" With a derisive laugh the man advanced, one fist cocked. Before he was quite close enough to land a blow, Harry lashed out with one foot, hooking it behind the other man's knee and toppling him to the ground.

"Or that, among other things."

Letting loose a string of profanities, the man tried to scramble to his feet, but again Harry was too quick for him, thrusting a knee into his midsection when he was halfway up, again landing him flat on his back.

Two more thugs now crowded into the mews behind their companion. "We was warned you might be a tricky one," one of them said. "Let's see if you can take all three of us with one arm, eh?"

So saying, the man launched himself at Harry, only to encounter a boot heel to the stomach that effectively knocked the wind out of him. Then, as the one on the ground finally struggled upright, the second newcomer charged.

The ensuing melee required all Harry's remembered battle skills. He made devastating use of his right fist, elbow and both feet as he fended off the trio of assailants. Fortunately none appeared to have brought weapons.

At first it seemed Harry might prevail. The first two times he was knocked down, he immediately sprang back up to plant the man a facer. Gradually, however, the evening's heavy drinking began to take its toll. His initial surge of energy and alertness at facing danger faded, making him slower and slower to rise and react. In addition, the three ruffians were now proceeding more cautiously after discovering Harry wasn't nearly as easy a mark as they'd been led to believe.

A kick to the back sent Harry staggering yet again, though he managed—barely—to keep his feet. He turned to aim another punch at his nearest attacker but before he could land it one of the others snatched up a discarded horseshoe and delivered a vicious blow to Harry's right temple—at which point everything went dark.

PORTUGAL—MARCH, 1809

Freshly promoted from ensign to lieutenant, Harry returned to his regiment flush with success from leading his first mission in northern Portugal. By dint of a surprise dawn attack, he and his men had freed a nearby village from its French occupiers. The grateful villagers had hailed his platoon as heroes, though in truth they'd bested a unit no larger than their own.

When Harry hurried to the officers' mess to report on the skirmish, his company commander was warm in his commendation. But then, with raised eyebrow, Captain Malthus suggested Harry might wish to wash off the mud of the fields before joining the other officers at table.

Only slightly chastened, Harry headed for his tent. Just before reaching it, he spotted a lad whose dull red coat, devoid of insignia, declared him a newly-enlisted private.

"You there, boy," he called out, for the soldier looked no more than fifteen, with his smooth, beardless chin and close-cropped dark hair. "Help me off with my boots."

Turning, the stripling coolly regarded him with gray eyes surrounded by rather remarkable black lashes. "If you're not capable of removing your own boots, sir, you surely have no business leading a platoon into battle," came the reply, in a voice undeniably feminine. "Did they not warn you that an army camp would lack many of the comforts you were accustomed to back in England—to include a bevy of servants at your beck and call?"

"Beg pardon, ma'am." Examining the slim figure before him more closely, he realized the voice was not the only feminine thing about it, despite the uniform she wore. "But you must admit my mistake was an honest one. Nor have I seen you about the camp before—for I'd surely remember such a face as yours."

She tipped up her chin to regard him haughtily down the length of her shapely nose, making him far more aware of his dirty and disheveled state than his captain's comment had done.

"My father, Colonel Maxwell, arrived a few days since to advise Colonel Flagston on the regiment's movements as they prepare to engage the French."

Harry had of course heard of Colonel Maxwell, the brilliant strategist who had helped more than one commander turn the tide of battle —but not that he'd brought a daughter with him.

"And is it at your father's behest that you wander about camp dressed in male attire?"

Now she colored slightly. "It seemed silly to change when I was only leaving the tent long enough to fetch more water. And I do not 'wander about camp.' I assist my father in his record-keeping and in nursing any wounded who are brought in."

"In other words, the answer is no. You'd best return to your tent before your father sees you, then." Harry allowed himself a hint of a smirk, at which the girl before him visibly bristled.

"I'll do as I damned well please," she snapped.

His brows rose. "So it would seem. Now I must beg your pardon for mistaking you for a lady, for none would use such language."

For a long moment she glared, then spun on her heel and stalked away. Harry watched her appreciatively from behind, making note of which tent she entered. Whether he would have opportunity to make use of that knowledge in future he didn't know, but he rather hoped so.

Over the next day or two Harry caught only fleeting glimpses of Miss Maxwell, dressed more conventionally in a drab gray gown that had clearly seen much wear, but she was again in male attire when he spotted her one evening upon leaving the company mess.

Hands on slim hips, Miss Maxwell was glaring at Ensign Phillips, a brash and rather irksome newcomer to Harry's company. Curious, he moved to join the small crowd already gathered around the pair.

"You'll apologize for that remark, sirrah, or you'll name your seconds," she declared.

Phillips burst out laughing. "Seconds? My dear Miss Maxwell, simply because you fill out those breeches more alluringly than any man does not mean you, a mere woman, can match the skills of one."

"I propose we put that to the test," she retorted. "Will it be pistols or swords?"

He shook his head disbelievingly. "Oh, come. You can't seriously—"

"Pistols or swords?" she repeated. "Or are you so great a coward you dare not face a 'mere woman' on the field of honor?"

"Now see here—" He took a menacing step toward her, but Captain Malthus stepped between them.

"It'll be swords, and you'll stop at first blood," he informed them both. "As my company is already understrength, I'll not risk losing another soldier, no matter how much he might deserve it."

Phillips stared at his commander. "But sir, surely you can't—"

"Time you learned to mind your tongue, Phillips," Malthus curtly informed him. "Miss Maxwell, fetch your weapon and I'll see this fool's is brought as well."

A few minutes later the two faced off in the center of camp with the better part of three companies—all who weren't out on maneuvers—in a large ring about them. Colonel Maxwell, Harry noticed, was watching the proceedings with an expression of mingled exasperation and pride—but no trace of alarm.

Captain Malthus took up position as *arbitre* and called out, *"En garde! Prêt? Allez!"*

The amused smirk on Phillips's face abruptly disappeared when Miss Maxwell opened with a bold thrust that he barely sidestepped in time. She instantly followed up, forcing him to parry. Within seconds it was obvious he was overmatched, his longer reach no compensation for her superior quickness and skill.

Barely a minute into the match, Captain Malthus called a halt. The surrounding crowd broke into applause while Phillips clutched his shoulder, his face contorted with pain…and embarrassment.

"Perhaps in future you'll be less quick to underestimate a woman," commented his opponent, who was not even winded. Then, with a courtly bow to Captain Malthus and the assembled soldiers, she headed for her tent.

More intrigued than ever by the remarkable Miss Maxwell, Harry made a point the next day of seeking her out in the surgery tent, where she was laying out instruments in readiness for the next batch of wounded that might be brought in.

"Give you good day, Miss Maxwell. Dare I ask whether you were required to patch the rent you made in young Phillips's shoulder last night? Well done, by the way."

Her dark brows drew down. "You see now what can come of insulting me. And no, Ensign Phillips preferred to have the orderly dress his wound."

Harry chuckled. "Can't say I blame him. For myself, I feel compelled to retract what I said to you at our first meeting, for you are clearly a dangerous woman to offend."

She continued to regard him suspiciously. Then, apparently deciding he was at least somewhat sincere, she allowed a small smile to play about her remarkably well-shaped lips.

"Apology accepted. Though I fear you were correct that ladylike speech is a skill I singularly lack, much to the despair of my *ayah*, who has tried her best to teach me."

"You appear to have spent your time cultivating rather more useful skills." Harry carefully kept all trace of amusement from his expression. "If I am indeed forgiven for my rash words, perhaps you would consider indulging me in a fencing or shooting match? I should quite like to match my skills against yours."

Her gray eyes narrowed, but then she gave a slight nod. "Perhaps that can be arranged, though when I finish here I still have two days of notes to transcribe for my father. Brilliant as he is, he rarely takes the time to make his hand legible to anyone but myself."

"At your convenience, of course." Harry leaned a shoulder against one of the tent poles. "One of the men mentioned that you spent much of your youth in India, Miss Maxwell. Is that where your father encountered General Wellesley?"

Deftly folding a canvas cloth on which the surgical instruments had been laid to dry after washing, she nodded. "My father was there pursuing his archaeological research and the two discovered a shared passion for military history, though my father's research has been far more extensive. I overheard exceedingly long discussions between them about ancient battle tactics when I was eight or nine years old. When General Wellesley left Calcutta, they continued those discussions by correspondence."

"And where did you travel after India?"

She furrowed her brow. "Persia, then Tibet for nearly a year—that is where I learned many of the methods I use with the wounded. Twice to Greece after that and once to Italy, Arabia briefly, then finally back to England."

Harry took the folded canvas from her and added it to a stack on a nearby table. "Is that when Wellesley persuaded your father to serve as an advisor to his regiments?"

"Not immediately. General Wellesley was in Ireland, then Denmark, after which he'd intended to sail for the West Indies. Meanwhile, I was attempting to persuade my father to allow me to enlist as a man to help fight against the French. I quite fancied myself a modern day Boudicca or Joan of Arc, who would single-handedly lead the

British forces to victory." Her throaty little laugh sent a sudden flicker of desire through him.

"You may do so yet. Indeed, Miss Maxwell, I begin to believe there is very little you could not accomplish, should you set your mind to it."

She frowned. "I have little patience with flattery, sir, for I am not so exceptional as you seem to think. In truth, most women are capable of far more than they realize, certainly more than most men would care to believe. The mere fact that we are barred from training as surgeons, lawyers, or even soldiers, does not mean we are incapable of learning, and excelling, as well or better than our brothers."

Harry was careful not to allow his surprise at this unorthodox view to show in his expression. "After seeing what you did to Phillips last night, I don't dare disagree."

Privately, however, he had no doubt that Miss Maxwell was a most unusual woman indeed…and one who increasingly attracted him. Though alert for any opportunity to spend time with her, he at first only managed a few words here and there. He was often out on maneuvers, and she seemed to have even less idle time in camp than he did. In addition to transcribing notes, she spent long hours translating various texts of her father's from Greek, Latin and even Sanskrit into English.

When wounded were brought into camp from occasional skirmishes with the French, she faced more pressing work, for she proved to have far more medical knowledge than the orderly assigned to the 45th, whose sole prior experience had been two months as a surgeon's mate.

While days were generally spent drilling or marching, evenings in camp were often enlivened by the soldiers adding to their rum rations any wine or spirits taken from French troops or gifted by the locals. Harry never partook, however. Liquor had been largely responsible for his father losing the small estate he'd received as an earl's second son, giving Harry an aversion to the stuff.

That abstinence freed his evenings to learn more of Xena Maxwell's life history—and a fascinating history it was. From the time of her mother's death when she was but five years old, Xena had traveled the globe with her father, gaining a familiarity with foreign peoples, languages, cultures and geography that few male scholars could boast.

Her unusual first name, Greek for "welcome stranger," stemmed from both parents' fascination with an obscure Greek myth about the goddess Athena, who allegedly masqueraded as a beggar woman, then showered gifts upon the only family that welcomed her into their home.

Though Harry knew he was by no means the only man in camp who admired Xena, after a week or two he began to believe—to hope —that she was coming to prefer his company to any of the others.

"How did you convince your father to allow you to come to Portugal with him?" he asked one evening as he helped her pack up the surgery tent in preparation for the next day's march.

The grin she flashed him over the stack of linens she held made his pulse quicken. "He knew full well I'd pass myself off as a lad and enlist the moment he was gone, otherwise."

"Able a soldier as you'd be, your skill in the surgery doubtless saves more lives. I don't like to think how many more of those recently wounded would have died if left solely to the tender mercies of Corporal Jenkins."

Xena shook her head. "That man creates far more work than he saves me, for I must keep half an eye on him at all times to prevent him causing more harm than good. Why, just last week he tried to begin an amputation before compressing the artery—poor Private Miller would have bled to death in minutes had I not intervened."

"Jenkins is no worse than what passes for a surgeon in most camps," Harry reminded her. "Ours is possibly the luckiest regiment in all Wellesley's army to have you."

That was too direct a compliment for Xena's taste, for she frowned warningly. "I am simply fortunate that my travels in Asia and else-where provided me with greater knowledge and better methods than most attempting to act in that capacity. I also have the advantage of being a woman."

"Advantage! How so?"

At his startled tone her smile returned. "I was no more than twelve when it became clear to me that women are far the more rational sex the world over. Men frequently allow their judgment to be clouded by passion or pride, while women take a more practical view of life."

Though her declaration went counter to all he'd previously believed, Harry did not laugh. Xena's views, as refreshing as her manner of speech and dress, were part of what he found so irresistible about her. "On what do you base such an, ah, interesting conclusion?" he asked, wanting to hear more.

"Study, experience and careful observation. No matter the country or culture, women learn at an early age to do whatever is necessary in order to survive and prosper. Indeed, they must, as they rarely have much, if any, *lawful* say over the disposition of their own persons or property. That is true even in such a supposedly civilized country as England."

Harry supposed he could not deny that. "And you conclude that the male sex as a whole is responsible for this widespread injustice?"

"Who else? 'Tis they who wrote the laws that ensure they hold all the power, despite being so very prone to corruption by it." She shook her head in resigned disgust. "In all my travels, I have encountered a disappointingly small handful of men, other than my father, worthy of my respect or trust."

Harry made no further attempt to argue with her but silently resolved to someday be numbered among that handful.

CHAPTER TWO

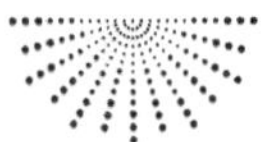

AS THE 45TH AND OTHER REGIMENTS UNDER GENERAL WELLESLEY'S command marched eastward across Portugal toward Spain, Harry's persistence with Xena Maxwell paid off. What had begun as a case of mistaken identity eventually progressed to friendship…and more.

One evening the two of them happened to be alone in the tent Xena shared with her father and *ayah*. A rare occurrence, but her Indian servant was off washing their linens in a nearby stream when Colonel Maxwell was unexpectedly summoned to meet with two regimental commanders sent over by General Wellesley to discuss tactics for an upcoming battle. As Harry had not been asked to leave, they continued their discussion of Shakespeare's sonnets.

"Surely you must wonder what all the fuss is about?" Harry teased when she expressed disdain for the very concept of romantic love. "Aren't you curious to know what might inspire a person to write such poetry or even go to war, as Paris and Menelaus did over Helen?" He had discovered that references to ancient classics generally kept her talking.

"Lust, I presume. *That* obviously exists, if only to ensure the continuation of the human race—and appears to be the cause of many regrettable decisions. I can't imagine why so many wish to elevate it with the name of *love* and hold it up as a pure and elevating passion to be sought above all others." She shook her head with a smile.

Harry smiled back, holding her gaze with his. "Very well, call it lust, if you prefer. Have you no wish to experience it for yourself, if only in the name of research?"

One eyebrow went up and for a moment he feared he'd been too bold—but then Xena laughed, throwing her head back and giving him a delicious view of her lovely white throat above the collar of her frumpy gray work dress.

"From what I've read—and witnessed—lust is an affliction far more common to men than to women." She then stunned him by adding, "But never let it be said that I am less than thorough in my research. If it is indeed possible for a woman to feel lust, I should like to experience it first hand. You seem knowledgable about such things, Lieutenant. You may *attempt* to inspire lust in me. What is the first step?"

Heart hammering, knowing he might never again have an opportunity like this, Harry moved to sit next to her on her father's trunk.

"This." Slowly, softly, so as not to alarm her, he leaned in and touched his lips to hers.

She did not resist, but nor did she respond. For several seconds he maintained a light pressure, then drew back slightly to examine its effect upon her.

Xena quirked a shapely eyebrow. "I have *seen* kisses before, Mr. Thatcher. That scarcely qualified, unless you meant to show me how you might bid goodnight to a child."

Harry grinned. "I didn't wish to frighten you."

Again, she laughed. "You have yet to frighten me in the least, Lieutenant, even when menacing me with a weapon rather more lethal than your lips."

"Will you allow me to try again?"

She nodded, her expression both skeptical and amused.

Daring all, he put both arms around her and drew her to him for the kind of kiss he'd dreamed of for the past several weeks. "For a kiss to *qualify*," he murmured, "it must be mutual."

Xena responded with a tiny, uncertain nod and he covered her mouth with his. She stiffened for an instant, but before he could release her with an apology, she put her hands on his shoulders to pull him closer. Hesitantly, experimentally, her lips began to move under his, causing a desire beyond anything he'd ever experienced to rocket through him.

Fighting the impulse to deepen the kiss, Harry held himself back, allowing her to explore this new sensation. Finally, cautiously, he moved his own lips, parting them, touching his tongue to the corners of her mouth. Instead of stiffening again as he'd half feared, she mimicked his motions with her own tongue until his and hers entwined.

Tightening their embrace, he probed the sweetness of her mouth while his hands savored the curve of her back. She made a slight sound of pleasure, deep in her throat, then deepened the kiss further herself, her hands now moving over his shoulders, his sides, his back. Fire bursts seemed to explode in his brain, his loins. Even when he'd lain with a woman, he'd never experienced such bliss.

He was reaching up to undo the top button of her gown when sanity abruptly returned. Belatedly recalling that someone might appear at the flap of the tent at any moment, he forced himself to draw back.

She stared at him, her face slightly flushed, her gray eyes wide. "What...interesting sensations. So that is what a real kiss is like? A normal kiss between a man and a woman? I had no idea."

Harry nearly blurted out that there had been nothing the least bit *normal* about that kiss, at least not in his own, admittedly limited, experience. Uncertain whether she had been as profoundly affected as himself, however, he simply nodded.

A smile now played at the corners of her delicious mouth. "I believe I begin to understand what all the fuss is about. And kissing is only the start, is it not?"

"Er, yes," he said cautiously. "But a nice start, don't you think?"

"Much nicer than I expected," she admitted. "Indeed, it was quite enjoyable. I rather think I should experience everything else that occurs between a man and a women. For *research* purposes, of course."

Startled and gratified, Harry returned her mischievous grin. "Of course. But…this is perhaps not the best time and place to continue. Your *ayah* will be returning soon, will she not?"

"Oh. Yes. I'd nearly forgotten." Xena blinked and glanced around the tent. Though larger than most other officers' tents, it was far too small to afford any more privacy than the cloth that had been hung to screen Xena's cot from her father's.

She thoughtfully furrowed her brow. "To avoid any risk of being pressured to a commitment neither of us desires, we'd best be discreet —something I'm certain we can manage with a bit of imagination. And then…" Her smile made his pulse, which had barely begun to slow, accelerate again. "Then we can continue my *research.*"

And so they did. As the regiment advanced inexorably toward Spain, where General Wellesley planned to engage Napoleon's forces sweeping down from the North, Xena proved her cleverness was not limited to ancient texts and healing. With admirable ingenuity, she created frequent opportunities to be alone with Harry so that he could continue educating her in the ways of love.

"I begin to understand how lust might possibly cloud the judgment of women as well as men," she observed during a stolen moment when he was allegedly helping her to gather local herbs for use in the surgery.

He smiled, caressing her bottom through the fabric of her dress as he pulled her closer. "You find this sensation pleasant, then?"

"Indeed. Does my touch inspire lust in you as well?" As she spoke, she ran both hands along his sides.

His arousal pressed against her stomach. "Can you not tell?"

In response, she slipped a hand between them to feel it through his breeches. He nearly gasped aloud with pleasure, then retaliated by doing the same, massaging the juncture of her thighs through her skirts.

"Oh, my," she exclaimed, pressing herself more firmly against his hand, then startled him by adding, "'Tis a shame we cannot dispense with the encumbrance of clothing, for I should rather like to experience more of this sensation."

He chuckled at her naiveté. "A shame indeed. But perhaps as well, for if I were to show you all I wish to, we could indeed find ourselves obliged to wed."

She tilted her head back to look up at him. "Because I might become pregnant, you mean?"

Surprised yet again by her plainspokenness, he nodded. "There is also the risk that our, ah, lust might develop into something more profound, breaking down *our* resistance to such an outcome." In truth, his own initially-voiced disinterest in marriage had changed some days ago.

Xena, however, laughed. "Small chance of that, given our mutual feelings toward matrimony. And as for the other, a Persian wise-woman shared with me some secrets to prevent conception. The main challenge will be to find a safe venue. Meanwhile, I suppose I must be content with this." Again pressing close, she lifted her lips to his for another kiss.

After two more days marching, the regiment was again encamped when Harry found a small, folded slip of paper in his mess kit one morning. Curious, he unfolded it. *One hour past sunset. Thicket near largest chestnut.* He recognized Xena's hand, distinctively clear and bold for a woman's, from the various transcripts and translations he'd seen in her tent.

That day seemed to move with preternatural slowness. With every passing hour, Harry feared some order might arrive that would send him away from the camp before sunset. When the appointed time finally approached, he could scarce contain his eagerness.

Already he'd made certain to mark the chestnut tree she'd mentioned, some hundred yards beyond the boundary of the camp on the edge of a steep riverbank. Passing rows of tents, he heard the beginnings of the usual evening revelry now all the men had finished their sparse evening meal. Even so, he moved casually but with purpose, as though going to answer a call of nature—which, in a sense, he was.

On reaching the thicket of tall ferns between tree and riverbank he slowed, listening. "Xena?" he whispered, when he heard nothing but the river below. No answer.

A knot of disappointment settled in his stomach. She must not have managed to slip away after all. Still, he moved into ferns nearly as high as his head and sat down, unwilling to give up so easily—and not two minutes later heard soft footfalls drawing near. Peering between the fronds, he saw Xena hurrying toward him, something bulky in her arms. Disappointment instantly gave way to elation.

"Over here," he called softly when she paused to glance about.

Immediately she plunged into the ferns and an instant later was beside him. "My apologies. I meant to be here before you, but Yamini —my *ayah*—asked rather more questions about my supposed errand than I expected. She knows me well and is far more difficult to deceive than my father. Indeed, I believe she may already suspect. I dare not stay out more than half an hour, lest she come hunting for me. Here."

She handed him her burden, which proved to be one of the rough wool blankets from the surgery tent. Harry quickly spread it upon the ground. As she settled down next to him, his heart began to hammer with anticipation.

"Have you something in particular in mind for tonight's research?" He tried to keep his tone light, but feared he failed at that.

Xena smiled up at him through the near-darkness. "I thought we might begin with a review of my lessons thus far and, ah, proceed from there."

Chuckling, he drew her into the circle of his arms. "A most logical plan." He lowered his lips to hers and she responded instantly—and eagerly. Her lips were warm, pliable and delicious, causing pleasure to spin dizzily through him. Long, blissful minutes passed before they finally paused for breath.

More profoundly affected than ever, Harry longed to know whether she felt the same.

"Surely every kiss cannot be like the ones we've shared thus far, or I can't conceive why men and women would ever do aught else," she breathed wonderingly before he could think how to ask.

He smiled, when elation made him want to shout for joy. "I fear I am not the expert you have assumed, but judging by what little experience I have had, I should say no—every kiss is by no means like this." He again covered her lips with his own and again she participated wholeheartedly.

Desire built within him to a fever pitch—and now there was little risk of interruption. He fumbled with the buttons of her gown, aching to touch her flesh, and she made no move to stop him. Soon the front of her drab work dress parted far enough to allow his hand access and he discovered with an exultant shock that she wore no chemise beneath it. Gently, he cupped his hand over one small, taut breast.

Xena gave a little gasp and he froze. "That…that feels wonderful. Pray don't stop!" She quickly undid the rest of her buttons, freeing both breasts. Lowering his head, he tentatively took one into his mouth while continuing to massage the other. "Oh. Yes," she breathed. "More, please."

Obligingly, Harry reached under her skirts to slide a hand up her inner thigh until he touched the soft curls at the top, then delved a finger into her already-moist cleft. Now she gasped more loudly.

"I…I had no idea." One hand ceased stroking his back, instead moving to cover his bulging arousal. "This means you wish for more too, does it not?"

"Of course," he fairly panted. "But surely you don't wish to risk—"

She leaned up to kiss him. "Pray do not worry I mean to trap you into marriage, Lieutenant. I have taken steps to be certain we'll face no unwanted consequences. Now, I believe I mentioned I haven't much time?" So saying, she began unbuttoning the front of his breeches.

Though Harry knew he should stop her, should at least demand to know what sort of precautions she had taken, his desire for her now burned too fiercely for caution. In a fever of eagerness, he worked with her to divest both of them of the majority of their clothing. Still, just enough sanity remained for him to whisper, "Xena, are you sure?"

"Yes, Harry." It was the first time she'd used his first name. "I wish to know *all*."

With a groan, he gave himself up to what they both wanted so desperately. So aroused was he, he'd barely entered her when he felt his climax coming. Determined that her first experience of the act of love be an enjoyable one, he reached between them to pleasure her, but there was no need. Already she was gasping and bucking against him as she reached her own peak. He followed only seconds later, clasping her tightly to him as he drove into her one final time.

"That was…remarkable," she murmured once their breathing had slowed. "If there were time right now, I should rather like to do it again."

Harry, still completely overcome by the experience, managed a shaky laugh. "I, ah, fear I would not be able to oblige you for some minutes, in any event."

"Oh, yes, I seem to recall hearing… 'Tis just as well, for I really must get back before Yamini comes in search of me."

With a sigh that sounded sincerely regretful, she pulled her dress back around and began buttoning up the front. "Thank you, Harry, for a *most* instructive and enjoyable lesson. I quite look forward to my next, for I should like to further expand my education as soon as may be."

The very next day, the 45th was again obliged to pack up and continue their grueling eastward march across northern Portugal. Nevertheless, Xena's eagerness for more lessons in "lust"—she still refused to admit the existence of love—continued unabated.

Though no true privacy could be contrived while on the march, she used the excuse of discussing Shakespeare, on whose works Harry was fortunately well-versed, to walk a bit apart with Harry so that they could at least talk without being overheard.

"I have thought quite a lot about my lesson in the fernbrake," she commented on the third day of the march. "Now that I better under-stand the pleasure involved, I see how women might be lured by such into the slavery of marriage, as most cultures give them no other acceptable way to enjoy such a wondrous experience regularly."

"You, however, feel no such lure?" Harry couldn't help asking. Occasional fantasies had begun to intrude into his waking as well as sleeping hours wherein Xena wished to continue their exclusive relationship even after they were safely back in England.

She snorted derisively. "I'd like to think myself far too rational to be seduced into lifelong subjection by a mere fever of the flesh, no matter how pleasurable I find it. Men frequently partake of such delights without being obliged to marry. Should not a woman also be allowed to enjoy a purely physical relationship without trading her freedom for the privilege? I mean to prove it possible."

"Given a choice, most women seem to prefer the married state to spinsterhood," he carefully replied. "Surely that must mean there is *something* to be said for it?"

"They simply believe what they've been told by their fathers and brothers: that they are incapable of handling their own affairs, so must allow some man to provide for them—as well as their progeny, since most *English* women have no idea how to avert pregnancy."

During a previous conversation, she had confided to him that a surgical sponge soaked in juice from the lemons so prevalent in Portugal, combined with the added precaution of ingesting wild carrot seeds, was known to prevent such a consequence. Harry could only hope she was correct.

"Then you still maintain that love is a mere invention of poets and playwrights?"

For the first time, she shrugged rather than nodding. "Given how much has been written about it, I cannot completely discount the possibility of its existence in specialized cases. Though it's likely many infer that emotion simply because they happen to find more pleasure in the company and attentions of one particular person in comparison to others."

Harry kept his smile to himself, privately thinking there might yet be hope of changing her mind on that particular issue.

.   .   .

As the days passed, Harry had cause to be grateful that their first coupling had been under such relatively ideal conditions. Even when they again made camp, never again did they have the luxury of a blanket or the leisure of knowing they were unlikely to be discovered. They instead had to settle for the occasional private moment behind a tent or quick interlude in some nearby woods for any subsequent lovemaking.

Even so, despite the war raging around them, Harry's focus increasingly centered on Xena and the stolen moments she contrived for them. If he had any illusions that her aversion to a permanent commitment might be fading, however, they were disabused one evening when he stopped by her tent to return a translated Greek battle account she'd lent him.

"Your young man is here," Colonel Maxwell called out teasingly when Harry appeared at the tent flap. "Have you come courting again, Lieutenant?"

Before he could respond, Xena emerged from her side of the tent with a frown. "Pray do not be ridiculous, Father. Lieutenant Thatcher is not *courting* me. What would be the point, when he knows as well as you do that I've no intention of marrying? We simply share several common interests."

Harry was impressed that she could claim that without a blush, given their *primary* common interest. At the same time, he was disheartened to learn she had not unbent her stance on matrimony at all, despite her obviously increasing fondness for him.

Just how engaged his own feelings had become was driven home to him the following week during one of their increasingly frequent clashes with the French. Having recently crossed into Spain, the 45th was beset by a fairly large force less than a mile from camp. After a sharp engagement, the British proved victorious, though with losses. Harry was escorting a cart full of wounded back to camp when a shout from ahead warned him it had also been overrun by the enemy.

Xena!

His heart in his throat, he wrested the reins of the closest horse from the soldier leading it and leapt astride. Heedless of the rough terrain, he urged his mount to a gallop, his only thought to reach her side and assure himself she was safe. If she were not...

On reaching the camp bare minutes later, he saw Xena, dressed in her private's uniform and wielding a pair of pistols, holding three French soldiers at bay. Two others lay bleeding at her feet. Behind her huddled the few other women in the camp, while a patient or two sound enough to hold a weapon appeared to be assisting in the defense.

Just as Harry came thundering up, another French soldier came round the corner of the surgery tent, rifle raised. Without hesitation, Xena shot him dead. A moment later more of the 45th arrived and the three still standing threw down their arms to surrender.

That evening Xena was hailed by the entire regiment for her heroism in preventing the massacre of those left behind in camp, for it was she who had sounded the alarm and rallied those able to the defense. Though he cheered with the rest, Harry was more than a little shaken by the discovery that, completely without intending to do so, he had fallen head over ears in love with her.

"It appears that my father is not the only one who has noticed how much time we are spending in each other's company," Xena commented two days later as they adjusted their clothing after a brief but passionate encounter in a deserted barn near the camp.

"And that concerns you?" In truth, Harry would as lief the other soldiers recognized Xena's clear preference for him, as it would make them less likely to pursue her affections.

"Of course. I've no more wish than you to be pressured into a commitment neither of us desires. Perhaps it would be wisest if we avoid being seen together for a while. In public, I mean. I have no wish to curtail *this* sort of activity." She winked at him.

"Nor I." Though it cost him an effort, Harry winked back. "Very well, if you think it best, I will keep my distance and strive to conceal how you affect me. In public."

Over the next week or two, Xena all but ignored Harry in public while making a point of talking frequently to others in camp. He would have found the change impossibly hard to bear were it not for the notes she continued to slip into the hollow of the little elephant-shaped clock he kept near the flap of his tent, naming the time and place of their next rendezvous.

Suspicions against them seemed to subside, just as Xena intended, their names no longer linked in the conversations he overheard in the mess. He was startled, therefore, to return to his tent one evening to find Colonel Maxwell waiting for him inside.

"Sir?" he inquired in what he hoped was a tone of respectful curiosity, though his stomach clenched with sudden nervousness. Only two hours earlier, he and Xena had enjoyed one of their most passionate encounters yet, in the copse behind the livery tent. Surely her father's visit could have nothing to do with that?

He was wrong.

"Lieutenant Thatcher. I understand you and my daughter have entered into a liaison that can only end in marriage—and quickly."

Harry swallowed, hard. "Entered… Did Xena—?"

"She has admitted the whole to me, yes, and agrees that a speedy marriage is the only option."

He could hardly believe it. "She…she does?"

"Of course. I assume you also see the necessity. But whether or no, you will reveal no reluctance you might feel to my daughter. I have already sent for the chaplain from battalion headquarters."

Though he'd hoped to change Xena's views on marriage once the war was over, Harry could scarcely believe that Xena herself would force the issue by telling her father about their activities! This was no time for questions or arguments, however, unless he wished to be run through or court-martialed.

"Of…of course, sir."

Half an hour later, he found himself facing the battalion chaplain in Colonel Maxwell's tent while Xena was led to his side by her father. Still perplexed by this sudden turn of events, Harry turned a curious glance her way. She did not meet it, instead staring straight ahead, her face set—seemingly determined to forge the very bond she had claimed to despise.

Persuaded that she would soon explain the reason for her apparent *volte face*, Harry repeated the vows steadily, as did Xena. But the instant they were pronounced wed, Colonel Maxwell stepped between them before Harry could so much as kiss his new bride.

"Thank you, Chaplain. You may go. And you, Lieutenant, will come with me. Xena, bide you here until I return." So saying, the colonel took Harry by the arm and frog-marched him from the tent and all the way to headquarters.

"Major Thorne," he addressed the startled officer on duty, "I request that this man be posted to another regiment. The 48th is currently below strength, is it not?"

The major nodded, his eyes darting curiously from Colonel Maxwell to Harry and back. "It is, sir. I, er, can see to it first thing in the morning."

"Tonight would be preferable. I'll leave him with you until the reassignment can be effected. Send an orderly to pack up his tent."

Colonel Maxwell turned on his heel and left both Major Thorne and Harry to stare after him—one merely curious, the other stunned.

Harry never saw Xena again.

On arriving at the 48th, bivouacked several miles to the north, Harry was greeted by two other young lieutenants he recognized from his days at Oxford—Lord Peter Northrup and Jack Ashecroft. Sharing the dangers and challenges of battle soon strengthened their earlier acquaintance into bonds of friendship. Even so, Harry never revealed the true reason he had been transferred to the 48th.

For the first week or two, he daily expected some word from Xena —a note of apology or explanation, or perhaps a demand for half his pay. Nothing came, however, and as skirmishes with the French intensified, his attention was necessarily diverted to other concerns.

Not until a week after their unexpected and spectacular victory over the massed French forces at the Battle of Talavera did Harry finally receive a letter—but from Colonel Maxwell rather than Xena herself.

Lieut. Thatcher, regret to inform you my daughter, whom I sent back to England as a result of your actions, never reached her homeland. I have just received word that the frigate Mary Anne, on which she sailed, was sunk by the French on the eighteenth of July and all souls aboard her lost. I write with the assumption that you held her in some degree of affection and therefore extend condolences, despite your being nearly as much at fault for her death as the French.

Yours, etc.

Colonel Geo. Maxwell

Jack and Peter stopped by Harry's tent while he still sat stunned, the letter in his hand. Jack jovially called out that they were on their way to the mess tent, but Peter, unusually perceptive even then, waved him to silence.

"Bad news from home?" he asked sympathetically.

Harry stuffed the letter into his pocket. "You might say that." Hard on the heels of shock, grief and guilt, came the realization that he would likely never know why Xena had decided to marry him. Perhaps it shouldn't matter now, but…

"Occurs to me I never did celebrate our recent victory properly. I'm minded to get roaring drunk tonight. Care to join me?"

Though by then his friends were well aware that Harry never drank, they both agreed without question—Jack enthusiastically, Peter with reluctant concern. It was the beginning of a pattern that was to endure for the next seven years.

CHAPTER THREE

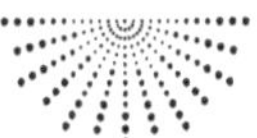

LONDON—NOVEMBER, 1816

A SLIGHT SOUND JARRED HARRY AWAKE. CONFUSED, HE TOOK IN HIS unfamiliar surroundings: dark blue bed hangings and matching drapes, a cheerful fire burning on the hearth, an ornate clock ticking on the mantelpiece above it. The luxurious chamber was a far cry from the army tent he'd just been dreaming of—or even his own modest lodgings in London.

"Where the devil am I?" he asked the medallioned ceiling.

"In one of my spare bedchambers," Lord Peter Northrup startled him by replying. "Glad to finally see you conscious, old boy. Must say you gave me rather a turn, remaining insensible for the better part of two days, though the physician claimed no permanent damage had been done."

Harry tried to struggle into a sitting position but abandoned the attempt when the dull throbbing in his temples became acute. Collapsing back against the piled pillows, he turned his head just enough to see his friend, sitting at his ease in an overstuffed chair near the head of the bed.

"Two days? How did I get here?" he demanded, then winced at the sound of his own voice, louder than he'd intended.

"When you didn't turn up night before last, Brewster went out looking and discovered you face down in the alley behind your lodgings," Peter explained. "He couldn't rouse you, so sent a stable lad to fetch me—at a most inconvenient hour, I might add." The relief and concern on his best friend's face undercut the mock-recrimination. "It seemed more prudent to bring you here to Curzon Street than to attempt hauling you up three flights of stairs, particularly since I didn't know whether whoever did this to you might return."

Harry frowned, trying to remember precisely what had happened. "Doubtful. I imagine the fellows who attacked me took all I had, so they'd have had little incentive."

"It was a simple case of robbery by footpads, then, and not an act of revenge by some jealous husband? You can no doubt understand why that might be my first assumption." Peter grinned, though worry still lingered in his eyes.

"Aye, wouldn't be the first time, would it?" Harry agreed. "But no. I'd won rather a nice sum at the tables half an hour earlier and clearly failed to watch my back well enough on the way home. Someone must have tipped them off." Recalling how he'd humiliated Phillips, a suspicion sprang to mind. Not that he'd ever be able to prove it.

"Someone from the club?" Peter was clearly startled. "Or were you at one of your hells in Seven Dials?"

"Guards. But you know as well as I there are a few members who'd sell their own mothers if they thought it might profit them."

Peter sighed. "You're right, alas, much as I hate to think it of fellow officers. But enough of that. How are you feeling?"

"Like the very devil," Harry admitted. "Though likely better than I should, considering." Carefully, he flexed each muscle in turn, testing every part of his body. "M'head's the worst. Bastard bashed me with a horseshoe."

"Anyone you recognized?"

Harry shook his head and immediately regretted it. "They looked like common ruffians—three of them. Held my own for a good bit, even so."

"I don't doubt it. Never knew drink to impair you in a fight."

Except that it had last night—no, night before last. Not that he'd give Pete the satisfaction of saying so. He was in no mood for another homily on his dissipated lifestyle.

After another searching look at Harry, Peter stood. "I'll have a tray sent up, after which you should rest a bit more. The doctor said he'd call again in the morning. Then, depending on his verdict, I may have a proposition to put to you."

Lord Peter quitted the room, leaving Harry to wonder what fresh plot for his reformation his friend might be hatching now.

Another night's sleep reduced the pain in Harry's head to a dull ache. The doctor, when he came, pronounced himself satisfied.

"It's a hard head you have, Mr. Thatcher," he declared in a faint Irish brogue. "The cut over your ear should heal well enough and the skull beneath suffered no crack, as it might well have from such a blow as you describe. Another two days' bed rest and you'll be nigh fit as a fiddle, I dare say."

Peter, standing just behind the man, grinned ear to ear at the pronouncement. "I'll see he stays put, never fear. And thank you."

As soon as the doctor left, Peter turned back to Harry, still grinning. "Excellent news, eh? Told him you had a skull of iron. Now, care to hear my idea?"

"Not if it involves flinging yet another debutante at my head. It's taken enough abuse already. Even so, I've no intention of lying idle for another forty-eight hours."

"Of course you will. I'll do my best to make the time pass quickly for you."

Harry snorted. "Fine. You can begin by leaving a bottle or two within reach."

As he'd expected, that request drew a frown and a shake of the head from his friend. "It's nine in the morning, Harry. Perhaps this evening I'll join you for a glass of sherry. But now, about my proposal —and no, it doesn't involve any debutantes. Perhaps you recall how I briefly became obsessed with discovering the identity of the Saint of Seven Dials, after we returned from the Congress of Vienna?"

Though this was not at all what Harry had expected, he nodded. "Yes, you were determined to show up the Runners. I assumed you were missing all that Austrian intrigue—though I missed other delights a good bit more. I recall one wench in particular—"

"Yes, well. Do you also remember that fellow working with the Runners poking about last summer, questioning various members of the *ton*?"

"Aye, we both thought it hilarious when he went after your brother Marcus. As though he could be capable of exploits like that." Harry chuckled at the memory. "Do you mean to say you've finally discovered who the Saint really is?"

Peter merely lifted a shoulder and glanced out the window. "In a manner of speaking. As it turns out, there was no *one* Saint. Not this past year, at any rate. It's been a shared role—or, I should say, a sequential one, as there was only ever one at a time. Now, however, the role of Saint stands empty and the poor of London are feeling the lack. Might you consider stepping into it?" he concluded in a rush.

Harry stared at his friend in astonishment. Belatedly realizing his jaw had dropped, he closed his mouth and swallowed. Twice. "You're mad, Pete," he finally said. "I may have more than my fair share of vices, but thievery has never been among them. Why the devil would you think *me*, of all people, a likely successor to the Saint of Seven Dials? I've no aptitude for that sort of thing."

"What about those missives you stole for Wellington in Vienna? Or the dispatches you intercepted, read and sent on with no one the wiser?" Peter shrugged with exaggerated nonchalance. "I merely thought the job might amuse you. Give you something interesting to do while your closest acquaintances are busy setting up their households, as you're dead set against ever doing the same yourself."

"Won't deny playing the Saint of Seven Dials appeals far more than parson's mousetrap, but my life's interesting enough without either. Besides, there must be a dozen better candidates out there. Men with an actual bent for philanthropy—and two good arms." He couldn't quite keep the bitterness out of his tone.

"So I should simply leave you alone to drink and wench yourself to death?"

"Aye, just as I've been saying these three years past," Harry snapped, more bothered by the sadness in his friend's eyes than he cared to admit.

With a terse nod, Peter turned to the door. "Very well. Should you change your mind before leaving here, let me know."

"Hold on, you never said who all those Saints have been. Was Marcus actually one of them? Who else? Anyone I know?"

Peter glanced back over his shoulder, one eyebrow raised. "If you agree to take on the role I can arrange for you to meet them. Otherwise, I'm bound by my pledge to keep their secrets. Give you good morning, Harry."

"You cannot be serious." Xena gestured at the half-dozen small items spread across the polished wooden counter. "Any one of these is worth three or four times what you're offering for all six."

The antiquities dealer merely shrugged. "It might be a different thing, madam, if I had specific buyers in mind for any of these items. As it is, I have no way of knowing how long it may take me to sell them, so cannot justify an upfront outlay of the sort you suggest."

With a huff of disgust, Xena began transferring the ancient coins and statuettes she'd brought as samples of her late father's extensive collection back into their velvet-lined box.

"Then I'll find a dealer with better business sense and a finer appreciation of rare artifacts." Head held high, she strode from the shop, kicking impatiently at the constricting skirts convention dictated she wear while in London.

Back out on the pavement, however, a modicum of her bravado deserted her. This was the second antiquities dealer she'd approached, and he'd offered her an even smaller sum than the last. Would they all prove so ignorant—or greedy? How was she to raise the money to repair the roof of Moorside Grange or the broken mill wheel in the village?

Still walking as briskly as her outmoded dress would allow, she consulted her all-too-short list of possibilities. Unfortunately, even a city the size of London boasted few shops dealing in the sort of arti-facts her father had collected over his lifetime.

"Beg pardon, ma'am," a gruff voice exclaimed as she inadvertently jostled a tall gentleman as she passed him from behind.

She glanced up to make an apology—for, tall as Xena was, the gentleman was much taller—and froze, startled.

Not nearly as startled as the man she'd bumped, however, for he stared as if seeing a ghost. "By Jupiter! Is it really Miss Maxwell, and in the flesh? But we all heard you'd gone down on that frigate the Frenchies sank off the coast of Corunna, back in '09. How the devil…?"

Compelled by long-ago habit, Xena very nearly saluted before gath-ering her wits enough to instead sink into a clumsy curtsey before her former General Wellesley, now the celebrated Duke of Wellington. "It is good to see you again, your grace. I, ah, assumed my father would have informed you of the mistake, though he himself did not discover the truth for more than two years."

"Two years! But surely you sent him word you were alive?"

"Certainly, once the news reached me about the frigate, but my message never reached him. When he returned home in '12, he was exceedingly astonished to discover me there, and alive."

"But how did you survive that sinking? It was reported that all aboard were lost."

"Alas, I believe the report was correct. The heavy rains in Spain that summer caused me to miss my intended sailing, forcing me to take a different ship to England. The delay proved fortunate for me, if not for the men aboard that frigate."

The Duke continued to stare at her in bemusement. "Fortunate? I call it a miracle! You were greatly mourned in the Peninsula when news of the sinking filtered back to us, not least by the many men whose lives were saved by your exceptional nursing skills. I'd never seen your father so thoroughly cut up. How does Colonel Maxwell, by the bye? Still gadding about the globe unearthing moldering bits of parchment and pottery?"

She shook her head. "I'm terribly sorry to be the one to tell you, your grace, but a year ago last summer my father succumbed to a fever during yet another Eastern excursion."

"Ah, a sad loss, that. Your father had a remarkable mind. I daresay he knew the details of every major military campaign conducted over the past two millennia. It made him a crack advisor on the battlefield, I can tell you."

She smiled wistfully, remembering those relatively carefree days—before her life had become the veritable cage it was now. "He had planned to write up an exhaustive account of your own campaigns, your grace, upon his return to Yorkshire. It is a great pity he was never able to do so."

"A pity indeed. Old Max would have put all those other would-be chroniclers to shame, no question about it. My condolences, Miss Maxwell. Or is it still Miss? I forget you are no longer the little girl I knew in India, nor even the young firebrand who once bullied her father into letting her wear a soldier's uniform. Surely by now you are married?"

Xena hesitated for a heartbeat before replying. "I...no. I am not married, your grace." A truthful answer, if not the *entire* truth. "I, ah, have instead endeavored to carry on my father's cataloguing of arti-facts and hope to write a book of my own one day."

The Duke's eyebrows rose above his distinctive hooked nose, then he smiled. "I shouldn't be surprised, as you were ever an Original, Miss Maxwell. You have remained in Yorkshire since returning to England, then? What brings you to Town?"

"Some of those same artifacts." Suddenly conscious of how shab-bily she was dressed, Xena glanced down at the wooden box in her hands. "I find myself obliged to sell a few of them, as my father left rather less in the way of funds than he perhaps intended."

"I see." Her former commander regarded her sympathetically. "Tell me, how long do you remain in London? Tomorrow I'm off to Paris again for a week or two, but on my return I'll be hosting a reunion of sorts for officers who served under me on the Peninsula. I would be exceedingly honored if you would attend in your father's stead."

"Oh! Er, thank you, your grace. I hadn't necessarily intended to be in London many more days, but—"

"But now you will stay, as a favor to me." It was a statement, not a question. "I daresay you'll see quite a few familiar faces there, and they'll all be as delighted as I to discover the news of your drowning was false. Indeed, I predict you will be the talk of the evening, something to lend an otherwise dull gathering a deal more interest. If you'll give me your direction, I'll have an invitation sent round."

Not daring to contradict so great a man, she told him the address of the house where she was staying—though unless she could sell at least a piece or two from her father's collection, she would not be able to afford her rooms there beyond the week she'd already paid.

"Splendid, splendid. I give you good day then, and trust you will enjoy your sojourn in Town." With a deep bow, the Duke departed.

For a long moment, Xena continued to stare after one of the few men she'd ever held in esteem, a thousand recollections crowding her brain. Then she turned on her heel to head back to her temporary abode on Rundel Street, walking faster and faster in her effort to outstrip the ghosts from her past that suddenly threatened to overwhelm her.

Not until she'd mounted the four flights of stairs to her apartments did she pause to catch her breath and, more importantly, to compose herself. It would never do to allow her mental disquiet to show. That would invite questions she felt in no way prepared to answer. After several deep, calming breaths, she finally opened the door.

"She's back!" A well-grown lad of some six-and-a-half years, clad in knee-breeches and a simple shirt, came running to greet her. "Mother, London is a wonderful place! Why, just this morning I have seen from the window fifteen liveried carriages, twelve drays and ten high-perch phaetons. And so many horses! Horses of every color and breed you can imagine. Can't we please stay here always? It is ever so much more interesting than Yorkshire."

Xena allowed herself to be led to the aforementioned window to witness these wonders for herself, exchanging an amused glance with Yamini, her onetime *ayah* and now Theo's nurse. Still smiling, she glanced fondly down at the still-chattering boy by her side—the only thing that had made seven years of veritable exile bearable.

~

Well before his forty-eight hours were up, Harry was heartily bored. He'd have escaped back to his lodgings the first day if Peter hadn't taken the simple precaution of spiriting away his clothes. Little as Harry cared for convention, he didn't much fancy wandering about Mayfair in nothing but his nightshirt.

Worse than boredom, though, were the memories. Memories, released by his recent dreams, and without sufficient distractions to keep them at bay, of a time when he'd been a whole man and a damned good soldier, with all his life to look forward to.

Worst of all, those recollections threw into unpleasant relief the relative pointlessness of his current existence.

Those excesses he'd adopted to put Xena Maxwell from his mind gradually became ingrained habits, increasing after he was invalided out of the army. At first he'd enjoyed scandalizing polite Society but by now even Peter expected him to act the wastrel. Where was the fun in being so predictable?

In truth, his nightly drinking, gambling and wenching had already begun to pall before this enforced inactivity provided so much unwelcome time for reflection. Not so long ago, while deep in his cups, he'd briefly considered putting a period to his existence, as his chosen method of self-destruction was taking far longer than expected. That moment of madness passed quickly, but remembering it still had the power to unsettle him.

Perhaps what he needed was a completely new path to Perdition, one that hadn't already been trodden by thousands of men before him. Becoming the next Saint of Seven Dials might be exactly that—and likely amusing, besides.

That evening, when Lord Peter again came to join him in a single glass of sherry after dinner, Harry picked up his glass—which wasn't nearly full enough—and raised it.

"Very well, Pete, you've beaten me down with this damned captivity. I'll do it."

"Try your hand as the Saint, you mean?" Eyebrow raised, Peter regarded him piercingly.

"Aye. I've flouted convention by all the accepted methods long enough. Time to try a new way to outrage Society—though I suppose I won't be able to take credit for it, more's the pity." He shrugged and forced a grin.

Peter wasn't fooled. "I felt sure you'd eventually grow bored with night after night of dissipation, though I confess it took longer than I expected. It's why I was very much hoping you would agree to take up this gauntlet—not only for the sakes of the poor denizens of Seven Dials, but even more for your own."

Harry's grin faded. "Already trying to take the fun out of it, are you? Surely you can't claim that becoming the Saint will be for my own good when a slip up would lead to the hangman's noose. I've seen the rewards posted for his capture."

"True enough," Peter admitted. "But wouldn't that be a better way to go out than by drinking yourself into an early grave—or otherwise by your own hand?"

So Peter had suspected, even without Harry telling him. As usual. Harry shrugged.

"It'd be a tolerably heroic death, at least. Thought I'd managed one at Salamanca before that Spanish family pulled me through."

"And a hell of a scare you gave us all, too." Peter's eyes were shadowed with remembered worry. "For more than three months everyone believed you dead, you know. Jack swore there was no way you could have survived after the French overran that diversionary maneuver you led."

"Wouldn't have if the Corsican's boys had noticed me. Playing dead is what kept me alive, though it cost me an arm. But enough of that. Now I've agreed, exactly how do I go about becoming the Saint of

Seven Dials? Will you finally tell me who else has played the part? Burning curiosity is half the reason I'm agreeing to this, you know."

Grinning now, Peter stood. "I'll do better than that. As soon as I go down, I'll send Brewster up with your clothes. Join me in the library in half an hour and you'll be able to meet a couple of prior Saints face to face."

CHAPTER FOUR

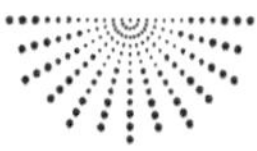

XENA HAD A DIFFICULT TIME GETTING THEO TO BED THAT EVENING, HE was still so wound up with excitement over the sights of London. Not till he was asleep did she finally give way to the memories that had been pressing at her since her unexpected meeting with the Duke.

Those two years in Portugal and Spain under Wellington's command had been the most exciting and fulfilling of her life, even compared to her previous wandering existence. On the Peninsula she'd enjoyed nearly as much liberty as the men until she foolishly allowed passion to overcome judgment—something she'd previously considered a uniquely masculine failing.

For that error she'd paid with the very freedom she so cherished.

"I find you have been less than truthful with me, Xena," her father unexpectedly confronted her one evening. "You've repeatedly insisted to my face that you and Lieutenant Thatcher are merely friends, while all along you have been engaging in activities that should be reserved for husband and wife—which you will become at once."

Xena was appalled. As lenient as her father had always been in allowing her to dress and behave as she wished, she'd persuaded herself he would be reasonable about this as well, should he discover it.

"How—? Did Harry…I mean, Lieutenant Thatcher tell you—?"

"Aye, but not to worry. He is more than willing to do the honorable thing."

She *had* begun to suspect Harry's feelings had progressed beyond friendship and simple lust—nor could she claim her own emotions were completely uninvolved. But that Harry might go so far as to trap her into a marriage he knew full well she did not want had never entered her mind!

In vain did she point out to her father that she'd done no worse than most of the soldiers around her. Angrier than she'd ever seen him, he vowed to have Harry court-martialed unless she agreed to marry him that very night—which she grudgingly did. When Harry neither hesitated nor asked her forgiveness before saying the vows that were to irrevocably bind them, she felt even further betrayed.

Furious at the two men she'd most trusted, Xena had refused to submit tamely when Colonel Maxwell ordered her back to Yorkshire on the next available ship. On landing at Plymouth she used the money her father had intended for a post chaise to Yorkshire to instead outfit herself afresh in male attire and enlist as a cornet in the 66th out of Cornwall, bound for Poland.

That, however, was as far as her desperate bid for freedom progressed.

Xena had been somewhat unwell on her delayed voyage from Corunna, which she attributed to the roughness of the crossing. When her courses failed to occur for a second month, however, Yamini gently pointed out an alternate explanation. Though Xena had been diligent in her use of lemon-soaked sponges and wild carrot seeds, her pregnancy was soon undeniable.

That unwelcome discovery put paid to her dreams of a brilliant military career. With little in the way of funds or options, she was forced to return to Yorkshire after all, traveling by mail coach rather than the more comfortable journey her father had originally provided for.

By the time she reached her father's estate in late 1809 there was no hiding her pregnancy. Though Xena herself cared not a fig about her reputation, Yamini was more foresighted, putting about a story that

Xena's husband had been killed in battle. Because Xena adamantly refused to be called Mrs. Thatcher, Yamini also implied that her mistress was still too distraught by his death to hear his name spoken aloud.

Contrary to what she'd told Wellington that afternoon, it was not until after Theo's birth that Xena finally unbent enough to write to her father. When he failed to reply, she assumed even news of a grandson was not enough to overcome his anger at her indiscretion. Refusing to grovel, she made no further attempt at communication, leaving it to her father to notify Harry Thatcher—or not.

Upon her father's eventual return to Yorkshire she had cause to regret that stubbornness, for his joy at finding her alive and at meeting his two-year-old grandson was clearly genuine. It did not, however, prevent Colonel Maxwell from resuming his travels after a mere three months at home, this time to Africa—and without Xena.

She was still stinging from a renewed sense of betrayal a week later when her convenient local fiction of widowhood unexpectedly became fact. While scanning the newspaper lists of war casualties, as she did daily, she spotted Major Harry Thatcher's name among those killed at the otherwise-victorious Battle of Salamanca.

Xena was completely unprepared for the shock and sorrow she felt at the news. So intense was her grief that she was forced to admit that what she'd declared impossible had occurred—she had fallen in love with him. How Harry would crow if he knew! Though she could scarcely don mourning without admitting her earlier deception to the district, she wore a black armband in the privacy of her home until she was able to push Harry Thatcher's idea back into the corner of her brain and heart where it belonged.

Now, with so many old memories newly-awakened for the first time in years, Xena wondered if she'd been wrong to suppress them for so long—along with what was perhaps the best part of her character.

Thus far, Theo had been raised with no knowledge of his father's identity, though he had recently begun asking questions. As Yamini frequently reminded her, he would soon need to be told, if not the exact truth, then some plausibly respectable version of it. It suddenly occurred to her that, by neglecting to mention his existence to the Duke of Wellington, she might possibly have done her son a disservice.

After all, it would not be many years before she would need to apply to schools on her son's behalf, and a highly-placed recommendation could make all the difference, not to mention other assistance he might receive later on. Could she perhaps make use of the connections she'd formed during her time on the Peninsula to Theo's advantage? The Duke of Wellington's upcoming reception might be an opportunity to do just that.

Not, however, attired as she was right now. Ruefully, she glanced down at her ensemble, nearly ten years out of date and shabby besides. No wonder the shopkeepers she had visited refused to take her seriously.

She could scarce afford *new* clothes, given what these rooms were costing her, but a few modest purchases could surely refurbish her appearance somewhat. She hoped so, as it seemed more necessary than ever that she convert a portion of her father's vast collection of artifacts into a source of funds for both immediate and future needs.

"That'll do, Brewster. Never mind about my cravat, just tie it any old way."

Harry's valet nodded and two seconds later stepped back. "There you are, sir. I must say, I am relieved to see you on your feet again."

"So am I." Harry smiled at his onetime batman and now literal left hand. "Lord Peter tells me I have you to thank for that. With any luck, I'll soon be able to not only catch you up on your wages but throw in a more tangible token of gratitude, as well."

If there was skepticism behind Brewster's smile he hid it well as he bowed Harry out of the room.

Eager as Harry was to finally leave his luxurious prison, he was even more curious. Two Saints of Seven Dials in this very house? How the devil had Peter arranged *that* on such short notice? He suspected it meant his friend had again read his mind and knew he would accept the challenge even before Harry did.

On entering the library a moment later, Harry was disappointed to see only four people awaiting him: Peter, his new wife, her young brother who now lived with them, and Peter's brother, Lord Marcus Northrup. No new faces at all.

"I take it I'm early?" Harry moved casually to a chair, hoping to disguise his lingering weakness before Peter noticed. He had no desire to play the invalid any longer.

"Not a bit of it," Peter replied with a broad smile and a glance at the others in the room. "Allow me to introduce the second and fourth Saints of Seven Dials. No doubt you'll meet the first and third once they return to London."

Harry blinked. "Second and—? *You*, Pete? And never say this young fellow managed some of the exploits I've read about?" He pointed at Lady Peter's brother.

"Nay, guv, though I wanted to give it a go—and might yet, someday." He shot a frown at his sister, who frowned back.

Peter laughed. "Wrong on both counts, old chap."

Now Harry was even more confused. "But surely—"

"That's why I acted the Saint," Peter's wife astonished him by saying. "To keep William from doing so. But for barely more than a week, so perhaps I should not be counted among the actual Saints."

"Certainly you count," Marcus declared, grinning as broadly as his brother at Harry's stunned expression. "Was it not your activities that reunited the three previous Saints a few days after your wedding? I'd say you proved yourself more than capable, both before we caught you and afterward, during our joint rescue of young Flute, here."

"Flute?" Harry echoed.

The boy, who looked no more than fourteen or fifteen, nodded. "Aye, it's what I've gone by 'most all my life. It's only Sarah here what calls me William."

"So you were a Saint of Seven Dials as well?" Harry asked Marcus directly, determined to be perfectly clear this time.

"The second, as Peter said. I took over after Luke—Lord Hardwyck, that is—retired his mask, so to speak. Not that he literally handed that over. Only a card, so I could copy it to create my own."

Harry had met Lord Hardwyck on multiple occasions when he was plain Luke St. Clair, as he and Lord Marcus had been close friends from their school days onward. Remembering a few things that had come out when Luke had claimed his title, Harry found it rather easier to believe that *he* had acted as the legendary thief.

"And the third Saint?"

"Noel Paxton," Peter said. "He hounded both Luke and Marcus in the mistaken belief that the Saint and the Black Bishop—you remember that traitor?—were one and the same. When he discovered his error, he asked their help in becoming the next Saint that he might use the role to track down the real culprit. He gave it up once he brought the villain to justice."

Slowly, Harry nodded, as various perplexing events from the past year or so fell into place. "And you, Flute. You've been associated with the Saints as well?"

"Aye, along with a few other boys. But I was the first, helping Lord Hardwyck almost from the start. I'm the only one that knew who the first Saint really was." He puffed out his chest proudly. "Used to be, I'd sniff 'round Seven Dials, see who was needing some brass sharpish like and pass the names along. Then I'd fence whatever booty the Saint nicked and dole it out in his name. His main accomplice I was, starting when I was no more'n twelve or thirteen. If anyone can show you the ropes on how to become the next Saint it's me!"

"So it would seem." Apparently the boy was a bit older than he looked. "How do we start?" Now that Harry had made his decision, he was eager to get on with it.

Peter grinned. "By getting you a bit stronger. Meanwhile Flute here can start filling you in on the history and requirements for the job. Once you're ready, I'll turn you loose with your new tutor."

Flute blinked at the title, then grinned. "Got some ideas already, I have. Lord Peter here says you're already a dab hand at picking locks and such?"

Harry shot a glance at his friend. "I did a bit of espionage work while in Vienna, yes. Didn't know it was common knowledge."

"Common? Hardly that," Peter assured him. "Doubt anyone but Wellington and I actually *knew* and few would have guessed, given your usual state between missions."

"I was bamming most of that, to put off suspicion."

"Most?" Peter raised an eyebrow.

"All right, some of it." While it was true Harry had done more than his share of carousing during the Congress of Vienna, he'd never let drink cloud his wits when serving his general. "What other skills will I need?" he asked the boy Flute.

"Why don't we leave you both to it?" Peter suggested, rising. The others did likewise. "Don't keep him up too late, however," he cautioned his young brother-in-law. "I imagine his head's still a bit sore, among other things. He'll need his rest if he's to be ready to pick up the Saint's mantle by year's end."

Harry was determined it would be much sooner than that, however —by week's end, if he had anything to say in it. Without ready funds for his usual pursuits, he was increasingly keen to try this new one.

Several days later Xena resumed her mission, this time clad in a gently-used but fashionable gown she'd obtained for ten shillings from a stall in Soho. Confident that she now looked, if not her best, then at least respectably well-off, she opened the door of the next shop on her list.

"D. Gold & Sons, Dealers in Unique and Unusual Treasures" appeared a similar establishment to the first few she'd visited, if rather dustier. The white-haired man behind the counter looked up as Xena entered, then favored her with a kindly smile.

"You'll have lost your way, surely, miss? The ladies' shops are mostly in the neighborhood of Bond Street."

Xena bit back the retort that rose to her lips. Back in Yorkshire, gentry, merchants and farmers alike knew better than to patronize Mistress Maxwell but not so, here in London.

"No, this is the shop I want," she said firmly. "Might you be Mr. Gold?"

One white brow went up. "I am." His voice held a trace more respect than before, but only a trace. "Have you been commissioned to purchase something in particular, madam?"

"I am not here to purchase today, Mr. Gold, but to sell." She stepped forward to peer through the glass fronting the long display cabinet beneath the counter. "It appears you deal in just the sort of antiquities I can provide."

As she'd done at the previous shops, Xena set her wooden box on the counter and opened the lid to reveal its carefully stored contents. "This you may recognize as having come from Persia, dating to the second century." She lifted out a small ceramic leopard.

Now both eyebrows went up. "Ah! May I?" Gingerly, Mr. Gold took the tiny, priceless statuette from her and turned it this way and that, examining it minutely, all the while making small, happy sounds in the back of his throat. Then, setting it carefully on the counter, he peered into the box. "And what else have you here? Surely this is not a genuine Caligula denarius, and in such fine condition?"

"It is, indeed. I see you are well versed in ancient artifacts, sir. Might these be the sort of items you would be interested in purchasing for resale?"

Mr. Gold now leaned away to take a better look at Xena herself while thoughtfully stroking his scanty beard. "Do you mean to say you have more?"

"I do. My father left an extensive collection—his life's work. Some of the pieces are duplicates, however, with which I am willing to part. For the right price."

The shopkeeper nodded, still peering at her over his half-moon spectacles. "It's possible I'd be willing to take some of those items off your hands, Mrs—?"

"Maxwell."

"Very well, Mrs. Maxwell, why don't you send your father, or your husband, to discuss the particulars with me? I'd not want it said that I took advantage of a lady in such matters."

Xena bristled. "I have neither father nor husband, Mr. Gold, but I assure you I am more than capable of handling these or any other affairs myself. If you are not willing to deal with me directly, however…" Letting her words hang, she picked up the Persian figurine and placed it back in the box.

"Now, now, miss, no offense meant," said the man quickly—though still patronizingly, Xena thought. "But you must admit it's not usual, nor seemly, for a pretty young lady like yourself to come alone on such a mission, and to this part of London."

"Seemly or not, if you have an interest in the items from my father's collection, you will deal with me, Mr. Gold, for there is no one else I trust to negotiate on my behalf. Now that my father is gone, no person alive knows his collection as I do."

There was no mistaking the increased respect in Mr. Gold's watery blue eyes now. "So it would seem. Very well, Miss Maxwell, let us see if we can come to a mutually agreeable arrangement, shall we?"

Pulling a dusty ledger book, pen and ink from beneath the counter, he smiled. "Now. If you would be so kind as to describe some of the items you are looking to sell?"

Forty-five minutes later Xena emerged from the shop, her velvet-lined box empty and her purse rather satisfyingly plumper than it had been an hour earlier. In addition to what he'd paid outright for the items she'd brought with her, Mr. Gold had agreed to take on consignment the rest of the objects now residing in a chest in her rented bedchamber.

Unless she missed her guess, the money he estimated she would eventually receive should cover nearly all necessary repairs at Moorside Grange as well as a few needs in and around the village that looked to it.

She was tucking her purse into the pocket of her cloak when an unshaven man in a threadbare coat blocked her way on the narrow pavement.

"'Ere now, missy, whyn't you just hand that over, eh?" He held out a grubby paw.

Startled, Xena took a step back. "Excuse me?"

"I said, give me yer purse—and that box, too, while yer at it."

Instead, she shoved the box into her pocket after the purse. "I'll do no such thing. Get out of my way."

The rough-looking man laughed. "My, ain't you a feisty one? But I'll have yer brass all the same." One hand shot out and grasped Xena's arm.

Though there were people about, it did not occur to her to call for assistance. Not when she had bested trained soldiers in contests of arms, once upon a time. Raising her newly-purchased secondhand parasol, she whacked her assailant smartly on the ear.

"Oi!" he exclaimed, releasing her. "What—?"

Before he could finish, she gripped the handle of the parasol as though it were the hilt of a sword and thrust it at his chest. With a yelp, he scrambled backward into the street and was nearly run down by a passing dray. Xena took a step toward him, still wielding the parasol menacingly, but he'd had enough. With a strangled cry, he turned and ran away.

"Well done, miss!" exclaimed a portly businessman, hurrying up just then. "Was coming to offer my help, but you can obviously handle yourself."

"My thanks anyway," she told the well-meaning merchant with a smile. "Good day to you."

"And to you!" Tipping his hat, he bowed.

Heartened by the encounter—and the first bit of real excitement she'd had in years—Xena continued on her way. Reaching into her pocket, she patted her purse with renewed satisfaction, anticipating her son's excitement when she told him they might indeed remain in London for the winter.

CHAPTER FIVE

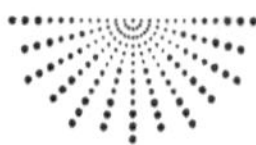

A BARE WEEK AFTER LEARNING THE IDENTITIES OF THE FORMER SAINTS OF Seven Dials, Harry felt ready to take on the role himself. He was completely recovered from his attack, save a half-healed scar over his right eyebrow and a slight limp that was improving daily.

At Flute's suggestion, he'd removed from his lodgings in Swallow Street to Lord Hardwyck's old quarters in the heart of Seven Dials. Despite the crumbling building's unprepossessing exterior, the flat itself proved perfectly livable.

"Lived here m'self, till Sarah insisted I stay with her," the boy had explained on their arrival there two days since. "More convenient for you to operate from here and easier to convince the other lads to accept you as the new Saint, too. Might even cozzen 'em into thinking you're the original, come back again."

Under Flute's tutelage, Harry had now successfully managed a few smaller thefts—pockets picked, an unattended package purloined from an empty carriage, that sort of thing—but tonight would see his first attempt at house-breaking.

In time he hoped to equal such fabled Saintly exploits as the filching of Lady Jersey's diamonds from her very neck while she hostessed a ball. First, however, he'd need to work his way back into the heart of Society, as he'd drifted rather to the fringes since returning from Vienna last summer.

To that end, Peter promised to include him in any likely invitations on condition Harry cut back on his drinking. Not counting the one spree to celebrate his first night out from under Peter's roof, he'd done so. Most of the time he felt the better for it, too, though it occasionally made sleeping difficult when those imaginary pains from his missing arm recurred.

"Ye'll do, guv'nor," Flute said as he put the finishing touches to Harry's costume. Brewster, his valet, had been sent off to visit his widowed mother in Surrey for a few days rather than risk his implication in any crimes while Harry was still learning the ropes. "Don't forget to slouch, mind."

"Right." Here in Seven Dials, Harry went about disguised as one of the many beggars infesting the area. His missing arm lent authenticity to the ruse, as a disturbing number of those beggars were indeed wounded soldiers who'd come home from the wars only to find little in the way of tangible assistance from the country they'd served.

Luckily, Harry had practiced similar deceptions during his time in Vienna, in order to infiltrate coteries that would never have welcomed someone known to be associated with Wellington.

"You have the direction of tonight's target?"

"Aye, it's not far. Just off Golden Square on Carnaby Street." Flute gave Harry's homespun shirt a tweak. "A cheat of a shopkeeper what turned Skeet off without reference or wages two weeks back," Flute continued. "A customer dropped a pot and broke it but the owner made like Skeet done it rather than blame the lady, then beat him for good measure. Skeet's better off away from him, but there's no denying the bloke's deservin' of the Saint's attention."

"Let's be off, then." Harry's thrill of anticipation was not unlike what he'd felt before battle during his time in the Peninsula. By thunder, he'd missed the feeling more than he'd realized.

Flute clambered down the rickety stairs that clung to the side of the building then glanced back at Harry, clearly concerned about his ability to maneuver with only one arm. But while Harry still cursed his infirmity every time he needed assistance shaving or tying a lace, he had no difficulty navigating these stairs—as he'd already proven more than once. Tonight he meant to prove he was capable of far more.

Reaching the filthy pavement, he hunched his shoulders and exaggerated his limp. "Lead on."

Staying a dozen paces back, as Flute was well known to the denizens of Seven Dials as the Saint's sometime accomplice, Harry dragged a leg and occasionally pretended to stumble. The boy's distinctive shock of straw-colored hair and jaunty stride made him easy to keep in sight.

When the maze-like alleyways of Seven Dials gave way to streets progressively better lit, better maintained, and more crowded, Harry dispensed with his limp and straightened his coat, the better to fit in. But not until they arrived in Carnaby Street did he catch up to Flute, waiting in the shadows of a narrow alleyway leading to a set of mews.

"That one?" Harry glanced up at the narrow house Flute was watching, the third one along the row. It looked much the same as the others in this area. On the fringes of Mayfair proper, most were inhabited by a mix of lower gentry and wealthy merchants.

"Aye," Flute whispered. "Tig should be by any minute."

Not two minutes later, a small boy, younger than Flute, appeared behind them in the alleyway. "Is this him?" He looked up at Harry with round eyes.

"Shh!" Flute admonished. "He's helpin' out, that's all. So? Is old Garamond gone out?"

"Aye, left nigh half an hour ago. C'n I help? I'm a dab hand at—"

"Not now, Tig." From Flute's long-suffering tone, it appeared this sort of conversation happened often.

Harry hid a smile. "Maybe in the future." Flute rolled his eyes. "Tonight's my first attempt, so I'd as soon go it alone. For pride's sake, you know."

"Oh, aye, guv, I ken." The boy was still grinning. "I'll just wait here with Flute then."

Harry fleetingly wondered if he was setting a poor example,

allowing the boys to act as lookouts, then shrugged. "Right, then. I'll be back soon."

He headed down the alleyway between tiny back gardens and a row of stables to survey his target from the rear. All the windows were shut—no surprise, given the chill November night air.

No matter. It would be easier to pick the back door lock than clamber one-armed through a window, though he'd run a greater risk of encountering servants. Creeping silently through the garden to the door, he put an ear to the keyhole and thought he could discern a faint murmur of voices from within, though not near the door. Gingerly trying the handle, he was startled but pleased to find it unlocked.

Quickly, he slipped inside, then softly closed the door behind him before peering down the dim stairs leading to the kitchens to listen again. No voices now, but the unlocked door proved some servants must still be about, if only a scullery maid or two washing up below.

He hesitated only a moment, then tiptoed past the kitchen stairs and along the narrow hallway to the first door—which was locked. That seemed promising, as it meant not even servants were welcome within. With a smile of anticipation, Harry pulled a thin, flexible blade from his pocket, fitted it into the keyhole and gave it a practiced twist or two.

Softly stepping through the door, he found himself in a study or office, as he'd hoped. A large desk was littered with papers and two big ledgers, one open, one closed. Curious, Harry glanced through both and discovered they were the shopkeeper's account books—identical, except for the expenses listed, which were far higher in one than the other. Apparently Flute had been right about the man's cheating tendencies.

Feeling doubly justified now, Harry turned his attention to a strongbox in the corner. That lock proved more challenging, but after several minutes an audible click rewarded his efforts. Inside he found rolls of coins and neat stacks of bank notes. He drew the canvas bag he'd brought along from inside his shabby coat and began filling it.

Ten minutes later he triumphantly rejoined the two waiting boys in the alley.

"Success!" he whispered. "Now we'd best get well away before any of us are spotted."

Though Tig had a tendency to chatter and clearly wanted to accompany them all the way back to Seven Dials, Flute managed with some difficulty to dissuade him. After taking separate, circuitous routes back, eventually both Harry and Flute were again ensconced in the little third-story flat.

"Let's tally up tonight's takings, shall we?" Grinning, Harry dumped the contents of the bag on the low table in the center of the room.

Flute gave a low whistle. "Cor! You must have cleaned the blighter out!"

"Not quite, but I took over half and left a card in its place. Care to join me in a glass or two to celebrate the new Saint of Seven Dials?" Lord Hardwyck had made him free of the collection of bottles he'd left behind but Harry had been sparing since his first night there.

"Nay, guv, I don't touch the stuff." Flute wrinkled his nose. "I seen what gin and such does to folks hereabouts. 'Twas the death of Tig's mother, and that's no lie. Anyways, I'd best get started spreading a bit of this around. There'll be a right number of happy families hereabouts tonight, I'm thinking!"

Once Flute had put a quarter of his haul into a smaller sack and left again, Harry shrugged.

"Better a solitary celebration than none at all," he said to the empty room. Plucking a glass and a corkscrew from the shelf behind him, he opened his first bottle of the evening and poured.

"This should be acceptable for tonight, don't you think?" Xena turned this way and that before the inadequate looking glass in her bedchamber to get a better look at the low-cut, midnight-blue gown that had been delivered just that afternoon from the most *au courant* modiste in all London. Though it had cost several times more than any garment she'd ever possessed, Madame Fanchot had been quite right when she said the color would complement Xena's dark hair and fair skin.

"You look so different." Theo regarded her dubiously from his perch on her bed, his own dark head tilted to one side. "But pretty," he finally conceded.

Young Gretchen nodded enthusiastic agreement. "Aye, a fair princess you look, mum, right enough!"

Yamini had insisted Xena bring a lady's maid to London for propriety and Gretchen had readily agreed to abandon her post as a maid-of-all-work in Yorkshire to fill what was a far more prestigious role. Once in the city, however, the girl was so frightened by the teeming streets she'd scarcely ventured outside their rooms.

Xena had not pressed her, as she much preferred going out alone whether it was the accepted thing or not. Tonight, however, was different.

"The carriage I've hired should be here in half an hour," Xena reminded Gretchen now. "I mustn't be seen arriving at Apsley House alone, so you *must* come along. Once we arrive you may join the other servants for some refreshment below stairs or even return to the carriage."

"Yes, mum. I'll...I'll decide once we gets there." Gretchen's dark eyes were wide with anxiety.

"That will be fine," Xena assured her. "Now, help me on with these wretched half-boots. It will be a mercy if I don't trip myself up. Why women wear such things instead of sensible shoes, I can't fathom."

"May I not come, too, Mother?" Theo pleaded, not for the first time. "I should very much like to see all the officers and especially General Wellington!"

Smiling, Xena shook her head. "As I've already told you, it wouldn't be appropriate tonight. But I will do my best to introduce you to the Duke before we leave London."

A short time later she and Gretchen clattered through the streets of London in the handsomest carriage Xena could reasonably afford to hire. She'd spent much of the past week planning her strategy for this evening, which included making the best possible first impression on her arrival.

To that end, she had spent a shocking sum on her appearance. It helped only slightly to remind herself that most women of her station spent far greater amounts on a yearly, if not a quarterly, basis. Ever preferring economy and comfort over fashion, at home Xena wore whatever old gown lay to hand when her preferred breeches were not an option. Here in Town, while inexpensive secondhand gowns might be enough to impress shopkeepers, tonight demanded something substantially better.

And though she knew it was foolish, she did almost feel like a princess in her costly new gown and the first modish hairstyle she'd ever worn in her life. Just as well, perhaps, for she would need every ounce of confidence to face down so many ghosts from her past over the next few hours…assuming she did not kill herself trying to walk in her fashionably impractical half-boots.

When the carriage drew up before the imposing entrance to Apsley House, some of her hard-won confidence evaporated. Where were the other carriages, all the officers and their wives who were supposed to see her emerge from her expensively hired equipage?

"The do were tonight, weren't it, mum?" Gretchen whispered, echoing her own sudden doubt.

"It says so on the note the Duke sent round." She pulled the square of hot-pressed paper from her reticule to read again by the blazing lamps on either side of the portico. "November nineteenth at half past six. We are perhaps a minute or two early, but no more than that."

The coachman opened the carriage door and lowered the steps, so she hesitantly stepped out to frown up at the house, which blazed with lights from every window. *Someone* was here, at any rate.

"Wait you here a moment," she told the coachman before proceeding up the broad stone stairs to the front door, Gretchen trailing anxiously behind her. Before Xena touched the ornate brass knocker, the door was thrown open from within.

"Miss Maxwell," exclaimed the Duke of Wellington himself in

obvious delight. "So pleased you didn't elect to come fashionably late. T'would have spoiled my surprise."

"Er…surprise, your grace?"

"Aye. I asked you here half an hour before anyone else so we can spring you on them after they're all assembled. Won't that be famous?"

Apparently Xena would have her grand entrance after all, though she now regretted the expense of the carriage. "I, ah, yes. I suppose it will. I'm relieved not to have mistaken the night."

He laughed and waved her coachman on to the stables. Extending an arm, he led her to a small but luxuriously appointed anteroom just off the entryway.

"I'll summon you once enough people have arrived for an effective announcement. Shouldn't be too long."

With a nod and a wink, he left before she could implement the next stage of her plan—explaining to Wellington about her son, then delivering a carefully worded request for his assistance in ensuring Theo's admission to Eton when the time came.

After half an hour of reassuring the quaking Gretchen, overcome by the splendor of Apsley House, the door to the anteroom finally opened again.

"Come," said the Duke. "I believe enough people are here now for my announcement. Let's astonish them, shall we?"

Xena rose so quickly from the gilt chair that she nearly tripped over her unaccustomed skirts. The Duke caught her by the elbow before she could fall flat on her face.

"Easy, now. Never tell me the indomitable Miss Maxwell is nervous?"

She managed to return his smile. "Of course not. It's these ridiculous boots the modiste insisted are all the rage. I've no idea how women navigate in them."

The Duke gave a shout of laughter. "Ah, yes, I recall you always seemed more at ease in male attire, whenever you could convince Old Max to allow you to wear it—which was far more often than most fathers would have, I'm certain. And I won't deny it became you. But come, I'll not let you fall off your stilts."

As the boots boasted a mere inch and a half of heel, Xena could not suppress a chuckle. "I thank you, your grace. I shall do my best not to embarrass you tonight—in light of which, there is something I must tell you before we go in."

"Oh?"

"Yes." Swallowing, she plunged on. "When we met on the street the other day, I was so surprised that I fear I spoke in error. If you recall, you asked then if I was married."

"Are you saying that surprise at seeing me made you forget you have a husband?" The Duke looked quizzically down at her.

She forced a small smile. "Not precisely. I am a widow, you see. My husband was killed at Salamanca."

"I'm terribly sorry to hear that. He was a soldier, then? What was his name?"

"Lieutenant Thatcher when we married, though according to the newspapers he was Major Thatcher by the time he was killed."

"Major...Would that be Major Harry Thatcher?"

She nodded. "You knew him then, your grace?"

For a moment he simply looked at her, his expression difficult to decipher. "Yes. I, er, did. This is an evening of surprises, indeed." Another pause, then, "Tell me, would you mind terribly if I introduce you as Miss Maxwell anyway? My speech is already prepared, you see, and it is the name everyone attending knew you by. I can't help thinking my announcement will be more of a stunner without any tedious explanations."

"That will be perfectly all right, your grace, as I've continued to go by Mistress Maxwell in Yorkshire. There is one other thing I need to tell you about, however."

"Whatever it is will have to wait. Heads are already turning this way and I won't have my surprise ruined." Tucking her hand securely into the crook of his arm, he led her out into the entryway. "Chin up, now!"

"But—"

It was too late. Already the Duke was addressing the crowd, raising his voice to battlefield level to command the room to silence.

"Your attention, everyone, if you please! You may recall that I promised you something special this evening, and here she is. The woman to whom more than a few of you owe your lives and whom I'm sure many of you mourned, as I did, when we thought she was lost to us forever. I give you the heroine of Vimeiro, Porto and Grijon: Miss Xena Maxwell!"

Stunned silence greeted Wellington's announcement, then the enormous room erupted into tumultuous applause. Every bit of Xena's wartime courage was needed as dozens of officers surged forward to greet her, several with eyes suspiciously bright with unshed tears.

"My dear Miss Maxwell!" exclaimed one, whom she belatedly recognized as the same Lieutenant Greevey she had nursed to recovery from a bullet wound after Porto. "You can't imagine how delighted I am to see you alive and well after all. You must allow me to introduce my wife. Cora, dear, this is the woman I told you about, without whose nursing skills you would have never met me."

The petite brunette at his side smiled, though not quite as warmly as her husband. "Then of course I must thank you as well, Miss Maxwell. I've heard much about you since our marriage. I'm sure my husband is not the only one happy to learn that news of your demise was false."

"Ecstatic, more like," he loudly assured them both as Xena murmured a polite acknowledgment. "It's like a miracle seeing you again after all this time!"

"Here, now, Greevey, give others a chance to pay their respects, won't you?" A much taller man shouldered him aside, beaming from ear to ear. "Don't know if you remember me, Miss Maxwell, but you saved my leg when the camp medic wanted to take it clean off. Can't thank you enough for that. I'm not ashamed to confess I cried like a babe when I heard you'd drowned."

Xena smiled in return. "Of course I remember. You were Ensign Paddymore then, were you not?"

The big man nodded eagerly. "Major by the time the war ended. All thanks to you, as I'd have been invalided out after my first three months if that idiot orderly'd had his way with my leg."

More and more officers crowded in to express their gratitude and delight at discovering she hadn't died after all and, in many cases, to introduce her to their wives or to fellow officers who hadn't previously met her.

Though Xena did her best to be gracious, she could not but be aware of the awkwardness of her situation. How on earth was she to solicit the influence of any of these people on Theo's behalf when they all believed her unmarried? If only she'd told the full truth to General Wellington upon first meeting him on the street…

Several times, when yet another man hailed her as "Miss Maxwell," a correction was on the tip of her tongue, but she feared the Duke might prefer to make that correction himself, and in his own time. Unfortunately, though she occasionally caught sight of him across the crowded room, he had not been near enough for conversation since announcing her.

With a slightly strained smile, she turned to the latest group of officers accosting her to yet again recount the circumstances leading to the false report of her death.

"As I feared, your dallying has made us late," Lord Peter commented as the carriage rolled up to Apsley House. "I did mention that this reception would be key in reestablishing you in Society, as many of those attending are extremely influential. Or had you forgotten?"

Harry scowled. "I needed a bit of a wash after this afternoon's activities. *That* aspect of my campaign is going well, by the way. Been doing good deeds with a vengeance, though certain members of the Quality may not agree."

His scowl faded into a grin as he remembered the expression on that arrogant marquess's face on discovering his pockets unexpectedly empty. Glancing wildly about at those nearest him on the street, his eyes had briefly lit on Harry but hadn't lingered, clearly considering him too impaired by drink and disability to have been the culprit.

"Glad to hear it," Peter replied drily. "William, through Sarah, has reported much the same." He glanced over at his pretty wife, who nodded. "But you know how Old Nosey feels about punctuality, even in social matters. Perhaps we can contrive to slip in unobserved."

"I've become quite adept at that lately," Harry informed him, still grinning. "But you're right. Let's join the throng." It was clear the Duke of Wellington's reception was in full swing but Harry was glad to see a few other latecomers. At least they'd not be the very last to arrive.

The haughty butler at the door handed them off to a smartly dressed footman to be shown into the grand ballroom. At the sight of so many of his erstwhile army comrades in their regimentals, Harry frowned. He'd not worn his own uniform since leaving service.

"The invitation said nothing about dress," he muttered. Peter hadn't worn his, either, but was decked out in his customary colorful style, wearing a peacock blue coat over a scarlet and silver waistcoat.

"No, it didn't." Peter looked less than pleased as well. "No matter. If some wish to relive what they consider past glories, let them. I intend to enjoy showing off my new bride, instead. Look, there's Jack, and in normal evening wear."

Together they made their way across the floor to Jack Ashecroft, now Lord Foxhaven. They'd seen little of their friend since his marriage two years since, as he'd spent the majority of his time at his estate in Kent.

"Wasn't sure you'd manage to get to Town, what with the recent rains," Peter greeted him as they reached his side. "Is Lady Foxhaven with you?"

Jack slapped both of his old friends on the back in greeting, then shook his head. "Nessa remained behind. She's been a bit poorly in recent days. Didn't feel up to travel."

Peter frowned. "Sorry to hear it. Nothing serious, I hope?"

A huge smile spread across Jack's face. "I suppose you might call it serious, but nothing to be sorry about. She tells me she's increasing again. She won't admit it, but I believe she's hoping for a girl this time."

"From what you've told us of young Julius's exploits, can't say I blame her," returned Peter, laughing.

"If you two are going to discuss nursery matters, I'll find someone else to talk to," Harry declared, rolling his eyes.

Both of his friends turned to grin at him. "Your time will come, Harry, mark my words," Jack said with a chuckle. "Then you'll wonder why you were ever so averse to the idea of a wife."

Harry snorted. "Leave off with your dire prognostications, won't you? I've escaped parson's mousetrap this long and have every confidence I can continue my evasions indefinitely. Can't imagine why you'd wish a wastrel like me on some poor unsuspecting chit anyway."

"The right woman could be the very thing to help you finally mend your ways," Peter chided him, still smiling.

"God forbid!"

With a shake of his head at such a reprehensible idea, Harry turned away to investigate whether their host had broken out his best bottles for the occasion…only to be accosted by Wellington himself.

"There you are, Thatcher," his former general exclaimed. "Began to wonder whether you meant to turn up at all. Afraid you missed my big announcement twenty minutes since, but perhaps that's just as well. Now I can spring the surprise on you personally. Come along, Foxhaven, Northrup. I daresay you'll want to see this."

With a gesture for them to follow, the Duke began thrusting his way through the crowd toward the far side of the enormous reception hall.

Once her initial discomfort began to fade, Xena rather enjoyed hearing story after story of a time she was now able to remember with fondness. Mindful of her plan to create useful connections for her son, she smiled, laughed and related a few stories of her own, confident that an opportunity to disclose the truth of her situation would soon present itself.

Observing that some wives seemed less delighted by her "miraculous" survival than the officers, she related only those stories least likely to offend overly-sensitive feminine ears. The men, unfortunately, were not so restrained.

"Remember the time you taught young Phillips here a lesson, Miss Maxwell?" laughed an officer she at first had trouble recognizing, he'd grown so portly since she'd last seen him.

She had no trouble recognizing the former Ensign Phillips, however. He had the same thin, sly face and peevish expression he'd worn seven years earlier.

"Decked out in soldier garb you were, and challenged him to a duel for a comment he made about your posterior," the older man continued with a chuckle. "Put a nice little hole in his shoulder with your rapier, and well deserved, too." He punched Phillips in that same shoulder.

All the men within earshot laughed uproariously while Phillips managed a tight smile. "I merely made a jest about her unfeminine attire. How was I to know she had such a thin skin?"

"As I recall, Mr. Phillips, 'twas *your* skin that proved thin on that occasion," Xena retorted swiftly. "Shall we discover whether that is still the case? I wager I can still best you with either sword or pistol."

"I'll have you know it's *Sir* Barney Phillips now," he snapped, scowling, then quickly moved away.

The officers laughed again but most of their wives appeared scandalized. "Surely you did not actually wear breeches in the camp, Miss Maxwell?" one matron asked in shocked tones. "Nor handle weapons?"

Before Xena could reply, three or four officers confirmed that indeed she had, and a good thing, too, as she'd been of help in defending the camp.

"Breeches seemed far more practical than skirts for such conditions," Xena explained to the affronted young matron. "I'd like to think that someday there will be no stigma attached to a woman who dresses for comfort and practicality rather than convention."

The woman's eyes grew wide and she moved hastily away.

"But clearly that day is not yet come," Xena murmured, watching her decampment with mingled chagrin and irritation.

A few officers close enough to hear were quick to assure her that they saw nothing wrong with a woman donning breeches when necessary. Xena barely heard them, for she had spotted the Duke of Wellington approaching through the crowd. She *must* seize this opportunity to tell him about Theo!

"Your grace," she began eagerly, but again he cut her off before she could finish.

"Miss Maxwell, I've a latecomer here whom I suspect you will be *particularly* happy to see again."

With a flourish, the Duke stepped aside to reveal three men just behind him. "Gentlemen, allow me to personally present tonight's guest of honor—our own Miss Maxwell, returned to us from the dead!"

Xena's breath left her body as if she'd taken a cannonball to the stomach, so sudden and intense were the shock, joy and disbelief that lanced through her in rapid succession. Before her, in the flesh, stood her onetime lover, husband, and Theo's father.

Harry Thatcher.

CHAPTER SIX

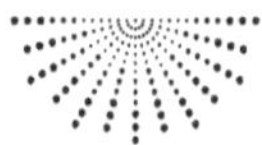

HARRY'S CURIOSITY WAS PIQUED BY WELLINGTON'S BARELY-suppressed excitement as he led their party across the room to see the "surprise" he had hinted at in the invitation for this evening. When the Duke slowed, he braced himself, suspecting some joke to pay them all out for their tardiness.

However, nothing could have prepared him for abruptly finding himself face to face with Xena Maxwell!

A wild happiness swept through him at seeing her alive—alive!—after all these years before he was assailed by a sense of unreality so intense he felt suddenly lightheaded. Surely this was impossible? She must be an apparition…or another dream. Or perhaps that blow to his head two weeks since had unhinged his mind?

From the corner of his eye he saw Peter step forward, one hand outstretched as though to save Harry from a fall, which made him realize he'd started to sway. With a supreme effort, he strove to pull himself together. Whether dream or insanity, all he could do was brazen it out.

A slight shake of his head served to clear the fuzziness threatening the periphery of his vision, bringing the woman before him into sharper focus. No longer was she the boyish figure with cropped hair and cocky smile who had so intrigued and beguiled him seven and a half years ago. This new Xena Maxwell was fully feminine in both body and face, with long, ebony locks artfully arranged and a far more modish—and flattering—gown than she'd ever worn back then.

Finally, he found his voice. "It, ah, would appear that news of your demise was somewhat exaggerated…*Miss* Maxwell, was it?" Dragging his gaze from her face, he glanced at Wellington, whose expectant grin had begun to fade.

Xena's voice, a bit lower than he recalled, snapped his attention back to her. "I…I might say the same, Mr. Thatcher, for the newspapers reported you killed on the battlefield at Salamanca." She darted a quick glance at his empty sleeve.

Wellington cleared his throat. "Hem. Yes. Well. Perhaps it was rather unsporting of me to spring you upon each other without warning. My apologies. No doubt you have much to say to each other, so I will leave you to it." Now looking almost sheepish—an expression Harry had never before seen on the Iron Duke's face—Wellington took himself off.

Almost at once, Jack stepped forward. "Harry, old boy, you must introduce me to the celebrated Miss Maxwell. Foxhaven, at your service." He executed a smart bow. "Though you and I never met, I heard much about you while serving in the Peninsula. I am delighted to finally make your acquaintance."

Her eyes still on Harry, she made a stammering response, whereupon Peter came forward as well.

"Give you good evening, Miss Maxwell. I am Lord Peter Northrup, and this is my wife, Sarah. She is but recently arrived in London, something I presume you have in common? Where have you been keeping yourself these few years past?"

"My…my home is in Yorkshire," she replied, her voice slightly stronger now. "Though I lived there but little prior to my time on the Peninsula."

Still dazed, Harry looked on as Xena—so like and yet unlike the girl he remembered—haltingly responded to Lady Peter's queries about her early life. He paid little attention to her answers, as he already knew that portion of her history leading up to their meeting in

Portugal. He was far more curious about the woman she was now—and how she came to be standing before him.

As his initial shock and disbelieving joy faded, uncertainty and suspicion began to creep in. How could Xena possibly have been alive all this time...and why had no one ever told him? Why had *she* never told him? He'd by no means lived in secrecy since his return from Spain, despite that false report of his death some months prior. Had she but bothered to inquire...

Now several other officers and their wives joined the circle about her. Harry tried to pick up the thread of conversation as Xena began to elaborate on that part of her history he burned to know.

"I still don't understand why no announcement was made once Colonel Maxwell learned you were never aboard the ship that foundered," Captain Findlay was saying. "He should have put a notice in the papers, to relieve us all."

Xena lifted a shapely shoulder, though her expression seemed strained. "I imagine he saw little point nearly three years after the fact, especially as he was off again to resume his archaeological pursuits soon after discovering me alive at home."

Or, Harry wondered, was it that neither of them wanted to dredge up memories of the old, hushed-up scandal that had led to their hasty marriage and subsequent banishment from the regiment?

"So you've been content to stay immured in the country all this time?" he suddenly heard himself asking, with an edge of skepticism he couldn't keep from his voice.

Turning, she met his eyes squarely with the thick-lashed gray ones he remembered so well. "*Content* is perhaps not the word I would choose, sir, but I have remained there, yes. My father and...circumstances gave me little choice." There was a question behind her gaze, and a challenge.

But what question, and what challenge? Surely she could not blame him for doing nothing to shorten her stay in Yorkshire when neither she nor her father had ever bothered to inform him of her survival?

The conversation moved on then to other reminiscences of the war years, with more than one officer recounting how the remarkable Miss

Maxwell had nursed him through wounds that would surely have proved fatal without her skills. Harry listened a few moments more, then stepped back to allow others to join the throng about her.

He couldn't imagine any "circumstances" that could have caged a spirit such as the one he remembered. Did anyone in Yorkshire—anyone *anywhere*—even know that she…they…were married? Wellington's behavior implied he did, for all he'd introduced her as "Miss Maxwell," and surely records of the marriage must still exist. Now that she knew Harry was also still living, what might she mean to do about it?

Somehow, he must contrive a word alone with her. In addition to burning curiosity, he very much needed to know where he—where they—stood.

"Are you all right, old chap?" Peter and Jack had also retreated from the group, though Sarah was still listening to the others' tales.

"What? Oh. Yes. Yes, I'm fine."

The glance his friends exchanged told Harry he wasn't the least bit convincing. He tried again.

"It's just…I knew her rather well when I served in the 45th. Her father was advising Colonel Flagston at the time, you know. Seeing her suddenly alive after all these years believing her dead was like being confronted by a ghost."

"Ah." That single word Peter uttered carried more understanding than Harry liked. "I hadn't realized that you and she were so close."

"Nor I," Jack echoed. "In fact, you never mentioned her once in all the time we served together, or since—not even when you first arrived from the 45th."

Harry shrugged, though it cost him an effort. "We were only acquainted for three or four months, but I suppose you could say we were…friends." A memory of their last, exceedingly passionate encounter assailed him.

Peter nodded sympathetically. "And you feel she should have somehow let you know she was all right." It was a statement, not a question.

"Yes. No! I— Damn it, Pete, you're too perceptive by half, as always. Very well, yes. It seems little short of deceptive she should have been living happily in the country all this time with never a word to…to those of us who would have liked to know."

Again, Peter and Jack exchanged a too-knowing glance.

"Her explanation sounded plausible enough." Jack shrugged. "She undoubtedly assumed her father would notify her closest friends once her letter reached him. That it never did is no great surprise, given how unreliable communications were back then. Surely there's no need to infer *deception* from a single missent message?"

"No. I suppose not. Though she might at least have written again." Or directly to him. He'd had as much right as her father to know she had survived. Of course, his friends didn't know that—nor was he about to tell them. "I've a mind to sample Old Nosey's cellars. What say you?"

Though his friends were clearly still curious, neither made any argument as they followed Harry in pursuit of a footman bearing a silver tray of filled wine glasses.

~

Xena watched Harry Thatcher's progress across the room while pretending to appear engaged in the conversation humming about her, though in truth she was still struggling to absorb the enormity of her discovery.

Alive! Harry Thatcher—her *husband*—was alive! Something the Duke had clearly known full well—which explained his rather odd reaction upon hearing the name of her "late" husband. Despite how retired she'd lived since returning to England, it seemed incredible that Harry could have been living openly in London all this time without her hearing so much as a hint of it.

Her gaze followed him about the room, a thousand questions crowding her brain. Was it at Salamanca that Harry lost his left arm? How long after the notice in the newspapers was he discovered to be alive? And, most importantly, now he knew *she* was alive, what might he intend to do about it?

It was disturbing to realize she had no idea what sort of man Harry Thatcher was now, and positively frightening that Theo's future as well as her own were now at the mercy of a virtual stranger's whims should he choose to exert his legal authority over them

Perhaps Harry's fellow officers could give her some idea of his character? She began to listen more closely to nearby conversations, alert for any opening that might allow her to learn more without directly mentioning Harry's name.

"Aye, look at old Tolliver over there." Viscount Linley, only a few paces away, nodded toward a portly man whose scarlet coat was stretched tight across his abdomen. "Let himself go to fat within two months of Waterloo."

Moving closer, Xena seized her opportunity, saying, "Many of the men here have altered almost out of recognition from when I knew them on the Peninsula, my lord. Though I suppose some of the most profound changes might not even visible to the eye. Whose behavior or outlook would you say has altered most since leaving the army?"

Lord Linley frowned thoughtfully. "Hm. Bit of a puzzler, that…"

"Not at all," protested Mr. Mellings, whose own uniform still fitted him well. "Sure to be Colonel Northrup, wouldn't you say? Transformed himself into a complete dandy within a month of selling out."

"Lord Peter Northrup, do you mean?" Xena's interest quickened, for he and Harry had appeared to be friends.

"Aye. On the battlefield he was hard as iron, giving no quarter to the enemy nor to his own soldiers if they disobeyed an order. But ever since returning home, he spends all his time choosing his colorful ensembles and chiding those of his comrades who've turned to more disreputable pursuits to while away their time."

Which comrades, she wondered. "Surely it is admirable of him to guide his friends toward more productive paths if they are going astray?"

Lord Linley chuckled. "Doubt Thatcher sees it that way! Though Foxhaven has cause to be grateful to him, I suppose. Word was, Northrup helped him reform enough to claim his inheritance a year or two back. Some condition or other of Foxhaven's grandfather, the way I heard it."

"But Mr. Thatcher refuses to be so guided?" Xena asked lightly, attempting to appear amused rather than worried.

The whole group around her laughed.

"Hardly Northrup's fault, that. Thatcher was known for his excesses even in the field," Mr. Mellings informed her. "I served in the 48th with him, along with Northrup and Foxhaven—Jack Ashecroft as he was then—and Harry was one of the chief carousers among us. After losing his arm he went from bad to worse. Daresay all he lives for now is drinking, dicing and wenching. Oh! Beg pardon, ma'am. Need to learn to mind my tongue better 'round the ladies, don't I?"

Xena forced a smile to her lips. "I heard far worse in field hospitals, I assure you. But if you'll excuse me, I believe I'll trouble that footman for one of those charming canapés and perhaps a glass of ratafia."

Her false smile still firmly affixed, she moved away, thinking furiously. Could it be true? The Harry Thatcher she'd known had never imbibed at all, nor had she ever witnessed him gambling. Had seven years truly transformed him into a drunken gamester...and womanizer?

If so, perhaps it was as well she'd had no chance to mention her son to anyone, for the thought of such a man having absolute authority over Theo was intolerable. In fact, the safest thing might be to keep Theo's existence a secret—though that would necessitate leaving London as soon as possible.

It was a shame, really. Mr. Gold had already found buyers for the original six items Xena had sold him, along with three others she had left on consignment. Why, just yesterday she'd written her steward in Yorkshire to commence repairs there, and to box up and send a few more treasures Mr. Gold had specifically requested. And Theo had been so very happy when she'd told him they could remain in London for the winter...

Lady Peter Northrup's approach interrupted Xena's anxious musings. "Miss Maxwell, do you suppose we might arrange an opportunity for more conversation than is possible right now? You've led far the most fascinating life of anyone I've ever met, between traveling the world and then spending time among the army camps. As my husband avoids speaking of his experiences during the war, I would be exceedingly obliged if you could tell me more of what it was like."

Xena swallowed. "Oh. Er, surely there are dozens here who can tell you far more than I, Lady Peter. I was on the Peninsula but two years. And though I believed at the time I lived just as the soldiers did, I suspect I was rather more sheltered than I knew. Well…except when it came to treating the wounded—but I cannot imagine you would wish to hear those gruesome details?"

Lady Peter paled slightly. "Perhaps not," she admitted. "But there is much I *would* like to hear. May I call upon you sometime this week? Where are you staying in Town?"

"Not in one of the more genteel areas, I fear, so it would probably be best if you did not." The last thing Xena wanted was for anyone even remotely connected with Harry to visit her rooms—and see Theo. Not before she had decided what to do.

"The more, ah, colorful areas of London do not frighten me." Lady Peter gave her an almost mischievous smile. "But if my calling upon you seems ineligible, might I persuade you visit me in Curzon Street? For truly, I should like to know you better. Were you the one to nurse Harry Thatcher when he was so dreadfully wounded? You both seemed quite strongly affected upon first encountering each other tonight."

"No, I…I never nursed him. His injury must have occurred after I left Spain—likely at Salamanca, as that was the battle where he was reported killed. In error, obviously." When had that error been discovered? She wished she knew. "He served in the 45th for three or four months while my father was there advising Colonel Flagston and our paths often crossed. That…that is all."

Though of course that was *not* all. Not remotely.

Unbidden, a far-too-vivid memory of the night Harry first introduced her to the pleasures of lovemaking made her knees go unexpectedly weak. Swallowing, she stiffened her spine to compensate, hoping her color hadn't risen.

"Even so, Miss Maxwell, I would be delighted if you would take tea with me one day this week," Lady Peter persisted, forcing Xena's focus back to the present.

"You are exceedingly kind, but I plan to remain in London only another day or two."

Lady Peter's beautiful face fell. "Oh, I am very sorry to hear that. I quite looked forward to our becoming better acquainted. If you *should* decide to stay longer, please don't hesitate to call upon me, even unannounced."

Xena murmured something noncommittal, then turned to greet yet another group of officers clamoring for her attention, glad to escape Lady Peter's insistence. Yes, the sooner she could leave London the better. Though if Harry should decide to follow her…

Would he? Did she want him to? No, of course she did not. Not if what those men said about him was true. Safer, surely, to convince him she had no fortune worth pursuing beyond a mouldering manor house in a remote corner of Yorkshire—nothing, in short, to tempt him away from his comfortably dissipated life in London.

To do that, however, she needed to contrive a moment or two alone with him. Not until she discovered his intentions could she effectively plan a counter-offensive, should one prove necessary.

More than an hour passed before such an opportunity presented itself. Though Xena tried to appear cheerful and animated while responding to continued expostulations about her miraculous survival and all the good she had done during the war, her attention was in fact centered on Harry's every movement—and the disconcerting memories sparked by seeing him again.

Unfortunately, every time she spotted him he was in the company of others, most often Lord Peter Northrup and Lord Foxhaven, and always, she noted, with a drink in his hand. Nor did the Duke's guests leave her alone for a moment. In desperation she finally excused herself to the ladies' retiring room, then found a quiet corner just behind the curve of the nearest elaborate spiral staircase.

Almost at once, she saw Harry approaching—also alone. "Give you good evening again, *Miss* Maxwell," he drawled, a sardonic edge to his voice. "Wonder if I might have a word?"

"Certainly, Mr. Thatcher." She fought desperately to keep her color from rising, reminded again of all they'd once been to each other. Seven years had certainly not made him any less handsome. Rather the reverse. "Here, or somewhere a bit more private?"

His mouth twisted into something that was almost—but not quite —a smile. "For what we need to discuss, an audience might be better avoided. Do you not agree?"

"I do indeed. There is an anteroom just back here—it is where the Duke had me wait until he could spring me upon his guests with a flourish."

"Pity I missed that. Back here, you say?"

Her heart unaccountably hammering in her chest—for surely she had nothing to fear?—she led him to the small, ivy-papered room she'd quitted some three hours earlier.

CHAPTER SEVEN

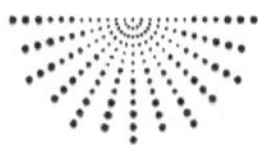

HARRY FOLLOWED XENA INTO THE ROOM, TRYING NOT TO BE distracted by the curve of her bottom as it moved under the thin silk of her midnight-blue gown. Now they were finally away from the prying eyes of all those damned officers and their gossiping wives, he needed to keep his mind clear if he was to get the answers he craved.

The instant the door was closed, Xena whirled to face him. "Now we are alone, perhaps you will tell me what you mean to do?"

"Do?" He blinked. "What do you mean? What the devil am I *supposed* to do when suddenly confronted by a wife who for seven years allowed me to believe she was dead?"

His words sounded harsh even to his own ears and Xena immediately bristled.

"*Allowed* you to believe? You are aware, are you not, that you were reported dead as well? I had no reason to disbelieve what I saw printed in the papers. Was I to write to a corpse?"

"The papers also printed a notice after I was found alive," he pointed out.

Xena averted her eyes—those same expressive gray eyes he remembered all too well. "I...canceled regular deliveries of the *Times* shortly after reading you were killed. Money was tight and it seemed an extravagance having it posted all the way to Yorkshire."

Thrusting away an image of her poring over the lists of dead and wounded frequently enough to have spotted his name, he returned to the main point. "Salamanca occurred a full three years after I left the 45th," he reminded her. "Three years during which you could have written to me after learning we all thought you dead. Why didn't you?"

She compressed her lips—lips that were fuller than Harry remembered. "I...wrote to my father. I assumed he would notify you."

"Ah, yes, that all-important letter that he supposedly never received."

"Do you accuse me of lying, sir?" she flared. "I assure you I did write to him, and before the end of '09. I had no idea he'd not received my letter until he returned home—barely a month before news reached England about the battle at Salamanca."

She darted a glance at Harry's left sleeve, then looked away—but not before he saw the flash of pain in her eyes...or was it revulsion?

"Why did you not write again when you received no reply?" Harry persisted. "Surely such momentous news was worth of at least one more attempt?"

Xena lifted a creamy shoulder, again averting her gaze. "He was still quite angry with me when I left Spain. I assumed that was why he did not reply. Writing again might have been seen as groveling for his forgiveness, which I could not bring myself to do. Not after he'd violated my trust by forcing us to wed."

"Do you mean that you did not expect him to insist upon our marriage when you informed him of our...activities?" Harry could hardly believe she'd been so naive, but it would explain much.

"Inform—? You cannot think *I* told him? Not after all my pains to keep our... activities, as you term them, secret? Even believing him as forward-thinking as myself, it was scarcely worth that risk—as ensuing events proved. You both knew my views on matrimony. I never expected you would resort to such underhanded stratagem to force my hand."

Harry stared, then slowly shook his head. "I assure you, I was as surprised as you claim to have been when Colonel Maxwell insisted we marry. He implied it was your wish, so I—"

"So you could not in honor refuse. My father told me it was *your* wish—and that he would have you court marshaled if I balked." Her dark brows drew down in a frown. "It appears we were both misled. He clearly owed his information to a third party. I wonder who?"

So did Harry. Aware that they might be interrupted at any moment, however, he shrugged. "That scarcely matters now, does it? The important question is, what do we do now? Announce the truth to the world and live from this day forward as husband and wife?"

"Don't be absurd," she snapped, looking suddenly alarmed. "After all, we barely knew each other seven years ago, and it's clear now that neither of us wished for that travesty of a wedding my father forced upon us."

Though true, her words stung more than he cared to admit. Seven years ago she had seemed to enjoy his company—and his love making— well enough. Alone with her, standing so close to her, he was rather too forcefully reminded of how very much *he* had enjoyed those encounters.

"What do *you* propose, then? Simply…pretend we were never more than chance acquaintances during the war and go our separate ways?" Harry supposed he should prefer that course, but…

The look she gave him was both suspicious and hopeful. "I…would not be averse to such a course. I've no particular desire to conform my life to yours at this late date, nor can I imagine you wish to conform yours to mine. I gather you have not married again, at any rate, under the misapprehension I was dead?"

Now *that* was a complication Harry hadn't even thought of—not that he'd ever been at the least risk of such a thing. "Me? No. And as you still call yourself *Miss* Maxwell, I presume you are no bigamist either." He let the implied question hang.

The Xena he'd known in Portugal and Spain had never been one to blush, but now her color rose ever so slightly. "I, ah, no. As no one in Yorkshire knew of our marriage—"

"You never saw fit to tell them. Can't say I blame you, as I never told anyone either. A bit awkward to admit the truth to everyone now, after so many years of silence on the subject by both of us, wouldn't you say? Though if Wellington suspects…"

Xena grimaced. "He doesn't suspect, he knows. I told him myself this very evening, just before he announced me. He neglected to mention you were still alive…and expected to attend tonight." She seemed understandably nettled by that omission.

"Old Nosey always did like his little jokes. Do you think he's told anyone else?"

After a moment's thought, she shook her head. "I feel sure someone would have mentioned it to one of us by now if he had."

True enough. If there were anyone Wellington might be tempted to inform, it would be Peter and Jack, as they'd done so much vital work for him in the past and were known to be Harry's best friends. Clearly he had not…yet. Harry imagined the glee with which the two would greet such news and cringed. Far better to tell them the truth himself than risk them learning of it at a venue such as this.

"I could ask Wellington to keep the story to himself," he mused aloud, "but even if he agreed to do so, he'd certainly want to know why. I confess, I was rather surprised *you* made no mention of our, ah relationship when Wellington first sprung us upon each other tonight."

"I realized, as you just pointed out, the awkwardness of such a revelation. Nor did I completely trust my judgment while recovering from such a surprise. As we cannot count on it remaining a secret, however, we must decide how we wish to proceed."

Harry regarded her thoughtfully. "You implied you would be happy enough to go on as we've done, living separate lives. Even should the truth out, we'd by no means be the only married couple to take that course. Wellington himself is a prime example, as it's well known he and his wife have lived apart for years. We could simply agree to do the same."

"Yes. That does seem the most reasonable solution." Her obvious relief was less than flattering, though Harry knew he should feel the same. "After all," she continued, "we were little more than children when we first met—I but nineteen and you not much older. Young and rash enough to play with fire, with the expected consequence. Surely we have both paid a severe enough penalty already for that youthful mistake?"

He'd never considered his time with Xena a *mistake*, though her father's learning of it certainly had been. Still, the course she suggested made sense, involving the least disruption to both their lives.

"Very well, we're agreed, then." Oddly, Harry did not feel nearly the satisfaction he ought to. "Shall we shake on it?" He held out his hand as he would to another man.

She hesitated only an instant before taking it. Though her grip was firm for a woman's, her hand felt distractingly small and soft in his. After a quick shake, she rather hastily let go and took half a step toward the door.

Harry felt strangely unwilling to let her go just yet, however. "If we are not to speak again after tonight, might I take this opportunity to appease my curiosity? What sort of life do you lead now, Xena? I was nearly as surprised to hear you've been fixed in Yorkshire all this time as I was to discover you still alive after so many years. I don't recall you ever speaking of your home with any particular fondness. Rather the reverse."

She bit her lip, as though debating how much to tell him. "I was… rather unwell when I first returned home, which kept me confined for a time. Once recovered, I discovered various tasks demanding my attention. My father's steward had died the year before and his replacement, hired by letter, proved rather incompetent. Between one thing and another, I never felt able to leave."

"Not even when your father returned? Surely at that point he could have taken over whatever duties you felt compelled to perform, freeing you to go a-roving as you always claimed to enjoy."

"He remained only a month, then was off on his travels again. He, ah, felt it best I not accompany him."

Harry had a distinct sense she was concealing something. "Surely he was not still angry three years later? Do you mean to say he was not happy to discover you were alive after all?"

Her smile did not quite reach her eyes. "I believe he was, but…not happy enough to remain at home. His was ever a wandering spirit."

Just as Xena's had been. It would be rather a shame if that were no longer the case, for the visible changes since he'd last seen her were all to the good. He ran an appreciative eye over the flattering—and expensive—lines of the midnight blue gown she wore, increasingly determined to learn more about the woman she was now.

Xena wondered if agreeing to a private conversation with Harry had been a mistake. Here, in close quarters together for the first time in seven years, she was finding herself far more affected—and attracted—than she cared to admit. Now, under his assessing gaze, her heart accelerated further.

"I still find it hard to believe you remained in Yorkshire all this time simply to manage your father's estate." His voice flowed over her with warm familiarity. "How prospers it now? Well enough for you to spend the winter in Town, it would seem."

His words reminded her that she mustn't let down her guard—not yet. If Harry was truly the womanizer those officers claimed, he likely recognized her gown was in the latest fashion and therefore costly. They'd also mentioned gambling…

"In truth, the estate does not prosper nearly so well as I should like," she replied firmly, "nor am I in Town for the winter. I simply came here in hopes of selling off a few of my father's antiquities in order to fund some much-needed repairs back home. I am certainly not in the habit of buying such fripperies for myself." She gestured toward her silk skirts. "But the Duke insisted I attend tonight, so it was necessary to dress presentably."

That drew a frown from him, no doubt because her apparent worth had decreased in his eyes—as she'd intended. "Then you mean to return home soon?"

The question was asked almost too casually, implying the answer might be important to him. But did he hope or fear she might stay?

She could not tell. "Fairly soon, yes," she answered after a slight pause. "As I said, there are matters in Yorkshire that require my attention."

"Have you still not found a capable steward, then?" he asked with a trace of skepticism. "Most people would rather winter in Town than so far north."

Tilting her head up to him, she produced a smile. "I am not 'most people,' Mr. Thatcher."

"True enough. You never were." His grin reminded her forcibly of the man he'd been seven years since. "Still, I can't imagine what a remote corner of Yorkshire might boast that would appeal to an adventurous spirit such as yours."

That came dangerously near the very topic she was determined to avoid. "London is expensive. I could not afford to stay all the winter even if I wished to." Not quite true, now she'd found buyers for some of her items, but she preferred he not know that. "What of you? As grandson to an earl, surely you have obligations as well?"

"None to speak of." He seemed suddenly wary. "M'father seems happier the longer we're apart, as we never did get on well. It's why I went into the army—and why he agreed to purchase my commission."

Xena recalled him once telling her that. It had been clear at the time that the estrangement pained him. "In the four years you've been back in England, you've never managed to mend matters with your family?"

"Can't say I've tried, particularly." His shrug dismissed the topic so she broached another she'd been curious about all evening.

"Your...injury." She nodded toward his empty left sleeve. "Did you sustain it at Salamanca?"

"Aye." His brusqueness told her it was another subject he was uncomfortable discussing. "The enemy left me for dead but a Spanish villager found me. Carried me back to his house, where he and his wife doctored me. If they'd had your skill at nursing, they might have saved my arm along with my life."

She tried to imagine how that must have affected so vigorous a man, remembering the despondency of other soldiers at facing such losses. "And afterward? When did you return to England and what have you been doing since?"

He hesitated for a moment before answering. "I was sent back three months after Salamanca, once I was more or less recovered. Invalided out on half pay. Between that and an occasional allowance from m'father I've managed well enough. So, you mean to return to Yorkshire quite soon, you say? I don't suppose—"

At that moment, the anteroom door opened.

"Ah, here you are!" exclaimed Captain Maitland. "Bad form, Thatcher, trying to keep Miss Maxwell to yourself. She must not know your reputation, or she'd never have consented to spend time in your company without a chaperone." His laugh was echoed by the group of other officers crowding behind him to peer into the room. "We can't have you sullying the name of the heroine of the hour, now, can we?"

"You'd never think it, given his handicap, but Thatcher here is quite the proficient with the ladies," another man put in.

"Not to mention the gaming tables," added a third.

Xena had begun to hope that the tales she'd heard about Harry earlier were, if not false, at least greatly exaggerated but that hope was dashed when he made no effort to deny them now—though he did look rather put out. As though he'd have preferred she not discover the truth about his current lifestyle. Having her fears confirmed now made her course all the clearer.

Striving to ignore the ominous prickling behind her eyelids, she nodded stiffly to Harry and the others before hurrying out of the anteroom.

On regaining the ballroom, she spotted the Duke in conversation with a small knot of officers near the buffet tables. With a deep, steadying breath, Xena moved his way. She would take leave of her host and have her hired carriage brought round. Tomorrow she would need to rise early to begin her sadly necessary preparations to leave London within the next day or two.

"Excuse me, your grace," she began upon reaching the Duke's side. "It grows rather late, and I—"

"Ah, Miss Maxwell, here you are! I've been wishing to have a word with you for the past hour and more. Gentlemen, if you'll excuse me."

With a curt nod to the other men, he guided Xena to an alcove at one side of the enormous room where he turned to face her, his expression contrite.

"Pray allow me to apologize for springing Harry Thatcher upon you without warning earlier. It was terribly unsporting of me to subject a lady to such a shock—even so stalwart a lady as yourself. While I rather hoped to catch Thatcher unawares, I failed to take your feelings into consideration, which was unpardonable in me. I, er, hope my little joke did not cause you pain, nor Thatcher either. It's true he's become a bit of a wastrel of late, with an eye for the ladies, but he has always proved himself honorable where it counted."

Which did not include said dealings with "ladies," Xena presumed, remembering what Harry had said of the Duke and his wife.

"I would have preferred that you had informed me in advance that my husband still lived and would be in attendance, your grace, but I accept your apology," she said stiffly. "As Mr. Thatcher and I have agreed to continue as we were before tonight, no lasting harm was done." She hoped.

"Very glad to hear it. After so many years apart, it is only logical you should wish to go on living independently—and Thatcher as well. It's an enlightened arrangement, and one I favor myself. But then, you always were a forward thinker." His expression grew warmer then, and in a way Xena did not entirely care for. "Would you care for another glass of something? Perhaps away from this crowd?"

Withdrawing slightly, she shook her head—though with a smile. "Thank you, no, your grace. I have a full day planned for the morrow so must take my leave. It is what I came to tell you."

"Ah. I will be in Town through the end of the month, so perhaps I'll have more luck the next time I see you." He seemed not at all offended, to her relief.

"I fear that is unlikely, sir, as I return to Yorkshire within a day or two."

"So soon? I assumed you were fixed in London for the winter. Have you not had success in selling off your father's trinkets?"

She managed a regretful smile. "Not so much as I'd hoped."

"You must give it more time," he advised, again with that too-warm smile. "London can be quite gay at Yuletide, though I'm bound to spend mine in Paris, alas. But I am keeping you. I'll have a footman call for your carriage and bring your wrap. Give you goodnight, Mistress Maxwell. I very much hope our paths will cross again sooner than you anticipate."

"I hope so, too, your grace," Xena lied, her previously high opinion of General Wellington slipping another notch. It appeared he was no better than the rest of his sex after all...no better than Harry had turned out to be.

Refusing to dwell on either disappointment, she headed toward the imposing front door of Apsley House to await her carriage, determinedly focusing her thoughts on the tasks now awaiting her—such as breaking the news to Theo that they would not be remaining in London for the winter after all.

CHAPTER EIGHT

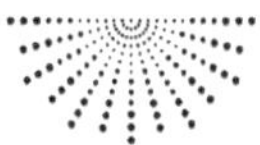

"GIVE OVER, YOU LOT." HARRY GLARED IRRITABLY AT THE FELLOW officers who'd been disobliging enough to air his indiscretions in Xena's hearing. "If you're all envious that I can do with one arm what most of you can't manage with two, simply say so."

They laughed and, after another ribald jest or two, drifted back to the party. Harry remained behind, trying to convince himself he was happy his interview with Xena had gone so well. What did it matter if she'd learned less than savory things about him, since they were to go their separate ways? His secret about the Saint of Seven Dials was safe, at any rate.

Emerging from the anteroom, he morosely observed the still-lively gathering, wondering what the devil was wrong with him. Then his gaze sharpened.

The Duke of Wellington was escorting Xena to an out-of-the-way alcove where they proceeded to carry on a conversation out of earshot of the other guests. Was Xena taking it upon herself to ask Wellington to keep word of their marriage private? He certainly wouldn't put it past her.

As he watched, the Duke nodded, spoke again, then smiled down at Xena—a smile Harry had seen his general employ on numerous occasions in Vienna when attempting to beguile a particularly comely wench or, more often, a highly-placed lady, into his bed. Was Wellington offering *his wife* a slip on the shoulder?

With a strangled oath Harry started forward before it occurred to him just how absurd his instinctive reaction was—and how unwise it would be to confront the Iron Duke in his own home, surrounded by dozens of officers who idolized him.

He checked himself, still frowning, just as Xena stepped back from the Duke. A moment later she headed toward the entrance, near where Harry himself still stood. Preferring not to encounter her while his emotions were in their current unsettled state, he slipped along the wall until he could become one of the milling crowd.

Some twenty minutes later, though he hadn't consciously intended it, Harry found himself face to face with Wellington.

"Thatcher," the Duke greeted him with a grin. "I imagine this has been quite an evening for you, no? Allow me to congratulate you."

"Sir?" What *had* Xena said to him? "You succeeded in handing me the biggest stunner of my life tonight, so surely I should be the one congratulating you."

"I did, didn't I? Must say, you carried it off better than I expected. Rather a disappointment, I confess—I was hoping for some real fireworks. But no matter. Your wife pointed out to me the error of treating a lady so, though it was you I particularly hoped to discomfit. But my congratulations were in regard to the situation in which you now find yourself, one most men would envy."

"How so?" Harry asked, more confused than ever.

The Duke's eyebrows rose. "Why, in having a wife who is as understanding as she is comely, which in her case is saying quite a bit. She has assured me she means to make no demands of you, nor interfere in your life in any way. As you've no succession to worry about, you are freer than ever to pursue your pleasures, with no risk of being inveigled into matrimony thereby. Well done."

"Ah. Yes. Er, thank you, your grace." Harry abruptly decided against asking Wellington to keep the marriage a secret. "We both agreed this course made the most sense."

"Miss Maxwell always was exceedingly practical for a female,"

Wellington agreed. "I knew her from a child, you know. She showed promise even then."

Harry did know—but the reminder made his onetime commander's leering at Xena even more unsavory. For an instant a correction as to Xena's proper name hovered on the tip of Harry's tongue before he bit it back. "A practical woman indeed," he managed lightly instead.

Others had now moved within earshot, clearly wishing a word with the Duke, so with a sketchy bow, Harry moved off in search of Peter. He'd had about all the polite mingling he could stomach for one evening.

A short time later, Harry, Peter and Sarah arrived back in Curzon Street, along with Jack, who had come along for a last chat with his old chums, as he meant to return to the country—and Nessa—on the morrow.

When they reached the first landing Sarah yawned. "If you gentlemen will excuse me, I will take myself off to bed. No need, therefore, to censor your conversation to avoid offending a lady's delicate ears." This last was said with an impish grin at her husband, who returned it before kissing her soundly and whispering something into her ear.

She swatted his knuckles with her fan, laughed, then continued up the stairs. Peter watched her with what Harry considered an unnecessarily besotted look on his face before turning back to the others.

"Let's have our port in the library, shall we? There should be a good fire and it has far the most comfortable chairs in the house."

Jack and Harry followed him into a room that somehow managed to be both elegant and cozy at once.

"Must say I'm impressed by what you've done with the place in just a few short weeks," Jack commented, looking appreciatively about before settling into one of the plushly upholstered chairs near the crackling fireplace. "Glad to see your taste in clothing doesn't extend to your furnishings." He shot an amused glance at Peter's colorful ensemble of peacock blue, scarlet and gold.

Peter grinned, well used to his friends' teasing about his attire. "I gave Sarah *carte blanche* to decorate the house as she wished, as her sense of style is nearly equal to my own. But for the breakfast room and one bedroom, it is nearly finished. But enough about such trivialities." He turned to Harry with a slight frown. "What on earth were you about tonight, closeting yourself into a room alone with the celebrated Miss Maxwell? Thought the point of the evening was to elevate your respectability, not to tarnish that of our host's guest of honor."

Jack let out a guffaw. "Never say you're still trying to turn Harry respectable, Pete? What's that saying about a sow's ear and a silk purse?"

As Jack was not privy to Harry's new occupation as Saint of Seven Dials, Peter responded, "Can't help m'self, I suppose. Always prefer to see my friends happy and I'm persuaded Harry is by no means as content to spend his life drunk and in debt as he'd have us believe. Even he should know better than to put a woman the Iron Duke clearly holds in esteem in a compromising position."

He frowned at Harry, who glared back—though less from Peter's words than at the memory of Wellington smiling suggestively down at Xena an hour since. As he'd not asked the Duke to keep word of his marriage quiet, he'd decided on the drive here to confess the whole to his two best friends tonight—which prospect contributed to his black mood.

Smoothing his frown with an effort, he put on as casual an air as he could summon preparatory to delivering his bombshell.

"You needn't worry, Pete. As it happens, Miss Maxwell's reputation was in no danger whatever—not when one considers that she and I have been legally married for some seven and a half years."

The complete shock that wiped all traces of jocularity from both his friends' faces was so comical it lightened Harry's spirits somewhat.

"What?" Jack exploded.

"Married?" Peter exclaimed at the same moment. "Impossible!"

"Of course it's impossible. He's bamming us, Pete. Look, he's grinning. Can't believe we were actually taken in for a moment."

Harry shook his head. "Though it would have been an excellent joke, I fear I'm quite serious. We were wed the very day before I joined the 48th, back in '09. We'd, er, let our passions get the better of our judgment and her father got wind of it. Needless to say, I left the 45th under a bit of a cloud, though no doubt Colonel Maxwell did his best to hush the whole thing up. It's why I never spoke of it."

Peter's disbelieving stare slowly became one of comprehension. "Then that letter you received, the one that started you drinking—"

"Was from her father, telling me she'd drowned when the frigate she had sailed upon was destroyed by the French."

"Which she was not aboard after all." Jack still looked thunderstruck. "So all this time you've believed her dead…until tonight? No wonder you reacted so when introduced. And Wellington—he knows, does he not?"

Harry nodded. "Xena told him we'd been married, believing me dead as well. Was rather a facer for both of us."

"I can imagine." Peter was frowning again now. "And while I can well believe Old Nosey would do such a thing to you, I'm surprised he would treat a lady so—particularly one so highly regarded by tonight's company as Miss Maxwell. Or, I suppose I should say…Mrs. Thatcher!"

At that, both Jack and Peter went off into peals of laughter that effectively blackened Harry's temper again.

"Very well, laugh. Can't say I didn't expect it. But don't think this revelation will affect my life in any way other than providing you two fodder for humor at my expense."

That only provoked more laughter. Indeed, it was at least two full minutes before either of Harry's friends recovered enough to speak.

"After the way you've chided us both for the way marriage has altered us, why should you think yourself immune?" Jack wiped his streaming eyes. "I assure you, dear fellow, you are not."

Peter, still helpless with laughter, simply shook his head.

"If this were what you two so sentimentally call a 'love match,' that might be true," Harry countered. "But while Xena and I were admittedly more attracted to each other seven years ago than was wise, we both regarded it as a mere passing liaison to while away the boredom and stress of camp life between skirmishes. While I was supposedly endangering my wife's virtue this evening, we were in fact agreeing to behave like civilized people and live our lives just as we've always done—separately. She means to return to Yorkshire within a day or two and I'll go on as before here in London."

That effectively quenched his comrades' hilarity. Both men now wore matching expressions of outraged confusion.

"What?" Peter demanded. "Surely you can't mean that! Why, you've just been reunited with the wife you lost and mourned all those years ago—and yes, we both knew you were mourning, though you never told us why. Now you mean to just...let her go again, without the slightest attempt to make a real go of your marriage? Are you mad?"

Now it was Harry's turn to laugh—though his heart wasn't in it. "Mad? Sane, more like—saner than either of you lovesick pups. Wellington himself pointed out how enviable most men would consider my position and I intend to take full advantage of it."

"Never say you mean to take Wellington as a model for happiness in the married state?" Jack snorted with disgust.

Harry shrugged. "He seems perfectly happy to me—wife comfortably tucked away in the country while he pursues his pleasures in Town. Why should I not do the same?"

"Because you've never even given your marriage a chance!" Peter nearly shouted at him. "True, Wellington might have done better not to marry at all on discovering the woman he'd courted a dozen years earlier was no longer the girl he'd fallen in love with. But once he did, he at least made a go of it before abandoning her for months at a stretch. Surely you owe yourself—and your wife—that much?"

"Xena didn't seem to think so," Harry retorted. "When I suggested we live apart she practically jumped at the idea." That still rankled slightly, though he'd never let his friends know it.

Jack made another attempt. "From what I heard of Miss Maxwell back on the Peninsula, she was even more unconventional and inde-pendent than yourself. Mightn't that make her your perfect match?"

Though once upon a time Harry had begun to believe exactly that, he refused to be drawn in by such a fantasy now. "No such thing exists," he said brusquely. "In any event, it's settled, as I already told you. She's leaving. I'm staying put. End of story." Standing, he downed the rest of his port in one impatient gulp, ignoring the burn in his throat. "Now, if you'll excuse me, I have my usual sordid pleasures to pursue. Give you good night, gentlemen."

Snatching up his hat and greatcoat, Harry stormed out of the library and down the stairs, slamming the front door as he quitted the house.

Not till he was nearly to Seven Dials did he slacken his pace, belat-edly remembering to act the drunken cripple so as not to be overly conspicuous to its denizens. Upon letting himself into Lord Hard-wyck's former rooms, he called out, "Flute? Are you here?"

"Aye, guv." The boy's straw-colored head popped around a corner. "Are you needing me to help you out of your evening things?"

"Yes, out of this costume and into a more appropriate one for housebreaking. The Saint has work to do."

A bout of burglary with perhaps a narrow escape for good measure would be just the thing to banish Xena from his mind.

Peter stared after Harry's rapidly-retreating form, blinking thought-fully as his best friend clattered down the stairs and slammed out of the front door. One brow raised, he then turned to Jack.

"Would you say he seemed a bit more put out than one might expect from a man who claims to have just achieved a so-called perfect arrangement?"

A slow smile spread across Jack's face. "He did indeed. Methinks he still has more of a soft spot for his long-lost wife than he's willing to admit—even to himself."

"My thought exactly. So the question now becomes, how do we go about convincing Harry of that?"

"Then you believe we should try?"

Peter nodded. "As I said, I cannot seem to help myself when it comes to forwarding the happiness of a friend—and you and I both know how much happiness is to be found in marriage to the right woman."

"But *is* this the right woman for Harry? If she's already decided she wants nothing to do with him or their marriage, what makes you believe we can change her mind? Or that we should?"

"How will we know—or, more importantly, how will *they* know—until they have spent sufficient time in each other's company to discover the truth?" Peter retorted with a grin. "You saw how they greeted each other tonight. I feel certain there was more at work in each than simple shock at discovering the other alive. If I'm wrong, so be it. She returns to Yorkshire and we leave Harry to his own devices."

Jack quirked an eyebrow. "And you'll really leave it at that?"

Sobering, Peter shrugged noncommittally. "I'll admit I'd prefer that not transpire. You've not been in Town enough in recent months to witness it, Jack, but Harry's been in a downward spiral of late. His drinking and gambling has reached new levels of excess, though it's increasingly obvious he enjoys it less and less."

He still hoped that becoming the Saint of Seven Dials would change that trend, but it was far too soon yet to know for certain. Besides which, as Harry himself had pointed out, it was an exceedingly risky pursuit with a distinct chance of landing him either in prison or at the gallows. Getting Harry happily settled with a wife was a far preferable option.

"From your thoughtful expression, I take it you are already planning a strategy to achieve this likely-impossible task?" Jack said, interrupting Peter's ruminations. "Will it require my assistance, or may I return to Fox Manor tomorrow as planned?"

Peter hadn't actually begun strategizing as yet, but now an idea began to form. "The first step, obviously, is to prevent Mrs. Thatcher from leaving London." Pronouncing her married name still made his lips twitch—and Jack's as well. "Nessa will be expecting you, so I'll attempt that stage on my own. Should I succeed, however, I believe it might be helpful to have you about for the next stage of our campaign —and Nessa, too, if she should feel equal to traveling."

"We had already discussed spending the winter in Town before she discovered she was increasing again. If her current indisposition proves as temporary as I hope—which she assures me is probable— we'll likely return before year's end. I can't imagine Nessa will wish to miss this campaign any more than I do."

Xena awoke with bleary eyes the next morning after an exceedingly restless night. She'd lain awake for hours, alternately wondering whether she were wrong to keep Theo's existence a secret from his father, then fretting that she would not be able to leave London quickly enough to do so.

Scenes from the evening kept replaying in her mind—that first, breath-stealing sight of Harry, his fellow officers' disclosures about the unsavory man Harry was now, General Wellington's disappointing fall from grace. Nor could she forget the way her heart had fluttered the whole time she'd been alone with Harry, all too reminiscent of how he'd made her feel so many years ago on the Peninsula.

When she finally did fall asleep, her dreams were all of Harry, past and present. At one point she'd come half-awake, convinced he was in the bed beside her—then experienced a most disturbing pang of disappointment on realizing he was not. Clearly it was high time she removed herself from his vicinity and such foolish fantasies.

With renewed determination, she arose, dressed and joined the others in the small, central parlor where they were already breakfasting.

"Mother!" Theo greeted her enthusiastically. "Mrs. Henderson says that if you will give your permission I may go out to the stables today with Mr. Beasley, the groom, to see the horses. I may, mayn't I? Please?"

Theo, as well as Gretchen and Yamini, had struck up a friendship of sorts with their landlady, and for the most part Xena had no fault to find with that, as it meant another pair of eyes to keep her active son out of trouble. Just now, however, she was struck by how very much Theo resembled his father.

Until seeing Harry again in the flesh last night, she'd almost forgotten the reddish highlights in his brown hair, so like Theo's, and his changeable hazel eyes—another trait Theo shared. Her heart tightened uncomfortably at the obvious similarities.

"Mother?" Theo prompted when she did not answer at once. "May I *please* visit the horses today? I promise to stay away from their hooves and to behave exactly as Mr. Beasley tells me."

"Oh, ah, yes, I suppose so, Theo, if you are careful."

He might as well have one last innocent pleasure, she reasoned, for he would be excessively disappointed to hear they must leave London within the week.

"Do you suppose I shall be allowed to give one of the horses a carrot or lump of sugar?" Theo's eyes sparked at the prospect. "I should like that very much!"

Xena smiled fondly at her son, deciding to wait until after she returned from her errands to give him the news about their departure. "As long as it is a very gentle horse, Mr. Beasley may allow it, if you ask politely."

He nodded vigorously, then jumped up. "I am finished eating. May Yamini take me downstairs now?"

"After your face is washed and your hair brushed."

"Will you come down, too?"

"Not just now. I must eat something and then I have a few errands to attend to. You may tell me all about it when I return."

A short time later, Xena again entered Mr. Gold's dusty shop. The old shopkeeper seemed delighted to see her.

"Ah, Miss Maxwell. I'd planned to send a message round today asking you to stop in, and here you've spared me the trouble. I've some very good news for you."

"Good news?" Xena echoed.

"Indeed. Someone has bought every Grecian item you've already consigned to me and has expressed interest in purchasing most of the ones you listed as available from Yorkshire, as well. All for a *most* handsome sum, I must say! I dare swear it is because the recent controversy over Lord Elgin's Marbles has sparked renewed interest in all things Greek."

Mr. Gold named a sum that made Xena gasp aloud. It seemed too good to be true—which meant she must be cautious. "Has he left any sort of surety against the items that are not yet in London?"

"Believe me, miss, his name alone is surety enough, but I fear he bound me not to disclose it as yet. He fears if word were to get out others might attempt to outbid him, though to my knowledge there are few currently residing in Town with resources to equal his."

Xena frowned suspiciously. "I can write to my steward in Yorkshire at once to request the shipping of the other items but should like some assurance first that this anonymous gentleman will not change his mind. I will not be remaining in London many more days, so it would be well if this business could be settled quickly."

Mr. Gold smiled indulgently. "His, er, the gentleman in question gave me his word, so you need have no worries on that head. He also expressed a wish to discuss the collection with you in person when his press of business allows it. Surely, with so much money at stake, you can see your way clear to extend your stay? I should be happy to do more business with you as well."

Xena thought hard. It was true that the total amount would cover every conceivable repair at home and ensure Theo's future as well, but did she dare wait for it all? If she were very discreet and stayed well away from the West End, perhaps the risk would not be so *very* great, as Harry would believe her already gone...

"I will see whether I can adjust my plans, Mr. Gold, though I would prefer to have that meeting as soon as can be arranged. You will send me word the moment it is possible, will you not?"

"Of course. Now, about those Turkish figurines you mentioned earlier…"

After another ten minutes discussion, Xena left the shop two hundred pounds richer than she had arrived, and with the promise of much, much more in the near future. She'd intended to stop by the modiste's to cancel the other two gowns she'd ordered but now decided against it. If she were to remain in London another week, there would be time for them to be made up and delivered, and she was now well able to afford them.

But who will I wear them for? a small voice whispered, introducing a note of disquiet to her otherwise improved outlook. Resolutely refusing to think about the one man she might *wish* to see her wearing them, she returned to Rundel Street. Only as she approached the entrance to Mrs. Henderson's house did she perceive the smartly dressed gentleman standing just outside—a gentleman she recognized with a start from last night.

"Give you good day, Miss Maxwell." Lord Peter Northrup stepped toward her with a broad smile. "Just the woman I was hoping to see. Might I have a word?"

Xena froze for an instant but it was too late to turn tail. "How did you find me?" she demanded.

Lord Peter's brows rose. "Not quite the cordial greeting I'd hoped for, but an understandable question, given that it did indeed entail a bit of difficulty. Fortunately for me, Wellington's secretary remembered where he had sent your invitation and was obliging enough to share your direction."

Belatedly recalling her manners, Xena dipped a grudging curtsey. "I give you good day, Lord Peter, and apologize for my initial rudeness. Might I also inquire as to your reason for seeking me out?"

"Of course. Perhaps you might invite me in so we may speak in rather more privacy?"

"I fear that would be most improper, my lord, for my abigail is out on an errand, which would leave us unchaperoned." Luckily Gretchen was not present to give her the lie, as Xena had not insisted the girl accompany her. "Surely we are private enough here, given how few people are about."

Lord Peter twirled his hat in his hands for a moment before nodding. "Very well, Miss Maxwell—or, I should say, Mrs. Thatcher. I come on behalf of your husband to ask that you not give up on your marriage so easily when there is a chance it might yet be source of happiness for you both."

Xena stared. "*Harry* sent you? He actually told you about—"

"No, no, you misunderstand. While it's true that Harry informed me last night about how things stand between the two of you, he has no idea that I am here."

"But you said—"

"That I was here on his behalf. I am. For it is primarily for Harry's sake that I am making this request of you. I am convinced you are the very thing he needs in his life just now. And who knows? You may discover he is just what you need in yours, as well."

A mirthless laugh escaped her. "I take leave to doubt both of those suppositions, sir. Harry made it quite clear last night that the last thing he wants is a wife hanging about. As for myself, after believing myself a widow all these years, I've grown quite set in my ways. I should imagine the same is true of Harry."

"Rather too set in his ways, I should say. It is my hope you might be able to change that."

"Then you do not deny that Harry enjoys a rather…unsavory lifestyle?" Xena held his gaze with her own, more than half expecting him to prevaricate.

He did not. "No, I don't deny it—except for the enjoyment part. It is my belief he does *not* particularly enjoy that lifestyle, but needs assistance in breaking out of a routine that is otherwise like to send him to an early grave."

Xena flinched, but strove to hide it. "Surely a wife's scolding is unlikely to convince him to give up his wilder pursuits for a dull, domestic existence. I should think the reverse would be true."

"I do not ask you to nag or scold—unless you wish to, of course." Lord Peter grinned. "But the, er, companionship of a woman such as yourself, a woman he once cared for enough to marry and then to mourn, might be the very thing to begin his transformation into a better—and happier—man."

Mourn? Harry had mourned her? She resisted a strong urge to ask for details. "I am afraid this sounds like wishful thinking to me, Lord Peter. Nor will I let you persuade me that it is somehow my *duty* to save Harry from himself. I have a home and a life in Yorkshire and I mean to return to it forthwith."

That life now struck her as depressingly empty and boring, after her brief taste of the bustle and variety of London.

"I had hoped to appeal to your sense of compassion, if not of duty," Lord Peter confessed. "I heard so many tales last night of your skill and dedication in nursing the wounded during wartime, it seemed likely to me that once you knew the dangers of Harry's current life-style you would seek to save him from it, just as you would seek to prevent a heedless child from drowning."

Xena swallowed. While it was true she had no wish for Harry to beggar or injure himself—or worse—she could not believe, after last night's conversation, that he would at all welcome her interference.

"Harry is no heedless child, but a grown man responsible for his own decisions, however unwise. I'm sorry, Lord Peter. I simply—"

Just then, a small form came barreling around the corner of the house, his dirty face alight with excitement. "Mother! You're back! I not only got to feed two of the horses, the groom let me help curry one of them as well."

Theo's effusions stopped abruptly on noticing Lord Peter standing there, but the damage was done. Xena's heart sank as she looked from her son's curious expression to Lord Peter's thunderstruck one.

CHAPTER NINE

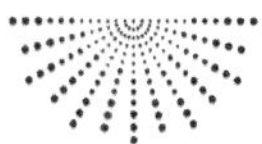

PETER STARED DOWN AT THE LAD NOW CLINGING TO HIS MOTHER'S skirts, feeling as though the earth had suddenly shifted on its axis. That hair, those eyes…there was no possible doubt. He was looking at Harry Thatcher's *son*.

With a Herculean effort, he tried to cover his shock with a smile. "Hello, young sir," he said, leaning down slightly. "I am Peter. What might your name be?"

The boy glanced questioningly up at his mother, but she was apparently too stricken to give him guidance. Squaring his shoulders, he let go her skirt and tilted his face—a childlike version of Harry's—up to Peter's.

"Pleased to meet you, sir. I am Theo. I mean, Theodore Maxwell."

Maxwell? He'd never even been told who his father was?

At that point, Miss Maxwell—no, Mrs. Thatcher, Peter reminded himself—recovered her capacity for speech. "Theo, dear, your face is dirty. Run upstairs and wash it, please. I will be up in a few moments."

She waited until the lad, with a last curious look over his shoulder, went into the house and closed the door behind him before turning back to Peter, her chin now lifting defiantly.

"Now you know my primary reason for wishing to leave London.

For…various reasons, I am persuaded my son will be far better off back in Yorkshire."

"I take it one of those reasons is to keep him in ignorance of his father's identity, as you have clearly done thus far?" Peter could not quite keep the implied accusation from his tone.

Glancing back toward the house, she lowered her voice. "I had intended to tell him as soon as we returned to Yorkshire—but that was before I learned that his father is still living, and had become, well, *you* know."

"And now you mean to continue keeping the truth from both Harry and young Theo? For how long?"

"I, ah, hadn't decided. Though now I suppose my decision is moot." Her eyes both challenged and pleaded with him. "Unless I can somehow persuade you not to mention him to Harry?"

Peter frowned. "I don't see how I can in conscience keep something so important from him. Nor does it seem right that you would do so."

She flushed visibly. "I am thinking only of my son's welfare. Would you have me cede authority over him to a man that you yourself have admitted is bent on drinking and gambling himself into poverty and an early grave?"

That gave Peter momentary pause, for he could not deny she had a point. She had also just given him the leverage he needed to achieve his original purpose in seeking her out. Though it went against the grain to make such a promise, if all went well he wouldn't need to keep it for long.

In fact, if his plan achieved the result he hoped for, he'd finally be able to tell Harry the truth about the state of his finances without fearing the money would merely fund more dissipation.

"I might be persuaded to keep my council, at least for a time," he said after a moment. "On one condition."

"And what condition might that be?" Wariness warred with the sudden hope in her eyes.

Quelling his misgivings, Peter smiled. "Why, the very thing I came here to suggest. I wish you to give your marriage to Harry a fighting chance for success by living together as husband and wife until, let us say, the first of the year. If, after that time, you both still prefer to go your separate ways, I will not seek to prevent it."

Appalled, Xena realized she'd fallen neatly into Lord Peter's trap, ambushed by her own carelessness in not more forcefully impressing upon her son the necessity of staying out of sight. Her first instinct was to refuse. If she could spirit Theo out of London immediately…

But that would be no permanent solution. Once Harry learned he had a son, he might well come after them despite his professed desire to avoid entanglements. Which pointed up a serious weakness in her enemy's position.

"Suppose I agree. How do you intend to convince *Harry* to go along with this ridiculous plan?"

A shadow of doubt appeared in his eyes, confirming her guess, but then it was gone. "I have my ways. Leave Harry to me."

Surely he was expressing more confidence than he felt. "If he should refuse, will you still abide by your promise to keep Theo's existence a secret?"

After a moment's hesitation, he nodded. "You have my word—but only if you will agree to the attempt."

Only partially reassured, Xena strove to further shore up her position. "Supposing you *do* somehow induce Harry to agree to your experiment, yet we still elect never to see each other again after the first of the year. What then?"

"I would still consider myself bound by my word. But surely the fact that you and Harry have a son gives you an added incentive to work toward a reconciliation—if that is the proper word, considering your long separation was due to misinformation rather than intent. If you will not make this attempt for Harry's sake or your own, perhaps you will do so for Theo's."

For a long moment she stared at him, various emotions warring for ascendancy—guilt, apprehension and, yes, a degree of longing that surprised her. Surely she did not *want* Harry to agree to his friend's plan—to be obliged to live intimately with him for a month and more? Of course she did not.

As she could see no other option, however, she gave a single nod. "Very well, my lord. I accede to your blackmail. It is very little else," she snapped when he started at the word. "When do you wish this foolish experiment to commence, and how am I to proceed?"

"I will send word when I've secured Harry's cooperation and will make all arrangements forthwith. It is my hope you can begin living as a married couple within the next few days. In the meantime, might you consider staying as our guest in Curzon Street? Sarah—Lady Peter —would like that very much."

Still hopeful that Harry would summarily refuse, Xena shook her head. "I can hardly leave Theo at a moment's notice, my lord, nor do I expect it will prove necessary. I will, however, agree to delay our departure from London for a week while you attempt to persuade Harry."

That should give her time to meet with Mr. Gold's client about her other Grecian items and perhaps receive some portion of the princely sum he promised. With such substantial funds at her disposal she could take Theo abroad, where they would be safe from pursuit should Lord Peter renege on his promises.

"Very well. But do not count on Harry's refusal. I'm known to be most persuasive when I believe myself in the right. I advise you to make whatever preparations will be necessary for the care of your son and your removal from these lodgings within the next few days. And now, Mrs. Thatcher, I give you good day."

With a smart bow, Lord Peter turned and headed up the street, whistling merrily.

Xena stared after him, shaken anew by his confidence. Though she could not at all believe Harry would agree to any such arrangement as his friend suggested, she supposed she had better speak privately with Yamini and Mrs. Henderson.

Just in case.

• • •

"Mother!" Theo greeted her when she returned to their apartments. "I was telling Yamini and Gretchen about the man you were talking to just now. He was dressed like a lord and so tall! And he spoke very nicely to me." Then, face still alight, he asked, "Is he…my father?"

Xena only just managed to keep her mouth from dropping open with shock. "Your—? Of course not, Theo! Why on earth would you think such a thing? I only met him for the first time last night, at the Duke's reception. He, ah, simply stopped to pay his respects."

Yamini, who knew Xena better than anyone alive, frowned but Gretchen clapped her hands.

"Oh, mum! He must have been quite smitten with you to seek you out the very next day! He'll be sending you flowers next, mark my words!"

"Don't be absurd, Gretchen." Despite her alarm at realizing Theo was far more curious about his father than she'd guessed, Xena almost laughed. "Lord Peter is married, and to the most beautiful woman I've ever seen. He was…good friends with a few of the soldiers I knew on the Peninsula and wished to give me further news of some of them. That is all."

Gretchen's freckled face fell, but Yamini's dark eyes sharpened. "Mum, if I might have a word?" She nodded toward Xena's bedroom. "We should discuss Theo's request of visiting the stables again."

It was clearly a pretext, but Xena followed Yamini from the room as Theo exclaimed to Gretchen, "He *was* a lord! I was right. The first lord I ever met!"

Softly closing the door behind them, Yamini turned a worried face to her mistress. "My dear, I could tell at breakfast that something is terribly wrong. Can you tell me what it is?"

Yamini had come to the Maxwell's grand house in India as a girl of eighteen to be nursemaid to the recently orphaned five-year-old Xena. Over the twenty-odd years since she had become far more than a servant, filling the roles of mother, friend and confidant. In desperate need of advice, Xena did not hesitate to unburden herself .

"I never have been able to keep a secret from you, Yamini, and you're quite right. I discovered last night at the Duke's reception that, after all these years of believing him dead, Theo's father is still alive."

The other woman stared. "Mr. Thatcher? But the newspaper—?"

"He was wounded at Salamanca and apparently believed dead for some weeks, but a Spanish family nursed him back to health. Yamini, he was *there*. I was never more shocked in my life than when we suddenly came face to face. He appeared equally stunned, for he had no idea I had survived, either. The Duke had saved that news as a surprise for his guests."

Yamini blinked several times, clearly trying to absorb the startling revelation. "So you and Mr. Thatcher spoke? What did he say? What do you plan to do?"

"At first we were both too startled to say much," Xena admitted, "but we did speak privately later and agreed we should simply go on as we'd been with no one else the wiser. Unfortunately, the Duke of Wellington knows the truth. So does Lord Peter Northrup, for he is apparently one of Harry's closest friends."

If Yamini felt surprise at hearing Xena's use of Harry's Christian name for the first time in many years, she did not betray it. "Then it was about your husband that Lord Peter came to speak with you?"

Xena nodded. "He, ah, feels that Harry and I owe it to ourselves, and to Theo, to give our long-ago unplanned marriage a chance to become a real one. He wishes us to live as husband and wife until the first of the year."

"And did you agree?"

"Not willingly. But Theo unexpectedly ran up to greet me, and when Lord Peter saw him he guessed the truth at once. When I asked him to keep Theo's existence a secret, he promised to do so only if I agreed to his suggestion."

Yamini's brows drew down. "Do you believe keeping Theo from his father is wise?"

"You sound like Lord Peter!" Xena exclaimed. "But last night I learned that Harry has become not only a drunkard but a gamester since last I knew him. How can I trust Theo's future to such a man?"

"I understand your fear of ceding any portion of control over your son's life—or your own life—to any man." Yamini regarded her shrewdly. "But Theo *must* learn who his father is at some point, if he is not to believe himself a bastard."

"Yamini!"

"Forgive my plain speaking, mum, but he'll be old enough to understand what the word means all too soon. Already he gives more thought to the question than you may realize. Out of your hearing, he has asked me countless times whether I have any idea who his father might be. Knowing your wishes, I've said nothing, but he grows more persistent by the week. Nor does it seem quite…right that his father be unaware."

Setting her jaw stubbornly, Xena shook her head. "I suppose in time they must both be told but that time is not yet come. Not unless I discover the tales I have heard about Harry are untrue."

"Your opinion is based on mere gossip? I thought better of your sense than that."

"It's not just gossip," Xena protested. "Harry himself implied as much. At least, he did not deny it." Even as she spoke the words, she recalled a certain softness she'd seen in his eyes last night…and the way being near him had made her feel.

"In any event, Lord Peter has yet to persuade Harry to go along with this mad scheme, something I consider highly unlikely."

Yamini gave her a knowing smile. "For myself, I hope Lord Peter will be successful, for there is no way better to learn what a man really is than by living with him for a time. Perhaps he will surprise you."

Did Yamini mean that he would surprise her by agreeing, or by proving himself to be a better man than Xena so far had reason to believe? She decided not to ask.

Harry rolled over in bed, then immediately regretted it. The sliver of sunshine making its way through a narrow gap in the thick curtains lanced directly into his eyes, exacerbating the pounding in his head. He groaned.

"Ah, you're awake, guv," came Flute's voice from the doorway of Harry's bedchamber. "Good. Couldn't figure which was worse—to wake you after such a night or leave Lord Peter waiting."

"What?" Wincing, Harry forced himself higher on the pillows to regard his young henchman and mentor blearily. "Peter's here? How the devil did he find the place?"

"Nay, guv, he just sent Renny with a message for you. Wants you at his house quick as you can get there, he said. Must be important?"

Harry groaned again, for he had a good idea what Peter wanted to talk to him about. The same thing that had driven him to over-celebrate after last night's successful housebreaking. Xena.

When purloining valuables from two different houses—both belonging to men who needed taking down a pin or two—failed to push Xena to the back of his mind, Harry had turned to his old friend, the bottle. That had eventually worked, but only by sending him to sleep after a maudlin period of alcohol-enhanced longing. Indeed, at three-thirty in the morning he'd nearly gone back out to find her. Luckily he'd passed out across his bed first.

The last thing he needed was more haranguing from Peter about "giving his marriage a chance." In the cruel light of day, he recalled only too clearly how relieved Xena had seemed when he'd told her he had no more desire to make their long-ago marriage public than she did. The sooner he could forget her again, the better—something he'd have to convey forcefully to Pete.

"I'll call on him after I've cleaned up a bit. And breakfasted." He didn't have much of an appetite after last night's excesses, and by the angle of that sunbeam it was well past noon, but no matter. Pretending to eat would delay the inevitable a bit longer.

It was nearly two hours later when, shaved, brushed and respectably clad, Harry presented himself at Peter's town house on Curzon Street. Given his tardiness in answering the summons, he was surprised by how affably his friend greeted him.

"Ah, Harry. I began to think my message missent. Take it you put in a rather late night after leaving us?" Though he smiled, Peter's eyes raked Harry's face, missing no detail—which meant he must know full well exactly how wretched he felt, and why.

"The job you persuaded me to tends to make for late nights," Harry replied shortly, in no mood for niceties. "What's so important it required rousting me from my well-earned bed?"

Peter's brows rose, though he appeared more amused than censorious. "It's past three, old chap. But come. We can discuss it in the library."

He led the way to the same room Harry had quitted in a temper last night. Harry flung himself into the best chair, his mood not improved in the least by the reminder. Before taking a seat himself, Peter went to the sideboard.

"Would you care for a glass of something first?"

Harry scowled, sure now that Pete was trying to soften him up for another assault. "Thanks, but no. Stomach's a bit tetchy just now."

He was still in that post-binge state of swearing off drink forever. The resolve never seemed to last much past dinner time, but at the moment it was still in force.

Though Peter was undoubtedly well aware of Harry's reason for refusing, he made no comment before taking the chair opposite. "I'll get right to my proposition, then."

Harry regarded him suspiciously. "Another proposition? Your last landed me squarely on the wrong side of the law—though I won't claim I'm not enjoying it. What's this one?"

"That you do what I suggested last night: give your newly-discovered marriage a chance of success. No, let me finish," Peter added quickly when Harry made an impatient motion to get to his feet. "I've already spoken with your wife, and she is willing to give it a trial if you are."

Slumping back into his chair, Harry stared at his friend in disbelief. "You've done *what?* Why—? How—? You had no right!"

"Concern for the welfare of a good friend gave me the right. After some discussion, she agreed it would be foolish to leave London without at least attempting to discover whether the two of you might rub along comfortably together. If nothing else, it may spare her the speculation and gossip that will inevitably arise once word gets out that the two of you were married."

"And why should word get out?" It was obvious from Peter's very nonchalance that he was not revealing all.

"Did you ask Wellington not to bruit it about?"

Damn. "Of course not. There were others by, and such a request would have required too much in the way of awkward explanation."

"By your account, he seems to believe being married will prove an asset, leaving you that much freer to pursue your usual, ah, variety of women. Given that, I believe it's fair to assume he won't hesitate to mention it, should occasion arise."

Didn't Peter ever tire of being right? Still, Harry attempted to mimic his unconcern.

"No matter if he does. Once back in Yorkshire, Xena will be safe enough from Town gossip. Doubt many of the locals there read the London rags. Can't believe she'd worry about such things, in any case." Certainly the Xena of seven years ago wouldn't have.

Peter regarded him from under furrowed brows. "And what of you? Can you honestly say it would not bother you to hear your wife's name bandied about? Have her caricaturized on storefronts?"

The thought made Harry's bile rise, but he strove to conceal it. "She's been guilty of nothing but wishing to live her own life. No fault to her for not wanting her name linked with mine. Who would?"

"Did you not hear what I said at the outset?" Peter's tone was irritatingly patient. "She told me she is willing to give your marriage a chance if you are. Given that, it would be ungallant in the extreme for you to refuse. Or perhaps the vaunted Miss Maxwell has a greater measure of courage than you do?" Peter leaned back in his chair while his words penetrated.

Though he could scarce believe Xena had agreed to any such thing, Harry couldn't see what Pete might gain by making such a claim if it were untrue. Was it conceivable she was as beset by old memories as he, after their first encounter in more than seven years? Or...

He now recalled her final encounter with Wellington last night, during which it had appeared the Duke was trying to persuade her to something. If they'd reached some sort of arrangement, that might account for her new willingness to remain in London.

Harry shook his head, striving to banish the unpalatable thought. "Impossible. How would we even manage such a thing? Have her come to live with me in Seven Dials? My flat on Swallow Street has already been let—not that it was much better."

If Harry expected that detail to be a stumper for Peter, he was disappointed.

"Of course not. That neighborhood is rather too rough for a lady, even one rumored to have shooting and fencing skills. As it happens, Marcus and his wife left Town two days since for their estate in Hertfordshire and that new school they're establishing, leaving the Northrup Town house empty. I make you and your bride free of it."

There were other difficulties, however, and Pete had to know it.

"How do you suggest I account for my sudden acquisition of a wife? Will that not cause as much gossip as Xena returning to Yorkshire?"

Peter smiled. "I've given that some thought, as well. We'll simply tell the truth, or a slightly censored version of it. Claim you were both too overcome by surprise and confusion last night at Wellington's do to mention it to anyone. Once you're seen amicably attending functions together, any early speculations will no doubt fade away."

Harry took leave to doubt that, but he was rapidly running out of arguments. Nor could he deny that the idea of living for a time in close quarters with Xena, who was even more bewitching than he remembered, held an insidious appeal. Not that he could allow Peter to guess that.

"Still sounds a mad scheme to me, and one more of your making than Xena's. What did you have to offer to get her to agree?"

"Offer? I promised no money, I assure you." He noticed Peter did not quite meet his eye, however, instead carefully adjusting the lace edging on one sleeve. "I won't claim she leapt at the idea when I first put it to her, but I eventually convinced her it was worth a trial."

"How long a trial?" Harry continued to watch his friend closely, hoping for more clues.

Peter continued to fiddle with his sleeve. "She, ah, suggested you give it until the first of the year. By then you and she should be able to determine whether or not my little experiment was a success."

A bit over a month, then. A month to become reacquainted with the woman Xena had become. A month to… No. Thinking along those lines would only drive him mad while making an already awkward situation more so.

"And what of my other pursuit, the one you persuaded me to only two weeks since?"

"Probably best if you curtail those activities for the duration. I am prepared to offer you five hundred pounds to offset any losses, however, which you may use as you see fit."

Harry regarded his friend through narrowed eyes. Clearly this experiment meant a lot to Peter if he was willing to offer such a sum in addition to his other arguments.

Though it chafed to accept what was essentially a bribe, Harry couldn't deny the plan held a certain appeal, apart from the money. In fact, a month of living in Xena's pocket might be the very thing to drive her from his mind once and for all.

"Very well. I'll attempt it…so as not to insult her. But on your head be it if she and I end up murdering each other."

CHAPTER TEN

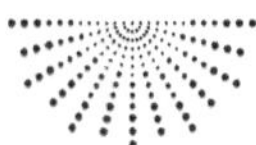

WHEN XENA HAD RECEIVED NO FURTHER COMMUNICATION FROM LORD Peter by that evening, she began to breathe easier. Clearly Harry had refused to go along with that ridiculous scheme, just as she had predicted. Though much relieved to be spared Lord Peter's "trial," she was nonetheless aware of a tiny thread of disappointment. It seemed Harry had been able to put her from his mind rather more easily than she'd been able to put him from hers.

That her dreams again prominently featured Harry did not help matters at all. To turn her mind to other paths, immediately after breakfast she set about preparing Theo's lessons for the upcoming week. Yamini was an excellent tutor, instructing him in the rudiments of Greek, Latin, French and mathematics, but Xena herself taught him history and geography as well as planning his courses of study. Back in Yorkshire she had also begun teaching him the basic principles of fencing, but that was scarcely possible here.

She had just written out Theo's mathematics curriculum when a tap came at the door. Glancing up as Gretchen answered, she saw one of Mrs. Henderson's housemaids. After a few exchanged words, Gretchen turned to her excitedly.

"There's a gentleman below asking for you, mum, like as not the same one who come calling yesterday. You're sure and certain he's already married?"

Xena's breath caught. Perhaps Lord Peter had merely come to release her from her bargain? She could but hope.

"Quite certain, Gretchen, so no spinning of romantic fancies, if you please. He likely brings more news of old comrades."

Bringing the more discreet Yamini along for propriety, she went down to Mrs. Henderson's tiny parlor, where her caller's delighted smile instantly banished her hopeful theory.

"How nice to see you again, Lord Peter," she lied.

He stood and bowed. "I am relieved to hear you say so, madam, as I come with what I consider excellent news."

"Oh?" She tried not to let her tension show.

"Indeed. As I predicted, Harry has agreed to my proposal. I would have sent word last night but thought it better to inform you in person."

For fear she might take Theo and flee London before morning? "Given how you obtained my agreement, I can't help but wonder at the means you used to secure Harry's."

"Once I told him you were willing, he was not so very hard to convince," Lord Peter assured her, flicking a speck of dust from his sleeve. "You will not, I hope, renege on our bargain?"

"Blackmail scarcely counts as a bargain in my view, but I never go back on my given word. Now we've both agreed, I presume you will begin working out how this experiment of yours is to proceed?" Though somewhat reassured by the possibility that Harry actually *wanted* to give their marriage this trial, she was curious about the logistics.

"On the contrary, my dear Mrs. Thatcher, everything is already arranged—another reason for my small delay in calling upon you."

Xena listened with growing dismay as Lord Peter outlined his scheme, both startled and grudgingly impressed by how many details he had worked out in only a day. He had even secured a house for them, to fulfill his conditions.

"Of course you need not spend all of your time there. You may go about whatever activities you like, so long as you both sleep in the house each night—though the more activities you share, the more likely this effort will be to succeed."

Did she *want* it to succeed? 'Twould be a good thing—for Theo's sake—if it prompted Harry to pursue a less licentious lifestyle, she supposed. Still... "You will not, I hope, require us to share a bedroom?"

Lord Peter looked startled. "Ah, no. I rather hope that in time you might *choose* such an arrangement, but that seems a bit much to insist upon before you have had a chance to become reacquainted."

That worry, at least, was allayed. Unless this house he spoke of was extremely small, it might be possible for them to share it without encountering each other at all, except in passing.

As though divining her thought, Lord Peter added, "I do, however, think it fair to insist that you dine together on those evenings you have no other engagements, as well as taking breakfast together each morning. That should provide ample opportunity for you to mutually determine how you wish to proceed as your time together progresses."

Xena wanted to argue that condition but something in his face told her that, despite his colorful dress and almost foppish appearance, Lord Peter was not a man to be easily swayed from a course he believed was right—as he clearly believed himself to be in this case.

"Very well. Two meals each day, whenever possible. When do you wish this experiment of yours to commence?"

"Tomorrow afternoon, if you can make arrangements to relocate by then."

"Tomorrow! I'm sorry, my lord, but I don't see how I can possibly—"

Yamini's soft voice interrupted her. "Begging your pardon, mum, I've taken the liberty of making all necessary preparations, save the packing of your personal effects."

Xena whirled to glare at the woman she'd always regarded as her closest ally. "Yamini! Why—? And what am I to tell Theo?"

"I have given thought to that as well, mum. An old acquaintance you met at the Duke of Wellington's reception has invited you to a house party here in Town. Attending will allow us all to remain longer in London. Given Theo's enthusiasm for city life, I doubt he will ask too many questions."

Feeling utterly betrayed, she turned back to Lord Peter. "It appears I can indeed relocate on the morrow. Where is this house you have arranged for me—us—to stay?"

"On Grosvenor Street. It is a house that has been in my family for several generations but is currently unoccupied, except for the servants. Not terribly large, but in a most eligible location, just around the corner from Grosvenor Square."

An eligible location indeed! The heart of Mayfair, in fact, where the very pinnacle of Society dwelt.

"Is there a particular time you would like me to arrive?" Despite herself, Xena could not suppress a tingle of eagerness. To see the house, of course. *Not* to see Harry again—especially in what would surely be an awkwardly intimate setting.

"As you will presumably have luggage, I will send a carriage for you. Shall we say three o'clock tomorrow?"

Xena swallowed. "I, ah, suppose that will be acceptable."

Lord Peter smiled broadly. "Excellent. Oh, Sarah asked me to mention again how very much she should like to become better acquainted. She is particularly eager to share with you the sights and amusements of Town, as many are still novelties to her, as well. The theatre, for example. I hope you—and Harry—will accompany us sometime in the near future."

That tingle of eagerness increased. Xena had always longed to attend a theatrical performance—perhaps to see one of Shakespeare's works on the stage, rather than simply read aloud, as she and Yamini had been known to do for amusement, and for Theo's benefit. She could even regale Theo with an account of the experience later…

"That might be pleasant, my lord. Thank you."

"Sarah will be delighted." Lord Peter stood. "And now, I'll leave you to your preparations. I give you good day, Mrs. Thatcher. Ma'am."

He bowed first to Xena, then to Yamini—a courtesy rarely offered to a servant, much less one of clearly foreign origin. Xena's opinion of him rose accordingly. Surely, if this man was Harry's closest friend, Harry could not be *quite* so debauched as those officers had implied?

She needn't wonder for long, she realized. Living in close quarters with him for a month should give her ample opportunity to observe his character for herself. As the great military tactician Sun Tzu had said in his writings, one should know one's enemies even better than one knew one's friends.

If a small voice whispered that she did not wish Harry to be her enemy, she ignored it.

~

"Is everything ready, Gretchen?" Xena asked from near the window as a crested carriage drew up in front of the house the following afternoon.

Her nerves were stretched taut despite telling herself repeatedly that she had little to fear. At the worst, she and Harry would have a falling out this very day and declare the experiment a failure at its outset—or would that be the best?

"Yes, mum, as I already told you three times. Begging your pardon," she added quickly when Xena shot her a frown.

Gretchen's excitement about the "house party" made her even less guarded in her speech than usual. Xena had therefore decided not to confide the truth to her until they were on their way lest the girl let it slip to Theo, something she preferred not happen just yet.

For whatever Harry might hope to come out of this attempted reconciliation, her own goal was clear—to learn everything possible about her husband's character and the state of his finances. Only then could she decide what would truly be best—for all of them.

"The coach is here. Theo, you must behave yourself and do as Yamini tells you."

He nodded, still half-pouting that he was not to go, too, though Yamini had promised to take him about to some of the sights of London while Xena was away.

"Now give me a kiss," she said, bending down.

Though at the great age of six and a half he often declared himself too old for such caresses, now he threw his arms about her neck. "I shall miss you, Mother. Will you truly be gone a whole month and more?"

"Possibly, but not so very far from here. I will arrange with Yamini to visit with you as often as I can. Perhaps we will go to a park together."

"Or the menagerie at the Tower?"

"We'll see." Giving her son another kiss, resisting the urge to clasp him to her again, she picked up her small valise and led Gretchen down to the waiting carriage.

The carriage driver strapped Xena's trunk to the back, with the help of Mrs. Henderson's man-servant, as she and Gretchen climbed inside. Lord Peter must be waiting for them at the townhouse he spoke of. At least, Xena hoped so. Her meeting with Harry might be a tiny bit less awkward that way.

"Gretchen, now we are private, I must tell you there is no house party—or, rather, the only guests will be myself and my husband, Harry Thatcher."

The girl's face fell at her first words, but then became a picture of blank astonishment. "Your…husband, mum? But he's been dead this many a year, ain't he? Or have you somehow gone and got yourself married over the past week?"

As the driver whipped up the horses, Xena briefly explained the double misunderstanding that had led to the current situation.

"Mind you, he knows nothing about Theo yet, so don't mention him to any of the servants at the house. I wish to, ah, become reacquainted with my husband before springing such a surprise on him. Or on Theo."

"I'll not say nothing, then, mum," Gretchen promised. "But lor' what a romance, to be sure! Reunited after all these years thinking each other dead! Like something out of a penny novel it is." Her brown eyes shone with renewed excitement.

Xena wondered whether she should discourage the girl from weaving such fancies, but just then the carriage drew to a halt before a handsome double-fronted town house.

"'Cor! Is this where we'll be staying, mum?" Gretchen exclaimed as the coachman opened the door and let down the steps.

Lord Peter had described the house as "not overly large," leading Xena to expect a far more modest dwelling. She should have known a duke's son would have rather higher standards than her own. Before she could give in to a sudden urge to have the coachman return her to Mrs. Henderson's, the front door opened.

"Welcome!" Lord Peter exclaimed, hurrying forward. "Come, let me introduce you to the principal staff." So saying, he put a firm hand to Xena's elbow and guided her up the front steps.

Several servants were lined up just inside. Completely out of her element, Xena nearly panicked again—then spotted Harry lurking in the shadows at the rear of the foyer. Courage—or perhaps it was pride —came to her rescue. Lifting her chin, she returned his wary gaze with a cool nod. Yes, she could do this.

Harry hid a smile. Despite Peter's assurances, Xena had looked ready to bolt before the courageous spirit he'd always admired reasserted itself. Now, standing suddenly straighter, she defiantly met his eye. No, his Xena had never been one to run from a challenge.

His Xena? Harry gave himself a mental shake. She was scarcely that anymore—assuming she ever had been.

Peter reclaimed her attention then. "This is Mrs. Walsh, the housekeeper."

The woman nearest the front door stepped forward. "Welcome, Mrs. Thatcher. I hope you'll be most comfortable here."

"And this is George." Peter indicated the young man next in line. "Though I suppose we must now call him Chambers, as he's just been promoted from footman to butler."

"Welcome to Grosvenor Street, ma'am." George executed a smart bow, clearly eager to live up to his elevation in status.

Pete went on to introduce the cook, Mrs. MacKay, and one or two others. "Your maid will undoubtedly need time to unpack your things," he said then, "so why don't I show you over the house?"

"Of…of course. Thank you." Xena's gaze followed the two footmen carrying her trunk upstairs to her bedchamber.

No. Xena's bedchamber was *not* something Harry dared think about.

Not yet.

Though Harry was as well acquainted with this house as any in London, he accompanied Peter and Xena on their tour in hopes of gaining some clue as to what Xena might be thinking and feeling.

As for himself, he was far more aware of her—physically—than he liked. The gown she wore fitted her admirably, suggesting her charms —charms he recalled all too well—without flaunting them. Then there was the faint scent drifting back from her, carrying that remembered hint of sandalwood and rosewater that still had the power to inflame him.

Damnation. This was going to be even more difficult than he'd expected.

"Here's the main dining chamber," Peter was saying. "The table is currently set for eight but can be expanded to hold twenty, should you wish to entertain. The breakfast parlor is across the hall. Marcus and Quinn often choose to eat there when alone, since it's rather cozier. Sarah and I, on the other hand, frequently had meals served in the library. Please don't hesitate to let the staff know what your preference might be."

At that, Mrs. MacKay, passing on her way back down to the kitchen, sent Harry a glance of barely-concealed delight. What the devil had Pete told the servants would be going on here?

After looking into each of the ground floor rooms, Peter led the way to the first story to see the library and formal drawing room, where guests were generally received. When he continued up to the second story, where the bedrooms were situated, Harry felt himself tensing.

"Here's where you'll be sleeping, for the time being." Peter opened a door to reveal the lilac-and-cream room that had been Quinn's—Marcus's wife.

When Peter moved toward the next room along, Harry finally spoke up. "I'll, ah, just use the same one I have in the past, across the hall."

Turning, his friend attempted a rueful expression, though his eyes danced. "I'm sorry, Harry, I fear that room is being used for storage just now, as is my old one, adjoining." He opened the door as proof.

Harry had forgotten this had become Sarah's room, redone in pink and yellow. Now, however, the new decor was all but concealed by the jumble of old furniture and rolled-up carpets, no doubt hastily hauled down from the attics for this very purpose.

"At the moment, I fear the only other bedroom fit for sleeping is that one." Peter nodded toward the chamber that connected to Xena's by a dressing room. "No doubt Brewster will already have unpacked your things."

Biting back an oath, Harry forced something like a smile to his lips. "I see. I suppose we can always rearrange things later."

"Of course, of course! I merely thought—"

"I know what you thought."

Peter's expression was carefully bland, though amusement still lurked in his eyes.

Xena, apparently no more charmed by the arrangement than Harry was, asked, "What sort of changes am I authorized to make, my lord?"

"Any you wish." Peter swept an expansive hand about. "M'mother will likely turn this into a Marland guest house eventually, as there are no more bachelors in my generation to make use of it. Meanwhile, do as you wish—redecorate, move furniture about, knock out walls…"

Xena raised an eyebrow. "I don't anticipate anything quite so drastic, my lord, but thank you. 'Twill give me a way to pass the time."

Biting his lip, Peter looked from Xena to Harry and back. "Yes. Well. I suppose I should leave you to accustom yourselves to your new, ah, situation. Give you good day, Mrs. Thatcher, Harry."

With a bow for Xena and a nod to Harry, he decamped down the stairs without a backward glance, leaving them alone in the passage.

"So." Harry thought it safest to keep things on a businesslike footing until he could gauge her feelings. "Here we are."

"Indeed." Though her chin was again raised defiantly, her eyes were wary. "Though our circumstances are…not precisely the same as when we last spoke, the same question applies. How are we to proceed?"

Caught off guard, Harry blinked. "How do you wish to proceed? What did you have in mind when you agreed to this scheme of Pete's?"

Now it was Xena who hesitated, not quite meeting his eye. "He, ah, persuaded me that we owed it to ourselves to get to know each other— the people we have become, that is—before going our separate ways."

"He said much the same to me. I, er, suppose he has a point." In fact, Harry was increasingly curious to learn all he could about Xena and what she'd been doing for the past seven years. That had played a far greater role in his being here than the money Pete offered him.

"I suppose he does." A slight frown formed between her dark brows. "Though we clearly cannot keep our, ah, status a secret, we earlier agreed not to broadcast it to the world. Is that still your preference?"

Harry opened his mouth, then shut it, not knowing what answer she wished to hear. Certainly, news of their marriage would be embarrassing to *him* in the extreme, as outspoken as he'd always been against matrimony. What sport everyone at his clubs would have at his expense! It seemed a cowardly reason to voice aloud, however.

"'Twould involve quite a lot of explanation, at the very least," he admitted cautiously, watching her expression. Was that a trace of relief in her eyes?

"True. Especially now I've been introduced as 'Miss Maxwell" to so many people, most of them no doubt acquaintances of yours. Have you given any thought to how we might prevent our marriage from becoming generally known while sharing a house in the heart of Mayfair for a month and more?"

He hadn't. "I, ah, suppose we could avoid being seen together in public. Refuse to receive visitors here. That sort of thing."

"That would probably be best." Now there was no mistaking her relief—which made Harry wonder why she'd agree to this trial at all. "We cannot count on word not getting about, however—the servants may talk, if nothing else—so we should decide what story we are to tell should we be questioned directly."

"Er, yes. I suppose we should."

Regarding her more closely, he now noticed that her jonquil day dress was not only flattering, it was also in the first stare of fashion, much like the blue one she'd worn that first night. Yet she claimed to be short of funds. A gentleman benefactor, perhaps?

Not that it should matter, as he'd by no means been celibate himself since their parting seven years ago. As lusty as Xena had been, he couldn't imagine she would have remained so, either. So why did the idea disturb him so mightily?

"Why are you really here, Xena?" he blurted out, hoping for a less repugnant explanation for the gowns. "Did Peter offer you money as well?"

Her gray eyes widened. "What? Of course not. Do...do you mean to say he actually *paid* you to stay here with me?"

Damnation! He hadn't meant to let her know that.

"How much?"

"Five hundred pounds," he admitted. "But that wasn't—"

"I believe I will help my abigail to unpack," she interrupted, her voice tight. Without another word she disappeared into her bedchamber, leaving Harry to wonder how he could have made such a botch of things already.

Xena felt like a fool.

She'd actually allowed herself to believe Harry was here because he wished to be. Really, she should have known—so why did learning the truth hurt so? Leaning against the closed bedroom door, Xena took several deep breaths. She would not cry, of course. She *never* cried.

"Mum?" Gretchen emerged from the dressing room. "Whatever is the matter?"

With an effort, Xena straightened, stepping away from the door. "I am a bit tired, that is all. I...I believe I should like to lie down for a while. Why don't you go downstairs, Gretchen, get to know the other servants and the layout of the house. In an hour or two, you may help me dress for dinner."

Though she still looked concerned, even alarmed, the girl nodded. "Aye, mum. Ring if you need anything." She gestured toward the bell-pull near the bed.

"I will. Thank you."

The moment Gretchen was gone, Xena took the precaution of locking the dressing room door before going to sit in the dainty lilac chair near the window to stare out at the mist still visible in the deepening twilight.

Why had she been so shocked by Harry's admission? He'd made it quite clear during their prior conversation that he had no more desire to be inconvenienced by marriage than she did. She could scarcely blame him for his reluctance when it had taken blackmail, virtually holding her son hostage, to induce her own cooperation. She should be *grateful* he still wished to keep their marriage private. Were it to become common knowledge, Theo might well learn of it.

All things considered, she had no reason whatever to be upset. Instead, she should be positively *relieved* to know Harry had not, in fact, come here in hopes of rekindling whatever they'd once enjoyed in the distant past.

Xena, who never, ever cried, put her face in her hands and sobbed.

By the time Gretchen returned an hour later, Xena had completely composed herself again. Though she would never admit to a soul that moment of weakness, the cry had done her good. After finally releasing those emotions kept in check since learning Harry was alive, it would surely be easier to discover all she could about his lifestyle and finances without any silly sentiment getting in the way.

"Did you have a nice nap, mum?" Gretchen asked cheerfully on entering. "I'll just finish your unpacking, then get you outfitted for dinner. Mrs. MacKay says it's normally served at seven, though when the young gentlemen lived here alone as they used, they more often than not ate at their gentlemen's clubs." She was clearly proud of knowing such worldly details.

"I've already finished putting everything away," Xena replied, "but if you could have water brought up, I'd like to wash my face before changing." Not for the world would she have Harry suspect she'd been crying…over *him*.

The moment Gretchen left to comply, Xena unlocked and opened the dressing room door so it would look as it had earlier, chiding herself for her earlier cowardice. She'd never been the least bit afraid of Harry seven years ago and had no reason to be so now, particularly given his undisguised aversion to being so near her bedchamber.

When Gretchen returned with a full pitcher and ewer, she was again in a chatty mood. "I finally got a good look at your Mr. Thatcher as I come up from the kitchens. Handsome as the devil he is!"

Xena couldn't disagree.

"A shame about his poor arm, though. Did he lose it in the wars?"

Nodding, Xena began splashing her face, enjoying the feel of cool water on her warm cheeks. "In the same battle where he was so badly injured that he was reported dead, leading me to believe myself a widow all this time." She saw no need to mention that her claim of widowhood had predated Harry's supposed demise by some three years.

Gretchen sighed happily. "And he thought you lost forever that whole time, too! This dinner tonight will be a special one, eh, mum? Your first together since finding each other after all those years."

"I, ah, suppose so." Before she could think how to disabuse Gretchen of her romantical notions, the girl switched topics abruptly.

"Such a fine house this is, mum! I'd heard tell of what servants' halls are like below stairs in London, but never quite believed it. True it is, though! Polly and Millie say Mrs. Walsh runs a tight household, but a fair one. They like her well enough, and Mrs.

MacKay, too. A couple of the footmen are quite nice looking, too." She giggled.

Though she knew she should admonish Gretchen to mind her tongue, Xena had no desire for her to return to her previous topic, so let her run on about the house and other servants while helping her mistress prepare for dinner. Once Xena was arrayed in a satin gown of lilac split over a silvery gray petticoat, however, the maid returned to her fancies.

"Pretty as a picture you look, mum, and that's no lie. If you're worried about winning back your Mr. Thatcher's affections, you needn't. One look and he'll be as smitten as he was when he asked you to marry him."

"Thank you, Gretchen. That will do."

Picking up her gloves, Xena quitted her chamber—though not without a quiver in her midsection. Sternly, she reminded herself that Harry had never *asked* her to marry him. Nor did she want him "smitten" with her.

Did she?

CHAPTER ELEVEN

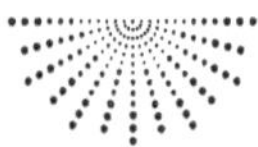

JUST AS HE'D DOUBTED XENA WOULD ARRIVE AT THE HOUSE THIS afternoon, Harry now half expected her to request a tray in her room rather than join him for dinner. Again, he was wrong. On the very stroke of seven she appeared in the dining room doorway, resplendent in a lavender confection that seemed to make her very skin glow. Swallowing, he sketched her a bow.

"Give you good evening, ma'am." He extended his right arm to escort her to a chair. "That's a most fetching gown you're wearing tonight." And likely as expensive as the one she'd worn to Wellington's do.

Xena regarded him warily. "Thank you. You're quite nicely turned out yourself."

Though Harry had taken rather more pains with his appearance than usual when dressing for dinner, he hadn't expected her to notice. "Er, thanks. Don't often get compliments from ladies."

"Oh? I was given to understand you have quite the reputation there." She removed her fingertips from his arm to seat herself at one end of the long table.

"It's not— That is— Very well, I suppose I have had." There was little point denying it, after what she'd heard at Wellington's. "Though men often, er, exaggerate about such things, you know."

He stopped before he could make things worse. He'd hoped to make amends for his clumsy admission that afternoon, not dig himself yet deeper into her bad graces. Moving the length of the table to take the chair opposite her, he attempted to look contrite.

"I'd like to, ah, clarify what I said earlier. Peter didn't actually *pay* me to come here. He simply offered to offset my probable losses at the tables while, ah, making this attempt at domesticity."

Far from appearing pacified, Xena frowned. "Then you've primarily made your living by gambling these past few years?"

Harry shifted uncomfortably in his chair. "Wouldn't say *primarily*, but it's come in handy as a supplement to my allowance and army cheques."

"I see."

Those two little words brought home to Harry the uselessness of his recent existence in a way nothing else had. Not that it was useless *now*, of course. His work as the Saint of Seven Dials surely counted for something. Not a defense he could use to Xena, however.

"Anyway, I'm sorry if I upset you earlier," he offered instead.

"Pray give it no mind." She spoke airily but did not look at him, instead adjusting her left glove where it touched her elbow. "It was no more than I had assumed, for you made it clear when we first spoke that a course such as this was never your wish."

A footman came in to fill the wine glasses and serve the soup course just then, so Harry delayed answering by taking several sips of his wine. "You made it perfectly clear it wasn't your wish, either," he pointed out once they were again alone. "Yet you haven't said what means Peter used to persuade you."

Xena took two spoonfuls of soup before answering—a surprisingly seductive act, though she clearly did not intend it so. "As you yourself pointed out, London is a more pleasant place to spend a winter than Yorkshire, though substantially more expensive. By offering this residence, Lord Peter gave me the means to stay despite my reduced circumstances."

Her sudden desire to winter in London made him more curious

than ever to know where the money for her gowns might be coming from.

"Then it seems your motivation was as mercenary as mine." He couldn't quite keep all trace of accusation from his voice.

She still affected nonchalance. "Yes, I suppose one might say that. There. We now have no pretense between us."

No pretense? Harry refilled his glass. Then, before he could stop himself, "Did Peter also give you the means to obtain such a fashionable wardrobe?"

Xena blinked, then glanced down at the satin gown she wore, a telltale flush creeping up her throat. "No, of course not. I've…learned that it is possible to obtain surprisingly fashionable clothing for very little, if one knows where to shop."

Not for a minute did he believe that was a second-hand gown she wore, but as he had not yet drunk enough to ask point-blank who had bought it for her, he merely said, "Very resourceful," and devoted his attention to his own soup.

"You mentioned an allowance as well as your army cheque," she commented after a moment. "I presume that comes from your father?"

"Through m'father, anyway. A portion of what he receives as second son." A distressingly small portion, but she didn't need to know that.

As Harry was no more willing to discuss the details of his finances —or lack thereof—than Xena seemed to be, he cast about for a safer topic of conversation than money, trying to recall what sorts of things they had talked about in Portugal and Spain. When they had been friends, if not yet lovers.

"Tell me, are you still a student of ancient literature?"

She looked up from her dish in obvious surprise. "I, ah, yes. Though less so since my father's passing, I must admit. These days I'm more like to reread Shakespeare or Homer than to delve into obscure Sanskrit texts."

"From what I recall you telling me, those do tend to be a bit more dry."

"Accounts of day to day doings or even retellings of old battles do not hold the same fascination that epic tales do, though they were occasionally a welcome distraction from the war." She scooped up her last spoonful of soup.

"Do you…ever miss it?" he asked softly.

Her gaze flew to his across the length of the table. "Miss it? The… battlefield, do you mean?"

That wasn't *precisely* what he'd meant, but he nodded.

Pursing her lips distractingly, she considered his question. "I certainly don't miss marching for days through the mud," she finally answered. "Nor seeing promising young men maimed or blown to bits by the enemy. But I won't deny there are things about it I do miss."

"Such as?"

Now she gave him a wry smile—her most genuine since arriving in Grosvenor Street and one that put him forcibly in mind of the Xena he'd known before—so much so that he almost felt the intervening years fall away.

"My freedom, for one. Though perhaps 'tis unreasonable to expect the same sort of liberty at six and twenty that I enjoyed at nineteen." The sadness in her eyes unexpectedly tugged at his heart.

"Why unreasonable? As a widow on your own, as you've believed yourself these four years past, you should have had even *more* freedom than before to dress or behave as you wished—or to go on adventures. Did your father become stricter on his return?"

She shook her head, the sadness still in evidence. "No. But as one grows up, one learns that circumstances can become far more confining than mere rules."

He assumed she meant the lack of funds to which she'd repeatedly referred. Unless, perhaps, she was now answerable to someone other than her father…?

"I mostly miss the camaraderie," he volunteered abruptly. "There's nothing like facing possible death together to forge strong bonds. Then there was the thrill that came with engaging the enemy, though that was often laced with a healthy dose of fear."

It was a thrill he'd managed to recapture to an extent during his exploits as the Saint of Seven Dials—one reason he was unwilling to suspend those activities completely for the next month. Especially if Xena persisted in pushing him away.

Xena's worst fears were in a fair way to being confirmed. Already Harry had admitted to being a gamester with little else in the way of income, nor had he denied womanizing when she'd given him the chance. As for his drinking, she had the evidence of her own eyes. He was already on his third—or was it fourth?—glass of wine since sitting down to dinner.

All of which served to strengthen her resolve to keep him ignorant of how much her father's collection was worth, or the money she'd already received for a portion of it. It had been beyond foolish to wear yet another new gown tonight in a misguided desire to look her best for him. Wastrel or not, Harry was no fool.

In addition, she recalled now how persistent he could be—and how he'd always known when she was being less than candid. The prickly exterior that had served to discourage the attentions of numerous men, both in the army camps and later in Yorkshire, had never worked with Harry. However else he'd changed, he'd lost none of his charm. She would have to be constantly on her guard to prevent him coaxing her secrets from her.

Therefore, though reminiscing about the war was stirring up emotions better forgotten, it was surely safer than discussing the true state of her finances or her real reason for accepting Lord Peter's bargain.

"The excitement I felt at the prospect of battle is something I've also missed since leaving Spain," she admitted to him after a moment. "Though my father tried to keep me well away from the front lines, we never knew when the enemy might overrun the camp."

"Requiring you to take up pistol or sword yourself—I remember." His look, both amused and admiring, so like the ones he used to give her, produced a disturbing tremor in her midsection despite her resolve. "In the one such incident I witnessed for myself, you acquitted yourself so well that the entire regiment celebrated you as a heroine."

Harry's smile became warmer, reminding Xena all too vividly of that evening—and of the private "celebration" she and Harry had enjoyed in his tent after her father and Yamini were asleep. In fact, it was that night she'd begun to suspect their relationship might be progressing beyond mere lust…

Swallowing, she hurried into speech. "I, ah, had little choice but to fight on that occasion, as no one else was at hand to defend the patients. I therefore did what was necessary to prevent the enemy killing more of our young men—but I cannot claim it was something I enjoyed. Besting an opponent in a fencing or shooting match is one thing, but taking a life is quite different."

"Can't say that was an aspect of war I enjoyed either." His penetrating hazel eyes became shadowed. "In the heat of battle, it was easy enough to forget the Frenchies were real people, with homes and families. But afterward…" He trailed off, shaking his head.

For a moment it was as though the years fell away and they were still the young, idealistic people they'd been back then, bound not only by mutual attraction but by the horrors surrounding them at all-too-frequent intervals. With an effort, Xena dredged up less dangerous memories.

"Even the long marches held a certain appeal," she said when the soup dishes had been replaced by platters of fish and meat, and they were again alone in the dining room. "The countryside in that part of Portugal and Spain was often beautiful and the local people we encountered along the way were interesting and sometimes quite colorful in their own right. Did you not find that as well?"

Harry agreed that he had and went on to describe a few sights and local experiences he remembered from later in the war, after Xena had left Spain. Thankfully, he seemed as willing as she to stick to safer topics for the moment.

Still, Xena found herself increasingly, uncomfortably, aware of him, even across the length of the table. Smiles, gestures, inflections in his voice as he spoke, even the way he occasionally raised only his left eyebrow, were constant reminders of the Harry she'd known so very well seven years ago. Evidence, surely, that something of the man she'd admired was still buried beneath the cynical, dissipated creature he now appeared to be?

But no, that was surely mere wishful thinking. She mustn't allow those long-ago emotions—emotions she'd denied at the time—to cloud her judgment and undermine her defenses.

Though the food was superb—the cook had clearly outdone herself—Xena was so distracted by Harry's presence and her own thoughts that she was scarcely aware of what she was eating.

"Shall I leave you to brandy and cigars?" she asked when the last course had been cleared away. Her father had rarely indulged in such things, but she knew it was the custom among the Quality for ladies to withdraw after dinner.

"Not much fun by m'self," Harry replied with a shrug.

He'd drunk an entire bottle of wine over the course of the meal, less the one glass Xena had barely touched for fear of having her wits dulled and perhaps letting slip something she shouldn't. Even so, he rose without the least sign of swaying and walked steadily to her side.

"Suppose we both go up to the library, instead? Always been my favorite room here."

She stood before he could take her hand, then kept a discreet distance between them as she accompanied him from the room. Given her already-heightened awareness of him, touching seemed…unwise. His sardonic glance told her he noticed her forbearance and perhaps even guessed at the reason, but she chose to ignore it.

"I take it you have been quite a frequent visitor here?" she asked when he moved confidently to the library sideboard to pour himself a measure of port.

He chuckled. "Daresay I've spent nearly as much time in this house as Pete has—or did until he got himself leg-shackled. Er, married, I mean."

Perhaps the wine had had an effect after all.

"Pray don't feel you must censor your speech around me, Harry. I did spend more than two years in army camps, you know."

He looked back at her with an expression she couldn't decipher but which threatened to bring color to her face again—something she refused to allow. She was *not* the sort of woman who blushed.

"Even so, that didn't come out the way I intended. Old habits and all that."

"Yes, well, *in vino veritas*. Perhaps after so much to drink you are merely revealing your true thoughts." Not that she was certain she wanted to hear *all* of those…

"So much—? Gadslife, Xena, I've barely drunk anything tonight. What are you on about? But if you think it likely to shake loose truths, I'll pour you a generous measure as well."

"Thank you, no." That he considered an entire bottle of wine "barely anything" lent additional weight to the conclusions she'd already drawn, further strengthening her resolve.

He poured her a glass anyway. "Come, Xena, we may as well try to be comfortable, as we've both agreed to give Pete's mad scheme a chance. He said you were willing to stay through the first of the year?"

She took the glass he proffered almost without noticing. "That is what I agreed to, yes," she said cautiously.

"Yet the other night, you claimed you could not remain in London long—that you had important business to attend to in Yorkshire. Is that no longer true?"

Caught off-guard, she avoided his penetrating gaze and lifted a shoulder. "'Tis…not quite so urgent as I'd thought, it turns out."

"You never were a good liar, Xena. In fact, you used to pride yourself on your forthrightness—though I suppose people do change over time."

Her eyes snapped back to his. "So I've noticed. When I knew you on the Peninsula, you never drank at all." She nodded toward his already nearly-empty glass of port. "If you wish to declare this experiment a failure at the outset—"

"Never said that, did I? I'm willing to give it a go if you are. Besides, five hundred pounds is more than I can afford to whistle down the wind." He said it jokingly, but she was unable to see any humor in it when her son's future potentially lay in this man's hands.

Unabashedly returning to the sideboard to refill his glass, he spoke over his shoulder. "So tell me, Xena, is there something in particular about London that convinced you to winter here after all?"

Did he hope she would say it was him? Moving to sit in one of the overstuffed chairs near the fire, she took a cautious sip of port, something she'd not drunk in several years. It was a good vintage, the sweet liquid warming her throat pleasantly as it slid down.

"I, ah, realized how much warmer it is here than in Yorkshire, for one," she finally said. "And of course there are numerous amusements to be found here that are sadly lacking at home."

"Of course." Regarding her intently now, Harry nudged the chair nearest hers a bit closer and sat. "Given those attractions, one wonders why you've never come to Town before?"

Xena frowned. "As I said, money has been rather tight. My main purpose in coming now was to remedy that."

"Ah, yes. By selling some of your father's foreign treasures. I do remember you saying so." Again he allowed his gaze to rove over her body—or, rather, her new lilac-over-silver gown. "I take it you've met with rather more success these past few days?"

"A bit, yes. Enough to allow me to refurbish my wardrobe, as you've clearly noticed, and to have the most pressing repairs begun at home. Another reason I prefer to stay in Town for the present," she added on sudden inspiration. "Some of those repairs are like to be disruptive and noisy."

It was only a slight fib, for she hoped to have enough money for those repairs and more within a week or so, which she would forward to Yorkshire with precisely those instructions. She had already written asking her steward to package up and send the Grecian items she had agreed to sell. She still needed to devise a way to communicate with Mr. Gold from this house without Harry learning of it...

He leaned in now, his gaze more penetrating than ever. "You seem distracted, Xena. Can it be you are finding this new arrangement as unsettling as I am?"

"How can I not?" Though she tried to keep her voice light, she was disgusted to hear a slight tremor in it, for his nearness was indeed unsettling her. "Only three nights since, we both agreed to behave as though that marriage, which neither of us sought, never occurred. Now, thanks to the machinations of your friend, we are sharing a house! Little wonder if neither of us is quite certain how to act."

His rueful smile admitted the truth of her words. "It's proving rather a challenge, I'll grant you. But whatever our motives for going along with Pete's experiment, now we are here, should we not make the best of it?"

"Exactly how do you propose we do that?" Again she heard that traitorous tremor in her voice.

"I can think of numerous ways." His voice was low, silken. "Can't you?"

His suggestive tone, his charming, slightly wicked smile, took her instantly back to a time when she'd eagerly looked forward to each secret liaison. A time when her greatest pleasure in life had been those stolen moments of passion—a pleasure she had never dared hope she'd experience again…

Desperately, sternly, she reminded herself that things were quite different now. Even if it *were* possible to recapture that passion, succumbing to Harry's charm now would be a mistake. Wouldn't it? Under his continued warm, searching regard, her resolve began to weaken.

"I…ah…" She gave her head a small shake to clear it.

Instantly, Harry's expression changed. "Never mind." Drawing back, he abruptly stood. "I've just remembered that I was to meet some friends this evening, so if you'll excuse me?"

"Oh. Er, of course." She felt more disappointed than relieved by his sudden withdrawal, which of course was absurd. "I wouldn't wish to keep you from the gaming tables." The acid that now laced her tone was aimed as much at herself as at him.

"Very understanding of you." His grin did not quite reach his eyes. "You're certain you don't mind me leaving you our first night here?"

"Not at all. As it happens, I have quite a bit of correspondence to attend to." Her resolve safely back in place, she stood as well.

Though she half feared—or hoped?—he would approach her again, he did not.

"I'll bid you good night, then." With a formal nod, he turned and left the room.

Xena blinked after him, chiding herself for her foolishly conflicting feelings a moment since. It was a good thing—a *very* good thing—that he was leaving before she could give into the temptation to do something she would almost certainly regret.

As soon as she heard the front door close downstairs, she released a sigh that she told herself was purely from relief. She then headed up to her bedchamber for a boring evening of letter writing.

CHAPTER TWELVE

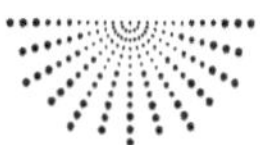

HARRY STRODE DOWN THE STREET IN THE DIRECTION OF ONE OF HIS more disreputable gaming hells, cursing his stupidity. What a fool he'd been to think Xena might still be attracted to him now! If she was receiving the attentions of some rich gallant, as he felt increasingly certain she must be, what possible interest could she have in a useless half-pay soldier with one arm?

A chorus of greetings met him as he entered the Black Crow, where he'd spent more debauched evenings than he could remember over the past two or three years. Clara, one of the pretty, buxom serving wenches the establishment was known for, hurried to plant a kiss on his cheek, pressing herself suggestively against him.

"'Arry, by my faith! It's been a month and more. What c'n I give you?"

Throwing his arm around her, he gave her shoulders a squeeze, then seated himself at an empty table. "Claret, as it's nearly your namesake." The squeeze and wink he gave her were from habit more than desire, for he was still preoccupied by thoughts of Xena.

The wench snatched a just-opened bottle off the next table despite complaints from the men sitting there. "This be a prime 'un. 'Twill put you in fine fettle for later." With a saucy wink of her own, she sauntered off to fetch the still-protesting group another bottle.

Over the next hour Harry tripled the money he'd brought with him. That, plus the excellent claret, improved his mood somewhat. Then the maxim, "lucky at cards, unlucky at love" floated through his brain. Abruptly, despite Clara's increasingly amorous overtures, he lost all appetite for remaining longer.

No, what he really needed to restore his spirits—and confidence—was a rousing adventure as the Saint. Flute still had long list of worthy families needing assistance.

Ignoring Clara's pout, he bid a pleasant good night to his unsavory companions and headed to Seven Dials. There, he quickly changed into the nondescript black furze coat and trousers he used for house-breaking and shouldered the black, cross-body sack that helped to compensate for his missing arm. Now to find a challenging target promising a suitably impressive prize as a reward.

As Mayfair was where such a prize was like to be found, he bent his steps back westward. He was scarcely away from Seven Dials, however, before he was accosted by Flute's young compatriot, Tig.

"Evenin', guv, remember me? Off to help the Saint again, eh? Is Flute meeting you there? Can I come?"

Harry frowned down at the boy. "Bit late for you to be out, isn't it?"

Tig shrugged. "No more'n usual. I'd as soon sleep when there's no fun to be had. So can I help again?"

Remembering how hard it had been to dissuade the lad last time, he cast about for a job he might do that would be unlikely to put him in danger. "Hm. There is something you can do for me, yes."

"What? There's lots I'm good at, just ask Flute. I c'n—"

"There's a, ah, lady I'd like to have watched, if you're willing. Do you remember where Lord Marcus used to live?"

"Oh, aye, guv. That ain't the house you'll be robbing, is it? He's a right'un. Fed me and me chums a treat once't or twice."

"No, no. But that's where the lady is staying. I'd like you to keep an eye on the place when you've time, let me know where she goes, who she sees, that sort of thing. Without being spotted, mind you." Xena was unlikely to suspect a grubby little urchin, but Harry knew that addition would appeal to the boy.

Indeed, he nodded eagerly, his face alight. "On it, guv! I c'n enlist a few o' the other lads to help out, too. How often d'you want me to report back?"

Harry hadn't thought that far, especially as he rather hoped there'd be nothing to report. Still, it would be good to know for certain, and it might keep some of these street urchins out of trouble for a bit. "I'll, ah, contact you through Flute, shall I? No need to start till tomorrow as she'll be asleep now. She may be up early, however, so you should hie off to your own bed."

Tig straightened importantly and sketched a salute. "Aye, guv, I'll be on the job bright and early. Good luck tonight!"

Harry waited until the boy was out of sight, then continued on toward the West End where, after half an hour of careful skulking, he was rewarded by the sight of Lord Gillyfather, an Irish upstart who delighted in flaunting his wealth, just leaving his ostentatious house on Berkley Square. A fitting target, to be sure.

The robbery itself went off without a hitch. An unlocked ground-level window and a few easily-picked locks later, he prepared to leave the way he'd come with a satisfyingly heavy haul of silver, gold, jewelry and notes bundled into the sack slung over his right shoulder. Silently returning to the window at the rear of the house, he lifted his booty through to set it outside on the ground. Then, as he was on the point of joining his sack of treasure, his luck turned.

"Oi! Who goes there?" came a shout from the hallway behind him. "Stop! Thief!"

With a stifled oath, Harry vaulted through the window into the kitchen garden. Snatching up his satchel, he ran to the back gate only to have his path blocked by a burly groom coming to investigate the clamor.

Without slowing, Harry lowered a shoulder and knocked the startled man aside even as voices and hurrying footsteps sounded behind him. A moment later he was running full tilt through the mews, his takings bouncing against his side, chased by at least three or four shouting men.

Luckily the night was exceedingly foggy, even for London in

November, providing a slightly better chance of escaping his pursuers. Though the burden he carried slowed him down, he stubbornly refused to drop it and admit even partial defeat. He ducked around corner after corner, hoping to confuse those following.

The leaders were close enough behind that his first two ruses failed. They were still hot on his heels and their companions not far distant when ahead, he saw an open stable door. Feinting as though going through, he instead ducked into the shadow behind it, still in the mews. It worked. The lead pursuers flung themselves into the stable with a yell of triumph to begin searching. When the other two men caught up and joined them, Harry moved noiselessly away down the mews before they discovered what he'd done.

He turned another corner, this one leading out to a larger street, when a shout from behind informed him the pursuit had begun again. Breaking into a run again, he headed for some bushes at the corner of Mount Street and ducked behind them to catch his breath. While he was still panting, he heard one of the men call to the Watch, demanding help to chase down the Saint of Seven Dials. Had a servant from the house he'd robbed discovered one of his cards so quickly, or were they just guessing?

Not that it mattered. If they caught him he was done for either way. The Northrup house on Grosvenor Street was his nearest refuge. Much as he'd prefer returning first to Seven Dials to drop off his bounty and change clothes, that did not appear to be an option.

First, however, he needed a distraction. Searching the ground at his feet, he found a largish stone. Carefully stooping so as not to drop or jangle his satchel of loot, he picked it up and waited his moment. It came when the group of pursuers—now including an elderly member of the Watch, wielding a rattle—passed an alleyway between two nearby houses. The moment their backs were to the alley, Harry took careful aim and heaved the rock down it, creating a noisy clatter.

In a flash, the men wheeled about and ran pell-mell into the alley, the watchman's rattle adding to their racket. Seizing up his prize again, Harry sprinted in the opposite direction, toward Grosvenor Street and safety.

Luckily Peter had given him a key, sparing him the need to ring and wake the household—or Xena. Slipping quickly inside, he shut the front door behind him and breathed a sigh of relief. Rather more adventure than he'd bargained for—his closest escape yet, in fact—but at least he'd come away with the fruit of his efforts. Passing a startled footman, he put a finger to his lips and made his way upstairs.

Xena couldn't seem to fall asleep. There was less of street noise here than outside Mrs. Henderson's house, and the bed was far more comfortable, but her mind was still too unsettled to allow her to relax.

She had written a detailed letter to her steward in Yorkshire, after which she had taken a candle to survey the unoccupied bedrooms across the passage with an eye to refurbishing at least one, so that she and Harry need not occupy quite such close quarters.

After that she'd made lists of possibilities, for both those rooms and for her life going forward. From the evening's conversation, it appeared Harry's circumstances and character were as bad as she'd feared. Given that, she was more than half minded to go abroad with Theo after all, as soon as she received the promised money from Mr. Gold's rich customer. But where, precisely? She'd written until her eyes grew heavy and the candle guttered. Yet she still could not fall asleep.

Restlessly, she adjusted the feather pillow beneath her head, then stiffened at the sound of stealthy footsteps and heavy breathing in the passage outside her door. Had Harry returned?

Though it should mean nothing to her either way, she slipped from under the down quilts and padded silently to her chamber door—first to listen, then to carefully open it a crack, so that she could peer into the hallway.

Harry, dressed in a rough-looking black coat he certainly had not been wearing earlier, was just entering his own bedchamber. When he spoke to his valet, Xena's ears sharpened.

"Yes, yes, I know, but never mind." He sounded out of breath, as though he'd been running. "I can fetch them tomorrow. For now, put this out of sight somewhere and for God's sake, have someone bring up a bath. I'm all of a sweat." The chamber door snicked shut, muffling anything further.

Quietly, Xena closed her own door as well, burning with curiosity. Harry must have done more tonight than play at cards or dice. He sounded as though he'd been running. Or—the thought caused an unpleasant lurch of her stomach—cavorting with a mistress? That seemed the most obvious explanation for him returning at this hour sweating and out of breath. If the woman was married and her husband returned unexpectedly, it would also account for him leaving his coat behind.

Resigned to at least another hour of sleeplessness, she crawled back under the covers to wait for morning, though she doubted it would bring many answers.

The morning was well advanced when Harry awoke the next morning, no doubt due to his unwonted late-night exertion followed by a hot, relaxing bath. Even so, the first thing he did on rising was to reach under the bed for the sack he'd stashed the night before to take full stock of his haul.

It was even better than he'd originally estimated. In addition to several expensive-looking rings and jeweled fobs, he'd come away with at least twenty pounds of silver plate and nearly half that in gold guineas, as well as some eight hundred pounds in bank notes. Enough to give relief to every needy family on Flute's current list and possibly many more for a deal of time to come.

Chuckling to himself, he shoved the sack deep under the bed again, then rang for Brewster. He might not be rich or titled but, by God, he was a far cry from useless.

When he went down to the breakfast parlor twenty minutes later, Xena was still at table, looking remarkably fetching in a rose and cream day dress.

"Good morning—though it is nearly afternoon now. I began to wonder whether you meant to come down at all." Though she smiled, her voice held a slight edge.

"My apologies. I fear I'm not in the habit of rising early. I hope you did not wait on me to break your own fast?"

"No, I ate more than an hour since but I will have another cup of coffee to keep you company." She motioned to the hovering footman, who immediately fetched the pot from the sideboard, where a selection of pastries and breakfast meats were still laid out.

Rather than display his awkwardness at serving himself one-handed, Harry took the chair opposite Xena and waited for the footman to bring him food as well as coffee. "What is all this?" he asked, gesturing to the pile of cards he now noticed on the table between them.

"Invitations. They began arriving only moments after I came downstairs this morning. Indeed, I'm surprised the frequent ringing of the bell did not wake you sooner."

Harry picked up the one nearest him, for a musicale to be held at the house of Lord and Lady Wittington the following week. It was addressed to "Major and Mrs. H. Thatcher." Glancing through a few others, he saw they were similarly addressed.

"How the devil can they all know about us already?" he wondered aloud.

Xena raised an eyebrow. "Precisely what I'd planned to ask you, given that last night we agreed to keep the matter as private as possible. Certainly *I've* had no opportunity to tell anyone who might—" She was interrupted by the sound of the front bell. "That will be yet more, I imagine."

A moment later, however, Lord Peter Northrup was announced.

"I'm glad I caught you both still at home," he greeted them jovially. Helping himself to coffee and a pastry, he joined them at the table without ceremony. "Ah, I see invitations have already begun arriving. Excellent."

Harry frowned at his friend. "Clearly you are far less surprised about it than we are."

"Yes, well, that would be because I was the one to send word round to the papers yesterday. Then I realized you likely hadn't arranged for deliveries yet after Marcus had them suspended, so I brought a few with me." He drew several folded newspapers from inside his coat and set them on the table.

Snatching up the *Times*, Harry thumbed to the Society news. There, among various betrothal announcements and recountings of last night's notable entertainments, he found the item Peter referred to.

"A Story Book Ending to a Star-Crossed Romance," he read aloud. "A battlefield wedding ended in apparent tragedy several years ago when Major Harry Thatcher's new bride, the former Xena Maxwell, was reported killed aboard a frigate sunk by Napoleon's forces. Mrs. Thatcher, who had sailed upon a different ship, was unaware that her husband believed her dead, so had not yet sent word to disabuse him when she read of his apparent death during the battle at Salamanca. Both Major and Mrs. Thatcher believed themselves widowed until unexpectedly encountering each other at a reception hosted by the Duke of Wellington four nights since. One can but imagine their surprise and subsequent joy at the discovery they are both alive! The happily reunited couple are currently residing at—"

Harry broke off with an oath. "What the deuce were you thinking to send out such romantical tripe without consulting either of us?"

"Knew you'd find it wearisome to keep repeating the same explanations over and over, so hit upon this idea to spare you the trouble." Peter grinned, not the least bit abashed. "Now, instead of the awkwardness you no doubt anticipated, you will be in demand as the novelty of the season, coveted by every hostess in Town—as you already perceive." He waved a hand at the invitations scattered across the table.

Xena finally spoke, her voice slightly higher than normal. "I'm sure it was very kind of you, Lord Peter, but I must agree that you would have done better to speak with us before taking such a step." She exchanged a glance with Harry, her face reflecting his own dismay at this turn of events.

"Yes, yes, I suppose I should have done," Peter said airily. "Now it's out there, however, I advise you both to take full advantage of the amusements offered. Which reminds me of the other reason I called. Sarah and I wish you both to accompany us to the theatre tonight, if you've no other engagement as yet. We thought you might prefer such an outing, with friends, to ease you into Society in your new roles before being pitched in headfirst by some of these ambitious hostesses." He nodded again at the accumulated invitations.

Though Harry's first instinct was to refuse, Xena's quick intake of breath stopped him.

"The theatre?" Eagerness had replaced her dismay. "Tonight?"

Peter nodded. "*Othello*" is being performed at Drury Lane. Are you familiar with the works of Shakespeare?"

"I certainly am," she replied, her eyes now fairly sparkling.

Harry's protest died on his lips. No matter how little he looked forward to providing all his acquaintances fodder for endless hilarity at his expense, he could not deny her the chance to see her beloved Bard played out on stage.

"What time shall we meet you there?" he asked, wondering what it would be like to see that eager, happy expression turned upon him. There were those occasions in Portugal, then Spain… He hastily pushed such thoughts away before his body could visibly betray him.

"Why don't you join us for dinner beforehand in Curzon Street so we can go there together? Sarah will like that above all things. Let us say half past six?" Peter stood.

Harry did likewise. "I'll see you out." He accompanied Peter to the front door before saying in an undertone, "Tell Flute I'll be stopping by the Seven Dials flat within the next hour or two. I have something to give him for, er, distribution."

Peter quirked a knowing eyebrow. "I somehow thought you might. I'll let him know." With a parting nod, he departed, leaving Harry to wonder how he could have already guessed about last night's successful foray.

∼

Xena picked up the nearest of the newspapers Lord Peter had brought as he and Harry left the breakfast parlor, her momentary excitement over attending the theatre subsiding as her earlier dismay reasserted itself. She'd hoped to keep her marriage to Harry relatively quiet, if only for Theo's sake, but it seemed that was no longer an option. Determined to learn the full extent of the damage, she began skimming through the articles about them.

Though the wording varied from paper to paper, each one carried essentially the same story Harry had read aloud, complete with their direction and sentimental hopes for the future of the supposedly ecstatic couple. The *Morning Chronicle* even went on to say, "A tale such as this is bound to revive the romantic spirit of even the most jaded soul. May it turn everyone's thoughts more hopefully toward the future, now that England is finally at peace."

Her marriage with Harry was to be held up as a symbol for the future happiness of the entire realm? Her coffee tasted suddenly bitter, for a more unlikely symbol could scarcely be imagined.

To distract herself from that thought, she turned the page of the paper she held to read something else and a moment later was engrossed in an entirely different story.

"Damned interfering nodcock," Harry muttered, rejoining her at table after Lord Peter had gone. "He claims to mean well, but—"

"Did you see this?" Xena interrupted him, feeling no need to hear yet again how very little Harry appreciated being saddled with her. "I recall hearing about this Saint of Seven Dials a few months ago, back in Yorkshire, but I had no idea he was still in business, so to speak."

The flare of alarm in Harry's eyes startled her. "What? I, ah, he's mentioned in the papers?"

Watching his face curiously, she nodded. "It seems he ransacked the house of some Irish peer last night and made off with a great deal of money and other valuables. Some servants and even the Watch gave chase, but claim he eluded them as if by magic." She glanced down at the paper again. "The robbery occurred quite near here, on Berkley Square. I daresay the pursuit may have come right by this house."

"More like he ran back to Seven Dials, as that's where he's said to be based." Harry shrugged, now appearing utterly uninterested—though Xena had an odd sense he was exaggerating that. But why?

"You were out rather late last night," she commented, pretending to pick at a pastry while gauging his expression from the corner of her eye. "You didn't happen to witness any of the commotion, did you?"

Again, she detected a quick frown of concern before Harry shook his head. "Not a thing. I hope I didn't wake you, coming in at such an hour?"

"No, you were quite stealthy." She chose the word deliberately and was rewarded by another flash of apprehension in his expression. "It took me an unusually long time to fall asleep, so when I heard your voice in the passage I was still awake."

He again affected complete indifference—and this time she was sure it was an act. "I didn't mean to stay at the tables quite so long but as I was having a particularly good run of luck I couldn't bring myself to leave sooner. Should I be out so late again, I'll endeavor to be quieter upon my return. If you continue having difficulty sleeping, ask Mrs. McKay for a draught. Pete says she brews a capital one."

"Yes, I'll do that," she murmured, letting the subject drop, though she continued to think back over what she'd heard and witnessed last night.

Harry, in what could well have been a disguise, and out of breath, as though he'd been running...as the Saint of Seven Dials must surely have done to escape pursuit. Was it conceivable that *Harry*...? Surely not!

Still, when Harry went out a short time later, Xena couldn't resist going into the library to peruse the months' worth of newspapers and magazines she found carefully stacked there, eager to learn a bit more about the mysterious Saint of Seven Dials. Though there were no papers from the past week or so, previous ones detailed his more daring exploits, or those involving particularly highly-placed members of Society.

Several stories mentioned the widely-held belief that the famed thief gave the majority of his ill-gotten bounty to the poor—thus the "Saint" moniker and frequent comparisons to the legendary Robin

Hood. Though popular opinion hailed him as a hero, various authorities doubted more than a tithe of what he stole actually left his own pockets.

In an hour she'd exhausted everything the library held on the subject without finding anything to support the possibility that Harry might be the Saint. Certainly, if those authorities were correct, the man would have no need to *gamble* for funds, which Harry, by his own admission, did regularly. Nor was there a single mention of the Saint having but one arm, which surely would have been noted by at least *one* of the numerous witnesses claiming to have seen him.

No, she'd clearly leapt to such an absurd guess in hopes of a more palatable explanation than the obvious one for Harry's late return and disheveled appearance last night. Chiding herself for her disappointment, Xena carefully replaced the papers as she had found them and returned to the breakfast room to devote her attention to her far more pressing problem—and the now-towering stack of invitations awaiting a response.

Harry was just as happy to head to Seven Dials with last night's booty shortly after breakfast. Now word was out about his longtime marriage, it would not be long before his friends and acquaintances began tweaking him about it. This task would put that inevitability off a bit longer and get him away from Xena's disturbing presence, besides.

"If what I read is true, you're like to equal Lord Hardwyck before long," Flute greeted him with a grin when he reached the flat a short time later. "That was a bang-up disappearing act you pulled, from what them blokes told the papers. M'sister showed me the story this morning."

Harry chuckled, successfully diverted from his earlier concerns. "Luckily for me, their wits were no quicker than their feet. A simple distraction put them off my trail long enough to make my escape—

though I can't deny it was a near thing. If many more had joined the chase, I doubt I could have shaken them all even in the fog."

With that, Harry opened his satchel to display its contents. Sorting through the jumble of coins, notes, candlesticks and jewelry, Flute gave a low whistle.

"I'll be able to fence this lot for enough to feed and clothe near everyone what needs it…those what deserve it, anyway…for weeks to come. Well done, guv!"

Though the boy's frank admiration helped to soothe his pride, Harry shrugged. "That's as well, as it's likely to be the last chance I'll have to play the Saint for a while."

Flute nodded knowingly. "Aye, I heard you got yourself a wife now. Must've been a right facer when she popped up alive after all this time! Guess you'll have better ways to spend your nights now, eh?" He waggled his eyebrows, reminding Harry that the lad was older than he looked.

"It's not— That is, it will be much harder for me to slip out without anyone the wiser. Especially her." How much *did* she suspect? He'd done a pretty poor job hiding his emotions when she'd mentioned the Saint earlier, and Xena was no fool.

"At any rate," he continued after a moment, "I'll resume my activities as soon as I safely can. In the meantime, I'll trust you to put last night's takings to good use."

A few hours later, watching Xena descend the stairs prior to leaving for Peter's, Harry couldn't help remembering Flute's innuendoes and fervently wishing they were correct. As she joined him in the front hall, clad in the same midnight-blue evening gown she had worn at Wellington's do, he was struck anew by how very beautiful his wife was. So alluring were the creamy shoulders and throat displayed by the low-cut dress, he had to swallow convulsively in order to moisten his suddenly-dry throat to speak.

"You, ah, look quite nice in that gown. The color suits you," he finally managed, then mentally cursed himself for the clumsiness of the compliment. One would never guess he had a reputation for being smooth-tongued with the ladies.

"Thank you. You're very kind, considering you saw me wearing it only four nights since. I fear it is the only evening gown I currently own, though I hope to have another delivered in a day or two." She smoothed the silken folds self-consciously.

Delivered? By whom? Harry stopped himself from asking the question aloud. Despite his suspicions, he had no proof she was carrying on an intrigue with anyone. For the moment, he would give her the benefit of the doubt. An argument would surely ensue were he to start flinging accusations and he wished her first visit to the theatre to be a pleasant one.

"Shall we go?" He extended his right arm.

CHAPTER THIRTEEN

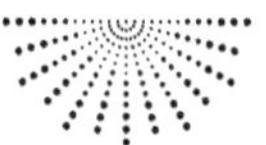

DESPITE HER MISGIVINGS ABOUT APPEARING PUBLICLY AS HARRY'S WIFE, Xena could not help being charmed by the warm manner in which Lord Peter's beautiful wife greeted her on their arrival in Curzon Street.

"How lovely to see you again," Lady Peter exclaimed the moment they were shown into the elegant drawing room, jumping up to hurry forward, hands outstretched. "I am delighted that you agreed to join us tonight and that we shall have a chance to know each other better after all."

"Thank you, my lady." Xena returned her hostess's infectious smile. "You are most kind."

"Please, you must call me Sarah. Peter and Harry are the very best of friends, and I would very much like us to become so, as well."

She pulled Xena over to sit on the claw-footed couch beside her while the men conversed near the fire. "Now, I know what the story Peter sent to the papers said, but pray tell me how it really is with you? You seemed amazingly composed at Apsley House, given what an enormous shock you'd just received, but I don't blame you at all for wishing to gather your wits before announcing your marriage to the world."

Reassured by Sarah's sympathetic, confiding air, some of Xena's initial nervousness dissipated. "If I appeared composed it was entirely by luck," she admitted. "Inside I was a mass of confusion, with not the slightest idea how I should proceed. It seemed…prudent to keep my counsel on the matter until Harry and I had opportunity to speak privately. Needless to say, it was rather an eye-opening evening for us both."

"And now you are living as husband and wife—or, at least, sharing a roof." Sarah's look and tone held a question.

Xena wondered how much Harry had told Lord Peter about the actual circumstances of their long-ago marriage—and how much he, in turn, had told Sarah. Did she know her own husband had been the one to orchestrate their current, uncomfortable situation? She could at least hope that his given word prevented him mentioning Theo to his wife.

Then another thought occurred to her. Surely, as wife to Harry's most intimate friend, Sarah must see him in unguarded moments. Perhaps she could reveal more about what sort of man Harry had become? Now was not the time to ask, however.

"We are giving it a trial, at least," she said instead. "'Tis far too early yet to say whether it will be a successful one, despite the rosy predictions in the papers. We have both grown rather set in our ways over the past seven years."

"I can well imagine. My younger brother and I were separated for eight years and scarcely recognized each other when next we met. Of course, we were still children when we parted."

Over dinner, Sarah told Xena the fascinating tale of how she had progressed from an orphaned street urchin to the wife of a duke's son, who in turn was able to rescue her brother William from a dangerous life on the streets.

"And all because Peter believed so strongly in me that he refused to give up. He was certain there was more about me than even I knew, and he proved himself correct. My husband can be very persistent when he believes himself in the right." She laughed.

As she'd already seen evidence of that persistence herself, Xena could not disagree—but did not find it particularly humorous. Especially as she was not at all certain Lord Peter *was* right in the matter of her marriage—or her son.

"Is he so stubborn when he proves to be mistaken?" she could not help asking.

Sarah blinked. "I do not know. He so rarely seems to be mistaken, you see. Of course, we've known each other only two months, so perhaps I am not the best judge. However, his friends all say the same, do they not?" She directed that question to Harry, who had been listening.

He snorted and frowned at his friend. "He's right more often than is good for him, that's certain, but he's hardly infallible. As will likely be proven again before long."

This, Xena knew, was a veiled reference to Peter's current "experiment." Though she should be relieved to know Harry held out no more hope for a successful outcome than she did, hearing him say so aloud stung far more than it should.

Suddenly desirous of changing the subject, she turned to their host. "Lord Peter, you are the one responsible for our receiving so many invitations. Perhaps you would be willing to advise me on which I might safely decline, as I fear it will be quite impossible to accept them all."

"Nor should you," he agreed. "As highly in demand as you two are at the moment, you can well afford to be selective. Between us, Sarah and I can give you some idea of which entertainments—and hostesses —you might be happier to avoid."

"Such as Lady Mountheath?" Sarah's blue eyes twinkled, but Xena detected a trace of bitterness behind them as well. "I know firsthand how unpleasant she can be. Indeed, she quite delights in the shredding of reputations, as do her two daughters."

Xena had heard that name before, and recently, but where? Ah, yes. Lord and Lady Mountheath had been mentioned in more than one of the old newspaper articles she'd read this morning, as they had been victimized by the Saint of Seven Dials on two separate occasions.

"I will certainly keep that in mind," she said. "What other invitations ought I to decline?"

As Lord Peter named several other people he personally knew to be either unsavory or unpleasant, Xena was startled to realize most of them had also had valuables stolen by the Saint. Could that be coincidence, or did the Saint of Seven Dials intentionally target those who most seemed to deserve his attentions? She wanted to ask, but did not quite dare in front of Harry, on the off-chance her silly suspicion was correct.

Once she and Sarah left the gentlemen to their port, however, it seemed safe to broach the subject.

"I have been reading in the papers about this Saint of Seven Dials and find him quite an enigma. What do you know of him?"

Though Sarah regarded her rather strangely, she answered after only a moment's hesitation. "If you've read what the papers have been printing, you'll know there are differing opinions as to his motives as well as widely varying speculations on who he might be. Some say he's merely a very skilled street thief, some a clever servant, others a peer or other highly-placed member of Society."

"Have you formed your own opinions?" Xena asked, though Sarah had been in London but two months herself.

"I won't claim to know which of those guesses is true, but certainly I can't fault his choice of victims. And, according to a few people I am still in contact with from my impoverished girlhood, he does distribute a great deal of money to the poor."

"Then it's true that he restricts his thefts to those who, ah, need to be taken down a peg or two?"

Sarah nodded. "At least, I know of no one who claims to have been burgled by the Saint for whom that could not be said."

The gentlemen rejoined them then, as it was nearly time to leave for the theatre, so Xena pressed no further. But she had learned enough already that she found herself rather admiring this Saint of Seven Dials, no matter who he might be.

～

Harry endeavored to conceal his trepidation on arriving at the Theatre-Royal at Drury Lane a short time later. As they followed Peter and his wife toward the stairs leading up to their box, Xena's gloved fingertips resting lightly on his extended arm, head after head turned to mark their progress. This, he knew, was only the beginning.

Just up ahead a group of his compatriots from the Guards' Club—and their wives—stood chatting. Remembering the delight with which Harry had tweaked each fellow officer upon his marriage, he now braced himself, watching the group from the corner of his eye as his party approached.

As luck would have it, Findlay spotted him first. "Why look, it's the celebrity of the hour!" he exclaimed. "What ho, Thatcher! Parson's mousetrap looks a bit different once you've been caught, does it not?"

The others chuckled, but the one unmarried gentleman in the group, after an admiring glance at Xena, sent Harry a look that might have been slightly envious. That emboldened Harry to respond.

"I was caught before I knew better. Even so, I'd defy any man to resist capture by such a crack shot and expert fencer as my wife was when first we met." To complete the effect, he cast a proud smile Xena's way, which she returned with a look of extreme surprise.

She recovered quickly, however. "Yes, I fear I gave him little choice, once I'd set my sights on him," she quipped. Harry hoped he was the only one who detected the brittleness in her voice.

"Such a thrilling and romantic story," Findlay's wife said with a syrupy smile at them both. "I do hope to hear more about it soon. You received our invitation for next week?"

Xena nodded. "I've not yet had time to respond, but yes. You are very kind."

They continued on, Peter murmuring, "Carried that off well, both of you. Knew you could."

"You needn't be so smug about it," Harry muttered back. Peter only smiled.

The play was already begun by the time they were settled in their box, but few people were watching it anyway. Most seemed far more interested in staring and pointing at *them*, then scurrying from box to box to make certain all of their acquaintances had noticed as well. In fact, the only person who appeared to be attending to the performance was Xena.

"Amazing," she whispered in awed tones half an hour later. "I know every word of this play, but actually seeing it performed is a completely different experience from reading it, even aloud. I am discovering an even deeper appreciation of Shakespeare's work."

Without thinking, Harry put his hand on hers. "I'm glad you are enjoying it."

That drew her attention from the stage for the first time since sitting down. Her gray eyes, wide with surprise, flew to his face, but though her hand twitched under his, she did not snatch it back. "I am. Thank you. And thank you, Lord Peter, for inviting us."

Before his friend could turn his head to reply, Harry removed his hand. Xena, he noticed, moved hers to her lap at the same time. Was she disappointed or relieved to be rid of his touch? He wished he knew.

At the first intermission, a steady stream of friends, acquaintances and virtual strangers descended upon them, cramming Peter's box to bursting as they vied for the chance to appease their curiosity under the guise of paying their respects. Several mentioned invitations already sent, while others invited them on the spot to whatever events they were hosting during the winter.

For all that she claimed to be unaccustomed to Society, Xena was charming to one and all, contriving to appear pleased and grateful for each invitation without positively committing to any of them.

"I fear I've not had time to look over my calendar properly," she said repeatedly, always with a smile. "Everything has happened so quickly, you see."

Not everyone who visited the box was so agreeably solicitous, however. Lady Grant, with whom Harry had dallied once or twice when Sir Charles was from Town, took the opportunity to run a critical eye over Xena and deliver a sly allusion or two.

"You must be as brave as the tales say, Mrs. Thatcher, to attempt the domestication of this fellow." She tapped Harry flirtatiously on the shoulder with her fan. "But no doubt one with your experience following the drum will have the fortitude to bring him back into line should he revert to form—and a most *amusing* form it can be."

She cast a seductive glance Harry's way—which he returned with a glare. He was about to send Lady Grant to the rightabout when Xena spoke up.

"I don't doubt it." If that bland smile cost her an effort, it did not show. "The Lieutenant Thatcher I knew on the Peninsula was nothing if not amusing. 'Tis good to know he is still considered so."

"Indeed, you might be surprised at the *range* of amusements he has added to his repertoire by now." With a parting wink at Harry that was clearly as much for Xena's benefit as his, she sashayed out of the box.

He looked back at Xena with a worried frown, wondering how to undo the damage, but she had turned to greet someone else as though she'd already put the exchange from her mind. Unless she was a far better actress than she used to be, she apparently gave not a fig what Harry might have done—or do?—with other women. Which he told himself was all to the good.

While most of the other ladies spoke politely to Xena, various gentlemen—not all of them unmarried—heaped lavish compliments upon her, congratulating Harry repeatedly on securing such a prize.

Despite his oft-stated aversion to matrimony, he could not bring himself to disagree, even privately. That aversion, he now realized, had only begun after he'd believed Xena lost to him forever. The same could be said for the acquisition of those habits that gradually changed him from optimistic to cynical, upright to debauched. A disturbing thought, and not one he had any desire to dwell upon just now.

When the play resumed, Xena found it much harder to give it her full attention than she had during the first act. Though the performers were superb, *Othello,* with its theme of a marriage gone horribly wrong, was not her favorite among Shakespeare's works— particularly just now. Still, she was careful to keep her eyes directed toward the stage, even while acutely aware of Harry, so close beside her.

Last night, she believed she'd taken his full measure as a drunken, gambling womanizer. Still charming, still *far* too handsome, but no longer worthy of her respect or confidence. Tonight, however, he was displaying a very different side to his character—polished, erudite, even gallant. She had not missed how coolly Harry had behaved toward that odious Lady Grant, even while Xena struggled to conceal her own reaction to the woman's innuendoes.

Nor was he drinking overmuch tonight. At dinner, he'd been sparing, and though she noticed many of the occupants of other boxes imbibing during the performance, Harry had brought no bottle nor so much as hinted he wished Lord Peter had done so. Could her criticism have effected a change so quickly, or was last night an aberration? She wished she knew.

To forestall another crush of people in their box, Lord Peter suggested they move to the upper Rotunda during the second intermission. The moment they appeared, they were besieged by yet more members of Society eager to meet the celebrated Mr. and Mrs. Thatcher. As before, Xena tried to be unfailingly polite, while on her guard against another assault like Lady Grant's.

None occurred, but when she heard the Saint of Seven Dials mentioned, she pricked up her ears, still cherishing a faint—surely foolish—hope that Harry might have been doing something other than visiting a woman the previous night.

"Not surprised he's up to his old tricks again," Lord Plumfield was commenting to any who would listen. "He's laid low before, you know. Always comes back as soon as the Runners move on to other matters."

Xena moved closer as two younger women nearby tittered. "I, for one, hope they never catch him," simpered Miss Melks. "I know you feel the same, do you not, Lady Emma?"

Lady Emma, wife of the wealthy and influential Viscount Rockingham, nodded, her golden curls bouncing. "I confess, I've had a soft spot for the rogue ever since—" Pinkening, she broke off.

"Ever since what?" Xena couldn't resist prompting in an undertone, though at the moment Harry was not close enough to overhear. "Never say you have actually encountered the Saint yourself?"

"She likes to hint that she has," said Miss Melks with a toss of her head, "but I take leave to doubt it."

Lady Emma made a face at the other girl. "That's all you know, Lucinda. I am careful not to speak of it within Lord Rockingham's hearing, as it occurred the very night we met and I'd not have him jealous."

"Jealous?" Xena repeated as the other girl flounced off with a laugh. "Do you mean to say something occurred between you and the Saint that might cause your husband uneasiness?"

The young matron pinkened further. "Certainly not," she replied quickly, though in a tone that gave the lie to her words. "But you know how men can be. It *is* a fact that I once met and spoke with the Saint, and that we were not precisely chaperoned at the time."

Xena burned to know more. "What is he like? Tall or short, dark or fair, uncouth or cultured?" Unfortunately, she couldn't ask outright whether he had both his arms without instantly arousing suspicion.

Lady Emma's face took on a dreamy expression. "Tall, dark and very *definitely* cultured. Whatever his detractors may say, he's no common thief. 'Tis my belief he is a gentleman in disguise—perhaps a very highly placed one. Indeed, he appeared to have quite intimate knowledge of the Upper Ten Thousand."

"How very interesting. I suspected it might be so, from what I've heard of how easily he slips in and out of exclusive gatherings. But did he have no, ah, distinguishing characteristic by which you might recognize him again, were you to see him at a gathering such as this?"

"Alas, he was masked at the time, and the room was dim. I can say without reservation, however, that he was perhaps the finest figure of a man I ever encountered…excepting Lord Rockingham, of course."

She turned doting eyes on her husband, who stood discussing politics a short distance away.

"My brief encounter with the Saint is a memory I'll always cherish fondly," Lady Emma concluded with a wistful smile. "But if I've crossed paths with him in company since, he never made the slightest sign, nor can I claim to have recognized him. In truth, I am perfectly content to leave his identity shrouded in mystery. 'Tis more romantic that way, don't you think?"

"Oh! Certainly."

Xena forced an answering smile as she regretfully relinquished her last hope that Harry might have been the one who'd robbed that Irish peer's house. If the notorious Saint of Seven Dials possessed but one arm, Lady Emma would surely have mentioned it. 'Twas not a feature easily missed, however dim a room might be.

She was forced to conclude that Harry had exerted himself last night with something far less heroic than playing Robin Hood. Surely it was as well she'd been disabused of such a foolish fantasy. Otherwise his improved behavior this evening might have weakened her determination to keep her very necessary secrets to herself.

"I'd say your first appearance in Society as man and wife was quite the success." To Harry's disgust, Peter positively preened as they waited for his carriage afterward. "As I predicted, you are become the hit of the winter Season."

"Peter, dear," Sarah admonished before Harry could think of a retort. "Isn't it enough to be right, without gloating about it?"

He grinned down at her fondly. "As you've reminded me before. And you're right, of course. Sorry," he said then to Harry. "I know there were some awkward moments for you both tonight, and I must take responsibility for that, as well."

"Well you should," Harry replied. "Can't deny I'll be glad when you've found someone else to make a project out of. Young Flute, er, William, perhaps."

"Yes, he's next on my list." Completely unabashed, Peter grinned and began talking of Sarah's hopes for her brother—with no mention of the Saint of Seven Dials, of course—until the two couples parted for the night.

Back at their temporary lodgings in Grosvenor Street, Harry cast about for some topic that might stave off the awkwardness that threatened now he and Xena were alone again. He was about to suggest another glass of port in the library when she forestalled him.

"I believe I will head to my bed," she said with a barely-concealed yawn. "After years of country living, I fear it may take me some time to become accustomed to Town hours, and tomorrow I must begin replying to all those invitations."

"I, ah, can help with that if you wish," Harry offered, though he knew it was customary for wives to handle that sort of thing.

She sent him a smile of thanks but said nothing, instead turning to make her way up the stairs, the heaviness of her steps confirming her weariness.

Harry followed as far as the library where he paused, thinking to have a glass or two of port himself, at least. But then he decided against it. If he were truly going to assist Xena with those blasted invitations tomorrow, best he get a decent night's sleep himself.

He therefore surprised Brewster by achieving his own bedchamber some hours earlier than was his wont. His valet did not comment, however, simply helping him off with his evening clothes and on with his nightshirt before leaving him.

Rather too restless for sleep, no doubt because most nights he would still be gaming—or housebreaking—for some time yet, Harry began pacing the room in his stockinged feet, attempting to plan his next foray as Saint. Instead, he found himself beset by visions of Xena as she'd been this evening—sitting rapt in the theatre box, thoroughly enjoying the play; laughing lightly at the outrageous compliments paid her by various gentlemen; turning her head so that a dark curl bounced against her elegant throat...

Suddenly, he became aware of soft sounds in the next room—the sounds of Xena preparing for bed. Without intending to, he padded to the dressing room door, which happened to be ajar, that he might hear better. He heard the murmur of her voice as she spoke to her maid, then a slither of fabric over fabric—her gown being removed? Though he knew it was madness, he put his ear to the crack, imagining Xena in only her shift…then without it.

Giving himself a stern shake, Harry pulled away and betook himself to bed. There was no point tormenting himself when Xena had not so much as hinted at even the least desire to treat their marriage like a real one.

It was a long time before he finally fell asleep.

CHAPTER FOURTEEN

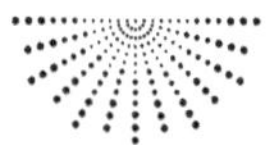

XENA WAS SURPRISED TO FIND HARRY ALREADY AT BREAKFAST WHEN SHE came downstairs the next morning—nearly as surprised as she'd been on hearing him come upstairs mere minutes after she'd begun getting ready for bed. At the time she'd sleepily assumed he meant to change and go back out.

"Thought you'd want to get an early start on all those infernal invitations," he greeted her without the least appearance of someone who'd been out carousing until all hours.

"Oh. I, ah, yes. We may well have callers later, so the more we can manage beforehand, the better, I suppose." Uncertain how to behave in response to his unexpected cordiality, she busied herself with filling a plate from the sideboard.

After they'd breakfasted, Harry did indeed help by reading invitations aloud to her, with an occasional opinion on whether one should be accepted or declined, while Xena penned replies. She'd been relieved when Lord Peter had informed her that only dinners and other entertainments where guests would be seated required a written response. Balls and routs could be attended or not, as other engagements allowed, as no one was expected to spend an entire evening at any given one.

Even so, more than a dozen necessary responses had yet to be penned when the first "morning" callers were announced, well past noon. Harry was quick to make himself scarce, his helpfulness apparently not extending so far as playing the polite in the parlor with his wife all afternoon.

Xena could scarcely blame him. In fact, after three hours of sharing tea and gossip with a succession of curious Society matrons, she positively envied him his escape. Morning calls, she decided, were yet another unfair burden English society placed upon women.

When the last caller finally left it was nearly time to dress for the evening, for they were expected for dinner at the Heathertons' before continuing on to Lady Gascombe's rout.

During both events, Harry proved the changes she had observed in him last night, however temporary, had at least survived their first outing. Over dinner, he proved himself well-versed in the topics of the day, delivering opinions intelligently while adjusting his manner according to his listener.

When ribbed about his customary habits, he was quick with a witty, though not ill-natured retort. Nor did he drink any more heavily than most of the other gentlemen—though by Xena's standards that still seemed rather excessive.

Lady Gascombe's rout was so crowded that conversation was nigh impossible, but Harry stayed close by Xena's side—which was as well, or they would likely have been separated by the press of people. They stayed little longer than was necessary to make their way into the small ballroom, filled to bursting, greet their hosts, then make their way back outside to wait for their carriage. Even so, it was nearly two before they returned to Grosvenor Street and Xena was again too tired to do more than bid Harry good night before seeking her bed.

Sleepily, she wondered whether she should comment on the positive changes in his behavior, or if doing so might embarrass him into reverting to form. She was asleep before she could decide.

• • •

After breakfast—which was considerably later than yesterday's—Harry again stayed long enough to help with the last of the initial flood of invitations before excusing himself.

"Promised to meet Pete and a few others at Gentleman Jacksons Saloon for a bout or two," he explained.

"Boxing, you mean?" Xena recalled hearing Gentleman Jackson's mentioned last night.

Harry nodded. "Figure I can use the exercise, what with all this rich food."

Again Xena rather envied him, this time for an activity she would have liked to learn more about, but which, as a lady, she could not. Determined to put her time to good use nonetheless, she gave instructions to Chambers that she would not be at home to callers, as she was expected at her modiste's for a fitting.

Then, once in the carriage, she directed the driver to take her to Mrs. Henderson's house in Rundel Street. After three days away, she fairly ached to see Theo again. Her fitting could wait.

Her son was delighted to see her and full of news, eager to tell her all about the various things Yamini had taken him to see and do.

"We visited a circulating library yesterday and Lincoln's Inn Fields the day before. I wanted to see Astley's Amphitheatre but Yamini says it is too far. May I visit Hyde Park, however? Mrs. Henderson says that is where all the most famous people in London are to be seen of an afternoon."

"She is likely quite right," Xena admitted with a smile. "I've not been there myself yet, but perhaps we can visit it together next week. I'll send Yamini word."

Though Theo continued to chatter, Xena's old *ayah* seemed unusually quiet. When Xena regretfully bade her son goodbye again after an all-too-brief visit, Yamini accompanied her partway down the stairs.

"You put on a good face for the little one, but I can see you are not easy in your mind," she told her mistress when they reached the first landing. "Perhaps, after three days in company with Mr. Thatcher, you finally realize I was right that they both should be told without further delay?"

Xena regarded her oldest, most trusted friend with surprise. "No! That is, not yet, for most of the rumors about him appear to be true. Since last I knew him, I fear my husband has become a ne'er-do-well who lives most by gaming and…and has been in the habit of associating with all manner of unsavory sorts."

She could not bring herself to admit even to Yamini that many of those were women.

"In addition, he drinks far too much." That was still likely true, despite his attempts at moderation the past two nights. "To be honest, I've wondered if I wouldn't be wiser to take Theo completely out of his reach the moment I have the funds to do so."

Yamini frowned. "And what *will* you tell Theo of his father? Surely you cannot think removing him from England will stop him asking and wondering? It is not as though your husband is a criminal, for all his lifestyle in recent years may not meet your approval. Do not forget that Mr. Thatcher believed himself unmarried far longer than you did. Depriving him of his son seems a harsh penalty for behaving as most young men of his class do."

Xena felt certain Harry's behavior had been worse than most, but refrained from saying so. Yamini would only point out that Xena had too little experience in Society to know how other young men behaved —which was, unfortunately, true.

"I'll do nothing irrevocable right away," she grudgingly conceded. "Indeed, I cannot afford to do so just yet. By the bye, I don't suppose Mr. Gold has sent any word?"

"He did, mum. 'Tis another reason I wished to speak with you privately. He sent a message around late yesterday asking you to call on him at your earliest convenience. Had you not come by today, I planned to ask one of Mrs. Henderson's servants to deliver a note to you in Mayfair."

Devoutly hoping that meant Mr. Gold had heard again from his wealthy buyer, Xena smiled. "How very timely. I had already intended to stop there, as I've had no opportunity to give him my new direction."

Giving Yamini an affectionate hug, she took her leave.

Just as he had the last time Xena had visited his shop, Mr. Gold greeted her with a wide smile. "Ah, Miss Maxwell. You received my message, then?"

"Yes, though future ones will need to be sent elsewhere. For the next few weeks I will be residing in Grosvenor Street."

The old shopkeeper nodded sagely. "I wondered whether you might be the same Miss Maxwell referenced in that rather remarkable story in the papers. Why did you not bring your husband with you today?"

Xena knew Mr. Gold meant no offense, but she could not prevent the tightening of her lips. "He has no involvement in my business with you, sir. Indeed, I would prefer he not learn of it at all just yet, as we are still sorting a few things out between us. Therefore, I pray you will be discreet in any messages you might have occasion to send to Grosvenor Street."

Though one white eyebrow went up, he nodded. "Very well, if you feel that is best. In any event, the reason I wished to see you was to deliver something I imagine you will be most happy to receive." Reaching under the counter, he pulled out a paper-wrapped parcel. "My buyer sent this by, with word it was to be delivered to you as soon as possible."

Opening the parcel curiously, Xena stared at the contents with a sense of disbelief. "Is this everything he had promised? So soon?"

Chuckling, Mr. Gold shook his head. "Nay, lass, it's but a downpayment. One fifth of the total, his note said, to help defray transportation costs for the rest of the artifacts and your added expenses for remaining here in London longer than you had originally planned."

Still dazed, Xena met the shopkeeper's twinkling blue gaze. "Thank you, Mr. Gold. Thank you very, *very* much! This will help enormously."

"He still wishes to meet with you, though he could not say when the press of business would allow it. The, ah, this gentleman is busy with extremely important matters, so I trust you are willing to be patient, given what he has already forwarded."

Xena smiled. "Yes. Yes I think I can now afford to be quite patient."

She bade him a cheerful goodbye, but with a parting reminder that all future messages be sent as discreetly as possible. It was still too soon to know whether the recent change in Harry's behavior was a permanent one. Until she did, she dared not risk him learning of this windfall for fear he might be tempted to gamble it away.

Suddenly, she realized that she now had ample resources to take Theo abroad, should she wish. Did she? Yamini insisted it would be a mistake, and her *ayah's* counsel had rarely proved wrong in the past. Then there was the matter of her promise to Lord Peter. No, she must stay a while longer, if only to give Harry the benefit of the doubt. Still, it was good to have options.

Her heart lighter than it had been in a long, long time, she bade the carriage driver take her to Madame Fanchot in Bond Street, where she impulsively ordered two more dresses in addition to the ball gown she was being fitted for. That she could afford ten times as many without appreciably depleting her funds was rather a delightful thought.

If anything other than the money contributed to her buoyed spirits, she preferred not to think about it.

Harry was beginning to wonder if it was worth the effort to play the unaccustomed role of polished sophisticate evening after evening without receiving at least a bit of encouragement from Xena. Being near her again *did* make him wish to become a better man than he'd been of late—a man more like the one she remembered—but he was finding old habits devilish hard to shed.

He'd cut his drinking nearly in half, yet she gave no indication she'd even noticed, much less cared. Nor had he gone out gaming again after that first night, which effectively removed him from all temptation by the women who frequented such establishments—not that he'd felt any particular inclination in that direction since commencing this experiment of Peter's.

Far from giving him a disgust of living practically in her pocket these past few days, being so near her only increased his yearning to recapture the passion they'd shared in their youth. It was for that reason he'd taken to going out after breakfast most days for some sort of exercise, in hopes of taking the edge off his desire. Not that it was working. He couldn't help thinking another stint as the Saint might help, but with all these infernal engagements every evening, he had no idea when he'd manage one.

Preparing to leave yet again after breakfast, he was therefore relieved to be told that a boy was asking for him at the back door. Xena had already repaired to the drawing room to receive yet more interminable morning calls, so he readily accompanied the footman through the house.

Perhaps Flute had news of another family in desperate need of assistance, or word of a particularly ripe target for the Saint? When he stepped out into the barren kitchen gardens a few moments later, however, it was Tig who awaited him there.

"I told you I'd contact you through Flute," Harry whispered, guiding the boy toward the back gate, where they were less likely to be overheard.

"Aye, guv, but I had to change where I been sleeping so I worried he mightn't find me. Figured I'd best bring my report to you personal-like, just in case."

Harry didn't have the heart to scold the lad for over-eagerness to carry out his task. "Very well. What have you to report?"

"Been watching the house all along, like you said, guv'nor, but yesterday was the first time the lady you described went out without yerself. Thought you'd want to know."

Suppressing a grin at the boy's self-important air, Harry nodded. "Yes, she went to Bond Street for a fitting. She told me." What she hadn't mentioned was where she was getting the means to pay for yet another dress.

Tig shook his head emphatically. "Nay, guv, that she didn't. Least-aways, not till the very end. I trotted along after the carriage she was in to see where it went."

"Trotted— You were able to keep up on foot?" Harry regarded the undersized urchin skeptically.

"Oh, aye, there were enough traffic it couldn't go but at a walking pace most of the time. Anyways, she went direct from here to a boarding house in Rundel Street, stayed there close on an hour, then went to a shop near Aldergate. Wasn't in there long, but it was only after that she finally headed for Bond Street. She spent the better part of two hours in that shop before coming back here." He beamed up at Harry.

It was all Harry could do to smile back. What the devil was Xena up to? Clearly she'd met with someone at that house...and in a questionable part of Town. Did her wealthy protector perhaps keep a set of rooms there for the sole purpose of conducting discreet *affaires* away from the prying eyes of Society?

Given Harry's own past, a fair argument might be made that he had no right to be jealous even if his suspicion proved true, but he still burned to know.

Though her extravagance at Madame Fanchot's gave Xena more than one pang of guilt over the next two days, she was glad she hadn't stinted when she and Harry arrived for Lady Ellerby's ball—Xena's first. The ladies fairly glittered with silk, satin and jewels, while the gentlemen provided elegant counterpoint in their dark tailed coats and breeches.

Harry was no exception, looking as distinguished as she'd yet seen him in his best evening attire, this coat specially tailored to make his injury less noticeable, with the left sleeve nonexistent rather than pinned up. Not even in his scarlet regimentals, shaved and brushed for the Commander's review, had he ever looked more outrageously handsome.

In her new ball gown of shimmering silver satin over a pure white underskirt, delivered only that afternoon, Xena felt confident that she at least *looked* the part of a proper gentleman's wife...even if she didn't feel much like one.

Indeed, her excitement at attending her very first ball was

tempered by more than a thread of trepidation. Dancing was by no means her forte and she'd had precious few chances to practice since being taught the basics as a girl. She rather regretted never attending the local assemblies in Yorkshire when numerous gentlemen approached nearly as soon as she was announced to request the honor of partnering her.

When she looked to Harry for guidance on how to respond, he merely shrugged. "Don't let my disinclination for dancing keep you from enjoying yourself tonight. Save me the supper dance and I'll be more than content to spend my time in the card room."

With that encouragement, Xena was soon bespoken for every dance of the evening. Harry partnered her for the opening minuet after which, true to his word, he retired to the sidelines. That one dance had proved his skill far superior to her own, however, making her rather wish she could do the same. She wished it even more as she found herself apologizing to partner after partner for her frequent missteps.

"I can't tell you how delighted I am that you've chosen to extend your stay in Town," said the Duke of Wellington as they began a waltz midway through the evening. "Rather had a feeling you might."

She looked up at her former commander in surprise and some misgiving. After their last encounter she'd been reluctant to agree to so intimate a dance as the waltz with him, but refusing the man England currently deemed second in importance only to the Prince Regent was out of the question. At least the waltz was less complicated than most of the country dances.

"You did? Why is that?"

He smiled down at her with the same warmth that had previously made her uncomfortable. "You implied a lack of funds compelled your return to Yorkshire, but I had already taken certain steps to help alleviate that concern."

"You took... Do you mean to say that *you* are the person who has offered to purchase my father's Grecian collection, your grace?" Xena was not sure whether to be grateful or aghast.

The Duke tightened his grip on her waist, his smile broadening. "My secret is out. Initially, I merely thought to help out the daughter of an old friend, but on seeing you at Apsley House last week, it is possible my motive became a trifle less pure."

Though her instinct was to pull away and leave him there on the dance floor, she could scarcely do so without causing a scene and giving rise to speculation. Before she could frame a diplomatic rejection of his implied offer, the Duke twirled her and Xena, considerably less than expert at the waltz, stumbled.

He caught her before she could fall and embarrass herself further. "I fear I have shocked you, my dear," he said with a chuckle. "Most women would be quite flattered."

"I am not most women," Xena retorted stiffly, repeating what she'd told Harry during their first conversation. "I am also married, your grace—as you are well aware."

"Oh, aye." He dismissed that argument with a shrug. "But as your husband will by no means desist from pursuing his pleasures on that account, you may see your way clear to do likewise."

Xena was startled—and more upset than she cared to admit—that the Duke could be so certain Harry did not intend to abide by his marriage vows. Still, she had no intention of being persuaded to similar indiscretions. Even were she tempted to do so—which she most definitely was not—she had her son to think of.

"I'm sorry, your grace," she said frostily. "If your purchase of those artifacts is contingent upon my agreement to a dalliance, I fear I must—"

"No, no, of course not," he interrupted her with another laugh. "I'll buy the demmed knick-knacks, never fear—least I can do for Old Max's daughter. Looks as though you've already put my downpayment to good use, in any event." He cast an approving eye over her ensemble. "Nor did I gain my reputation in battle by surrendering after the first setback." The dance ended then and he released her with a wink.

Her face no doubt pinker than usual despite trying valiantly not to blush, Xena dipped the Duke a hurried curtsey and turned away, wishing fervently she could return every penny to him. Unfortunately, after spending a goodly portion on herself, she had already sent the balance of his money to Yorkshire. Upon hearing her name spoken as she left the floor, that wish intensified.

"Mrs. Thatcher is angling to trade up, it would seem," Mrs. Mellings whispered loudly.

"I daresay," agreed Lady Digby, wagging her turban. "Though that may well be a source of relief rather than concern to her husband. Wellington is known to be most generous to his lovers."

Mrs. Mellings nodded. "Aye, I can't imagine Mr. Thatcher would turn away a bit extra, no matter the source." She tittered.

"It will also give him more leisure to resume his own interests, which I overheard Lady Grant saying he has been forced to neglect of late."

Xena determinedly moved out of earshot, pretending not to have heard, though she suspected she'd been meant to. Let the gossips say what they wished. She'd done nothing wrong. Nor had she formed any foolish illusions about Harry or their marriage, despite the apparent—and no doubt temporary—change she'd seen in him these past days.

Even so, she was turning instinctively to scan the crowded room for Harry when her next partner stepped forward. With a bow and a fulsome compliment on her nonexistent "grace" in the dance, Mr. Pottinger led her back out for the cotillion just forming. For an instant she thought she spotted Harry near an archway, but when she looked again he was gone.

Not until the supper dance did she again encounter her husband, by which time her distress over the Duke's suggestive remarks had faded somewhat. Harry proved as adept at the waltz as General Wellington, though of course he could not take her right hand in his left, instead directing her to place her hand against his chest.

When she commented on his skill, he smiled down at her. "I do my best, considering." He grimaced toward his left shoulder. "'Twas something Wellington expected of all his officers. It stood me in good stead in Vienna, though I can't claim to enjoy it."

Xena tried not to look conscious at mention of Wellington's name, but feared she was not entirely successful. "Was the card room to your liking?" she asked quickly, hoping he would not notice.

"Not particularly. Our hosts decreed but penny stakes for the evening, which takes most of the fun from it. Pity, that, or I'd be well up by now."

She mentally congratulated their hosts on their wisdom while contenting herself with nodding in mock sympathy.

Supper was a noisy affair, allowing for little in the way of real conversation. The knowledge that she was engaged for another dance with the Duke immediately afterward prevented Xena from properly enjoying the assortment of dainties available.

When the dancing resumed, she was pleased to discover the first was not another waltz. Her relief was short-lived, however, for the country dance had scarcely begun when the Duke reopened his earlier topic.

"I must apologize for shocking you earlier, my dear," he said while deftly stepping through the figures. "I confess, I did not believe it possible after the time you spent in army camps. Old Max must have done a better job shielding you from the baser instincts of my soldiers than I expected of him, absentminded as he could often be."

As Xena had managed to carry on an affair with Harry for nearly three months practically under her father's nose, that was scarcely true but of course she did not say so. "I was merely…surprised, your grace," she forced herself to say before the movements of the dance separated them.

When next they came together, he took the opportunity to say, "I don't suppose I might persuade you—and Thatcher, of course—to come to Paris? I'm bound there this Tuesday and would be happy to show you all the delights that city has to offer."

Though Xena had long wished to visit Paris after all she'd heard about that city, accepting an invitation such as this was obviously out of the question. "I fear my *husband* and I are fixed in Town for the present, your grace."

He smiled, turning about as the dance required. "I hope once you've acquired a bit of Town bronze you'll reconsider, my dear. As for

Thatcher, I've no doubt he would enjoy Paris enormously. All his favorite vices are to be found there, multiplied a hundredfold."

Stung by this reminder of how generally known Harry's indiscretions were among the *ton*, she completed the dance in silence, her enjoyment of the evening effectively quenched.

~

Harry watched balefully from the sidelines as Xena exchanged flirtatious banter with Wellington during their second dance of the evening. It had seemed only fair to encourage Xena to dance with other gentlemen tonight as this was her first ball and he disliked the exercise himself. Now, however, he was beginning to regret his generosity.

That Xena proved less skilled a dancer than Harry himself mattered little, for she covered her blunders well, with humor and grace. He supposed he should be grateful his former general had danced with her *only* twice thus far, but the way he looked and spoke to her made it abundantly clear he regarded her as far more than the daughter of an old friend.

Xena's feelings were less easy to decipher, but she would scarcely have accepted him a second time were she attempting to discourage him.

A sudden, hearty slap on his back, made Harry spill half the wine in his nearly-untouched glass.

"What ho, Harry!" exclaimed Lord Fernworth. "Looks like your missus is making quite the conquest, eh?" He waved his own glass toward the dance floor, slopping wine himself, though he appeared not to notice.

"Don't know what you're talking about." Harry turned his back on the dancers. As usual, Ferny was nearly too drunk to stand—though that never kept him from talking, and far too loudly.

Fernworth snorted a guffaw, then hiccuped. "Can't fool me, Harry, m'boy. Saw you watchin' 'em. But buck up! Wellington's known to do quite handsomely by the husbands of his lady-loves. With luck, you'll soon have extra blunt for the tables, not to mention more time to pursue your own pleasures, eh?"

Heads were beginning to turn their way so Harry attempted to usher his sometime-friend away from the floor. "Let's get some coffee into you, what do you say, Ferny?"

He received a pitying look in return. "That the way of it, then, Harry? Leg-shackled only a week and already under the cat's paw? Turning priggish as Lord Peter, you are, and no doubt just as besotted by your wife. Poor blighter." Blearily shaking his head, he wandered off to refill his now-empty glass.

Harry frowned after him. Ferny was a drunken nodcock, of course, worse than Harry had ever been, but he was uncomfortably aware that only a month ago he'd uttered similar words to Pete—and before that, to various other friends. Was Ferny right that Harry was beginning to exhibit the very symptoms he'd previously deplored in Jack and Pete? Worse, was he right about Wellington and Xena? It would explain much.

Still beset by those troubling thoughts, Harry was silent on the carriage ride back to Grosvenor Street. Xena, who'd danced every set, was already nodding, so seemed not to notice. On their arrival, she made no protest when he merely bid her good night before shutting himself into the library with the port decanter.

Half a bottle brought him no closer to figuring out what, if anything, he should do, so he finally made his disgruntled way up to bed.

The arrival of two more dresses the following day—and from Madame Fanchot's, the most exclusive modiste in all London—served to sharpen Harry's suspicions further. Xena happened to be out returning calls when the boxes were delivered, so on impulse he took them from the footman to carry upstairs himself. Outside her chamber door, he peeked inside to see whether a card might be enclosed, but none was.

Wellington was both smart and discreet enough that the omission proved nothing, but without firmer proof he could scarcely confront

Xena about an affair. Nor was he certain he would—or should—do so even if he obtained such proof. They had never pledged fidelity to one another, unless one counted those wedding vows they'd been forced to recite, once upon a time.

Upon their return from Lord and Lady Varens' soiree that night, however, his resolve to keep his own counsel on the matter was shaken when Tig greeted Harry at the back gate with news that Xena, while supposedly making calls that morning, had again visited the boarding house on Rundel Street.

Giving the boy a few shillings for his trouble, Harry walked back to the house, wondering how he might discover who she was meeting there. A frowning glance at Xena's window showed it already dark. Just as well, he realized. For a moment, he'd been tempted to demand the truth from her this very night.

Instead, he again retired to the library after calling for a fresh decanter of port.

CHAPTER FIFTEEN

XENA FELT AS THOUGH SHE'D SCARCELY CLOSED HER EYES WHEN Gretchen opened the curtains late the next morning.

"It's that sorry I am to wake you, mum, but you said as how I wasn't to let you sleep past eleven o'clock."

"No, no, it's fine." Xena yawned cavernously. "'Tis an at-home day, so I must be ready to receive callers soon."

After nearly a full week in Society, Xena felt as though she'd been sucked into such a whirlpool of morning calls, afternoon teas, and evening musicales, card parties and balls that she scarcely had time to draw breath. She and Harry rarely had a moment alone. Even breakfast was often only a hurried bit of toast and coffee before her first visitors arrived.

Every dinner since their first had been committed elsewhere, which she sincerely hoped Lord Peter would not consider a violation of the terms of their agreement, as it was a result of his interference. And every night they returned home so late that it was all she could do to make her way up the stairs before collapsing into bed.

Harry was still surprisingly attentive in public, always making certain she was well supplied with refreshment—though she noticed his own glass was always full as well, generally with wine or something stronger rather than her usual orgeat or lemonade. In private, however, he had grown increasingly aloof.

He was not in the breakfast room when she descended and a casual query revealed that he was still abed. Either Harry was as exhausted by their recent schedule as she was…or he'd gone out again last night after their return from that soiree in the wee hours. At the moment, she could scarcely summon the energy to wonder which.

After three cups of coffee she felt awake enough—barely—to remove to the drawing room, resolving that for the remainder of her time in London she would have but *one* at-home day in a week. That resolve was strengthened when Lady Mountheath was announced, mere seconds after she'd seated herself on the divan.

"My dear!" The overbearing matron greeted her with a too-broad smile that boded ill. "I am glad to see you are alone as yet. Indeed, I came rather earlier than my wont in hopes of finding you so."

"Good day, my lady." Xena rose only long enough to dip a quick curtsey. "You have come with a particular purpose, then?"

"Indeed, and I wish it were a more pleasant one." Lady Mountheath now affected an expression of deep concern that looked no more sincere than her smile had. "I am here to put you on your guard."

Xena's initial misgiving deepened. "On my guard? Against what?"

"Against opening yourself to rumor and gossip. The other night, at Lady Ellerby's ball, I overheard something that worried me exceedingly on your behalf."

"Oh?"

Lady Mountheath nodded sententiously. "Perhaps, being so very new to Town, you are unaware that, for all his heroism, the Duke of Wellington has…less than an impeccable reputation when it comes to his dealings with ladies. To be publicly seen receiving marked attentions from him is sure to give rise to speculation."

"The Duke was an old friend of my father's," Xena primly informed her unwelcome visitor. "He asked me to dance so that we might speak of those shared memories. That is all." With an effort, she refrained from glancing down at her new morning gown—purchased with money the Duke had sent her through Mr. Gold.

"If you say so, Mrs. Thatcher. However, it is not *my* opinion you need fear, as I am the *last* one to spread gossip. You should consider instead how others might, ah, misconstrue a pair of dances accompanied by overt admiration." Her expression conveyed clearly that *she* believed the rumors.

Nor could Xena claim that they were completely unfounded, given the Duke's stated intentions, however blameless her own behavior had been. "What others?" she could not help asking.

"Your husband, for one. I overheard him speaking with Lord Fernworth at the ball. It sounded as though he is already quite looking forward to both extra time to indulge his own disreputable pursuits and the money to better fund them, all as a direct consequence of Wellington's improper interest in you."

Before Xena could summon an appropriate response—if one even existed—more callers were announced. Lady Mountheath immediately rose, donning a sunny smile. "I will bid you good day, Mrs. Thatcher, for I have several more calls to make."

Several more ladies' days to ruin, you mean. Xena bid her a frosty goodbye, then turned to greet the newcomers, striving to put the hateful woman's insinuations from her mind—though with limited success.

By the time Harry made his way down to breakfast, well past noon, the first of Xena's morning callers had already arrived. Not only had he stayed up too late and drunk too much, but once in bed he'd slept poorly, tossing and turning till well past dawn.

He tried to convince himself that his black mood this morning was due to lack of sleep, aggravated by the fact that it had been a week since he'd had opportunity to play the Saint. Damn Pete's interference, anyway, persuading him to the role, then obliging him to abandon it just as it was becoming enjoyable. Though his last haul had been a particularly a good one, he was positively itching for another foray.

Deep down, however, he knew the real root of the trouble was Xena. The thought of another full month of going about together, pretending to the world that they were a normal married couple while he was torn in two between desire and suspicion, was unbearable.

He would have to contrive a private moment with her to finally get some answers. If she meant to leave him for Wellington, better to know at once and end this torment. And if she did not?

He honestly wasn't sure.

"I decided to cry off from Lady Jeller's dinner and musicale this evening," Xena surprised him by announcing later that afternoon when they chanced to pass each other on the stairs after her last callers had gone. "I fear I would be likely to embarrass us both by nodding off during the performances, as little sleep as I've managed the past several nights. I hope you do not object?"

"Object to being spared a boring evening of mediocre music and tepid lemonade?" The Jellers were teetotalers and known for enforcing their preference on their guests. "Hardly."

Looking closer at Xena—something he'd avoided lately, as the effect she had on him only led to frustration—he realized she did look rather drawn.

"I believe an evening's rest will do you good," he said with sudden concern. "Our schedule has been rather frenetic thus far and I'd not have you make yourself ill by doing too much."

Her brows rose in surprise, but then she laughed. "'Tis a sad commentary on how a few years can change one, is it not? Time was, I could march fifteen miles in a day on less sleep and *far* shorter commons than I've had here in Town."

"Yes, well, I doubt I'm up to such exertions myself these days. There's a reason soldiering is primarily an occupation for the young, you know."

"Not that we are so very old, either one of us." She sounded almost wistful. "I should say Town living is more to blame than age for our comparative lack of vigor. Were we to make a habit of long walks and fewer, simpler meals, we might discover ourselves as capable of such as we ever were."

Was that a veiled reference to his drinking? Nothing in her expression indicated that, but he wondered. After cutting back the first day or two, his consumption had gradually increased again until it nearly rivaled its previous level.

"Shall we ask Mrs. MacKay to send up nothing but chicken and vegetables tonight?" He kept his voice light and bantering. "Perhaps we should also tell all the Society biddies to go to hell and schedule a series of marches for ourselves instead of this endless succession of parties."

Xena laughed with him. "I won't deny the idea holds a certain appeal. Though I wouldn't dream of insulting Mrs. MacKay's excellent cooking by asking for such a meal, I confess that a quiet dinner at home will be a most welcome change."

An entire evening alone with Xena, something they'd not managed since their first night in the house, should give him ample time to ferret out the truth of where her money was coming from…and where her affections lay. That was surely why his heart quickened at the thought —not because of some foolish hope that this evening might end differently than their first.

Swallowing hard, he stood. "I've a few matters to attend to just now, but I'll return in good time for dinner. Until then?"

"Oh, ah, certainly. I've fallen sadly behind in my correspondence, so will have plenty to occupy me in the meantime."

Harry went downstairs, calling for his hat and coat. Those "matters" he referred to were fictitious, but he needed air—and distance from Xena—to work out a strategy for achieving his aim later on.

Deep in thought, he bent his steps to the Guards' Club. He'd avoided the place in recent days but by now most of his old comrades had already had opportunity to give him a hard time about his marriage. On entering, he was met by a chorus of greetings, though not without a sly allusion or two.

"How does it feel, now the shackle is on the other leg, eh, Thatcher?" quipped Thomas Westercott, whom Harry had mercilessly tweaked upon his own marriage a year since. "Not quite so bad as you expected, I'll warrant."

Before Harry could respond, Sir Barney Phillips gave an ill-natured laugh. "Not so bad? I can't imagine anything worse than being saddled for life with a shrew like that, no matter how comely she's become."

"Clearly my wife pricked your pride as sharply as your shoulder, once upon a time," Harry shot back. "Won't deny she's got spirit, but a *real* man isn't put off by that. Rather the reverse."

That got a general laugh, for the story of Xena besting Phillips in that duel back in '09 was well known to most there. Harry joined in, though privately he was startled by the unreasoning anger that swept through him at hearing Xena termed a shrew. It wasn't as though she needed a husband or anyone else to defend her honor.

Though the glowering baronet left a moment later, the banter about Harry's abrupt transformation from bachelor to seven years married continued unabated. Regretting his decision to come here after all, he was moving toward the door to follow Phillips out when a new arrival changed his mind.

"Jack! When did you return to Town? Thought you were fixed in the country for the winter."

Lord Foxhaven stepped forward to clap Harry on the back. "Nessa insisted. She claims to be feeling better, though right now she's having a lie-down, as the trip to London rather tired her. Thought I'd make myself scarce rather than racket about the house unpacking and such.

"So," he continued, with what Harry considered an ominous gleam in his eyes, "I understand you've set up housekeeping for the rest of the year?"

"Ah, that's why you've come back, is it? To witness my domestication firsthand?" Harry lowered his voice. "Sorry to disappoint you, but the true tale is the one I already told you, not the long-lost-love faradiddle Pete sent to the papers."

Jack frowned. "But it *is* true you and your wife are living under the same roof, is it not? I had that from Peter himself."

Harry snorted. "Only because he bribed us both to make the attempt. She's no happier about it than I am." If it cost him a pang to admit that aloud, he strove to hide it.

"In that case, why did you both agree?" Jack now looked skeptical. "Pete couldn't possibly have thrown that much money at you. He's well off, I grant you, but—"

"Come, let's share a bottle and talk of something else." Turning his back on his friend, Harry moved to a table in the corner.

Jack obligingly ordered a bottle from a passing servant before sitting down, but refused to change the subject. "Don't tell me that after living for a week in such close proximity you haven't managed to recapture any of the early attraction that ended in your marriage?"

Shifting in his chair, Harry shrugged. "Won't say I'm not attracted. You've seen her—I'd have to be blind. Haven't seen much evidence it's mutual, however, so I can't very well press the matter, can I?"

Jack started to chuckle. "Oh, of course not! The upstanding Harry Thatcher would *never* pay the least bit of improper attention to a woman unless she expressly invited it. No, wait. I must be thinking of someone else, not the greatest flirt and seducer at the Congress of Vienna."

"This is different," Harry snapped, nearly as irritated as he'd been by Phillips's insult. "Xena is not some lightskirt to be tumbled for an evening. She—"

"Is your wife," Jack finished with a grin. "Play your cards right, and the tumbling may well go on for a lifetime. A most *enjoyable* lifetime."

Harry opened his mouth to retort, then closed it again, having no good answer other than to voice his suspicion about Wellington— something he had no mind to share with even his closest friends…even if it turned out to be true.

Instead, he considered the possible merit of Jack's words. He'd proven dozens of times since the war that he was more than capable of charming a woman. What might happen if he focused those vaunted skills on Xena? Might he finally persuade the full truth from her or…more?

Perhaps it was worth a try.

~

True to his word, Harry joined Xena in the drawing room nearly half an hour before dinner.

"Give you good evening, my dear." He executed an elegant bow. "My, what a fetching frock that is. That particular shade of pink brightens your complexion and makes your hair appear even more lustrous than usual."

Xena regarded him suspiciously. Lately, no matter what pains she'd taken with her appearance, Harry seemed not to notice. "That is kind of you, considering that this dress is in fact secondhand. I'm told it is not quite the thing to be seen publicly in the same gown twice, so I must needs save my few new ones for when we are out in company."

She carefully did not mention her two *newest* ones. After Lady Mountheath's comments earlier, she felt more than a little conflicted about wearing those dresses at all, as she'd bought them with the Duke of Wellington's money. In fact, had she not already forwarded the bulk of that money to Yorkshire for needed repairs, she'd be tempted to return it to him forthwith. As it was, she'd written to Mr. Gold that afternoon, telling him she had reconsidered selling the balance of her father's Grecian collection to his "mysterious" buyer.

"Then may I say that you wear a secondhand gown better than most ladies wear the costliest creations from the finest modistes." Harry poured them each a glass of sherry from the sideboard and moved to sit on the sofa.

Ignoring her glass, Xena moved to a chair that was near, but not too near, him. "What are you playing at, Harry? You know better than most my opinion of flattery."

Rather to her surprise, he chuckled. "I wasn't certain whether you still felt the same. I've heard any number of men heaping you with praise this week without having their ears pinned back for it."

She couldn't suppress a smile. "I've wished to do so on several occasions but stifled the impulse to avoid giving offense. It would seem most gentlemen of the *ton* find it safer to lavish empty compliments upon a lady than to attempt actual conversation with her."

"To be fair, I've known hardened battle veterans, brave enough under enemy fire, to cower in the face of your incisive discourse on certain topics. These pampered London dandies wouldn't stand a chance." His hazel eyes twinkled as they used to during all their spirited discussions of her unorthodox opinions. Discussions she'd quite enjoyed...and missed.

"It is difficult to give them any reason to cower when they never ask my opinion on anything weightier than the state of the weather or the cut of their coats. Speaking of which, you look rather fine for a dinner at home. Do you have other plans for later?"

"None whatsoever. Who deserves my best, if not my wife?" he replied with a hint of a wink.

She might have asked that exact question, had he not deflected it so neatly. Vaguely unsettled by the look in his eyes—one she remembered rather too well—she changed the subject.

"Were you able to deal with your business this afternoon?"

Still smiling almost—but not quite—suggestively, he nodded.

"Merely a meeting with friends at my club, whom I'd been neglecting. Lord Foxhaven and his wife are back in Town—you met him at Wellington's do, I believe?"

There was a slight edge to his tone when mentioning the Duke's name, though if what Lady Mountheath reported overhearing was true, she couldn't think why.

"They intend to host a dinner and perhaps a small ball once they're settled in and would like us to attend, if our schedule will allow."

"He is one of your closest friends, is he not?" she said, glad to be on safer ground. "I'm certain we can arrange to be there. However, as we are neither of us particularly fond of dancing, I rather hope it will only be dinner."

Those two dances with the Duke of Wellington had rather dimmed her enthusiasm for balls. In fact, it was partially to avoid encountering him again tonight that she'd decided to decline the Jellers' invitation, for he'd commented in passing at the previous evening's rout that he looked forward to seeing her there.

"Did you never attend balls in Yorkshire?" he surprised her by asking then.

"I, ah, no. I rarely mingle with the local gentry, as we have little in common."

"You spend all of your time at home, then? On your estate?"

Was he digging for information as to the extent of her property? Property that, according to the law, was now his…

"I have plenty to occupy me there, as I've been able to afford few servants," she replied cautiously. "This year's harvest was poor after such a cool summer, which has had an effect on rents from the tenant farms."

He nodded, though his expression was too knowing for her comfort. "Surely you must do something for amusement? You used to enjoy fencing…among other things." Again, a ghost of a wink, reminding her of just how much she—they—had enjoyed those "other things."

Swallowing, she glanced away. "I tend my herb garden and teach those of the village women willing to learn which ones are most useful, and for what ailments. And I read, of course."

"Of course. What of your fencing and shooting? I'd hate to think you have neglected those, given your previous level of skill." His smile suggested he was recalling other skills as well but she refused to blush.

"I occasionally still shoot, as I can devise targets. Fencing is more difficult without proper opponents, though I've recently begun to teach—" She broke off. Great heaven, she'd nearly said Theo's name! "—some of the local village lads," she continued after a too-long pause.

One raised eyebrow proved he'd noticed her hesitation. "Only the lads?"

"I, ah, haven't been able to persuade any of the girls' parents to let them learn," she improvised, still rattled by her near-slip.

"Pity. The world might be a better place if more shared your enthusiasm for experiences outside their normal sphere."

There was no mistaking his meaning now. Longings Xena had believed long buried began to stir—longings she dared not indulge. Did she?

To her relief, a footman appeared just then to announce dinner. Instantly, Harry was at her side, his arm gallantly outstretched.

"Shall we?"

As they went down to dinner, Harry chided himself for attempting flattery to win Xena over, for she'd never been one to have her head turned by pretty speeches. Clearly he would do better to continue engaging her on other topics that might subtly remind her of what they once were to each other—and try to discover all he could along the way.

When they entered the dining room, he was pleased to see that, per his instructions, the two place settings were indeed at right angles to each other at the head of the table rather than at opposite ends. At Xena's questioning glance, he grinned down at her.

"I thought this would be cozier and make conversation rather easier. I hope you don't mind?"

"Of...of course I don't mind." Her tiny hesitation implied he'd flustered her a bit with his earlier allusions.

That was all to the good, as it might cause her to reveal more than she intended, as he suspected she'd nearly done a few moments ago. Was she perhaps teaching fencing to local gentlemen, as well as boys? He pulled out her chair before seating himself practically at her elbow. Unstoppering the decanter before him, he poured the ruby liquid first into her glass and then his own.

"My favorite vintage," he commented, raising his glass. "A fitting one with which to salute you."

One brow skeptically raised, Xena saluted him as well, then took a small sip of the excellent wine. "It's very good," she admitted.

"I'm glad you like it. You see, we do still have a few things in common."

She took another small sip, now avoiding his eye. "Our mutual dislike for dancing, for example."

"That, too." He let his amusement show in his voice. "Though I must say that for one so disinclined to dance as you claim, you carry off the necessity famously. I've meant to compliment you upon it."

At her frown, he quickly added, "A compliment is only flattery if untrue, you know." It was an argument he'd used more than once in his defense in the past—most particularly after an enjoyable session of lovemaking. She obviously recalled that circumstance as well, for she looked suddenly conscious, her protest dying on her lips.

"Who knows?" he continued. "With a bit more practice you may come to quite enjoy dancing. I have rather a better excuse for avoiding it, alas."

"Yet your dancing is far more polished than mine, when you give yourself the trouble," she retorted. "Indeed, you do an excellent job of making one forget your injury entirely. I've been...extremely impressed by how well you've adapted."

Now it was Harry's turn to be discomfited by a compliment. "I, ah, suppose I am beginning to, at any rate. In the early days my attempts were quite laughable, I assure you. I'd no idea how many tasks require both hands until I was forced to make do with one. The simple act of tying a bootlace is still completely impossible." Forcing a laugh, he tossed back the rest of his wine.

"Still, it is clear you have worked hard at it." Her expression was both admiring and sympathetic. "I knew more than one soldier who simply...gave up after a loss such as yours. Poor Private Miller became so despondent he put a pistol to his head. A terrible pity, for he was otherwise quite healthy—and so young." She sighed sadly.

"Won't say I wasn't tempted to do the same early on," he startled himself by confessing, as it was something he'd never told a soul. "If it weren't for Pete and Jack—Lord Foxhaven now—I likely would've. They pulled me through the worst of it."

"I'm happy they were there for you," she said softly, the sympathy in her eyes deepening to something almost like pain.

Harry refilled his glass, glad of an excuse to look away. He was well on his way to becoming maudlin—not at all what he'd intended for tonight. As the soup was brought in, he reverted to their previous topic.

"As there are doubtless more balls ahead of us, perhaps we should devise a strategy that will get us both out of dancing."

To his relief, the pity left her expression. "I'd be quite relieved if we could come up with an acceptable ruse that will not offend our hosts. What do you suggest?"

"I generally use the card room as a refuge if one is provided, but that would leave you on your own—unless you'd care to join me there?"

Xena regarded him uncertainly. "Ladies don't, do they?"

"Not that I've noticed, but are you so very concerned with observing the proprieties? You never used to be."

Instead of responding, she took a hasty spoonful of soup, a faint flush creeping up her throat.

Harry pressed his advantage, leaning in a bit closer. "We could always look for an unused room or corner and get up a game on our own, well away from prying eyes. 'Twas a skill we both excelled at, once upon a time."

Though she pinkened further, she now met his gaze squarely. "I presume you are not referring to cards now? Though that might solve the problem of dancing, I should think it would create others. I'd not wish to risk embarrassing or insulting our hosts, should we be discovered—particularly the Foxhavens, as he is such a close friend."

"Jack's in no position to object after a certain story I heard on my return from Vienna," Harry said with a chuckle, remembering the tale of Jack and Nessa inadvertently displaying themselves *in flagrante* at a prominent ball. "Besides, he was the one who—" He broke off with a cough. No, Xena did *not* need to know what Jack had suggested earlier. Not yet, at any rate. "Ah, well, I suppose we needn't decide until the problem next arises, eh?"

He refilled his glass—it was somehow empty again—and planned his next assault on Xena's defenses, which he was almost certain were starting to crumble.

CHAPTER SIXTEEN

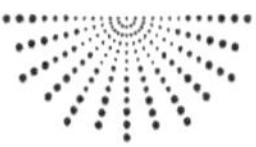

UNSETTLED BY HARRY'S INNUENDOES—OR, RATHER, BY HER BODY'S response to them—Xena finished her soup in silence. Harry did the same, though his was accompanied by a deal more wine. Already he'd lowered the level of the initially full decanter well past the halfway point.

A fresh decanter of white wine was brought out with the fish course and Harry proceeded to make heavy inroads into that as well, while asking a few more questions about her home and habits in Yorkshire. Xena limited herself to a single glass, reasoning that she'd best keep her head clear tonight if Harry was determined to drink enough to impair his judgment.

When the pheasant was served, Harry again shifted topics. "I know you don't much care for compliments, but I can't help noticing what a very fine string of pearls you are wearing. I suppose new jewelry was necessary for your entree into Society, as well as dresses?"

He'd already seemed curious—even suspicious—about the new gowns she'd worn this week. And not completely without cause, as it turned out. Unlike the dresses, however, the pearls she could explain without blushing.

"They were my mother's. My father presented me with what little jewelry had been hers on my sixteenth birthday. As you might imagine, I had no occasion to wear it on the Peninsula, so left it in Yorkshire."

"Ah. I presume their sentimental value prevents you attempting to sell them as you've done with your father's artifacts?"

Though in fact the thought had once crossed her mind after her initial lack of success at the latter, she nodded. "I have little else to remember her by."

"Yes, I recall you lost her at an early age, while in India. I... remember everything you've ever told me about yourself, Xena. It is why I am now striving to fill in a few details of these past few years."

Had she misjudged him? Was it possible that, instead of a mercenary or suspicious motive, his curiosity was sparked by a gentler impulse? Not for the first time, she wondered whether Yamini was right and that she was doing both Harry and Theo a disservice by keeping them ignorant of each other.

She had not exaggerated when telling Yamini about his drinking, however, for he'd nearly emptied the second decanter now.

"What say you we have the sweetmeats served in the library, where we can sit at our ease?" he suggested as the last course was cleared away.

Though his unusual mood tonight made her a bit uneasy, Xena offered no objection. Perhaps it would be as well if no servants were at hand to hear whatever he might say next, as Harry seemed well on his way to becoming drunker than she had ever seen him. Likely he'd begun while at his club earlier.

He escorted her up to the first floor, the footman following with a tray of confections. As soon as the servant left, Harry closed the library door. "Private, as I said."

Smiling seductively over his shoulder, he again poured two glasses of port, carrying them both in one hand to where she stood near the fire. "This is better, is it not?"

"I...ah...yes." To her disgust, her voice came out higher than she intended. She was a woman grown and a mother, not some green girl to be flustered by a man's attentions—especially a man she happened to be married to!

"I'm glad you agree." Setting both glasses on a low table, he lightly touched her cheek. "For a while, I feared you had completely lost your thirst for new and exciting experiences."

Her heart accelerating in spite of herself, Xena swallowed. "Perhaps not...not completely," she whispered. The longing she'd felt earlier that evening returned, stronger than ever. In vain she tried to remind herself that she mustn't give in. Harry was clearly drunk—he'd not be saying these things otherwise.

He leaned in closer. "I wouldn't have thought it possible for you to become even more intoxicating than I remembered, Xena, but you most assuredly have."

Feeling oddly intoxicated herself, though she'd drunk but little, she swayed toward him. Gently, so gently, he touched his lips to hers, just as he had the first time they'd ever kissed...and now, as then, she was nearly overwhelmed by the riot of sensation that assailed her. This, *this* was why she had become so addicted to Harry all those years ago. It was an addiction she'd thought long cured...but she'd been wrong.

For a long moment she clung to him, reveling in the spiraling pleasure she'd thought never to feel again. But as he pulled her tighter against him, a tiny thread of sanity intruded. Striving desperately to calm her racing pulse, her desperate longing for more, she leaned away. "I...I can't."

"Can't you, Xena? We are husband and wife, you know." The passionate yearning in his expression was tinged with a sadness that tempted her on a whole different level.

"I know. But—" The truth about Theo hovered on her lips. No! This was *not* the time for such a confession. He'd had far too much to drink and her own judgment seemed nearly as questionable as his at the moment.

He seemed to sense her decision, for the sadness in his hazel eyes increased. "I'd rather hoped we could put an end to pretense tonight."

"To—?"

"I know, Xena. I know about your visits to Rundel Street and who you've been seeing there."

With a gasp, Xena's hand flew to her throat. Harry already *knew* about Theo? How? Had Lord Peter broken his promise after all?

"I…I'm so sorry, Harry. I never should have—"

He released her then, almost pushing her away. "Never should have what? Lied to me?" His voice turned harsh but there was still more of pain than anger in his eyes.

Miserably, she nodded. "Please, let me explain," she began again, but he swung away from her.

"No need. I'd as soon not hear the sordid details of exactly what favors you've been granting Wellington in return for the money he's been lavishing on you. Give you good night, madam wife." Turning on his heel, he stalked out of the room, slamming the door shut behind him.

Harry stormed out of the house without hat, overcoat, or any idea where he was going. His only thought was to put as much distance between himself and Xena as possible.

For a few delicious moments it had seemed they were close to recapturing the passion they'd once shared, the affection that had existed between them. Then, when he'd almost convinced himself he'd been mistaken in his suspicions, she'd confirmed them—had *admitted* to carrying on an affair with Wellington and lying about it.

Turning a corner, he staggered slightly. Perhaps sharing that second bottle with Jack at the club had been a mistake—especially since Jack had barely touched it. Between that and the wine at dinner, he was drunker than he'd been in over a fortnight—because he'd felt the need for a bit of liquid courage to bolster his attempt to storm the citadel that was Xena.

Not that it had helped. A more spectacular failure he could scarcely imagine. It appeared that even his most practiced overtures couldn't hold a candle to Wellington's. Was she even now laughing at his pitiful attempt at seduction? He doubted she scoffed when *he* complimented her….

Still with no clear destination in mind, he quickened his steps, trying to outpace his humiliation.

When Xena had last undermined his confidence, he fuzzily recalled, the Saint had successfully restored it. He might as well try that same solution tonight…and he knew precisely which target would serve his purpose best. With a grim smile, he directed his steps toward Hyde Park Corner and Apsley House, Wellington's new Town residence.

~

Xena stood stock-still in the middle of the library staring at the door Harry had slammed shut as understanding belatedly dawned.

It appeared Lady Mountheath had been absolutely correct about Harry's belief that she was having an affair with the Duke of Wellington—but completely wrong about his feelings on the matter!

She breathed a sigh of relief, not only that her secret about Theo was still safe, but even more that Harry was by no means *happy* about her supposed dalliance with their former general. A moment later, however, indignation supplanted that relief.

How dared he make such an assumption on so little evidence? Her behavior had been above reproach, whatever Wellington's intentions— she'd done nothing more than dance with the man! True, the Duke had indirectly paid for her newest, most expensive dresses, but she had traded no "favors" for them. She hadn't even known he was the one buying the artifacts until the night before last.

Had Harry given her a chance to explain, she likely would have told him all about Theo, thinking he already knew. By reacting as she had to that erroneous assumption, Xena had surely given Harry what he would consider proof that his suspicions were correct.

But…so what if she had? she thought defiantly. *Harry* had no right to pass judgment on *her* given his own reputation for promiscuity! Surely a wife had as much right to extra-marital dalliance as her husband.

At any rate, she could see no way to convince him of her fidelity without telling him the truth about Theo after all. *That,* she now had no inclination whatever to do, even if her seeming admission of guilt drove Harry straight into the arms of one or another of his mistresses.

Bitterness rose up in her throat at the thought but she would never willingly abide by the horridly unequal standards of acceptable behavior for women compared to men.

Clinging to that grim vow, Xena headed upstairs to her bedchamber to ponder her options—only to be met by a smiling Gretchen.

"I've laid out your prettiest nightgown, mum, as it seemed likely you might have company tonight." She tittered, a hand over her mouth.

Xena frowned at the maid. "Whatever do you mean, Gretchen? Company?"

"Why, your Mr. Thatcher, of course, who else? Everyone below stairs was abuzz with how famously the two of you was getting on over dinner. Matthew, the footman what served you, told us. 'Course, Mrs. MacKay and the others have said all along as how things were bound to turn out right for you both."

Unfortunately, the servants could not have been more wrong.

Still, Xena was curious. "Why should they think so?"

"Because this here's a lucky house for romance." Gretchen spoke matter-of-factly. "No doubt that's why Lord Peter wanted the two of you to bide here."

Snorting a mirthless laugh, Xena shook her head. "Lucky? Come, Gretchen, you must know that is mere superstition."

The maid shook her head vigorously. "Not a bit of it, mum! Why, Lord Peter and his wife, they married sudden-like after knowing each other barely a week and after just a few days here in this house, they turned out happy as larks. Same for his younger brother, Lord Marcus. Him and his bride was *forced* to marry because of some scandal or other. They was at each other's throats at first, too, from what Millie says. Yet they're happy as anything now, too—and the change happened whilst they was living right here."

"Two instances is scarcely proof," Xena pointed out.

"How 'bout three, then? Lord Edward, another one of their brothers, lived here before his marriage, too, and after. He and his wife scarce knew each other at all—one of them marriages for money, I think—but now they've a little one and so in love it's hardly decent, by all accounts. And Mrs. Walsh, who's been here nigh forever, says there's more what found love in this house in generations past. Mark my words, mum, the luck will work for you and your Mr. Thatcher, too."

Though it was clearly all gammon, Gretchen spoke with such certainty that Xena's mood lightened slightly in spite of herself. Still, she shook her head. "If so, 'twill be a near miracle, I fear. Though our evening may have begun well, it did not end so. Mr. Thatcher left a few minutes ago, and in quite a temper."

"You do tend to be a bit too plain-spoken for your own good, mum, begging your pardon."

Xena's lips twitched. "You are a fine one to talk, Gretchen. But I've ever been one to prefer honesty to polite untruths despite the consequences."

"Yet you won't tell Mr. Thatcher the truth about you and him having a son?"

Ouch. "I will. But only when the time is right. Tonight…was not that time."

Would that time ever come now? First she would have to somehow mend things with Harry—while at the same time making him understand that she'd not tolerate his double standard. If he wished her to remain faithful, he must be willing to pledge the same, something she doubted he would do.

Still, if she could stay awake until his return, she would confront him over the issue this very night. What had she to lose?

On reaching the ornate iron railing surrounding Apsley House, Harry paused to take stock and determine his best way to proceed. It was only then that he noticed the white cuff of his shirt protruding past his coat sleeve, like a beacon in the dark. His high-point collar was likely even more visible.

He supposed his wisest course would be to change clothes before making this undoubtedly risky attempt, but the thought of the long walk to Seven Dials and back in his current unsteady state decided him against it. How difficult could this be, really? It was just another housebreaking—and Wellington surely had it coming. The Duke himself must admit that cuckolding a fellow officer was bad form.

By way of compromise, Harry pulled off his cravat and stuffed it in his pocket, then detached his collar and did the same. Not much he could do about the cuff, as it would require another hand to tuck it into his sleeve. He'd simply keep it as close to his body as possible until he'd gained the inside of the house.

Only one or two windows in the front of the house showed lights, so Wellington was likely still out at some do or other, leaving only servants for Harry to elude—something he was fairly confident he could do despite his narrow shave a week since. Slipping through the open front gate, he went around to the back of the house, keeping to the shadows.

No rear windows had been left conveniently ajar—not surprising, as the night was uncomfortably chilly—but that did not concern him unduly as by now he was nearly as skilled at unlocking windows as doors. Not until he reached the dark window farthest from the lit kitchens did he remember that, in addition to his usual disguise, his housebreaking tools were back in the flat in Seven Dials.

Muttering a curse at his own stupidity—and again regretting that last bottle of wine—he went to work on the window anyway, jiggling the sash to discover its locking mechanism. A simple small drop-bar— easy enough to dislodge with a thin strip of metal slipped between sash and frame...which was among his other tools in Seven Dials. What might he use as an expedient?

Searching through his trouser pockets, he found a pair of his Saint cards left over from a previous caper—a bit of luck, as those were something else he hadn't thought to bring along. Carefully, he jimmied the rectangle of stiff parchment through the crack along the edge of the window, then slid it up until it contacted the locking bar. So far, so good.

Thoroughly absorbed in his task, he nearly forgot his surroundings until a shout from the direction of the kitchens recalled him. He'd been spotted! With a muffled oath, he ducked behind some ornamental bushes and scurried, still crouching, close along the side of the house toward the gate where he'd entered. With any luck, whoever had seen him would be content with having driven off the intruder…

But luck was not with Harry that night, it seemed. He'd barely reached the corner of the great house when more shouts came from behind, then the sounds of hurrying feet. A moment later he heard remarkably military-sounding orders called and remembered something he should have considered sooner—many, if not most, of Wellington's menservants were former soldiers.

As recognition would be nearly as disastrous as capture, Harry broke and ran full-tilt for the gate, making sure to keep his left side out of view from any who might come round the corner before he could make his escape. Running as hard as his inebriated state would allow, he achieved the gate and sprinted off down Constitution Hill along the edge of Green Park, thinking to take a circuitous route East toward Seven Dials.

For a dozen steps he thought he'd been successful in eluding pursuit—then the sound of a shot shattered the night, accompanied by a cry to halt. His heart now fairly in his throat, Harry swerved to the park railing and vaulted it, wishing Green Park boasted more trees. Perhaps if he cut straight across and back up to Piccadilly…? But already it was too late. From the corner of his eye, he saw at least two of those after him veering left to cut off that avenue of retreat.

"Damned soldiers," he panted, swerving back to the right to fling himself over the railing again, now aiming for St. James's Park, which offered more chance for concealment.

"Tally-ho!" came a shout from behind. "I've spotted 'im, men! After me!"

By now Harry's right side felt as though seized by a large claw. Drawing breath grew more and more painful, but he dared not slacken his pace. Darting into The Mall between the two parks, he dodged and wove through the trees, hoping thereby to confuse his pursuers before hurling himself over the railing into St. James's Park.

The trees here were widely spaced, offering little cover, but he made use of what he could as he approached the lane bisecting the park. On the verge of collapse, Harry whisked behind the next good-sized tree he came to in order to catch his breath and better hear what the ex-soldiers were shouting to each other. It sounded as though none were quite positive where he'd gone. Yet.

By now his exertions combined with the excitement of the chase had gone a long way toward clearing his head. What a complete dolt he'd been! Madness to attempt robbing such a well-guarded house, so ill-equipped and clad for the task and after over-imbibing as he had—the primary cause of that error in judgment. If he were apprehended or even killed, it would serve him right.

Still, they didn't have him yet. Peering cautiously around his tree, he saw six or seven men milling about near where he'd jumped the railings while their apparent leader ordered them to make a methodical search of the park.

"I saw a shadow go over the fence. He's in here somewhere. If we get him and he turns out to be the Saint, think of the reward!"

Thus motivated, the group fanned out to search among the trees. He would certainly be found in moments if he remained where he was, but moving would bring them even quicker. Which was the better option?

A low laugh followed by a feminine giggle a short distance away reminded him that despite the Regent's recent efforts to clean up the Royal Parks, St. James's was still popular with whores and those who partook of their wares. In hopes of duplicating the ruse that had served him so well a week since, Harry scanned the ground near his feet and was rewarded by the sight of several chestnuts within easy reach. Stooping, he snatched one up and hurled it in the direction of the trysting couple—and was rewarded by a shriek.

As he'd hoped, Wellington's servants converged on the sound, giving Harry his chance. Not far ahead was the ornate yellow bridge

Prinny had commissioned for some celebrations two years since. If he could duck behind it, he might have a chance of remaining concealed until the hunters gave up the chase.

On the very thought, he ran as quickly yet as lightly as he could toward the bridge. He was just crossing to its far side when more shots rang out, immediately followed by a searing pain in his side. He'd been hit!

Acting on nearly-forgotten battle instincts, Harry ran a short way up the bridge, then pitched himself off the side away from his pursuers. He hit the frigid water with a splash, then ducked under the scummy surface to swim as far from the bridge as he could manage before his air gave out. When it did, he carefully raised only his mouth and nose above the water for one deep breath, then continued swimming underwater, repeating the process again and again until he reached the far end of the canal, near the Horse Guards.

At that point, he finally dared raise his head far enough to look back and was gratified to see half a dozen men still milling about the foot of the bridge. Though he could not make out words from this distance, they sounded excited and pleased, clearly believing he'd been badly enough wounded to drown. Drawing a shaky sigh of relief, Harry waded through the shallows to a low copse by the bank where he was able to crawl out of the water within the cover it offered.

Though shivering violently by now, Harry forced himself to remain where he was until the men left the park entirely. Every muscle in his body seemed made of heavy stone when he finally forced himself to his feet to go…where?

Seven Dials would likely be his safest refuge and the distance was only slightly more than that to the house on Grosvenor Street but only at the latter could he be assured of a hot bath. In addition, Brewster had some experience at patching minor gunshot wounds, which his must surely be. Numb as he was from the icy water of the canal, he scarcely felt it now, especially in comparison to his aching legs and feet.

After traversing a few hundred yards, however, the burning in his side returned, a streak of fire in the otherwise frozen block that was his body. Though the distance was less than a mile, it took Harry the better part of an hour to reach the servants' entrance of the Grosvenor Street house, by which time he was in considerable pain.

He unlocked the door as quietly as he could, peering down into the kitchen as he passed. As it was near midnight, only a single scullery maid was still there, putting away the last of the dinner pots and pans. Tiptoeing was quite beyond him but she was luckily making enough of a clatter to cover his clumsy footsteps. Availing himself of the back servant staircase, he made his weary, shivering way to the second story.

CHAPTER SEVENTEEN

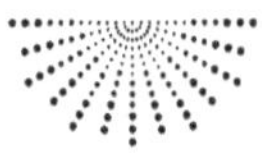

A THUD FROM OUT IN THE HALLWAY JERKED XENA AWAKE. SHE'D FALLEN into a doze while reading in the chair near her bed, awaiting Harry's return. Judging by how little remained of the candle burning on the table next to her, she must have slept an hour or more. Rubbing the sleep from her eyes, she pulled her wrapper more tightly around her and hurried to fling open her door.

Harry was still in the hallway, leaning heavily against his door as he groped for the handle. He appeared even drunker than when he'd left, but she was determined to speak with him nonetheless, for fear she might lose her resolve by morning.

"Now you are home, there are a few things we must—"

She broke off, startled. "Goodness, Harry, you are soaking wet! What on earth happened to you?"

He glanced down at his dripping clothes. "Tripped. Fell into horse trough," he mumbled. "Hot bath'll help." As he reached again for the handle of his chamber door, a violent shudder shook his frame.

"Yes, and without delay, I should think." Stepping to his side, Xena opened the door for him. "Have a bath drawn at once," she instructed his startled valet. "And extra blankets brought up, as well."

Brewster glanced at Harry, who nodded, apparently shivering too much now to form words. The man disappeared.

"Now, we must get you out of those wet things at once, or you will certainly catch a chill." Xena spoke matter-of-factly, tamping down her curiosity…and worry. "Here, let me help you," she added impatiently when Harry fumbled ineffectually with the buttons of his coat.

Quickly, she undid the buttons herself and stripped off his sopping coat, and waistcoat, then gasped at sight of his shirt, stained crimson along one side. "You are bleeding!"

Not waiting for him to force an answer through his chattering teeth, she gently tugged the shirt off over his head, then bent to examine the wound. Relief replaced the horror that had initially swept through her, more intense than any she'd felt in any battle surgery, on finding it less critical than she'd feared. Her curiosity intensified, however.

"Do not try to tell me a fall caused this, for I know a bullet wound when I see one, Harry, better than most. What really happened?"

He blinked a few times as though having difficulty bringing her face into focus. "C-c-caught a fellow cheating at cards," he managed after a moment. "We fought and he grazed me. J-j-just a scratch, I think."

"I will be the judge of that." Already, she was gently exploring the area with her fingertips. "The bullet is still lodged, but barely below the skin. You were fortunate it did not go deeper, though you appear to have lost a lot of blood."

Brewster returned then, his arms piled with blankets. Behind him were two footmen, one carrying a large copper bathing tub and the other two steaming kettles.

"That was very quick," Xena commended them. "Thank you."

"Water was still hot from the washing up." The valet motioned the footmen to set up and begin filling the bath while he fetched the water pitcher from the dressing table. "Still, 'twill take a few more trips before— What—? How—?" He'd seen Harry's wound.

"Your master has been shot," Xena confirmed. "I don't suppose any forceps are available in this house?"

Again, Brewster looked to Harry for an answer and again his master was no help.

"No matter." Xena spoke briskly, as though addressing orderlies back on the battlefield. "Sugar tongs should do for this. Bring them up with the next pair of kettles."

"Aye, mum. Right away, mum." With respectful bows, the three men scurried back out.

Picking up Harry's ruined shirt, Xena tore a wide strip from the bottom. "Let's get this cleaned up, shall we?"

She folded the cloth, dipped it into the tub, then gently laid it against his side. He winced, tensing, then slowly relaxed, his eyes beginning to drift closed.

"No, you mustn't sleep, not yet. You're half frozen still. Once we've warmed you up you can go to bed, but not before."

After a moment, she decided the bullet hole in his side was clean enough and turned her attention to pulling off first his boots, then his breeches.

Harry had a vague feeling he shouldn't allow Xena to undress him… that he had some reason to be upset with her…but could not at the moment recall what that reason was. As she methodically stripped his sodden nether garments from him, he again felt a pleasant lassitude overtaking his senses.

"Ah, good," she startled him by exclaiming. "Yes, these should do."

Harry was dimly aware of several people moving about the room, pouring kettle after kettle into the copper tub. Then Xena put a firm hand on his shoulder.

"This will likely hurt a bit, but I promise to be quick," she said. He felt a sudden, sharp pain, and then it was gone. "There. The bullet is out. Now, let's get you into this bath. Gentlemen, if you can assist me? I fear he hasn't the strength to do this under his own power."

Hands, some more gentle than others, grasped him about his knees, thighs and chest and then the warmth of the bath enveloped him— painful at first, as it thawed his extremities, then heavenly as the warmth penetrated to his very core. His eyes drifted shut with the sheer bliss of it. When he opened them, only Xena remained in the room and the water was merely tepid.

"Did I—?"

"Only for a few minutes," she assured him. "Not to worry, I wouldn't have let you drown—much as you deserve such a fate after behaving so foolishly."

She didn't know the half of it! His mind now noticeably less fuzzy than it had been at first, memory of the evening's events—all of them —came flooding back…along with the realization that he was completely naked. At his instinctive movement to cover himself, Xena's lips quirked up.

"It's a bit late for that, Harry. Remember that I've seen quite a lot of male bodies before this, in surgery…and I've seen you thus before as well, though it's been quite some time. Would you prefer I turn my back while you get up and dry off, or will you need my assistance?"

In answer, Harry struggled to his feet with some difficulty, turning half away from her. "There. Now where's the blasted drying cloth?"

Still smirking, Xena turned her back and handed it over his shoulder. He took it, still feeling absurdly vulnerable and more foolish than ever.

"I thank you for your assistance but as you can see, I am fine now."

"Not quite," she retorted. "I still need to bandage your wound, but you may put something on first, if you wish, so long as you do not cover it."

He glanced down to see the long bullet graze still oozing blood, though slowly. Muttering under his breath, Harry wrapped the damp drying cloth around his waist before turning to face Xena. "You're enjoying this far too much, you know."

"No doubt I shall pay for it later," she said lightly. "Now, hold this against your side."

While he pressed a thick pad to the wound, she deftly wound long strips of cloth around his body, binding the pad in place.

"You'll likely be sore for a few days, but if you don't attempt anything too active you should heal well enough. If it becomes at all inflamed, however, you must let me know."

"I will. Thank you," he said again. Then, as she turned to the dressing room door to go back to her own room, he burst out, "Xena, *are* you having an affair with Wellington?"

She spun to face him. "Of course not," she snapped, but then her eyes narrowed. "But what if I were? *You* are scarcely in a position to censure me, given all the lurid tales of your own indiscretions I've heard this week. If you expect fidelity from me, Harry, you had best be prepared to promise the same. Sleep on that, if you will."

So saying, she turned back around and disappeared into the dressing room, closing first his door, then hers behind her.

Harry gazed after her, stunned, before a slow smile curved his lips. *That* was the Xena he remembered so well—fiery, untamable...and brutally honest. If the Xena of old were under Wellington's protection, she almost certainly would have thrown it in his face.

But then he recalled her reaction—stricken, even apologetic—when he'd mentioned her visits to Rundel Street earlier. Did that mean she was carrying on a dalliance with someone *other* than Wellington? He took two steps toward the dressing room door before a wave of weariness washed over him.

Perhaps tomorrow would be soon enough for more questions.

Xena's first impulse on rising the next morning was to check on Harry, to make certain his condition had not worsened in the night. Pulling on her wrapper, her hand was on the handle of the dressing room door before she realized it would be unwise to wake him, as rest would help him to heal more quickly. Still, she was unwilling to go downstairs, where she would be unable to hear any sounds from next door, so requested a tray in her room.

During the dark watches of the night, the dreadful sight of Harry covered in blood had repeatedly recurred, disturbing her sleep with thoughts of what could have happened had his wound been more serious. Thus, it was increasingly difficult to restrain herself from popping into his chamber to assure herself he was merely asleep.

Finally giving into temptation, Xena crept through both dressing room doors as quietly as possible. On finding him sleeping peacefully, his breathing slow and even, she was startled and dismayed by the rush of relief she felt. When had he come to mean so much to her?

Reminded of the similar anxiety she'd felt during Theo's bout of scarlet fever the previous year, she realized this was a perfect opportunity to see her son again without arousing Harry's suspicions. After cautioning Brewster to let Harry sleep as long as possible and to discourage him from too much activity when he finally awakened, she called for the carriage.

As it went along, she several times glanced behind her, wondering whether Harry might still be having her followed. She noticed no one suspicious but the very idea sparked a renewal of the indignation she'd felt last night. They still had quite a bit more to discuss once he was recovered.

On her return to Grosvenor Street two hours later, she immediately inquired after Harry only to be told he had gone out half an hour before. Disgruntled at having missed him, Xena asked to have tea brought to the drawing room, where she sat down at the desk to sort through a few more invitations. She'd scarcely begun, however, when the young butler, Chambers, appeared in the doorway.

"Lady Foxhaven and Lady Peter Northrup to see you," he announced.

Welcoming the interruption, Xena rose with alacrity to greet them. "How nice to see you again, Lady Peter."

"Sarah, remember? And I've brought someone who very much wished to meet you—Nessa, Lady Foxhaven."

The newcomer took Xena's hand, her brown eyes warm. "As your husband and mine are such close friends, Mrs. Thatcher, it is my hope we might become so as well—particularly as, from what Sarah tells me, you are likely dealing with some of the same challenges I faced in the early days of my marriage."

Xena's interest quickened. "Sit down, do," she said, ringing for more tea. "To what challenges do you refer, Lady Foxhaven?"

"Nessa, please. Perhaps I should begin by telling you that I first met

Jack, Lord Foxhaven, at a masquerade—one I should never have been attending in the first place, but I was simply dying for some excitement after the dull life I'd led to that point."

She laughed. "By marrying Jack, however, I got rather more than I'd bargained for. He had every bit as rakish a reputation as your Harry, whereas I'd lived so sheltered I was quite taken aback by evidence of his former, er, activities. Having spent time in army camps, you are doubtless more difficult to shock, but I'm sure gossip can be hurtful all the same."

Xena was by no means convinced Harry's rakish days were all behind him, but did not say so. "Er, yes, I suppose it can. I take it Lord Foxhaven mended his ways after he married you?"

"He did, though I confess I doubted for a while—mainly due to the backbiting of a former, ah, flame or two. That led to a few misunderstandings early on, but once we got those sorted our marriage became an exceedingly happy one. He has turned out the best father to our son I could have imagined and seems as eager as I that this next one might be a girl." She patted her middle confidingly.

"Oh! I hadn't realized—"

"No, we've made no announcement as yet, but we are both quite excited—though already I find sleeping more difficult than usual. Which reminds me, did either of you hear shots fired last night?"

The other two shook their heads, though Xena's interest was caught. "When would that have been?" she asked.

"Near midnight, I should say. I'd gone to bed early, still tired from traveling, and they woke me. Jack thought they might have come from Green Park or even Hyde Park Corner."

"A duel, perhaps?" Sarah suggested. "Or someone defending himself against footpads?"

Nessa shuddered delicately. "I don't like to think of them so close to Mayfair, but I hear that unsavory sorts frequent the parks at night."

Xena said nothing, remembering the bullet she'd taken from Harry's side last night. He'd said it happened in a fight—a duel?—over cards, but she was aware of no gaming establishments near Hyde Park. She would insist upon more details when she spoke with him next.

The conversation moved on to more general topics then and Xena was happy to find neither of her new acquaintances seemed prone to gossip. By the time the two women left, she felt she could indeed become close friends with both of them…not that she planned to remain in London after fulfilling her bargain with Lord Peter.

January would no doubt see her returning to Yorkshire—a strangely dreary thought.

After sleeping well into the afternoon and partaking of a hearty, belated breakfast, Harry felt very nearly himself again. On learning that Xena had gone out, he waved away Brewster's protests and headed to Tattersall's, where he'd yesterday agreed to offer his input on a pair of carriage horses Jack was considering. It would be unwise, he reasoned, to go into hiding after last night's incident and perhaps invite suspicion.

He and Jack stopped by the club afterward but even when they were joined by other old army comrades, Harry limited himself to a single pint of ale. Hoping for another evening at home with Xena so that he could make another attempt to learn her secrets, he returned to Grosvenor Street in good time for dinner only to learn they were committed elsewhere.

"Would you rather we cry off again?" she asked when he frowned at hearing he'd barely have time to change before leaving. "How are you feeling, by the bye?"

"Well enough, but I'd as lief be spared cavorting about a ballroom just yet."

"It's only dinner at Lord and Lady Plumfield's. We were invited to Lady Tinsdale's ball tonight as well, but given your recent injury I assumed we would give that a miss. Should we call in a proper physician? If you still—"

"No," he said quickly. He'd prefer no one else learn of his injury, as he had no way of substantiating the tale he'd given Xena last night should awkward questions be asked. "That is, I can't imagine any London physician giving me better care than you, my dear."

She continued to regard him for a long moment, brows now skeptically raised. "Very well. But you must tell me at once if your side grows warm or more painful."

"Of course. I, ah, suppose I'd best go change."

As Brewster helped him into his evening clothes, Harry chafed at the delay before he could question Xena further about her contradictory words and behavior last night. After all but admitting she was seeing Wellington on the side, she'd later denied it, then essentially threatened to do so anyway unless *Harry* promised to be faithful. What did it all mean?

As it happened, he'd not been with another women since learning Xena still lived—nor, oddly, had any particular desire to do so. Still, it was one thing to parrot the words in a wedding ceremony and another to give Xena his word now, years later. If he did so, he'd feel honor-bound to keep it—but could he? Few husbands did, he well knew. Jack and Pete were anomalies, and likely only because they were so recently wed.

Harry was still wrestling with such thoughts when he handed Xena into the carriage for the short ride to Lord and Lady Plumfield's house. Her first words once they were underway, however, effectively drove the matter from his mind.

"Lady Peter brought Lady Foxhaven to call today and she mentioned hearing shots fired last night near Hyde Park Corner. I don't suppose you know anything about that?"

Caught off guard, Harry hesitated, striving to remember just what he'd told Xena last night. "Ah, no, I'm afraid not. The gaming establishment where my, er, incident occurred was well East of here, quite in the opposite direction."

"No matter," she said, though he thought the look she gave him still held a hint of suspicion. "I was simply curious, as you hadn't mentioned where the fight that wounded you took place—nor much else about it. Was it an actual duel?"

"Certainly not a formal one." Relaxing slightly, he began embroidering his story. "Fellow was cheating, as I said, and when I called him on it he challenged me. Everyone around us was keen to see us fight on the spot—I fear most of us had been drinking more than was wise —so we stepped out into the street. Then, instead of waiting for someone to count off paces, the blackguard pulled a pistol and shot without warning. Luckily for me, he was in too great a hurry to make his escape to aim properly. Fired wild and ran for it."

"You'd have been luckier still had he missed entirely," she pointed out. "At least you admit drinking was partially to blame. Let that be a lesson to you in future."

Rather than protest her sermonizing as he would with Pete, he congratulated himself that she seemed to accept his account of last night's events. Unfortunately, his complacency was shattered mere moments later.

"I'll not believe it 'til they actually find his body," Lord Blenny was saying as they entered the parlor where the Plumfields' guests were gathered before dinner. "The fellow is slippery as an eel, everyone knows that."

"Corporal Mainwaring insisted to The Courier he scored a direct hit," Mr. Cheevers countered. "And half a dozen others of Wellington's men claimed he spoke truth. Just because there hasn't been time to dredge the canal, doesn't mean—"

"I hope you're wrong, Papa, and Lord Blenny is right," Miss Cheevers cried, clearly distraught. "'Twould be a great loss to us all if the Saint of Seven Dials were killed."

Her father snorted. "A loss to some of the riffraff in the slums, perhaps, but not to the rest of us. Can't think why you ladies insist on romanticizing the scoundrel."

Harry tensed but before he could think of a way to redirect the topic of conversation, Xena spoke.

"I fear I have not seen this evening's Courier. What happened?"

"The Saint of Seven Dials attempted to burgle the Duke of Wellington's house last night," their hostess, Lady Plumfield, informed her. "Only imagine, how brazen! But some of his servants saw him before he gained entry and gave chase. One of the men claims to have shot him as he fled across the bridge in St. James's Park. He tumbled off into the water and they believe he must have drowned. They searched for some time after but the men found no sign of him. 'Twas dark, of course, but they insist he could not have escaped without their seeing him. The Bow Street Runners are talking of having the canal dredged to confirm it."

"Indeed!" Xena shot a glance at Harry, who felt he did a creditable job of looking only politely interested in the conversation while carefully avoiding her eye. "A friend did mention hearing shots fired in the vicinity of Apsley House late last night."

Lord Blenny hmphed. "Only means Wellington's men chased and fired at the rascal, not that they succeeded in killing him. They'll not get any reward before that's proven."

"If they did not catch him, what makes them believe it was the Saint of Seven Dials?" Xena asked then. "Could it not have been some other housebreaker?"

"Not likely," Mr. Cheevers declared. "According to the article, on returning to the Duke's residence the men examined the window he'd been attempting to force and found one of the Saint's distinctive cards wedged between sash and frame. For myself, I believe we've finally seen the end of that bounder."

His wife and daughter gave twin sniffs into their handkerchiefs.

"I suppose we must hope so." Xena again looked pointedly Harry's way while he focused his attention on the precise fall of his cravat, adjusting it slightly.

Xena was no fool. The details matched far too closely for her to fail drawing the obvious conclusion. All he could do now was put her off as long as possible in hopes that inspiration might come to him before she had opportunity to confront him privately.

The topic of the possible demise of the Saint of Seven Dials continued to dominate conversation during dinner.

Xena could think of only one way to account for the similarities between the newspaper story and Harry's return home at midnight, soaking wet and nursing a bullet wound besides. No wonder he'd seemed uneasy in the carriage earlier when she'd mentioned shots fired near Hyde Park Corner—then spun that elaborate tale about a fictitious duel.

Nor was it difficult to guess why Harry had selected that particular target, given his assumption about the Duke of Wellington and herself. Though a week ago she'd dismissed the idea that Harry could be the Saint, it now appeared confirmed beyond reasonable doubt.

If any additional evidence were needed, the assiduous way in which he avoided speaking or even looking at her during the remainder of the evening must mean he knew quite well that Xena had deduced the truth: incredible, impossible as it seemed, her husband was indeed the notorious Saint of Seven Dials!

The moment they were safely shut into the carriage for the drive back, she rounded on him. "I knew you had accumulated your share of vices over the past seven years, Harry, but I had no idea you had become an arrant fool as well. What on earth were you thinking to attempt robbing Apsley House, of all places, particularly in the state you were in last night?"

Gazing fixedly out the window of the carriage, Harry shrugged. "No idea what you're talking about. Do you seriously believe a one-armed man could be capable of the exploits the Saint of Seven Dials is fabled for? I told you what happened last night. 'Tis scarcely my fault the Saint, whoever he was, managed to get himself killed at nearly the same time."

His words had a rehearsed sound, and no wonder. He'd undoubtedly been practicing them for the past two hours.

"You truly persist in denying you were anywhere near Hyde Park Corner or St. James's Park last night?"

A muscle in his jaw twitched but he still did not look at her. "As I said before, I was well East of Mayfair at that time last night. Guess I know well enough where I was shot. Would you like me to take you there and show you? I can even point out the horse trough I fell into afterward."

The conviction in his voice might have given Xena pause if not for her other bit of evidence.

"What of our first night in Grosvenor Street? I told you I was unable to sleep, but not that I saw you arriving after your supposed evening of gaming. You were dressed in completely different clothing than you'd worn on your departure and out of breath besides."

He swallowed visibly, then gave a mirthless laugh. "Believe what you will, then. If you cannot see the absurdity of my attempting house-breaking or gate-climbing or pocket-picking, handicapped as I am, I know not how to convince you."

Xena glared at him but said nothing else for the remainder of the drive, instead planning her next assault—for she was determined to force a confession from him. Once their cloaks were removed and they'd mounted to the first landing, she turned to him with a smile.

"Would you care for a glass of something in the library before bed?"

Clearly startled, then suspicious, he shook his head. "Though I thank you for the invitation, I'm feeling a bit pulled. Perhaps another night."

Eyes narrowed, Xena followed him up the stairs. Once in her own chamber, she allowed Gretchen to help her change for bed but as soon as her maid had gone, she put on her wrapper and marched through first one dressing room door and then the other.

Harry, already clad in nightshirt and dressing gown, stared at her in surprise, as did his valet, who was in the act of brushing Harry's dinner jacket. "Xena, what—?" Harry began.

"I wish to examine your wound so as to be certain no inflammation is setting in. Brewster, you may go."

Though Harry's brows drew down as though he might counter-mand that dismissal, his man departed without a word.

"As I told you, I feel fine. There's no need—"

"I have reason to believe my medical knowledge is superior to yours, so I will be the judge of that. Come, sit here on the edge of the bed and let me have a look."

Warily, he did as she asked, pulling the folds of his Banyan across his lap in a way that made Xena smile. Had he already forgotten she'd seen him in the altogether only last night?

"If it will help to preserve your modesty, you may arrange your attire in such a way as to expose your injury and little else. I'll even look away while you do so."

Harry's sheepish expression acknowledged her hit, but he still waited until she averted her eyes to adjust his nightwear to accommodate an examination.

Not even attempting to hide her amusement, Xena let her gaze rove about Harry's chamber, alert for any other bit of evidence she might find to assist in forcing an admission from him that he was indeed the Saint of Seven Dials. Not that he was likely to have left anything in plain sight, but—

Her gaze lingered a moment on an object she recognized from their army days, a small wooden clock carved in the shape of an elephant—a gift, he'd once told her, from his grandfather the Earl when he was a boy. The clock was rather more battered now, but still keeping time. On recalling something else about that clock, she took two quick steps toward the fireplace and plucked the clock from the mantel.

"Here!" Harry protested, surging to his feet. "What are you doing?"

Instead of answering, Xena turned the clock over and pressed the cunningly hidden catch on the bottom to expose the hollow cavity within—a cavity formerly used to conceal small articles of a valuable or incriminating nature.

Such as the handful of cards residing there now—cards etched with a numeral seven topped by a gold-ink halo.

CHAPTER EIGHTEEN

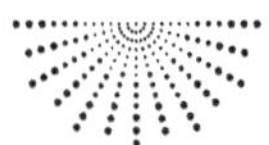

HARRY STEPPED FORWARD IN ALARM BUT BEFORE HE COULD intervene, Xena turned with a triumphant smile, holding one of Harry's Saint cards aloft between her fingers.

"Oho!" she cried. "Do you still protest your innocence?"

Scowling, Harry snatched his momentarily-forgotten dressing gown off the floor and pulled it back on. "I should have known better than to believe you came here out of concern for my health. It appears your intent was quite the opposite."

"Hardly that. I do wish to check on your wound but I'll admit I hoped to persuade you to tell me the truth in the process. Then I saw the clock and recalled how we used to hide…things…inside it." Primarily secret missives from Xena herself, once their relationship had progressed to the point of assignations.

"Now," she continued, "suppose you tell me the whole story while I have a peep beneath those bandages?"

Finally admitting defeat, he nodded. "Very well, I'll tell you. But there's little point now in worrying about this bullet hole festering. Once the world knows the truth I'll be swinging at the end of a rope anyway."

Xena blinked. "The world—? Why should anyone else guess you are the Saint?"

"There is a sizable reward for my arrest, you know," he pointed out. "Far more money than you're like to receive from the sale of your father's trinkets, or even from whatever gallant is buying you dresses from Madame Fanchot's. My execution would also secure you permanent freedom from the inconvenience of a husband."

"I am not a monster, Harry," she snapped. "No matter how foolishly you have behaved, do you really imagine I would turn in my own husband for money?" Her vehemence implied he'd not only startled but offended her—a hopeful sign.

"Even were I so inclined," she continued after a moment, "which I most certainly am *not*, it would do me little good. Do you not realize that if you are exposed as the Saint, my property will be forfeit along with yours?"

Confused, Harry stared at her. "What the devil do you mean? I've no property to forfeit. And what has yours to do with it?"

"In the eyes of the law, my property became yours upon our marriage," she explained, clearly surprised he would not know that. "Indeed, I have wondered why you never attempted to put in a claim after you returned from Spain if you truly believed me dead."

"Never even occurred to me," he admitted truthfully. "Was never much of a legal scholar, you know, unlike you, always crusading about such things. Shame, really. If I'd known, we might both have discovered our error years ago."

Xena blinked at his words, then swallowed. "Yes. Yes, I suppose we would have."

She couldn't quite keep the wistfulness from her voice, realizing the fault was at least as much hers. Had she not been too stubborn to write to him directly after returning to England, he would have learned at once that she had not died. She likely would have been informed he'd survived Salamanca early on, as well. Harry could have met Theo while he was still a toddler. They might have become a real family...

"Now, do let me examine your wound, as I suggested," Xena said with forced briskness. There was no point dwelling on such regrets now.

Resuming his place on the edge of the bed, Harry lifted his Banyan and nightshirt to expose the bandages still wrapped around his body, though Xena noticed he was careful to keep his lap and left shoulder discreetly covered.

"Very well. Take a look, if you must."

"Thank you." Carefully, she unwound the bindings and lifted the cloth pad covering his wound. Already the shallow gash was scabbing over and the edges of the deeper cut where she'd removed the bullet were clean. "Hm. It looks well enough so far, though it will be another day or two before the danger of infection is past. And now, if you don't mind, I should very much like to hear the story of how you evaded General Wellington's battle-trained servants last night."

As she replaced the pad with another, cleaner one and retied the strips holding it in place, Harry began his tale from the point where he was spotted behind Apsley House, then described his pursuit through two parks before finally being shot from behind.

"Luckily for me, I learned to swim quite well underwater as a lad. Never expected to need that particular skill again, but it stood me in good stead last night."

Rapt, Xena listened in silence to every word, still absorbing the remarkable fact that Harry, *her Harry*, was the fabled Saint of Seven Dials! Yes, she'd suspected it immediately on hearing the details of the legendary thief's near-demise, but she hadn't quite *believed* it. It seemed so completely unlikely, given the sort of man he'd become.

Over the past week she'd begun to doubt anything remained of the brash young lieutenant she'd once known. Full of grandiose plans for fame and fortune, if not as a soldier, then after the war, he'd borne little resemblance to the drunken gamester she'd recently observed. Now, hearing Harry tell of swimming for his life—with but one arm!—in freezing water, while already wounded... Yes, this was indeed the man she remembered.

As he finished his tale, she tied off his bandage, then moved to the chair by the bed. "Why did you become the Saint of Seven Dials to begin with? And how long ago?"

"I've only been playing the Saint a few weeks, so most of the stories you've heard about his exploits don't pertain to me, I'm afraid." He gave a self-deprecating shrug.

"Do you mean there were others before you?" she asked in surprise.

He nodded. "At least four, to my knowledge. Er, not at liberty to say who, of course."

"No, I suppose not." She regarded him thoughtfully for a moment. "And now yet another will have to take up the mantle, for your house-breaking days are surely behind you after an incident such as this."

"What? No such thing!" he protested, frowning. "Think you this was my first narrow escape? Far from it, though I admit it's the first where I've taken a bullet."

Xena raised an eyebrow. "I assume you hadn't attempted any other burglaries while so deep in your cups as you were last night?"

"Perhaps not," he admitted rather sheepishly. "But—"

"You cannot continue, Harry," she insisted. "Aside from the risk to you, have I not explained that my property, my home—" *and Theo's* "—would be forfeit if you should be caught?"

"I won't be caught." He sounded far more certain than he could possibly be. "It's true I went off half-cocked last night but I paid the price and learned my lesson. Won't do that again. But becoming the Saint has been the best thing that's happened to me since I returned from Spain, maimed."

"The best— What do you mean?"

"Sorry, should have said the best thing until finding you were still alive."

She grimaced. "Pray don't. You know I've never been one to seek compliments—especially empty ones."

"Nor sincere ones, either. Yes, I remember." He leaned forward to put a hand over hers where it rested on the arm of the chair. "Xena, please try to understand. This—becoming the Saint, I mean—is one of the few useful things I've done since leaving the army. It has allowed me to believe I might still make a mark in the world, do some good, despite..." He glanced toward his left shoulder.

Her heart twisted within her as she suddenly understood that the loss of his arm had damaged his spirit far more than his body, transforming Harry from that lighthearted, devil-may-care soldier into the cynical, embittered wastrel he'd become since the war. If playing the part of a modern-day Robin Hood was the way to restoring that spirit she'd so admired—yes, perhaps even loved—how could she not support him continuing?

Xena gave a decisive nod. "Very well. If it means so very much to you, I suppose you must carry on once you are recovered enough—on one condition. I will accompany you on all future forays, in order to make absolutely certain you are not captured."

Harry snatched back his hand to stare at her in outrage. "Accompany me? Are you mad?"

Xena raised her brows. "Not at all. Does it not make perfect sense that I should wish to have a hand in protecting my own property from seizure?"

"You can safely leave that to me," Harry informed her. "I refuse to chance your arrest or injury. The risk should be mine alone."

"But it isn't, don't you see?" She leaned forward persuasively, reminding him of how they used to fence with words as well as swords. "As long as you act as the Saint, my home, my future, is also at risk. Surely I should be allowed to assist in safeguarding it?"

"What makes you think I'll even tell you when I'm planning to make my next attempt? You can't—"

"Have you followed constantly, as you have apparently done with me?" she asked sweetly, making him frown. "Oh, but I can—and will. Even if it means discovering *other* activities of yours of which you might prefer I remain in ignorance. If necessary, I can even don male garb and follow you right into your gaming hells. You yourself mistook me for a man, once upon a time."

"Only for a moment," he snapped. "And that was before you'd become quite so—" He broke off but cast a glance over her body. That she caught his meaning was clear by the frowning awareness in her expression.

Abruptly, she stood. "I propose we both sleep on the idea for a night or two, as you are in no shape just yet to be leaping fences or clambering through windows. And now, Saint Harry, I give you good night."

With a mocking curtsey, she retreated through the dressing room, leaving him to stare after her, dumbfounded. *Saint Harry?* Did she think this a joke?

No, not a joke, he realized. An opportunity. A chance for her to recapture the excitement her life had apparently lacked these past few years.

He hadn't missed the light in her eyes, the smile she couldn't quite suppress, both while he'd recounted last night's adventure and while arguing her case. It was an expression he'd recognized from the Xena he'd known of old, with her insatiable thirst for adventure. She'd also been exceedingly stubborn, which suggested she would be difficult to dissuade from this dangerous course—though of course he must do so anyway.

Tired as he was, Harry spent some time rehearsing various arguments he might use on Xena before finally falling asleep. As he drifted off, however, what he found himself remembering was the unmistakeable respect in Xena's eyes as he'd told her about his escape—a respect he hadn't won from her since the Peninsula. His spirits lighter than they'd been in a very long time, he fell asleep with a smile on his face.

That a night's sleep had dimmed Xena's enthusiasm for becoming the Saint's "assistant" not at all was apparent at breakfast the next day.

"Good morning," she greeted Harry smilingly when he joined her downstairs. "I trust you slept well?"

He regarded her suspiciously. "Well enough, considering…everything. You seem unusually cheerful this morning."

"Because I've come to realize that the future may be full of exciting possibilities after all. Coffee?" She gestured to a footman to fill his cup.

"So you're quite looking forward to more balls and such, are you?" he asked casually, spreading butter on a piece of toast.

"Not balls, particularly. In fact, as neither of us is fond of dancing, I don't believe we'll attend any more of those. Another visit to the theatre might be nice, or perhaps a musicale. However, I referred to more...private activities."

Harry choked on his first sip of coffee and the footman disappeared as if by magic. "You...what?"

Still smiling, Xena continued. "It occurs to me that the strategy you yourself suggested two nights since might be the perfect way to divert all suspicion should we wish to, ah, disappear from the social scene occasionally. Perfect, because it will seem to confirm what most of the ton wishes to believe of us anyway."

"Oh. Then you didn't actually mean...?" He hadn't *really* believed she'd meant what she'd first implied, but still felt a pang of disappointment.

She shrugged. "What matters is what Society thinks we are up to, not whether they are correct or not. They wish to portray us as a pair of calf-eyed newlyweds, so why do we not let them?"

"So that you can pursue that ridiculous plan you mentioned last night?"

Taking a dainty bite of shirred egg, she nodded.

"I already told you I won't allow it," he growled.

She swallowed, then dabbed the corner of her mouth with a napkin. "Yes, you did. As if that might affect my decision. It does not. But come, you've barely touched your breakfast."

"Xena, I'm warning you..."

"And I thank you for your concern. Consider your warning taken under advisement."

With a last glare, he gave up the argument for the moment and devoted himself to his meal, furiously trying to come up with an argument—any argument—that might sway her.

The moment he finished eating, however, she immediately began asking question after question about his activities as the Saint of Seven Dials—most of which he grudgingly answered.

"So you were actually living right in the heart of Seven Dials before coming here to Grosvenor Street? Wasn't that terribly dangerous?"

"Less for me than it would be for you," he replied dampeningly, for there was more of eagerness than worry in her eyes. "A former Saint has a flat there and gave me the use of it, along with the guidance of his original assistant."

Her face fell. "Oh. Then…you already have an accomplice?"

"Flute doesn't help me steal, any more than he did for L— for the previous Saints. But he is thoroughly familiar with Seven Dials, to include which denizens are most in need of—and deserving of—the Saint's assistance. He's also suggested a few likely targets, along with sharing which methods the previous Saints found most successful."

"So this…Flute? He essentially trained you to become the Saint? At whose behest? You can't have simply run across him by chance."

Harry grimaced. It was far too easy to slip in talking to Xena. Already he'd accidentally mentioned Flute by name, then had nearly blurted out Lord Hardwyck's name as well.

"A, er, friend of the last Saint felt I might be a good successor, so arranged to have Flute sent my way."

"Might I meet this Flute? Oh, please, Harry," she pleaded when he immediately shook his head. "I already know about you being the current Saint, so what harm can it do? You can't deny I have the strongest of incentives to keep your secret, as well as those of anyone else connected in the business."

"I'll, ah, have to speak to the last Saint before I'd feel easy doing that. If…that person—" Blast it, he'd nearly said *she*— "feels it would be appropriate, then perhaps it can be arranged."

It would never do for Xena to learn the last Saint had been a woman, or there'd be no dissuading her at all from the dangerous course she seemed so determined to pursue.

Unfortunately, Sarah was delighted at the prospect of bringing Xena into the entire secret when he broached the subject. An hour after breakfast she stopped by, ostensibly to borrow Xena's translation of a particular Greek manuscript they'd discussed on a previous occasion. But the moment Xena went upstairs to fetch the translation, she turned to Harry.

"In truth, Harry, I came to see you, on Peter's behalf as well as my own, for we were both frightened to death when we read of the Saint's supposed demise in last night's paper. I can't tell you how relieved I am—and how relieved Peter will be—to know it was not you who was shot after all!"

Harry gave her a wry smile. "It *was* me, as it happens, but I luckily received little more than a scratch. Xena saw me arrive home wet and wounded, however, so when she heard the story yesterday evening, she drew the obvious conclusion."

"Then she knows?"

He nodded. "And has been peppering me with questions ever since. I made the mistake of mentioning Flute and now she wants to meet him, as well. I put her off, of course, saying I'd have to ask the previous Saint—but without mentioning any other names."

"Oh, but of *course* she must know all, Harry, she is your wife!" Sarah exclaimed. "Indeed, I've felt almost underhanded becoming her friend while keeping something so very important from her. Surely you don't believe she would betray you? Or any of us?"

"No, no, of course not. It's just—" He broke off at the sound of Xena's light step on the stairs, with a warning frown at Sarah.

Which she blithely ignored.

"Xena!" Sarah exclaimed the moment she re-entered the drawing room. "Harry tells me you have discovered his big secret. How wonderful!"

Xena stared at her in blank astonishment. "His…you knew? That is —" She sent a questioning glance at Harry, who grimaced and shrugged.

Sarah laughed gaily. "Of course I knew! 'Twas Peter who suggested Harry take over as Saint, as I only took on the role long enough to prevent my young brother—I believe Harry mentioned him to you as Flute?—from doing so."

Harry watched with a sinking heart as Xena's expression changed from shock to perplexity to pleased comprehension.

"*You* were the last Saint of Seven Dials, Sarah? Truly?" At Sarah's nod, Xena turned an accusatory glance on Harry. "So much for your protestations that a woman cannot so much as *assist* the Saint in his pursuits!"

"I, ah, never said that precisely," he protested, with a wary look at Sarah. "I simply said I'd prefer *you* not do so."

Xena raised one dark eyebrow. "Because I am uniquely less capable than the average woman?"

His huff of exasperation disguised a hint of a laugh. "Of course not. You know very well the reverse is true, particularly if you've kept up your wartime skills. It's just—"

"That you don't wish to share the glory?" she suggested.

"Don't be absurd. That's not it."

"Then—?"

"Blast it, Xena, it's bloody dangerous and I won't risk losing you again so soon after getting you back!"

The words were out before he could stop them—and as great a revelation to himself as to Xena, who looked every bit as astonished as she had upon learning Sarah had played the Saint.

"Harry." Her voice quavered slightly on his name. "I...I didn't think...that is, I didn't realize—"

Abruptly, Sarah stood. "Thank you so much for this translation, Xena. I've just recalled that I'm expected elsewhere, so if you two don't mind, I'll show myself out." With a barely-suppressed grin, she disappeared.

Xena barely noticed Sarah's departure. She was still staring at Harry, wondering if she had perhaps misheard him. His expression, half sheepish, half startled, told her she had not.

She took a step toward him, for his admission required one of her own. "I can't bear the thought of losing you again either, Harry. That's the real reason I want so badly to help you, to make certain you are not caught or killed. Two nights ago you nearly were and knowing how very close I came to never… I'm not willing to risk that. I won't."

"Truly, Xena?" His eyes were beseeching but wary, as though he wanted to believe her but didn't quite dare.

Suddenly shy—a feeling totally alien to her—she nodded. "Truly, Harry."

Swiftly he stood, closing the distance between them to place a gentle hand on her shoulder. "Then…why have we both been so stubborn about admitting it?"

Unable to break away from his mesmerizing gaze, she gave an embarrassed little shrug. "Both too fearful of looking foolish, perhaps?"

"Perhaps." His mouth quirked up in a smile, drawing her gaze from his eyes to his lips.

She put out her tongue to moisten her own, which had gone suddenly dry. With a groan, Harry slid his hand from her shoulder to her back and pulled her against him for a fierce—and achingly welcome—kiss.

Xena did not hesitate this time but returned it wholeheartedly, memories of all the passion they'd once shared flooding back as though it had been only yesterday. As he deepened the kiss, her blood heated, her pulse quickening. She had missed this—missed him!—so much more than she'd allowed herself to acknowledge.

"Harry, I—" she murmured against his lips, but he shook his head slightly.

"No words. No apologies or second thoughts. Not now." And he was kissing her again, as though he were drowning and her lips were his only chance of survival.

Her arms went around him almost of their own volition and she pressed her body tight against his, heedless of the open drawing room door or any servants that might be passing. His hand slid up her back to tangle in the hairs at the nape of her neck, inflaming her senses further.

Suddenly her clothes felt far too confining and his far too bulky between them, separating her from the insistent evidence that he wanted her as desperately as she wanted him. She began tugging at the lapel of Harry's coat, only to have her senses return just far enough to realize she could scarcely disrobe him here in the drawing room.

A low chuckle escaped Harry's throat and he tilted his head to regard her quizzically. "Perhaps not the best venue, eh? I find I could use a nap to aid in my healing. Would you care to join me?"

Silently, she nodded. There were surely a multitude of reasons she should demur, but her body was clamoring too loudly for her to hear them. With a sultry smile that promised all manner of delights, Harry moved his hand from her nape to her waist and guided her out of the drawing room and up the stairs to his bedchamber.

Once there, they could scarcely remove each other's clothing quickly enough. It was as though neither wished for time to reconsider. Harry made short work of the tiny hooks down the front of Xena's day dress while she fumblingly unbuttoned his coat and pushed it from his shoulders. He then went to work on the laces of her light half-corset while she undid the front of his breeches. In moments they were separated only by the thin fabric of his shirt and her chemise.

Seven years ago, in Spain, their clandestine couplings had been by necessity both hurried and mostly clothed. Now, however…

Harry shrugged his shirt off over his head in one fluid motion and Xena untied the top of her chemise so that it slipped down to pool around her feet. Then, bare skin to bare skin, they resumed where they had left off. His mouth again covered hers and now he was able to trace his fingers directly over her curves while she similarly explored his body, so much harder than she remembered, with her hands.

Pressing herself against him with increasing urgency, Xena was dimly aware that she still had another, bigger confession to make, but she was far too aroused to risk spoiling this moment by blurting out that she and Harry had a son. That revelation could surely wait until…after.

Taking two quick steps backward, Harry pulled her onto the bed—another luxury they'd never experienced on the Peninsula. By now Xena was nearly panting with her need for him, but despite his quite-evident eagerness, he took the time to pleasure her almost to the point of release so that when he finally entered her, she climaxed at once.

"Oh, Harry," she breathed as she crested her peak. "I—"

Again, he silenced her with a deep kiss that intensified as he reached his own zenith.

A long, blissful moment later, as her breathing and heartbeat finally began to slow, he tilted his head back to smile at her. "You were saying?"

"I…I've missed this." It was not what she'd nearly said in the heat of passion, but true, nevertheless. "So much more than I realized."

His smile broadened. "As have I. A shame that our mutual pride—or stubbornness, if you will—denied us both a week and more of such pleasure. If you'd care to join me in a real nap now, we can begin making up for lost time afterward."

Now? Should she tell him now? How would he react?

To put off the moment of reckoning a bit longer, she made a show of examining his bandages to make certain their activities had not reopened his wound. Then, still groping for the right words, she glanced up at the small elephant-shaped clock on the mantel—and gasped.

"Why, it's nearly three! Nessa—that is, Lady Foxhaven—will be here for tea in half an hour and I'm hardly in a state to receive her. Oh! Does she also know about—?"

He shook his head, disappointment evident in his eyes—which she took as a compliment. "Not to the best of my knowledge, as Pete and I have had no occasion to bring Jack into the secret."

"I'll certainly not mention it, then."

Reluctantly disentangling herself from him, she scrambled off the bed and scooped up her hastily-discarded gown and underthings. Her confession could wait another hour. "Have your nap and I'll make your excuses."

Dropping a last, quick kiss on his lips, she exited through the dressing room to make herself presentable for callers.

Harry drowsily watched her go, a smile—half pleased, half puzzled—lingering on his lips. His Xena had proved every bit as passionate as he remembered but not at all like a woman in the habit of taking lovers. In fact, if she hadn't all but admitted otherwise, he'd think she'd never been with another man since leaving Spain more than seven years since.

That fantasy pleased him, which was odd in itself. For in his own amorous exploits over those intervening years he'd never fancied despoiling innocents, instead limiting his pursuits to those women with more experience. He'd dallied with his share of lightskirts of the demimonde, of course. But his preference had tended more toward married women prone to straying, as they generally made few demands outside the bedchamber.

Many had been skilled in the arts of love—some exceedingly so—but none had ever affected him as profoundly as Xena. Once he'd rested a bit—for the combined effects of his recent loss of blood and his exertions just now left him surprisingly tired—he very much looked forward to resuming what they'd so pleasantly begun.

And if she *did* have some lover tucked away somewhere in Town, he felt confident he could soon make her forget him. No matter who he was.

CHAPTER NINETEEN

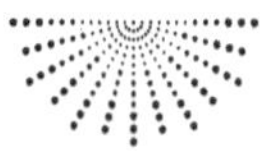

AFTER A QUICK WASH TO REMOVE THE LINGERING TRACES OF lovemaking, Xena hastily rang for Gretchen to help her dress. Though her maid commented on the becoming glow of Xena's complexion, she was apparently too innocent to divine the cause of it.

"It's clear living here agrees with you, mum," was all she said. "While I won't say I don't miss Moorside, I hope you'll be able to stay a good while."

"I rather hope so, too."

Xena smiled at her reflection, feeling an optimism for the future beyond anything she'd experienced since her teens. Not only were she and Harry finally coming to terms, she had new adventures to look forward to in assisting him as the Saint of Seven Dials. All that remained was determining how, exactly, to tell him about Theo. And when.

She reached the drawing room with barely enough time to ring for a tea tray before Lady Foxhaven was announced, along with Mrs. Orrin, a pretty, slightly overblown blonde Xena had not yet met.

"Dear Lady Foxhaven did not think you would mind if I joined her," Mrs. Orrin gushed, her brilliant smile at odds with the calculating way in which she took in every detail of Xena's appearance. "I only just arrived in Town and when I heard that dear Harry's, er, Major

Thatcher's long-lost bride had been resurrected, I simply *had* to meet her at once."

Over Mrs. Orrin's shoulder, Nessa gave Xena an apologetic shrug and mouthed the word, "Sorry," implying that if there had been a polite way for her to avoid bringing the other woman along, she would have done so.

"I'm pleased to meet you, Mrs. Orrin. I take it you've known my husband for some time?"

"Oh, my, yes. One might say we've been rather *intimate* friends, in fact." There was no mistaking her meaning, particularly given the spiteful smile that accompanied her words. "I can't help but wonder how one so very averse to matrimony is managing this discovery that he's had a wife tucked away in the country all these years. One *hopes* it may make him more discreet, if nothing else."

The tea tray arrived then, sparing Xena the necessity of responding before she could compose herself. Fuming inwardly, she requested a third cup and invited both ladies to sit down. Then, trying to ignore poor Nessa's horrified expression, she calmly seated herself opposite them at the tea table and began pouring out for her guests. *Never let an enemy know your weaknesses.*

"Rest assured, Mrs. Orrin, I've already been made well aware of my husband's past poor choices." Xena kept her voice pleasant and detached, as though discussing the weather, despite her anger and humiliation. It helped that by now she'd had a fair bit of practice fending off mean-spirited gossips.

Her unwelcome guest produced a tinkling laugh that grated on Xena's ears. "Past? Our Harry has indeed become more discreet if you believe *that*, Mrs. Thatcher, given the tales I've already heard since returning to Town."

Nessa, reaching for a tea cake, jogged Xena's elbow just as she was in the act of pouring Mrs. Orrin's tea, causing the hot, brown liquid to cascade over the other woman's bright yellow skirts.

"Oh dear, how clumsy of me," Nessa and Xena exclaimed simultaneously and with matching insincerity.

Springing to her feet, Mrs. Orrin let out a shriek and snatched up a napkin to dab at the spreading stains. "How…how *dare* you!"

It was Nessa who responded, drawing herself up until she looked every inch the marchioness she was. "I might ask the same of you, Mrs. Orrin, persuading me to bring you along with a false story of a family connection, then going out of your way to insult our hostess. You will not wish to stay, of course, now you've so foolishly sullied your gown. The butler can show you out."

At the chill in Nessa's voice, Mrs. Orrin seemed to realize she had crossed an invisible line, offending someone in a position to severely damage her social standing. Her face now an unattractive shade of puce, she moved quickly to the doorway, then turned, her pale blue eyes slits of fury.

"I do earnestly pity you, my dear," she spat at Xena. "For everyone knows the best lovers invariably make the *worst* husbands." With that, she flounced out.

Nessa quickly moved to sit next to Xena. "Oh, my dear, I am so terribly, terribly sorry I allowed that *awful* woman to deceive me! I should have been more on my guard, for when I first married Jack I was frequently subjected to similar attacks—though few quite so brazen. Pray pay her no mind, for it is clear she was motivated by nothing but spite and jealousy."

Xena managed a faint smile, though Mrs. Orrin's parting words had shaken her. Had she not just discovered firsthand how very skilled a lover Harry had become? Though passionate, he'd not yet acquired such skills when last they'd been intimate together. How *many* women—?

She broke off that thought in order to reassure Nessa, who was clearly still upset and concerned on her behalf.

"I spoke the truth when I said I was well aware of what Harry's reputation has been. I can scarcely reproach him with it, as he had every reason to believe himself unmarried these seven years and more."

Nessa grimaced. "Even so, he needn't have been quite so— But no, you are right, of course. He has known the truth less than two weeks and *I've* certainly heard no tales implying he is still carrying on…flirtations…with anyone else."

As Nessa was highly unlikely to have heard such gossip even if true, her words were less comforting than she no doubt intended them. Though Xena had no direct evidence Harry had continued his adulterous activities in recent days, she also had none to the contrary…nor had he promised fidelity, even when challenged to do.

"Thank you, Nessa. I admit I was rather taken aback, but more by Mrs. Orrin's vulgarity than by any new revelations. Now, shall we talk of something else? Your hopes for a daughter, perhaps. Have you begun to consider possible names yet?"

That successfully diverted Nessa from the previous uncomfortable topic and for the remainder of her visit they discussed how her current pregnancy differed from her first thus far. Once or twice Xena was on the point of mentioning her own, making her wish even more strongly that she had never kept Theo's existence a secret from everyone—particularly Harry.

After Nessa had gone, however, she couldn't help recalling Mrs. Orrin's insinuations. Perhaps she should attempt to discover whether or not the odious woman's claims were true before making such an important confession?

Or…was that merely an excuse, to put off a while longer what was sure to be an exceedingly awkward conversation? She honestly wasn't sure.

When Harry awoke, he was startled to discover it was past time to change for dinner. Though Xena had implied they would be eating in tonight, he had no wish to keep her waiting. Especially after…

He smiled at the memory—which affected other portions of his anatomy, as well. Now that they'd broken down the barriers between them, the night ahead—nay, all the nights ahead!—promised to be exceptionally enjoyable. Spurred by that idea, he rose with alacrity and rang for Brewster to help him dress.

A short time later he hurried down to the drawing room and found Xena already there, clad in a gown of silver-gray that matched her eyes and exposed just enough of her décolletage to tantalize without being the least bit improper. The smile she gave him was a shade less welcoming than he'd expected, however.

"Apologies if I have kept you waiting," he hastened to say. "I apparently needed that nap more than I realized."

Her expression warmed, though her eyes still held a certain wariness. "I'm certain you did. It would be well for you to get as much sleep as possible, as that is sure to speed your healing."

"Are we expected somewhere after all?" He glanced pointedly at her gown, which he was almost certain could not be secondhand. "After what you said at breakfast, I rather thought—"

"No, we have no engagement elsewhere. I wrote to cancel and trust my phrasing will spread the impression I intended." Did she color slightly, or did he imagine that?

Either way, Harry's blood quickened. "I'm glad to hear it. Dare I hope that means you wish to continue where we left off earlier?"

"Of course," she agreed with surprising coolness. "That is why I sent round to invite Lord Peter, Sarah and Sarah's brother to join us for dinner. There is still much I need to learn about your activities as Saint of Seven Dials if I am to effectively assist you."

Harry felt as though she'd dashed cold water on his ardor. "I, er, had something rather different in mind."

"Ah. Well. Perhaps we will have time for that later." She did not quite meet his eye.

"Xena." He reached out to trace a finger along the curve of her shoulder where it was bare above her gown. "I—"

The front door knocker sounded from below just then and she sprang up with nervous energy, moving away from his touch. "Ah! Our guests are here."

The meal was a far cry from the intimate dinner of verbal foreplay Harry had envisioned. Instead of trading flirtatious banter with him over the various courses, Xena took every opportunity when the servants were out of earshot to ply Flute and Sarah with questions.

"I had no idea the numbers requiring assistance were so great," she said to Flute at one point. "Do you really know the inhabitants of London's slums well enough to be certain only the most deserving receive whatever the Saint—Harry—gives you?"

Quickly swallowing a mouthful of roast potatoes, the lad nodded. "Aye, mum. I lived among 'em most of my life and word gets around who's in real need of a helping hand and who's just looking to buy more gin—or worse."

"And there are other boys who help you?"

"A few, aye. Some more trusty than others. I know you've had Tig doing a few things on the side for you, guv," he added to Harry, "but he's a talker, he is. Never means any harm, 'o course, but when he gets to boasting there's no knowing what he might say no matter who's listening. You'll want to be careful there, I'm thinking."

Recalling something Xena said last night, Harry realized Flute was likely right. He'd not like word to get about that he was having his own wife followed.

When Xena and Sarah rose to leave the gentlemen to their brandy, Flute asked if he might go out to the mews to visit his friend Renny, who'd been hired by Lord Marcus to work in the stables. Sarah and Peter both assented, which left Harry and Peter alone in the dining room with the decanter.

Harry poured his friend a generous measure and a much smaller one for himself, as he was still disinclined to over-imbibe after that disastrous outing. Peter noticed at once.

"Must say, Harry, this experiment of mine seems to be working out even better than I envisioned. I salute you." He raised his glass.

With a wry smile, Harry lifted his own. "Been waiting your chance to say 'I told you so,' haven't you? Very well, say it. Can't deny this idea of yours wasn't quite so daft as I thought."

Peter's grin broadened. "Glad to hear you admit it, though the way you and your wife look at each other already told the tale. I didn't suggest this course to torment you, you know. 'Twas in hopes you might finally find happiness. It gratifies me no end to see that occurring."

"I'd be happier still if Xena would give up this start of helping the Saint. Should have known she'd insist, once she learned the truth, but I don't like it." There was also the matter of her mysterious lover—or whatever secret she was keeping—but Peter didn't need to know that bit.

His friend nodded sympathetically. "Believe me, I understand how you feel. Why do you suppose I married Sarah so precipitately last month?"

"Because you were completely besotted?" Harry had teased him mercilessly about that at the time, but now…

Peter acknowledged the hit with a laugh. "I was, yes. I also wanted to get her away from that dragon of an aunt, Lady Mountheath. But the primary reason for my haste was to keep her safe once I discovered she was playing the Saint. It worked…eventually. Took a bit of effort to convince her I really had the means to support her, though."

"That's another thing." Harry frowned, for it was an issue that had begun preying on his mind. "I'm in no position to support a wife, even if I give up most of those pursuits you've deplored. Nor does Xena appear to have much beyond an impoverished estate. Wish now I'd let you continue investing what I got on cashing out instead of demanding it back so quickly. Maybe if the Saint manages another good haul, I'll give some of it to you to manage for me as you've proved to have a rare ability there."

Peter shifted uncomfortably in his chair. "Er, yes, well, surely it's time to let someone else take over as Saint, especially given you don't want your wife helping you? I'm sure Flute can come up with a few ideas—"

"Aye, you're probably right," Harry agreed heavily. "But I owe Xena at least one adventure first, she wants it so badly."

He hadn't missed the eager sparkle in Xena's gray eyes as she absorbed all the details Flute could give her over dinner. Watching her, he'd been reminded again and again of that enchanting nineteen-year-old girl with an insatiable thirst for adventure. He couldn't just snatch that away from her, however much he hated to see her at risk.

"How if we ask Flute to find a relatively safe target for one final caper?" Peter suggested. "Perhaps that will satisfy her wish for a bit of excitement with minimal danger to either of you."

"Very well. If Flute can find such a target sometime over the next week or so, I'll let Xena come along as lookout." Harry rather doubted Xena's appetite for new and thrilling experiences would be so easily sated, but it was surely worth a try.

"I'll speak with him tonight, then." Peter took a judicious sip of brandy. "Once that's settled, I suggest we sit down together to discuss the matter of your finances."

It was near midnight when Lord Peter and the others left to return to Curzon Street, but Xena's mind was so abuzz with all she'd learned, she doubted she would be able to sleep. The smile Harry turned on her once they were alone again in the drawing room told her at once that sleep was not precisely what *he* had in mind, either.

"Though I'm by no means resigned to you putting yourself at risk, I am happy you enjoyed yourself this evening." He moved toward her with a compellingly seductive look in his eyes that made her heart accelerate.

"I did. Indeed, the prospect of participating in your adventures makes me exceedingly glad I did not return to Yorkshire the day after our first meeting in London, as I originally intended."

He smiled, a smile that did nothing to calm her pulse. "I'm glad as well, though at first I also believed that would be best. Clearly, we were both mistaken."

As he had earlier, he traced a finger from just behind her ear, down the side of her throat to her shoulder, sending a delicious shiver of anticipation along her spine.

"What I still don't understand," he murmured, "is why, when you clearly crave adventure every bit as much as you did when we first met, you buried yourself in Yorkshire for seven years."

To answer that question, Xena would have to tell him about Theo—something she could not justify putting off any longer. Indeed, she should have done so before allowing this afternoon's intimacy, even as caught up in passion as they'd both been. It suddenly seemed downright dishonorable to keep something so important from him while enjoying his caresses.

"I, ah, had rather a compelling reason, actually," she said, seeking exactly the right words for such a revelation. "The same reason that finally brought me to London. You asked if I'd been seeing someone secretly, and I have. He..." Her voice caught in her throat. *He is your son* seemed too big, too shocking a statement to simply blurt out without warning.

Harry frowned at her hesitation, but now it was a curious, even understanding frown rather than an angry one. "He asked you to come? After convincing you to stay away before?"

"Not...precisely. It was my own choice to stay in Yorkshire, but he, ah..."

"Come, Xena, whatever it is, whoever he is, you can tell me. I promise not to react as I did before. I'm not drunk tonight. You were quite right that I've scarcely conducted myself as a married man all these years, when we both had reason to believe ourselves unattached. I've come to realize how unreasonable it was in me to expect such a young, beautiful woman to remain chaste when I...I've been anything but."

"As I've been made repeatedly aware." Reminded of those humiliating encounters, a touch of acid crept into her tone despite her resolve and Harry's conciliatory attitude. "Most recently this very afternoon, by a Mrs. Orrin."

Rather than look conscious, as she'd expected, he stared at her blankly. "Orrin? I don't..."

"Plump, pretty, blonde. She claimed to have known you quite *intimately*, and not so long ago, either."

"Orrin. Ah! Must've been Melisande. I vaguely recall she was engaged to that nodcock Orrin when we, er... Guess she married him after all when I wouldn't come up to scratch—not that I gave her reason to think I would. But that was—"

"So many women ago that you'd forgotten?" Xena didn't even attempt to hide her indignation. "You dallied with a betrothed women and then...*forgot*?"

Maddeningly, he shrugged. "We were only, er, together once or twice. And I didn't know she was engaged until she offered to break it off for me. Told her it wasn't necessary and stayed well away after that. The idea of spending a lifetime with such a shrew..." He shuddered. "Should have adhered to my rule of limiting my flirtations to married women. Much less inclined to cling."

Belatedly noticing Xena's horrified expression, he hurriedly attempted to backtrack. "There weren't so very many, I assure you, and there won't be any more now you're back. But as I've confessed so much, will you not share your own indiscretions as well? Then we can start afresh, with everything out in the open."

"But I..." No. She simply *couldn't* bring herself to admit she'd never had a single lover other than Harry himself. Not now.

"Come, Xena," he repeated, more seductively now. "I just told you I have no intention of straying again. Are you not willing to extend me the same courtesy?"

"Courtesy?" She nearly laughed at the inappropriateness of the word. "Very well. I also agree not to *continue* any dalliances going forward. However, I...I find myself quite fatigued. Good night, Harry."

She hurried from the room before he could become yet more persuasive, knowing full well that if she stayed she would again join him in his bed. Nor could she resist the impulse to let him believe, at least briefly, that there *had* been others. It made things seem more... equal, somehow, despite Harry's rather surprising promise.

At the door of her bedchamber, however, she hesitated, looking back over her shoulder. She'd been determined to tell Harry the truth about Theo tonight, had finally screwed up her courage to do so, but now felt far too agitated in her mind to attempt it. Surely tomorrow would do just as well?

Hearing Harry's tread on the stairs behind her, Xena whisked into her chamber and softly closed the door behind her, still agonizing. Theo would need to be told as well, of course. Perhaps Yamini could advise her on how to inform both father and son gently? It was she, after all, who'd insisted all along they both be told…

Relieved by that thought, Xena vowed to meet with her old *ayah* at her very earliest opportunity, and to do whatever she suggested.

As it happened, that opportunity came far sooner than she expected. Over breakfast the very next morning, Harry announced that he would be going out for a few hours. "Jack wants me to help him try out his new pair of chestnuts, but I'll be back well before dinner, I should think."

As soon as Harry went upstairs to change, Xena penned a quick note to Yamini. Enclosing enough money for a hackney, she summoned a footman and bade him deliver it to Mrs. Henderson's house on Rundel Street immediately.

When Harry took his leave some twenty minutes later, Xena pretended to be busy with other correspondence, as invitations had continued to arrive despite her excuses. After waiting long enough to be assured he'd be well out of sight of the house, she rang for her cloak.

Upon leaving the house for his fictitious appointment, Harry walked partway down the street. There, screened by the vine-covered railing of a nearby house, he watched the front door of the house he'd just left.

Denied the soporific he'd hoped for last night, he'd lain awake in bed for some time thinking over everything he and Xena had said to each other shortly before she'd gone upstairs…and cringing to think how he must now appear to her.

For a moment there, she'd seemed on the very point of revealing the name of her lover. He'd foolishly believed a casual confession of his own past sins might make her more willing to admit to her own—undoubtedly lesser—offenses. The effect had been quite the opposite, but now he was more determined than ever to discover, one way or another, who the man was.

In the course of his amorous pursuits over the past few years, Harry had faced more than one outraged husband across the field of honor. He'd seen those men as mere objects of pity—bloodless milksops unworthy of their lustier wives' fidelity. Therefore, he'd invariably ducked and fired into the air rather than risk killing—or being killed.

Now, for the first time, he had a most unwelcome insight into how those husbands had perhaps felt.

Knowing Xena as he did, he suspected that now he'd extracted a promise of fidelity from her, she'd feel honor bound to break things off with her lover face to face. This was her opportunity to do just that—and Harry's opportunity to discover exactly whose name she seemed so desirous of protecting.

"Mornin,' guv!" piped a voice at his elbow. "Not to worry, I'm still on the job. Did you think I'd forgot?"

In truth, Harry *had* temporarily forgotten the assignment he'd given to Tig—an assignment he rather regretted now, as he very well might have been happier not knowing.

"Not at all. But I won't be needing your services in this particular capacity any longer."

"Planning to follow 'er yourself today, are you?" The boy nodded with a wisdom that sat strangely on his young features. "Finally goin' to have it out with 'er? I didn't even 'ave a chance to tell you 'bout her last visit to Rundel Street two days since."

Harry frowned down at the lad, recalling what Flute had said about his tendency to speak out of turn. "You've not mentioned those visits to anyone else, have you?" Two days since...the very day *after* she'd denied having an affair with Wellington?

"Nay, guv, nay. I know Flute thinks I can't hold my tongue, but I can. 'Specially when— Look, here she comes now! I'll leave you to it, guv, shall I?"

Though Harry had hoped he was wrong, Xena was indeed emerging from the house, and with no maid in evidence. Harry nodded silently to Tig and motioned him in the opposite direction, back toward Seven Dials. This was a task—and possible confrontation —he preferred to handle alone.

Looking quickly left and right, she put up the hood of her cloak and began walking quickly westward along Grosvenor Street—the opposite direction from Rundel Street. Nor would she be likely to go there on foot. Could he have been mistaken after all?

Harry was by now adept enough at moving inconspicuously that he had no difficulty following Xena without her perceiving him, staying as far behind her as possible without losing sight of her distinctive burgundy cloak. Though she occasionally glanced over her shoulder, he was quick to turn away to watch a passing carriage or peer down an alley.

When she turned down South Audley Street, he wondered if she merely meant to call upon Sarah, perhaps to ask more questions of Flute. He clung to that hope until she turned again, just before reaching Curzon Street, to head toward Hyde Park Corner...and Apsley House.

Despite her denial, it seemed his initial suspicion had been correct after all. A sick knot formed in his stomach, and not only because Xena had lied to him about Wellington.

At the park railing he stopped, watching her retreating back with a sense of defeat. While he'd been confident his skills could make her forget any other lover, he could never compete with all Wellington could offer her, both inside the bedroom and out. Status, riches... Swallowing, he started to turn back—then saw Xena pass through the Chesterfield Gate into Hyde Park itself, rather than continuing on to Apsley House.

Had she arranged to meet Wellington away from the house? Or— insidious hope—might she have some other purpose here entirely? Though he didn't dare assume that, he was curious enough to resume shadowing her. Better to know the worst at once than cling to false hope.

By the time he reached the gate himself, Xena had moved well along the path leading to the Serpentine, a popular spot for families with children…and for lovers. At this season, however, there were few people near the river, making Xena easy to spot from even a furlong away. Positioning himself behind a conveniently placed shrubbery, Harry began scanning the area for Wellington's distinctive form.

Though the Duke was not in evidence, Xena suddenly quickened her pace to approach a pair of figures near the bank of the Serpentine —a woman dressed as a nanny and a small boy. As Harry watched, Xena stooped to embrace the child, then stood to engage in what appeared to be earnest conversation with the nanny.

"What the deuce?" Harry muttered to himself. Using the widely-spaced trees for cover as much as possible, he moved closer and closer to the unlikely trio.

Finally he was near enough to see them all clearly—near enough, in fact, that if Xena turned she would certainly spot him, though he was too curious to worry overmuch about that. The brown-skinned nanny he now recognized as the Indian woman who'd acted as her abigail on the Peninsula. Why, though, should Xena feel a need to meet with *her* secretly? And the boy…

Harry's gaze sharpened as he realized there was something disturbingly familiar about his reddish-brown hair and hazel eyes, though he was almost certain he'd never seen the lad before. He appeared to be about six or seven years old. And the way he clung to Xena suggested…

The shock of realization must have forced some sort of sound from Harry's throat, for Xena and her two companions turned as one to look his way.

"Harry?" Xena's hand went to her throat and she glanced wildly down at the boy by her side, then back at Harry, eyes wide, stricken— the same expression, in fact, that she'd worn that fateful evening when he'd accused her of having a lover and he'd gone out and got himself shot. "How—? You said—"

"That I was meeting Jack." Still dazed by his discovery, he spoke slowly, disbelievingly. "I…had an idea you meant to meet with someone and wanted to find out who. I thought—"

"I know what you thought," she interrupted him with another quick glance at the lad. "You were mistaken. Obviously."

"Obviously." *Was* this little boy with eyes and hair so like his own truly his son? He couldn't quite bring himself to ask such a question directly. "I remember your old abigail, but perhaps you would introduce me to your other companion?" His voice sounded stilted, formal, to his own ears.

When Xena hesitated, the lad at her side took the initiative. "I'm Theodore Maxwell, sir. Are you a friend of my mother's?" He sounded surprisingly mature for his age—as well as slightly suspicious.

"I…yes. A friend." Harry had no idea what else to say—what else he *should* say.

"Then why is she afraid of you?" the boy demanded, moving to place himself between Harry and the two women. "I won't let you harm her, or Yamini, either."

Xena put a hand on young Theodore's shoulder. "Thank you, Theo, but I am not afraid and he means me no harm." Her expression was less confident than her words, however. "This is…Mr. Thatcher. We knew each other before you were born. He…" Her voice trailed off as though she could not make herself say the words, either.

It was the nurse, Yamini, who broke the silence this time. "Tell him, mum. Tell them both. You know full well it is time. Past time." Her voice was firm, not at all like a servant addressing her mistress. Far from reprimanding her, Xena flushed and nodded.

"Yes. It is time. Though I think you've already guessed the truth?" Xena said to Harry, an apology in her eyes. She stooped to put both arms around her son. "Theo, dear, when you asked me about your father, I told you he was killed in battle, because that is what I believed to be true. It was only after arriving in London that I learned he…he survived after all."

"Then—" The boy's hazel eyes grew round as he stared up at

Harry, his small face now alight with disbelieving joy rather than suspicion. "Are you my father? Sir?"

With great effort, Harry managed to swallow the lump that had formed in his throat. "So it would seem. I'm happy to finally make your acquaintance...Theo."

CHAPTER TWENTY

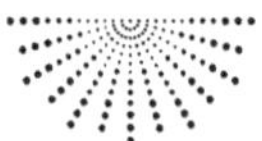

XENA WATCHED HARRY GREET THEIR SON FOR THE FIRST TIME, anxiety warring with relief. Theo regarded Harry with something like awe, then began peppering him with questions, his eyes—so like Harry's—fairly glowing with delight. But though Harry smilingly responded to everything Theo said, there was tension in the line of his jaw and in the way he held himself. Was he angry or merely stunned?

If the former, she prayed he would wait until they were alone to vent it. She knew now she'd been wrong to keep Theo's existence, and Theo himself, from his father. Though fully willing to face the consequences of that error herself, she desperately hoped her son would not be hurt in the process.

"What was it like to be a war hero?" Theo was asking now. "Did the French shoot off your arm when you led your troops into battle?"

"Er…something like that. I've been told my efforts contributed to our side winning the battle at Salamanca, at any rate."

"Wow! And did—"

"Theo," Xena broke in gently, for Harry was clearly becoming more and more uncomfortable. "That will do for the present. Mr. Thatcher and I need to discuss a few things privately now. No doubt you will have a chance for more questions later."

Theo's expression clouded slightly. "Then you are not both coming back with us? Or taking me with you?"

"Not…not just yet." She shot a pleading glance at Yamini, who gave her a small nod. "But soon."

"Tomorrow?"

She fought to keep her worry from showing in her face. "Perhaps. I will send word. Now, give me a kiss."

With an embarrassed glance at Harry, Theo complied, then held out his hand to Harry, who gravely shook it.

"I look forward to becoming better acquainted, Theo."

A grin broke across Theo's face. "So do I…Father."

The look on Harry's face almost made Xena laugh—but not quite. For she still had a reckoning to face.

Harry was silent as the two of them walked side by side toward the park gates. Xena longed to know what he was thinking but didn't quite dare to ask. Not until they reached Park Lane did he speak.

"How long did you mean to keep him a secret?" His voice was conversational, even casual.

Xena glanced up at him, trying to gauge his mood, but his face told her no more than his voice. "I, ah, not long. I've wanted to tell you for some days now. I very nearly did so last night, but—"

"But I began boasting of my past conquests," he said with a grimace. "Much as I'd have liked to know the truth at once, I suppose I can't fault you for trying to shield the boy from a disreputable scoundrel like me."

"I—" The pain in his eyes made her wish to deny that motive, though it was essentially true. "I simply wished us to become better acquainted before springing a son upon you—or a father upon Theo."

"Yet you initially meant to leave London without telling me." It was a statement, not a question.

Reluctantly, she nodded. "Not knowing what sort of man you had become over the past seven years, I…I feared you might try to take him from me—something I could not legally have prevented."

He looked startled, then thoughtful. "What changed your mind?

Surely not Peter's offer of a place to stay for the winter, as you claimed."

"It… Lord Peter happened to see Theo when he called upon me to ask that I remain in London. As you may have noticed, there is rather a strong resemblance and he guessed at once that he was your son."

Now Harry did look angry. "Do you mean to say *Peter* knows? Has known since the day after we met, yet never said a word to me?"

"That…was the bargain I struck with him," Xena confessed. "I agreed to, er, give our marriage a chance by living in the same house with you until the first of the year in return for his promise—"

"To keep *my son* a secret from me?"

Miserably, she nodded. "I realize now I was wrong. That you would never confiscate Theo out of spite, or some misguided belief that as a man you would know better than I what's best for him."

"And Peter had to know that even better. *He* knew I'd never attempt to take the boy from you, even if you didn't."

"Lord Peter did make it perfectly clear he disapproved of my keeping Theo a secret from you," Xena's sense of justice forced her to admit.

"Yet he agreed to help you do so." Harry continued to glower.

Afraid she might be the cause of a rift between the two friends, Xena hastened to explain further. "He only did so because I would have left for Yorkshire at once, without ever seeing you again, had he refused. You mustn't blame him. I was…rather stubborn, I fear."

"I have no difficulty whatsoever believing *that*. And now I know the truth…even if I can't quite believe it." Harry's expression softened to one of wonderment. "A son."

As they continued on to the house in silence, Xena began to breathe more easily. Was it possible the worst was already over? It was too soon to know, but she prayed it might be so.

∼

Harry was still wrestling with the enormity of discovering he was a father when they reached the house on Grosvenor Street. That, and trying to fit everything Xena had said and done this past week into this new, life-changing reality.

By unspoken agreement, once they'd handed off their outer things, they retreated upstairs to the library. The moment they were shut inside, he turned urgently to Xena to ask the question uppermost in his mind.

"Now your carefully guarded secret is out, do you regret your bargain with Peter?"

The worry faded from her eyes, a slight smile softening her mouth. "No. How can I? Theo has a father now. And you and I have, well... Perhaps Lord Peter understood us both better than we did."

"Which will make him even more insufferable than usual for a while. Being right—as he is far too often—generally does." He'd already seen some evidence of that last night, in fact. "I assume it was Theo you were visiting in Rundel Street and not some lover?" She nodded. "Yet you led me to believe otherwise. Why?"

Her chin snapped up indignantly. "Why? Why did you have me followed, when I'd given you no cause to suspect me of any impropriety?"

"Not directly, perhaps, but it was obvious from the first that you were hiding something. An affair seemed the most obvious answer. Especially given the way you and Wellington... Where *did* you get the money for all those dresses, if not from him?"

"As it happens, he did provide most of it, though I was unaware of the source until after I'd spent it. An anonymous, wealthy buyer offered to purchase my father's entire Grecian collection. Not until Lady Ellerby's ball did I discover that buyer was the Duke."

"And how did you discover that?"

"He told me himself."

Harry's eyes narrowed. "Ah. And what did he demand in return?"

Xena primmed her lips. "He did not *demand* anything, though he did...hint. However, I let him know in no uncertain terms that I was not interested, even when he attempted to convince me *you* would not mind."

Recalling Ferny's drunken congratulations that evening, he

supposed some husbands were indeed willing to look the other way while the Duke dallied with their wives, hoping to elevate their own status thereby. Given Harry's past, Wellington likely assumed he would be the same.

"He was wrong."

"Yes, I rather suspected that when you attempted to burgle his house." Her lips quirked up and Harry felt suddenly obliged to kiss them. Thoroughly.

Xena returned his kiss enthusiastically but when he pulled her body against his, she tipped her head back to look up at him. "I'm surprised you did not guess yesterday that I was not in the habit of taking lovers given my lack of…proficiency."

"I found nothing lacking, believe me." His gaze roved over her lovely, upturned face. So beautiful. So difficult to believe she was truly his and no other's. "However, if you wish to expand your, ah, repertoire in the bedroom, I am more than happy to be of assistance."

"You know how I enjoy learning new things." She grinned up at him, suddenly impish. "Though I could wish you'd led a less profligate existence in recent years, we may as well put your extensive experience to good use."

"Ever my practical Xena. Shall we retire to a more appropriate classroom for your next lesson?"

Still smiling, she nodded. "Yes, please."

Hand in hand, they again ascended to Harry's bedchamber. Yesterday, his need for her had been so great that he'd barely remembered to satisfy her before taking his own pleasure. Today he intended a more leisurely session that they might both enjoy every moment properly.

Accordingly, once they were safely in his room, he pulled her to him for another kiss, caressing her back, her shoulders, the nape of her neck. When she began urgently fumbling with his cravat, he put his hand over hers.

"One step at a time," he murmured against her lips. "Trust me."

Slowly, he undid the cravat himself, then unbuttoned only her top two buttons before again kissing her deeply. Though she was soon quivering with eagerness, he continued to take his time, alternating kisses and caresses, first through the cambric of her dress, then through her chemise, once she was free of the gown. Along the way, he allowed her to unbutton his coat and remove it. Then, still clad in shirt and breeches, he bade her sit on the bed.

"Why?" she asked breathlessly, leaning in for another kiss as she reached for the buttons of his breeches.

"Trust me," he repeated with a wink.

She sat and he knelt before her to unlace and remove one sturdy little boot, then the other, after which he one-handedly rolled down her stockings with sensuous slowness. As he bared her feet, he caressed each one, reveling in their dainty femininity. Finally, gliding his hand up her left leg from ankle to knee to thigh, he rose to his feet.

Xena regarded him with half-lidded eyes, her lips slightly parted with pleasure. When she fumbled again with the fastening of his breeches, he did not stop her but lifted the hem of her chemise further until it was up to her waist. The moment she'd freed him from his confining nether garments, she tugged him down onto the bed beside her.

"Now?" she whispered as he kicked his feet free of shoes and breeches.

"Soon." Again he covered her mouth with his own, now sliding his hand over her hip to her waist, then up to her breast, which he took the time to massage thoroughly.

Nearly panting with need now, Xena yanked her chemise the rest of the way off, over her head, then reached down to grasp his straining arousal, tugging him gently closer. Her touch nearly sent him over the edge but Harry sternly held himself back, determined to show her a little something new first. He lay back on the bed, pulling her down atop him. "Now you're the one in control."

Her eyes widened slightly, then she smiled. "Mm. Surely what every woman wants to hear?" Shifting until she straddled him, she pressed her mound against his shaft as she ran both hands over his chest. Then, frowning, she tugged at his shirt, trying to pull it off over his head.

Harry took one of her hands. "That's not necessary, is it?"

Yesterday they'd been in such a frenzy of passion he'd removed his shirt without thinking, something he'd never done for any other woman since losing his arm—not that any had ever insisted. Xena, however, had a most stubborn gleam in her eye.

"Did you not just say I am the one in control here? I shall decide what is necessary." She continued to tug and, after a brief struggle with self-consciousness, Harry raised up enough to allow her to wrestle his shirt up and off until he was as naked as she.

Her eyes now softening, she smiled, her ardor clearly not dampened in the least at the sight. "There now. That is more equitable, is it not?" She leaned forward until her breasts brushed his bare chest.

"Who am I to argue with the woman who holds all the cards?" He massaged her bottom for a moment, then slid his hand up her back to pull her down for a kiss.

Her full length now pressed against him, she maneuvered herself slightly so that the very tip of his shaft nudged at her moist cleft. Then, deepening their kiss, she slowly impaled herself upon him, causing him to gasp into her mouth.

Joined, they began rocking together in that rhythm as old as time, their breaths coming shorter and shorter. When his release was imminent, Harry slipped his hand between them to bring her to her peak simultaneously with his own and an instant later they both cried aloud in ecstasy.

Spiraling slowly down from the heavens, Harry decided his two best friends had the right of it about the advantages of a love match.

Not that the word *love* had actually been uttered by either of them...yet.

Xena was tired but happy by the time she and Harry made their way downstairs for an early dinner, which they elected to have in relative privacy in the smaller breakfast parlor. She'd found their afternoon of lovemaking as eye-opening as it was enjoyable. Who could have guessed at so many different ways a man and woman might pleasure each other? And Harry had promised yet more lessons to come.

Over the meal, he resumed the questions their passionate interlude had interrupted, clearly curious to learn all he could about those portions of her story she had previously omitted.

"When did you discover… That is, were you aware of your, er, condition when you left Spain? When we last—"

"No, I didn't learn I was pregnant until I'd been a week and more in England—and it came as quite a shock." She related how she'd planned to enlist in the 66th before that discovery forced her to retreat to Yorkshire after all.

"And that is why you never left. Because of Theo."

She nodded. "For the first year and more I was exceedingly resentful toward both you and my father—though eventually I was forced to admit that becoming pregnant would have prevented me continuing as I had even without what I perceived as your betrayal."

His gaze was sympathetic. "How hard that must have been for you. I wish more than ever word had reached me in Spain. Perhaps then—" He broke off, staring down at his plate.

A lump formed in Xena's throat, forcing her to set down her fork. "I'm so sorry, Harry. My stubborn, foolish pride is what prevented me writing to my father again, or to you. Because of it, I very nearly ruined both our lives. Perhaps not permanently, but… I have no one to blame but myself for cheating us both of what could have been years of happiness." A tear of regret slipped down her cheek.

Harry glanced up before she could dash it away and was instantly at her side. "Pray don't, Xena. While I wish I'd learned you were alive all those years ago—and about Theo—you did what you felt was best at the time."

Fiercely, she shook her head. "Best for whom? Surely not for Theo. I see now how selfish I've been all along. After discovering you alive here in London it was terribly wrong of me to keep you ignorant not only of your son but about the true state of my finances. Moorside is no grand estate, to be sure, but it is not quite so impoverished as I led you to believe."

"For fear I might stake a claim, drink and gamble it away from you —and Theo?"

She nodded, shamefaced.

"Given the tales you heard about me that first evening—none of them precisely false, alas—it is scarcely surprising your first instinct was to protect both your home and Theo from a scoundrel like me. Much as he tried to protect you from me in the park."

He grinned at the memory and Xena grudgingly smiled back, though her heart still ached for what might have been.

"I cannot believe you nearly so depraved as the gossips claim, Harry, not now that I know you better. Maintaining such a reputation was your way of thumbing your nose at the absurd expectations of Society—much like my own refusal to go along with most of their strictures."

Abruptly, he sobered. "Don't try to gild my past, Xena. While I plan to be a far better man going forward, I can't deny the gossips mostly had the right of it. Not only have I no lands or fortune of my own, I've been anything but a saint these past years, believe me."

Now it was Xena who grinned. "You did *become* one, however. The Saint of Seven Dials, in fact."

Acknowledging her hit with a wry smile, he resumed his chair. "Yes, about that. Given what I now know, I've come to believe you were right that I should give it up—pass the torch on to someone with less to lose."

Though she'd originally demanded he do just that, now Xena felt a stab of disappointment. "Oh. I, ah, suppose that *would* be the wisest course, but…"

"But you were quite looking forward to playing a role in my next foray?"

Feeling a bit sheepish, she nodded. "You can't know how very much I've missed excitement these past few years. The challenges of maintaining an estate with insufficient funds are poor substitutes for escaping an elephant stampede, scaling a Tibetan mountain or fending off French soldiers in camp."

"I'm sorry, Xena. Remembering your love for adventure, I *was* resigned to allowing you to assist me at least once. But now—" A tap came at the parlor door, interrupting him. "The next course, I presume."

Knowing they might be discussing sensitive matters, they'd instructed the footmen to knock.

"Enter," Harry called out.

Instead of a tray-bearing footman, however, Flute entered the room. "Beggin' pardon, sir, ma'am. Polly didn't mention as how you were at dinner, just that I'd find you here. I c'n come back later if—"

"No, it is quite all right," Xena assured the boy with a smile, wondering at Harry's sudden frown. "You have a message from Lord Peter or Sarah?"

"Er, not exactly, mum. Mr. Thatcher here said as how I should keep my ear to the ground for a sure thing and I just heard tell of a nice, plump pigeon that should be safe enough for the plucking."

Harry's frown intensified. "Yes, well, that was before— That is—"

Before he could send the lad away, Xena quickly intervened. "That was very enterprising of you, Flute. What target have you in mind?"

Twisting his cap between his hands, he darted a glance at the still-frowning Harry, then shrugged. "Tig heard a couple ruffians talking earlier today, saying as how some rich wine merchant's gone abroad, leaving his Town house empty. No servants there, even. They was planning how they could rob it themselves, maybe tomorrow, so I though the Saint might should beat them to it?"

"Who is this merchant, Flute, do you know?" Xena asked. "As I'm sure you're aware, the Saint tries to limit his targets to those who most seem to deserve his attention."

Flute nodded, grinning now. "No worries there, mum. He's a skinflint of a codger, name of Biddle. Has a hard time keeping servants, he pays so poorly. It's why the place ain't guarded now. Married a few months back and turned off those he had so he could spend the blunt saved on their wages to take his bride on a Grand Tour."

"Biddle?" Harry echoed. "Biddle. Hm. That name is familiar… Ah, I have it! Phillips was complaining about him a month or two ago—his new stepfather. Rich as Midas, he claimed, but too nip-farthing to help with Phillips's gambling debts."

"Sir Barney Phillips, you mean?" Xena pursed her lips in distaste. "I suppose it's a point in this Biddle's favor if he's not overfond of him."

Harry chuckled. "Too true. I won't deny it's a tempting target, Flute, but—"

"No, don't you see, Harry, it's perfect!" Xena exclaimed, growing excited. "Tonight, while Theo is still safe with Yamini, is the perfect time for the Saint to pull off one last caper. Can't we? Please?"

For a long moment he regarded her, clearly wishing to refuse. But then his hazel eyes softened and a smile touched his lips. "Very well, as it means so very much to you, my dear. But you are to serve as lookout only, mind! I'll not have you in harm's way." Then, turning to Flute, "Tell us more of this Biddle's house. Where is it, precisely?"

Three hours later, Harry still had strong misgivings about allowing Xena to come along as they approached the house near Tottenham Court Road that Flute had described.

From a distance and in the dark, she did look remarkably like a boy in her breeches and overcoat, her hair bundled up under a cap much like Flute's. But anyone seeing her face under any sort of light would guess the truth at once. She was well armed with a pair of pistols and a short-sword, however, so if she were threatened in any way she should be well able to defend herself—or so he repeatedly told himself.

"Remember," he whispered, "under no circumstances are you to venture inside. That way, in the unlikely event I should be captured and arrested, no blame can attach to you. I'm sure you've no wish to deprive Theo of both his parents in one evening."

"Of course not," she said, though the stubborn set of her jaw rather worried him. "You've been exceedingly clear as to how limited my role must be."

"Good." She'd likely pout for a day or two, but he would far rather that than risk her safety tonight. He had no doubt he could cajole her out of any sullens in short order.

Biddle's Town house was a goodly-sized one, lending credence to Flute's—and Sir Barney's—assertion that the man did a good business as a wine merchant. And it did indeed look vacant, with nary a light showing. Even so, two houses away he bade Xena stop.

"You can watch the back of the house well enough from here. I recall you used to be capable of rather a piercing whistle. Is that still the case?"

She nodded. "So if I see anything suspicious—?"

"Yes, whistle as loudly as you can, then head back the way we came. When you reach Oxford Street, you'll be able to flag down a hackney to take you back to Grosvenor Street. On no account are you to linger, even if I appear to be in difficulties. I've burgled far trickier targets than this and escaped unscathed, so I've no doubt I can do the same tonight, especially with a bit of warning."

"I understand." She sounded far too docile for his liking, but he could scarcely take her to task for that.

"Very well. Mostly likely I'll be able to rejoin you here inside half an hour without incident and we can return together to Grosvenor Street. Then tomorrow…we'll send for Theo?"

She smiled up at him in the dimness of the alleyway. "He'll like that very much. Do be careful, Harry." Rising up on her toes, she gave him a swift but very sweet kiss. "Now go."

Though sorely tempted to pull her to him again, he desisted, mindful of her disguise—not that anyone was in evidence at the moment. Still, there were windows. Turning quickly away, he continued on, through the tiny garden behind Biddle's house.

On reaching the back door, he peered down the well beside it to the kitchen window. No, no lights there, either. The place truly must be as deserted as Flute claimed. He'd considered asking the lad to come along to keep an eye on Xena but there'd clearly been no need. Just as well, as she would surely have taken issue with such a precaution.

The back door was locked but he'd come equipped with his picks this time and made short work of it. In ten seconds he was inside, the door closed behind him. He paused again to listen and utter silence met his ears. Though certain now the house was empty, he moved down the central hallway with extra caution for fear that if he knocked something over, Xena might hear, worry—and perhaps react.

Examination of the front parlor by the pale light of the street lamps across the way revealed expensive looking *objects d' art* adorning mantel, tables and walls. It appeared Mr. Biddle was given to ostentatious display. After dropping several smaller pieces into his sack, Harry crossed the hall to the sumptuously appointed dining room—and the plate closet behind it.

Warming to his work now, he again pulled out his lock-picks, only to find the key was already in the lock and the door ajar. Had those thieves Tig overheard beaten him here after all? Frowning now, he pushed the door open.

"Oi!" came a shout from within. "We got 'im!"

Quick footsteps sounded behind him, then a familiar voice drawled, "Let's have a light, shall we, blokes? I'd like to take a good look at my prize before we turn him over to the authorities."

Harry wheeled about, only to be seized from behind by whoever had been lying in ambush in the plate closet, a beefy arm around his neck. In the sudden flare of a tinder box, he saw Sir Barney Phillips standing in the dining room doorway, flanked by two larger men. Phillips, brandishing a small pistol, smirked broadly as one of the others lit a candle and held it aloft.

"You've fallen neatly into my trap, Thatcher. When I heard a rumor the Saint of Seven Dials was missing an arm, my suspicion immediately leapt to you. You can't imagine how gratified I am to learn I was correct. Now, in addition to that most substantial reward—which I will of course share with my compatriots here—I'll have the added satisfaction of seeing you swinging from a gibbet. Not a bad night's work, if I say so myself."

CHAPTER TWENTY-ONE

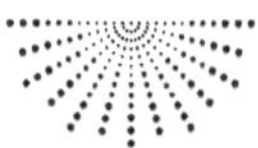

XENA HAD SCARCELY WAITED UNTIL HARRY'S BACK WAS TURNED BEFORE softly following him along the narrow alleyway leading to Biddle's Town house. Apart from how insulting it was to be told to wait such a distance away, she could surely watch and warn him more effectively from a closer vantage point.

She was also quite curious to see how he would gain entry, as the house was presumably well secured against its owner's lengthy absence—but she hadn't even reached the railing separating the small yard from the alley when Harry disappeared inside, closing the door behind him.

"Hmph," she snorted quietly, annoyed and impressed. He clearly hadn't been exaggerating when he'd claimed to know his business. She must remember to ask him where he'd picked up such skills, for he could scarcely have become so proficient in a mere matter of weeks.

Leaning against the wall separating Biddle's kitchen garden from that of the next house, she discontentedly settled in to wait. Where was the adventure Harry had promised her?

On that very thought, movement behind a ground floor window near the door caught her eye. Squinting through the darkness, she perceived at least two figures moving inside, perhaps even three. Had

Mr. Biddle left someone behind to guard his house after all? What if the man or men had guns?

Her heart beginning to pound, Xena moved away from the wall to creep through the yard to the back door, where she pressed her ear against the cold panel. She was almost certain she heard a faint whisper on the other side. Really anxious for Harry's safety now, she forced herself to remain where she was while she slowly counted to twenty.

Then, ever so slowly and carefully, she turned the handle and pushed the door just far enough to peer through the crack. Tiptoeing down the hallway ahead, silhouetted by the pale light coming through the fanlight above the front door, were three men, one fairly slight but flanked by two much larger ones. Taking a deep, silent breath to steel her nerves, Xena opened the door far enough to slip inside, then pushed it nearly to behind her in case they glanced back.

Just then, a shout came from up ahead and the three men quickened their pace, no longer bothering to be quiet. Thankful she'd taken the precaution of wearing thin-soled shoes, Xena softly hurried after them, pulling her pistols from the pockets of her coat as she went.

Harry, meanwhile, glared at Phillips. "Looks like you've done a bit of housebreaking yourself, unless 'Old Biddy,' as you've named him, had a change of heart and gave you a key to his house. Wonder how he'll like hearing about that?"

As he spoke, he desperately sized up his situation. It seemed hopeless enough, given the two louts on either side of Phillips and the one half-throttling him from behind. He wondered if there were any more. Either way, he had no intention of going quietly. If nothing else, a struggle would give Xena more time to escape.

Phillips chuckled. "I figured out weeks ago which window offered easiest access to this place. Think you I'd stay in a tiny flat in Cheapside while Biddle and m' mother gad about the Continent, leaving this palace empty? Long as I'm careful, they'll be none the wiser on their return—and it offered the perfect bait to lure you in. Had my friends here drop news of the place within hearing of that little urchin who's been helping you—the one who was so obliging as to boast of assisting the one-armed Saint only a few days since."

Tig, no doubt. Flute had warned him the boy had a tendency to talk too much. Too late for regrets now, however.

Without warning, Harry drove his elbow into the stomach of the man holding him, then immediately crashed the back of his fist into his captor's nose. Caught off-guard, the man doubled over, then went stumbling backward into the plate closet with a resounding crash. Harry kicked the door shut, turned the key, pocketed it, then set his back against the door, smiling grimly.

"One down. Who's next? These fellows already know my mettle from when you sent them to rob me of your voucher a few weeks since. Care to try me yourself, Phillips? Or was being knocked down once enough for you?"

Sir Barney moved forward, bringing his pistol to bear, his expression first stunned, then furious. "Surely you jest, Thatcher! One trick move won't get you out of this. Jim, Bill, hurry and bind him up—and don't be too gentle."

"I think not," came a voice from the hallway. Xena stepped into the dining room, a pistol gleaming in each hand. "I taught you a lesson once, Phillips, and won't hesitate to do so again—though this one is like to be more lasting."

Harry didn't know whether to curse or cheer. Before he could decide, Phillips whirled with an oath to train his pistol on Xena. Equally startled, his confederates turned as well.

"Gorblimey!" one exclaimed. "It's a woman!"

Immediately taking advantage of their distraction, Harry launched himself at the nearest thug, who'd already come halfway around the dining table to carry out Phillips's order. Hitting the man square in the back, he knocked him into a chair, which fell with a clatter.

As he'd hoped, it took Phillips's attention off Xena. The pistol swung back around and he again brought it to bear on Harry. A shot rang out…and the pistol flew from his grasp. Phillips cried out, wringing his now-empty hand. "You bitch! I'll—"

Before he could finish, Harry closed the distance and sent a fist crashing into his mouth. "I'll thank you not to speak to my wife like that, Phillips."

Recovering from their surprise, the other two men now entered the fray. The one Harry had pushed aimed a vicious kick his way while the other came around the table with a roar, to be stopped by the sight of Xena's other pistol pointed his way. Meanwhile, Phillips was struggling to get to his feet and two loud thumps sounded from the plate closet door as the trapped man hurled himself against it from inside.

The man nearest Harry swung a wild punch at his head. Harry ducked, caught him behind the knees and sent him crashing onto his back. Snatching up Phillips's pistol, Harry then moved back to keep the whole room in range.

Xena took two quick steps forward to press her still-loaded pistol into Phillips's side while Harry aimed his at the man she'd been covering before.

"You witnessed what I did to French soldiers who overran our camp back on the Peninsula," Xena reminded Phillips when he tried to pull away. "Don't think I'll hesitate now."

"Should have known Thatcher needed an accomplice to act as the Saint of Seven Dials. You can hang, too and I'll mourn you no more than I did the first time I thought you'd died." He spat at her.

She laughed airily, not at all as though they might both be facing the gallows. "The Saint of Seven Dials? Harry? I presume you have proof of that?"

"He's here, ain't he? That's proof enough. No one but the Saint would've known this house was empty and unguarded just now."

Following Xena's cue, Harry forced a chuckle. "No one? I knew, as did most everyone at the Guards' Club and likely elsewhere. You've made no secret of your resentment that your mother's wealthy husband took her off touring without helping you out of your numerous gaming debts—to include what you owe me, by the bye.

Concerned you might attempt to burgle your stepfather's house in his absence, I bethought me to check on the place."

Xena took up the story. "Aye, and I persuaded Harry to let me come along in case his suspicion was well-founded—as it clearly was. Mr. Biddle will no doubt be most grateful we happened by to interrupt your larcenous scheme, Phillips."

"What? You can't— That's a load of horse dung and you know it!" Phillips sputtered. "It was on *my* orders my men here let that boy, your helper, hear them talking about this place standing empty, pretending they meant to rob it, just so as to draw the Saint out."

"Boy? What boy might that be?" Harry asked mildly, keeping a foot planted on the downed man's chest, as a precaution. The silence from the plate closet suggested the third man was either listening or had managed to knock himself senseless.

"I don't know his name, blast it! But they heard him boasting of helping the Saint of Seven Dials a few days since, so—"

Harry raised his brows. "You're saying your so-called evidence consists of something these fellows—whom I can *personally* attest are thieves—overheard from some nameless street urchin? If necessary, I can bring numerous highly-placed witnesses forward to affirm my whereabouts during the Saint's various capers. Can you do the same?"

Now Phillips blanched. "I… You… I've never stolen anything in my life!"

"How upstanding of you." Xena's voice dripped sarcasm. "It's a shame your friends here can't claim the same. I'll wager they're already known to the Bow Street Runners—in which case the Runners are likely keeping an eye on you as well, Phillips. London may no longer be the, ah, healthiest place for any of you."

Phillips and his still-standing accomplice exchanged worried glances.

"'Ere, we won't say nothin' if you'll just let us go," the one on the floor grunted. "What's it to us if yer the Saint?"

"Let you go? I don't see how we can in conscience do that," Harry drawled, thoroughly enjoying Phillips's growing panic. "I suggest instead that you three join your companion in crime in the plate closet while we fetch the Runners. Shouldn't take us more than an hour or so."

With some grumbling but an air of general relief, the three men went docilely into the closet, clearly confident they could contrive to escape before the Runners arrived. Whether they escaped or not mattered little to Harry, as he had no plans to notify Bow Street in any case. His only concern was to get Xena safely away.

Once the closet was again locked from the outside, Harry extended his arm to her. "Shall we go?"

Lips twitching, she took his arm. "Let's."

Not until they were back outside did they start laughing.

"You were magnificent, Harry," Xena gasped, hugging him.

"I was about to say the same. I can't even be angry at you for directly disobeying my orders, as you likely saved my life by doing so."

She grinned up at him. "I never was very good at following orders."

"Don't I know it!" He began laughing again. "Can't imagine what I was thinking to expect it."

Sobering then, she leaned her head against his chest. "You wished to protect me—just as I felt compelled to protect you. Together we make quite a good team, do we not?"

"We do indeed. Even so, given Phillips's suspicions, I believe it would be wisest for this Saint to retire for good."

Xena sighed. "I fear you are right, much as I hate to say so. At least I was able to enjoy one real adventure first!"

"Far more adventure than I'd bargained for," he agreed.

In fact, he'd never been more frightened in his life than when Phillips threatened her with that pistol. He hoped never to feel that way again. Though, knowing Xena, he suspected it was a vain hope.

Xena strove to keep various other emotions at bay by reliving their triumph as they continued on toward Oxford Street. "I wonder if

Phillips and his footpad friends will manage to escape from that plate closet?" she mused.

"Though there's scarcely one brain between the four of them, there's easily brawn enough to break down a door. Not that I'll be stricken with guilt should they starve in there."

"Nor I. Especially after—" She broke off to look up at him. "Oh, Harry, I'm so terribly sorry I insisted we go there tonight. Had they succeeded, it would have been entirely my fault. When I think how close I came to losing you yet again, I—"

He silenced her with a kiss, then said, "It was thanks to you they did not. Pray don't forget that. I won't."

She managed a grudging smile in return but could not so easily ignore the fact that her stubbornness had nearly cost her all—again. Tonight's near-disaster finally forced her to admit what she'd attempted to deny for days...nay, years. She was totally and utterly in love with this man.

And he deserved to know it.

"Harry, do you recall what my views on matrimony were when we first met?"

Warily, he nodded. "You had extremely strong opinions on that... and other things. Such as love."

"Yes. I claimed it did not exist. As it happens, I was very much in error. I love you, Harry. I believe I loved you even back then, though I refused to admit it even to myself."

Incredulous joy spread over his face and then he pulled her to him for a long, passionate kiss. "I've wished to tell you the same for two days and more," he said after a moment, "but feared it was too soon. That you were not yet ready to hear it."

"More than ready, I think," she murmured against his lips before he again captured hers with his own.

After a few blissful moments, Xena drew back to smile up at him. "Er, perhaps we should get back? It will scarcely do for us to be seen embracing while I am clad thus."

Harry threw back his head and laughed. "An excellent point.

Though, as you were in breeches the day we first met, it seems rather fitting, somehow. Come, I'll hail us a hackney."

Xena was eagerly looking forward to more intimacies once they reached Grosvenor Street until an unwelcome thought intruded. "Do you suppose we would be wise to arrange an alibi for this evening, lest Phillips is foolish enough to speak out after all?"

"Doubt he will, but perhaps you're right. What do you suggest?"

"Lady Norville's ball is tonight. We may not arrive in time for supper, but can still put in an appearance. After changing into more appropriate attire, that is."

Harry laughed. "Yes, I imagine you'd create quite a stir appearing as you are now. Very well, let's pop home, change as quickly as we can and head back out. I'll even dance with you, to celebrate our narrow escape."

When they entered Lord and Lady Norville's ballroom some forty-five minutes later, the supper dance was just ending. At Harry's request, Xena was clad in the same midnight blue gown she'd worn at Apsley House—and feeling far, far happier than she had then.

Their plan was to slip in quietly and then be seen by as many people as possible, to give the illusion of having been there longer, but Lord Foxhaven spotted them almost immediately upon their arrival.

"Harry! Peter said you likely wouldn't be here tonight. Give you good evening, Mrs. Thatcher." He bowed to Xena, who curtsied in return.

"It is such a crush, I was beginning to despair of finding anyone we knew," she replied, smiling at Nessa, by his side.

"Believe it or not, this would be considered quite a thin crowd in the height of the Season." Nessa grimaced. "While I enjoyed my first well enough, since then I confess I've come to greatly prefer the country."

Lord Foxhaven turned and raised a hand, gesturing. "There's Peter now. Let's see if we can all find a table together for supper, shall we?"

Soon the three couples were seated around a table in an out-of-the-way corner that allowed for conversation without shouting.

"Rather surprised to see you here tonight," Lord Peter said to Harry as they served their wives lobster patties from a passing tray. "Know you're not much for dancing, especially given—" He broke off, apparently remembering in time that Lord and Lady Foxhaven knew nothing of Harry's recent bullet wound.

Harry shrugged, grinning. "Felt a need to get out and about. We both did." He winked at Xena, who grinned back.

Lord Foxhaven, noticing, raised his eyebrows. "I sense a new understanding has been reached. Could it be that you took my advice, Harry?"

"In a manner of speaking."

"What advice was that?" Xena asked, curious.

"I'll, ah, tell you later," Harry replied enigmatically, with a quick glance at the others.

Lord Foxhaven quickly stood to flag down a footman serving champagne. When everyone's glass was filled, Foxhaven held his aloft, his eyes fairly dancing with amusement. "To domesticity."

Harry hesitated, blinking, then lifted his glass as well. "Very well. To domesticity," he echoed. "I confess, I'm finally discovering its myriad benefits. In fact, I would like to invite you all to stop by this week to make the acquaintance of…my son."

Nessa and Sarah exclaimed aloud, Lord Peter's face broke into a broad smile, and Lord Foxhaven choked, spraying the table with champagne.

"You— Your— What?" he sputtered as Nessa gently thumped him on the back. "How—? When—?"

Xena took pity on the poor man. "Theo was born a few months after I reached Yorkshire. As I was not yet aware of my condition when I left Spain, Harry had no idea. In fact, he did not learn of Theo's existence until today…a circumstance for which I take full blame."

Because these were friends, she went on to explain how she'd been misled by pride to allow Harry and her father to believe her dead for so long, then by misplaced fears to keep Theo a secret after discovering Harry still alive after all.

"You were right," she told Lord Peter ruefully. "I should have made them known to each other at the outset."

Sarah stared at her husband in mild outrage. "You *knew*? And never said a word to me?"

He shrugged. "I made a promise. I did hope I'd not to have to keep it long, and am beyond delighted that was indeed the case." He lifted his own glass. "To the newly reunited Thatcher family!"

Everyone drank to that—Harry sparingly, Xena was pleased to note.

As they rose from the supper table a short time later, Lord Foxhaven whispered something to his wife, who nodded. He then turned to the group with a smile.

"Nessa and I have agreed that we would be delighted to invite you all to Fox Manor for Christmas, if your own schedules permit. And yes," he replied in answer to Xena's sudden frown, "your son is most welcome, as I should like him to meet Julius. Our boy may be rather younger than yours, but it is my hope they will grow up as friends."

Seeing Harry's delighted grin, Xena felt confident in accepting the invitation, as did Lord Peter and Sarah.

When the dancing resumed, Harry partnered Xena for the first three, after which they mutually decided they'd stayed long enough to provide the necessary alibi. Both were having difficulty stifling yawns by then, after such a long, eventful day and evening.

By the time they reached Grosvenor Street, Harry was weary to the bone. Judging by Xena's dragging steps as they climbed the stairs together, she felt much the same.

"I feel I could sleep for a week," she said with a yawn when they reached the hallway outside their bedchambers. "But first I'd like to check your bandages once more. I'll come in after a few minutes, if you can keep awake that long."

Tired as he was, Harry felt his pulse quicken. "I'll do my best."

Brewster made quick work of divesting his master of his evening wear before discreetly disappearing. Not five minutes later, a tap came at the dressing room door.

"You needn't knock, you know," Harry said, greeting her with a kiss. "Not now. Not ever."

She smiled sleepily up at him. "I thank you, though I wouldn't wish to surprise you on the chamber pot. Is your wound still bleeding at all?"

"It hasn't soaked through your wrappings, if so."

Without prompting, Harry shed his banyan so that she could unwind the bandages, no longer self-conscious at allowing Xena to see him completely unclothed. If he weren't so blasted tired…

"Hm. The spot that reopened during your melee with Phillips's men is still oozing a bit. One moment."

Fetching warm water from his ewer, she dabbed it, then applied another layer of her special salve before rewrapping the long strips of cloth.

"There. I doubt your healing has been set back more than a day. I'll let you get to sleep now." Going up on her toes, she kissed his cheek. "Earlier, I'd thought to demand another lesson tonight but we'll both enjoy it more once we've rested."

At the genuine regret in her voice, Harry pulled her against him. "Not to worry. We have a lifetime for more lessons." The thought made his heart expand with joy. "For now, I should be most pleased if you would consent to share my bed."

Xena had no objections whatsoever and a few minutes later lay curled beside him under the covers. "Mmm. This is nice," she murmured—and almost instantly fell asleep.

Gazing down at her peaceful face, it occurred to Harry that he'd never before slept with a woman without first taking his pleasure, yet he was perfectly content. More than content. In fact, he knew beyond doubt as he drifted off to sleep that he was happier than he'd ever been in his life.

The next morning, Harry discovered that Xena woke nearly as prettily as she slept—something he happened to know few women could claim.

"Mmmm." Stretching luxuriously, she blinked at the light filtering between the drawn draperies. "What time is it?"

"Time for your next lesson, Mrs. Thatcher, unless you have other plans," he replied with a smile.

Her gray eyes turned smoky. "No other plans whatsoever, Mr. Thatcher."

CHAPTER TWENTY-TWO

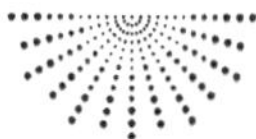

FOX MANOR, KENT—CHRISTMAS EVE, 1816

XENA HAD DISCOVERED LORD FOXHAVEN'S COUNTRY SEAT TO BE EVERY BIT as beautiful—and far grander—than Harry had described it. They'd arrived from London in time to join the Foxhavens and Northrups for a late luncheon that afternoon, after which Lord Peter insisted Harry accompany him to Lord Foxhaven's study to discuss some matter or other.

While the men were thus occupied, Xena and Sarah had eagerly accompanied Nessa on a tour of the house, exclaiming with delight over each exquisitely appointed room and prospect. Later, however, as she dressed for dinner in the sumptuous chamber provided for the duration of their stay at Fox Manor, Xena found herself missing London. The past three weeks in that house on Grosvenor Street had easily been the happiest of her life. Because of Harry.

He had suggested Theo join them the very day after their adventure with Phillips and Mrs. Walsh, with her customary efficiency, had the third story nursery and adjoining rooms ready to receive him and Yamini that very night. Needless to say, their son was overjoyed—as was Xena, watching the growing rapport between Harry and Theo with each passing day.

Lord Peter, ever the well-meaning meddler, had crafted a story for public consumption to account for Theo's sudden appearance on the scene, which warded off any awkward questions that might otherwise have arisen.

Mr. Gold had soon found other buyers for the remainder of her father's Grecian collection, sparing Xena any further obligation to the Duke of Wellington—who'd written a charming letter expressing his congratulations that, by all accounts, she and her husband had indeed achieved a true love match.

Now, watching Flute amuse Theo and little Julius with sleight-of-hand tricks on the hearthrug in the elegant parlor where the ladies had withdrawn after dinner, Xena sighed with contentment, despite her still-unappeased curiosity.

Harry and Lord Peter had been closeted together all afternoon. She was already dressing for dinner when Harry finally joined her, where-upon he'd greeted her with an ebullient kiss.

"What is it?" she'd asked when Harry released her, for he'd seemed unusually happy—but also a bit dazed. "Did Lord Peter have good news to impart? Oh! Is Sarah perhaps increasing?"

Smiling, he'd shaken his head. "If so, he didn't tell me. No, the matter he wanted to discuss was quite different. I haven't time to explain it all right now but I promise to share it with you later."

With that she'd had to be content, for no amount of cajoling as they finished dressing would induce him to say more. She was still trying to imagine what Harry's news could possibly be when the gentlemen joined them in the parlor, presumably having finished their cigars and brandy.

"What a pleasant picture of domesticity this is," Harry commented jovially as he entered just behind his two friends.

"Father, look!" Theo exclaimed from his place by the fire. "Flute—I mean, William—is pretending to pull pennies from our ears but I've figured out how it's done, haven't I?" He looked to the older boy for verification.

"Aye, he's a quick one, he is," Flute agreed. "Here, I'll show you something a bit trickier, shall I?"

As Harry watched the three boys, Xena in turn watched Harry with a loving, though still-puzzled, smile.

"I was just saying to Sarah and Xena how lovely it would be if we could spend every Yuletide like this one," Nessa said as her husband bent down to kiss her. "Don't you agree?"

"I do indeed. What is Christmas without friends?" Moving to the sideboard, Lord Foxhaven poured six glasses of sherry and began handing them around. "I propose we do exactly as Nessa suggests and make this an annual gathering. Can't think of anyone I'd rather have about me at this time of year."

"That's a handsome thought, Jack," Lord Peter said, accepting his glass. "I'd far rather be here than in Town or at Marland. Though should Sarah and I eventually purchase an estate of our own, we'll want to reciprocate, of course."

"I'm certain we should enjoy that, too." Xena smiled at Harry as he took the chair nearest her. "It's a shame Yorkshire is such a great distance from Kent. Look how well the boys all play together."

"There's no call for you to hurry back to Moorside Grange, is there?" Lord Peter asked, raising one brow at Harry with what almost seemed a prompting look. "Leave the place in the hands of your steward for the winter and find a nice little house in London. Then we can all visit frequently."

Xena darted a concerned frown Harry's way, for she knew his lack of fortune was rather a sore point. Only three nights ago he'd mentioned how unfair it seemed that she should bring an estate to their marriage— even a modest one like Moorside—while he had nothing to offer her but his love. It was the single off-note in the harmony they had enjoyed of late.

"I fear that once all the repairs are made, there'll be little left of what I received for my father's antiquities," she said before Harry could reply. "I've no doubt that in time, and with Harry's help, Moorside will become more profitable, but as of yet—"

"Actually, I believe a house in Town sounds like an excellent idea," Harry broke in. "Only for the winter, of course, after which we must have an eye for Xena's estate."

"*Our* estate," she quietly corrected him, wondering why on earth he should suggest such a thing when it was clearly beyond their means.

But Harry simply sent a quelling look at Peter and changed the subject by asking about plans for the morrow, Christmas Day.

Harry had been bursting to share Peter's amazing revelation with Xena all evening. Not in front of all the others, however. No, he wanted to experience Xena's surprise—and rapture—in private.

He'd mentally rehearsed how he wanted to deliver the news, but the very moment they were alone in the luxurious bedchamber that was to be theirs through the New Year, Xena turned to him with the same concerned frown she'd worn earlier.

"What were you thinking, Harry, to say we might take a house in London for the winter? You know full well we can't afford such a thing, though of course I hope we might someday."

Smiling broadly, Harry pulled her against him, his speech forgotten. "As it happens, my love, we can. Peter shared some rather remarkable news with me this afternoon when we were shut up all that time. Believe it or not, you see before you a wealthy man."

Her expression turned to one of blank astonishment. "What? How —? I don't understand."

"Neither did I, but Pete carefully explained it all. Even then, I refused to believe him until he produced the account books he'd brought along for that purpose. It then took us all afternoon to work through the details, which is why I was unable to rejoin you until you were dressing for dinner. Have I mentioned how much I like that dress, by the way?"

She narrowed her eyes at him. "You are stalling now. Please tell me the whole at once, sir."

"Not stalling, merely enjoying the moment." He dropped a quick kiss on her nose. "Very well, to put it briefly—when I cashed out, I gave some of that money to Peter to manage for me, as he has rather a remarkable knack with investments. I had no idea *how* remarkable, however! Heedless scoundrel that I was at the time, I ran through the remainder in less than a twelvemonth and demanded the rest back from him. He returned what I'd originally entrusted to him, allowing me to believe that was all, when in fact he had already more than doubled my money."

Xena's eyes widened. "Do you mean he continued to invest the remainder without your knowledge?"

He nodded. "Over the past three years, he has managed to parlay it into a tidy little fortune. Nowhere near his own, of course, as he had far less to work with, but quite respectable nonetheless. You'll now have no need to sell off any more of your father's collection for the sake of your estate."

"Our estate," she repeated, but now she was smiling. "Do you realize what this means, Harry? We really will be able to make Moorside profitable and in far less time than I'd imagined. And we will be able to send Theo to any school we wish in a few years...and to Oxford after that."

Thoroughly enjoying her mounting excitement, he decided to increase it further. "That is not even the best of it, my dear. Peter has agreed to continue investing a good portion for our future and Theo's, but meanwhile we should have enough to do all you'd like for Moorside...and to travel, as well. I thought we might give Theo the sort of experiences that helped his mother grow into the remarkable woman she is now."

Xena caught her breath, her eyes positively shining now. "Truly, Harry?"

"Truly. Consider it my Christmas gift to you, my love—the one thing I know you've longed for above all these past few years: the opportunity for more adventures."

"You know me so very well, Harry. I had no idea I'd married such a gallant scoundrel."

Pleased by her description, and even more pleased by the joy reflected in her face, he lowered his lips to hers. "I certainly intend to do my best."

Keep reading for a sneak peek at *Tessa's Touch*, book 1 of the **Seven Saints Hunt Club** series, set in the same world as the **Saint of Seven Dials** series!

TESSA'S TOUCH (PREVIEW)

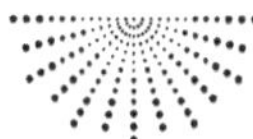

LEICESTERSHIRE, ENGLAND—OCTOBER, 1816

"EASY, FELLOW, IT'S ONLY AN OWL'S SHADOW," LORD ANTHONY
Northrup said as the horse he was leading along the deserted road
shied yet again.

Already he was beginning to regret the favor he'd done young
Ballard by purchasing this skittish hunter from him, but he was careful
to keep his irritation from his voice so as not to upset the beast further.
Justifiably famous for his skill in handling difficult horses, Anthony
had been sure he could handle this chestnut better than the inexperi-
enced Mr. Ballard.

Perhaps leading it back tonight hadn't been the best plan, however.
His own mount was a placid, well-trained beast, unlikely to react to
the nervousness of the new horse, but he'd underestimated the chestnut's spookiness. He'd be glad when he finally reached his hunting
lodge with both animals.

For several minutes he continued without incident, riding Cinder,
his gray gelding, at a slow trot through the gathering dusk with the
new chestnut following on the lead. The road from Melton Mowbray
was mercifully empty at the moment, but Anthony knew that was
unlikely to last with so many men arriving in the Shires for the start of
foxhunting season.

Sure enough, a moment later he heard hooves approaching from behind at a quick trot. He glanced back and saw horse and rider silhouetted against the rolling fields that were fading from green to gray in the twilight. Slowing Cinder to a walk, he maneuvered both horses closer to the verge to give the other rider ample room to pass, in hopes of avoiding an incident with the skittish chestnut.

His hopes were dashed when a rabbit suddenly erupted from the hedge bordering the road, right under the chestnut's nose. Predictably, the horse spooked and reared, then lunged forward, dragging the lead rein across Cinder's neck. Anthony's gelding shied away from the sudden contact, dancing sideways even as the chestnut reared again, nearly pulling Anthony from the saddle.

One of the chestnut's descending forelegs caught on the lead rein, wrenching it from Anthony's grasp. Cursing, he vaulted to the ground to make a grab for the lead before the horse could bolt, but he was too late. The chestnut swung away from him, then galloped away up the road, the lead whipping behind.

With another curse, Anthony turned back to Cinder but before he could remount to give chase, the other rider swept past him at a gallop, already in pursuit of the chestnut. Vaulting into the saddle, Anthony followed. He hadn't seen the fellow's face, but assumed it must be someone he knew, to spring so quickly to his assistance.

He and Cinder galloped only a furlong or so before reaching their quarry, for the chestnut had somehow managed to tangle his reins in the thick hedge that lined the road. Unfortunately, the horse was in full panic, bucking and kicking at the hedge, tangling the reins even more tightly as he whinnied with rising hysteria.

The other rider dismounted and took a couple of cautious steps toward the frightened beast. Judging by his stature, Anthony realized he could be no more than a lad.

"You'd best stay clear," Anthony said, dismounting as well. "He's in the devil's own temper and could do you an injury."

"Nonsense," came the reply.

Anthony stared, for the voice was undeniably feminine, despite the fact that the rider had been riding astride and wore breeches. Before he could process this remarkable anomaly, she took another step toward the panicked chestnut, leaving her roan mare standing quietly.

"Come then," she said soothingly, "what seems to be the trouble?"

To Anthony's amazement, the horse instantly stopped kicking and stood, trembling, with its ears pitched forward.

The woman continued to approach the still-jittery chestnut. "There, now. It's not so bad, is it? Look at what you've done to yourself," she said to the horse in a singsong lilt that seemed to hold the beast's complete attention.

A moment later she had the lead in one hand and with the other deftly untangled the reins from the hedge. When she laid one small hand on the horse's neck, it gave a great shudder, then stopped trembling. Ducking its head, it turned to nuzzle her ear.

Smiling, she patted the chestnut's nose and Anthony just caught her whisper of, "I miss you, too, Zephyr." Then she turned and said aloud, "I don't think he'll give you any more trouble, sir," and handed him the lead.

Anthony had been watching in amazement, but now he thought he understood why the horse had responded to her. "Thank you. You seem to have—"

He paused, for the rising moon gave him his first good look at her face—and a lovely face it was, framed by a few honey-brown curls that had escaped her riding cap. The breeches outlined a fine pair of legs, causing his thoughts to veer down a totally different path.

"Horses like me," she said simply, clearly not realizing he'd heard her whispered comment to the chestnut.

Her dark eyes met his and a spark of sympathy, of connection, passed between them. Anthony felt something deep inside him stir in response. Lust, of course. He was long familiar with that feeling. Anything beyond that was doubtless only the result of the moonlit setting and the unusual events just past.

"So it would appear," he finally replied. Shaking off his bemusement, Anthony managed a grin. "And I can't say that I blame them, Miss—?"

To his disappointment, she did not supply a name. "I'll be on my way, then," was all she said. With a fluid motion, she was back in her saddle and a moment later was cantering away down the road at a pace he had no hope of matching with two horses to manage.

He watched her appreciatively until she was too far away to discern clearly, then turned to remount Cinder and continue his brief journey, still bemused by the mystery of the beauty in breeches. Her accent had not been that of some local farmer's daughter. Was she perhaps the pampered mistress of some gent here for the hunting season?

Anthony received a generous allowance from his father, the Duke of Marland, as well as a quarterly stipend from the Army, where he'd attained the rank of major during the recent wars. Maybe the breech-clad beauty could be lured away from her protector. But no—if she was familiar with the horse, it was more likely she lived somewhere in the area. Besides, her manner hadn't been at all flirtatious—nothing like that of a Cyprian.

Busy with such thoughts, he didn't realize until he reached his hunting box that she'd been right about the chestnut. He'd given no further trouble. What had she called him? Zephyr? Ballard hadn't mentioned the horse's name, but he had no doubt that was it. He'd ask Ballard about it tomorrow.

Handing both horses over to a waiting groom, he warned him about the new gelding's skittishness. The man looked skeptical, given the chestnut's current placidity.

Anthony just shrugged, then turned to the house, one of the larger hunting boxes in the area, boasting six large bedrooms and a generous dining room. The half-timbered house had been left him by his great-uncle, an avid sportsman who had taught Anthony most of what he knew about hunting. Great-uncle Alden would be pleased, Anthony thought, to know his former hunting box now housed the Seven Saints Hunt Club, second in consequence here in the Shires only to Melton's Old Club.

"About time you returned," he was greeted by Sir Charles Storm, better known as Stormy, upon entering the parlor. "Rush insisted on holding dinner for you and I'm famished."

Anthony turned to Ryan Dean, Earl of Rushford, with a grin. "Good of you, Rush, but not really necessary. I'd no idea Ballard's beast would be so much trouble. That's what delayed me." He threw himself into an overstuffed armchair near the fire.

"Horse was a bad deal, then?" massive Grant Turpin, lounging opposite him, asked sympathetically. "That's what comes of doing favors for striplings. Warned you against that."

Anthony grinned, knowing his imposing friend would have done the same, for Thor, as he was known to his intimates, was a notoriously soft touch. "Yes, you did, but I knew I could handle the brute better than young Ballard. He's a damnably skittish thing, though. Starts at his own shadow. Or did, until—" He broke off, suddenly reluctant to mention the girl who'd come to his rescue.

"Doesn't sound like much of a hunter, though you'll set him right if anyone can," Thor said with gratifying confidence. "Is it temperament or training, do you think?"

"Too soon to know," Anthony replied with a shrug. "Could be a combination—"

"I say," Stormy broke in, "can't we discuss it over dinner?"

With a chuckle, the four men adjourned to the dining room, where they were joined by three other founding members of the Seven Saints Club. It was a jovial group, for among the requirements for inclusion were a lack of pretention and general amiability. Just now, everyone was in high spirits in anticipation of the first real hunt of the season four days hence.

Not until the roast beef was served did the conversation return to Anthony's new purchase.

"Where did Ballard buy that horse, anyway?" asked William Verge, Viscount Killerby. "There haven't been any auctions yet, have there?"

"Not that I know of," Anthony responded to the little bouncing ball of a man affectionately known as Killer. "He bought it from a local squire, a fellow by the name of Seaton."

"Seaton?" echoed Stormy from the opposite end of the table, where he'd been working his way steadily through the courses. "Of Wheat-stone? Someone else had a bad mount off him last year— horse refused the jumps. Now, who was it?" He frowned and took a sip of claret in an apparent effort to jog loose the memory.

"Porrington, wasn't it?" offered Rush. "I remember him landing in a ditch when that new bay of his balked last year. Thought the dunking did him good, personally."

There were nods of agreement, Anthony's included, for Porrington was notoriously high in the instep. In fact, he suspected it had been Porrington who had blackballed Killer from the Old Club several years earlier, the event that had ultimately resulted in the formation of the rival Seven Saints Club.

"Perhaps I'll pay this Seaton a visit." If the young woman he'd met knew the horse, she might well be found somewhere at Wheatstone. "See if the fellow is making a practice of selling half-trained horses."

He remembered how easily the girl had calmed the horse. Perhaps he hadn't made such a bad bargain after all . . .

"Good idea," Thor agreed. "We can act as though we're interested in buying and look into Seaton's setup. Could be Porrington and Ballard were isolated incidents, or it could be pattern. I'd hate to see any other striplings like Ballard taken in, if so."

"It's not as though we've anything else to do, with the first hunt still days away," Stormy added.

Anthony had intended to go alone, but now he nodded. "Very well. In the morning I'll have another word with Ballard, then we can give Seaton's stables a look."

This suggestion was met with general approval, and the coversation turned back to the hunt and a spirited discussion of the season's prospects for good sport.

On her return to Wheatstone, Tessa Seaton was careful to ride the strawberry roan mare in a wide circle around to the back of the stables, well out of sight of the main house, before dismounting. If she were quick, she could return Cinnamon to her stall and get back before her father noticed she'd been away.

"How did she go, then?"

Tessa whirled, startled, to see her cousin Harold leaning against the corner of the main stable block. As usual, his hat was pulled low over his forehead, a piece of straw dangling negligently from his lips.

"Fine. She went fine," Tessa replied with a shrug. "I told you she would." Regret tugged at her, for she'd already become rather fond of Cinnamon. It was foolish, since the horse had been bought for resale.

Her cousin nodded. "With those lines, I'm betting we can get a monkey for her once the hunt begins."

Tessa frowned. "I doubt she's worth five hundred pounds, though she is better-tempered than most of our beasts." She refrained from pointing out that the pervasive temperament problems were a direct result of Harold's inept training.

"She jumps well," she continued, "but she's not as fast as most huntsmen would prefer. Perhaps with another season's conditioning—"

"What the devil difference does it make?" Harold interrupted. "She's worth whatever someone will pay. Nimbus is flashier, though, so we should show him in the first hunt. He'll fetch even more, I'd wager."

"Nimbus? He's not ready. We've only had him since August and he's not shed most of his bad habits yet. He bit two stable lads last week, and kicked Rambler the week before that."

"The stable lads won't be riding him. You will."

"Me?" she echoed in amazement. "In the hunt, do you mean? Papa will never allow it." Sir George Seaton had very definite views on what constituted proper behavior for his daughter, and riding to hunt—or too much riding at all, for that matter —was not a part of it.

"Leave that to my father," Harold said with a smirk. "Your mother used to ride in the hunt, you know, and Sir George with her. He never objected to that."

Tessa shook her head. "That was different. If Papa could ride with me, perhaps—" But her father hadn't been able to sit a horse for six years, not since the hunting accident that had permanently crippled him.

"Father will be riding with you," Harold said. "He'll have to be there anyway, to negotiate the sale afterward."

Harold's father, Mercer Emery, brother to Tessa's late mother, had taken over management of Wheatstone shortly after Sir George's accident. Tessa had been sixteen at the time, and in no position to object, particularly as her father had remained bedridden for several months.

When Sir George recovered enough to take an interest in the estate again, Uncle Mercer confided to Tessa that Sir George's heart had been affected by his accident, making any sort of upset or exertion dangerous for him. He also informed Tessa that Wheatstone's finances were in far worse shape than her father had known, and that discovering the truth might be enough of a shock to kill him.

Tessa often regretted the decision she'd made then to help her uncle conceal the true state of Wheatstone from her father. The estate had continued to deteriorate over the years, until now they were living month to month, forced to buy and resell horses to supplement the meager rents from their tenants. It seemed clear that her uncle was no better an estate manager than his son was a horse trainer, but after six years, there was little she could do about it.

"Even if we can convince Papa to let me ride, Nimbus isn't trained for the hunt," she argued now. "His manners around other horses are atrocious."

Harold's mouth twisted for a moment with something that might have been bitterness, but then he smiled and put a hand on Tessa's arm. "He's gentle enough under you, just as they all are."

What he said was true enough, for Tessa had a special way with horses, just as her mother had. A gift, from their Irish forbears, her mother had once told her. It was a gift Harold, unfortunately, did not possess, for all he fancied himself a horse trainer.

Nor did his father possess it. That had been painfully clear last year when Uncle Mercer had ridden in the hunt. The horses had performed creditably only because Tessa had calmed them immediately before the runs. She didn't doubt that they would perform far better with her actually riding them. Still, did she dare agree?

"Uncle Mercer got Nimbus for a song because he was barely

broken," she said, stepping away from Harold's touch. "Even if we invest another year in his training, he'll make a tidy profit when sold. There are drawbacks to selling too early. Remember Zephyr, that skittish chestnut we sold to Mr. Ballard a few weeks ago? Apparently he's already sold him to someone else."

She paused, remembering how handsome that someone else had been— easily the handsomest man she'd ever seen.

"What's that to us?" her cousin said. "We made a nice bit off that sale, enough to fix that leaning chimney you've been fretting about. Oh, that reminds me— Father mentioned today that the west wing roof is beginning to leak."

Tessa stifled an unladylike curse. Roof repairs would not only be expensive, they'd be as difficult to hide from her father as the chimney repairs would be. There was no denying the estate needed money, however she might dislike the means of getting it.

"If we get a reputation for selling half-broken horses, it could harm future sales," she felt obliged to point out.

"All the more reason to sell as many horses as quickly as we can," Harold retorted. "We've enough beasts to unload this season to lay some money by against the future."

When she still hesitated, Harold added, "I'm thinking you'd rather I not let anything slip to Sir George about these evening rides —and what you wear for them." He nodded significantly at her breeches. "No knowing what it might do to that bad heart of his."

"But it was you who— Never mind." Tessa turned away before her temper got the better of her, handing Cinnamon's reins to a too-interested stable lad. "I must get back to the house."

Her cousin had suggested that she do some riding astride so that the horses wouldn't be solely used to a sidesaddle. It would be just like him to use it against her, however, with no regard for what it might do to her father's health.

Without another glance at her cousin, she strode toward the back of the manor house. Entering by the kitchens, she could reach her own chamber without her father seeing her, for he could not negotiate the stairs in his chair. It was how she always escaped his notice, but tonight she felt guiltier about it, for some reason.

Perhaps it was because of her encounter with that gentleman leading Zephyr, she mused as she nodded to the kitchen staff, who were well used to seeing her arrive in breeches just before dinnertime. It had been foolish of her to come to his aid dressed like this, but when she had recognized Zephyr, she had felt an obligation, both to the man and the horse.

Hurrying up the back stairs, she shook her head fiercely. Obligation or no, it had been stupid. Should the gentleman find out who she was, and word somehow get back to Papa, it would upset him far worse than anything Harold might say.

Sir George set great store on Tessa being accepted by the surrounding gentry in a way her mother, the daughter of his own father's horse trainer, had never been. Tessa cared little for the opinions of their neighbors, but as it was so important to Papa, she tried to at least pretend, for his sake. If the Leicestershire gentry whispered about "odd Miss Seaton," her father would never know—any more than he would know about the leaking roof of Wheatstone's west wing. Tessa would make certain of that.

What would he say if he knew that her lifelong dream was to take over management of the stables, where she could use her gift to train and breed the horses with which she felt such a deep connection? Not that she could ever suggest such a thing to her father, of course. Though undeniably proud of her skill as a rider, he discouraged her from even visiting the stables, preferring that her mounts be brought to the door.

To spend more time with her beloved horses and to give them a break from Harold's "training," she was forced to deceive her father. Her cousin, no doubt aware that her work with the horses mitigated his own ineptitude, was willing to keep her secret, with the help of his father.

She'd convinced herself that any sale was a good thing, not only for the money, but to remove another horse from Harold's cruel and clumsy methods. Now, though, she couldn't help questioning the wisdom of selling horses before they were ready. But what alternative was there?

With a sigh, she signaled Sally, her maid, to help her out of her male attire and into a demure blue gown suitable for dinner with her father.

❧

"Were you able to find out anything more from Ballard?" Rush asked Anthony as they and a couple of others cantered along the road leading to Sir George Seaton's estate the next afternoon.

"Not as much as I'd hoped," Anthony confessed. "He seemed disinclined to talk about the circumstances of his buying the horse. Only said that the chestnut 'showed well,' and he'd been mistaken about its temperament. I couldn't tell whether there'd been deliberate deception or if he's simply a wretched judge of horseflesh." He had also discovered that the horse's name was indeed Zephyr, but saw no point in mentioning that.

"I can't imagine how anything short of deception could have made that horse show well," said Stormy from behind him. "He's a nervous wreck, ruined by bad training or treatment, at a guess."

The others agreed, for they had all paid a visit to the stable this morning. The calming influence of the mysterious breech-clad beauty had not lasted the night, unfortunately.

"There's Porrington, too, don't forget," added Thor.

"At any rate, we'll know more soon," Rush said. "Here's Wheatstone now."

The four men slowed to a trot as they reached the long sweep of gravel leading to a fair-sized manor house that looked to have been built in Elizabethan times. The house stood on a small rise, surrounded by wide lawns, still green, and dotted with occasional trees. Beyond the house they could glimpse paddocks and buildings that must be Seaton's stables.

"Fellow appears to be doing well enough," Thor commented as they headed up the drive.

As they drew closer, however, Anthony wasn't so sure. One chimney leaned slightly, and the roof of the ivy-covered western wing sagged noticeably. The main, central block of the house appeared solid enough, however, and as they drew up to the front steps, a groom appeared from around a corner and a butler opened the oak and wrought iron front door.

"What might your business be, gentlemen?" the retainer asked with an admirable blend of haughtiness and respect.

As they'd agreed earlier, only Anthony dismounted and stepped forward. "I am Lord Anthony Northrup, come to speak to Sir George Seaton," he said. "I may be interested in purchasing a horse from him."

"And we'll just nip down and take a look at the stables," Rush added, he and the others turning their horses' heads in that direction.

The butler looked alarmed. "Gentlemen, please! If you'll just—" But Anthony's friends had already kicked their mounts to a trot and a moment later disappeared around the corner of the house.

Anthony turned to the distressed butler with a smile. "Don't worry, my good fellow. They know their way around a stable and won't alarm the horses. And now, if you'll announce me to your master?"

He still appeared upset, lending weight to Anthony's suspicions about the stables. "I'm sorry, my lord, but Sir George is rarely at home to visitors. His man of business, Mr. Emery, handles all transactions."

"Nevertheless, I should like to speak with Sir George himself, if that is at all possible." Why should the baronet leave such matters to his steward? That was rather unusual. In any event, if this Mr. Emery was selling inferior horseflesh, Sir George needed to be made aware of it.

Something in his tone apparently convinced the butler that further argument was pointless. "Very well, my lord. If you will step inside, I shall discover whether Sir George is able to receive you today."

He left Anthony to wait in the parqueted entry hall, where he amused himself by examining his surroundings. These presented a curious mixture of shabbiness and elegance, as though taste outstripped the money necessary to fully implement it. Faded draperies were artistically looped above the long side windows which illuminated two lovely Grecian urns in shallow alcoves. Closer inspection revealed that one of those urns had been cracked and carefully repaired.

Before Anthony could form a hypothesis to account for these anomalies, he heard quick footsteps coming down the staircase. He turned.

"I appreciate you seeing me on such short notice," he began, then stopped abruptly. Instead of the country squire he'd expected, he found himself facing a vision of loveliness with shoulder-length curls the color of honey and a trim figure shown off to advantage in a pale yellow day dress.

"I'm sorry, my lord, but my father is unable to receive visitors," she said as she reached the ground floor. "I have sent for Mr. Emery so that you may discuss your business with him."

He blinked. This was none other than the young woman in breeches who had come to his rescue the night before, for all she looked quite different properly clad in a gown. The sudden shock in her brown eyes showed that she had recognized him at the same moment, though she quickly tried to conceal it.

This had suddenly become a most interesting visit.

~

Order *Tessa's Touch* to keep reading!

I know there are many, many books out there to choose from, so I want to take this opportunity to personally thank you for choosing and reading *Gallant Scoundrel*. This book is the fifth installment in my "Saint of Seven Dials" series of Regency-set historical romance novels, all set in the same "world" as my traditional Regencies and *Scandalous Virtue*, with a few of the same (fictional) peripheral characters. Though each of these books stands alone, complete in itself, some readers prefer to read them in order. With all of my Regency historicals, I thoroughly enjoyed the opportunity to stretch my wings beyond the rather strict boundaries of the traditional Regency, while still preserving the feel and accuracy of the time period.

For this book, I did take a few small liberties with the historical timeline in that I could find no hard evidence that the Duke of Wellington actually visited London in late 1816, when he was based in France after the end of the Napoleonic wars. It seems plausible, however, that he might have traveled back and forth a bit, so I chose to make that assumption. Nor did he purchase Apsley House from his brother until 1817, but it was such a perfect setting for those early scenes (and the Duke is such a great character!) that I chose to think he might have taken up residence a bit earlier. I hope you'll forgive my minor fudging in service to providing an entertaining read.

If you enjoyed *Gallant Scoundrel*, I hope you will consider leaving a review wherever you buy or talk about books to let other like-minded readers know they might enjoy it, too.

ABOUT THE AUTHOR

Brenda writes novels of sparkling romantic adventure spanning Regency England, Americana, contemporary teen science fiction and more. Which ever you pick up, you'll find excitement, romance and, always, an uplifting happy ending. In addition to writing, Brenda is passionate about embracing life to the fullest, to include scuba diving (she has over 60 dives to her credit), Taekwondo (where she's currently working toward her 4th degree black belt), hiking, traveling…and reading, of course!

Connect with Brenda at:
brendahiatt.com